THE HADLEY ACADEMY

FOR THE IMPROBABLY GIFTED

THE HADLEY ACADEMY

FOR THE **IMPROBABLY GIFTED**

— CONOR GRENNAN —

Tommy NELSON®

An Imprint of Thomas Nelson

The Hadley Academy for the Improbably Gifted

© 2019 Conor Grennan

Published in Nashville, Tennessee, by Tommy Nelson. Tommy Nelson is an imprint of Thomas Nelson. Thomas Nelson is a registered trademark of HarperCollins Christian Publishing, Inc.

Cover art by Micah Kandros Design.

Illustrations by Alessandro Valdrighi.

Tommy Nelson titles may be purchased in bulk for educational, business, fund-raising, or sales promotional use. For information, please e-mail SpecialMarkets@ThomasNelson.com.

ISBN 978-1-4002-1534-8 (hardcover)
ISBN 978-1-4002-1537-9 (e-book)
ISBN 978-1-4002-1800-4 (audio book)

Library of Congress Cataloging-in-Publication Data

Names: Grennan, Conor, author.
Title: The Hadley Academy for the Improbably Gifted / Conor Grennan.
Description: Nashville, Tennessee: Tommy Nelson, [2019] | Summary:
Although his abilities are dormant, thirteen-year-old Jack Carlson is
drafted into an academy for future heroes where some believe Jack is the one prophesied to end the
    ancient Shadow War.
Identifiers: LCCN 2019020500 (print) | LCCN 2019022229 (ebook)
Subjects: CYAC: Ability—Fiction. | Self-confidence—Fiction. | Schools—Fiction. | Prophecies—
    Fiction. | Good and evil—Fiction.
Classification: LCC PZ7.1.G7424 Had 2019 (print) | LCC PZ7.1.G7424 (ebook) | DDC [Fic]—dc23
LC record available at https://lccn.loc.gov/2019020500
LC ebook record available at https://lccn.loc.gov/2019022229

Printed in the United States of America

19 20 21 22 23   LSC   10 9 8 7 6 5 4 3 2 1

Mfr: LSC / Crawfordsville, IN / September 2019 / PO #9549946

For Finn (Systemic) and Lucy (Kinetic)

CONTENTS

CONTENTS

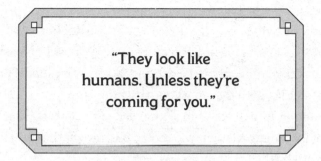

CHAPTER 1

"They look like humans. Unless they're coming for you."

CONSPIRACY

It's the best presentation I've ever made, Jack. Seriously. Mr. Robbins is gonna love it."

Jack's best friend, Freddy, was organizing the papers scattered across his desk in first period. "But you know what? It's not even about my grade. It's about *humanity*. I need to get the truth out there."

Jack reached down and picked up one of Freddy's fallen papers. "You're failing history, Freddy. You don't need to get the truth out there. You need to pass eighth grade."

Freddy twisted around in his chair. "You're beginning to sound like one of them, Jack—one of the people trying to silence people like me."

"Your final project is not the time for another conspiracy theory," Jack urged.

"This is the opposite of a conspiracy theory." Freddy tapped his notes. "These are facts, man."

"Just saying 'these are facts' doesn't turn things into facts. They have to actually be true—"

"Freddy Sanchez and Jack Carlson." Mr. Robbins made a zipping motion across his lips. "Okay, people. We're going to continue with your final projects on the rise and fall of civilizations. Brandon went yesterday with his report on Attila the Hun."

Brandon Jordan stood to acknowledge the cheers. That's what you got for having a father who rented out Yankee Stadium for your thirteenth birthday: a bottomless well of applause.

"Yes, it was quite the stirring tribute, Brandon," said Mr. Robbins dryly. "Today, however, we will move on to . . ." He checked the notebook on his desk. "Freddy Sanchez." Mr. Robbins peered over his glasses at Freddy. "Freddy will be presenting about the history of clandestine security."

Freddy hopped up and clicked on the laptop at the front of the room. The classroom screen sprung to life, displaying a title in oversized font:

THE SECRET MILITARY ACADEMY RESPONSIBLE FOR SAVING THE WORLD BY FREDDY SANCHEZ

A collective groan rose from the class. Most of the kids had been in St. Paul's since kindergarten. They had seen Freddy's work. This was pretty much par for the course.

Mr. Robbins shot a suspicious look at Freddy. "Is this a joke, Mr. Sanchez?"

Freddy's eyebrows popped up. "No, sir!"

Mr. Robbins paused, seeming to consider whether he should end the presentation before it got any stranger. But he sat back and waved Freddy on.

Freddy pushed his mop of curly black hair from his face and tugged his frayed khaki pants down to cover his ankles. Freddy and Jack were both on scholarship at St. Paul's. They made pants and shirts last as long as possible and dreamed of the day they would stop outgrowing their clothes.

Freddy cracked his knuckles and clicked the remote. A satellite map of the East Coast of the United States appeared on the screen behind him. "There are thousands of small islands off the coast of Maine," Freddy began. "Elk Island is one of them. It would be indistinguishable from all the other islands dotting this map except for one thing."

He clicked forward to reveal a detailed sketch. Drawing, Freddy would say, was something of a specialty for him, although he measured *specialty* in degrees of enthusiasm rather than actual talent. The messy image in front of the class now was of a colossal stone fortress in a pine forest. At the fortress's center rose a massive gate made of rough vertical beams bound together by iron. A single symbol marked the gate: an *H*.

Mr. Robbins put his feet up on his desk and leaned back in his chair, drawing muffled laughter.

"This is a photo-realistic rendering of a particularly unusual structure on Elk Island. This fortress is clearly ancient, and yet there is no public information about it."

Freddy strolled to the screen in a well-rehearsed move. "That's because this building is a military installation where teenagers are trained for active duty." Freddy pointed at the screen and paused for effect. "This is the Hadley Academy for the Improbably Gifted."

Snorts of laughter rippled around the class. Jack sighed.

For as long as he could remember, Jack had received a text from his friend every evening that read URGNT!!!! or FOTW!! (Freddy's code for "Fate of the World.") That was the signal for Jack to meet Freddy in the hallway of their apartment building in Jersey City's south side. Freddy would share some discovery from the Dark Web, something the government didn't want the world to know.

"You're the only one I can tell," Freddy would whisper.

On that front, at least, Jack believed him. Freddy's mother was a recovering meth addict, and his father worked three separate jobs to pay for her institutionalization. Freddy barely saw his father and hadn't seen his mother in over a year. Freddy's aunt helped out when she could, but she had three young kids of her own and lived a long bus ride away. So his dad had asked Jack's mom to keep an eye on Freddy.

Freddy's hallway whispers frequently drew the attention of Jack's mom. Jack was adopted, and his mother often told Freddy how grateful she was that his dad trusted her to take care of him too. She regularly poked her head out the doorway and invited Freddy to dinner. Freddy would make a beeline into the galley kitchen where he'd reveal the same secret to Jack's mom. She listened with the gravity one might afford a trusted anchor on the nightly news. She asked follow-up questions about yetis and aliens, probed him about his latest government conspiracy, and made Freddy feel that his information was utterly reliable.

When Jack had asked her about it once, her face softened. "Freddy lives in a different world, Jack. You can trust him without believing him."

"He's exhausting," Jack said.

"Imagine how exhausting it is for Freddy. He has to convince his best friend of things that he knows are true."

But this mysterious island military academy—Freddy had kept this a secret even from Jack and his mother.

Freddy, mistaking the groans of some of the more academically minded girls in the front row for awestruck murmurs, found Jack and flicked his eyebrows as if to say, "pretty good, right?"

"Where did you say this island was?" Mr. Robbins asked, interlocking his fingers behind his head.

"Somewhere off the coast of Maine. Other than that, I'm not exactly sure, sir."

Mr. Robbins looked up in mock surprise. "You can't find the island? Aren't you the founding member of the cartography club?"

The class snickered.

"That's Jack's club, sir," Freddy corrected him. "I only joined last week, when Claire transferred and Jack was the only one left."

Jack sucked in his breath. *Seriously, Freddy?* His friend had no filter between brain and mouth.

"Still want to tell me you don't have a crush on my girlfriend, little man?" Brandon called from the back of class. "It wasn't enough that you guys were cross-country buddies?" His friends cackled.

"That's enough," Mr. Robbins interrupted.

If Claire Lacoste had been there, she would have rolled her eyes, relaying a silent apology to Jack about how her boyfriend could be a jerk. She'd have cast a single glance back at Brandon, which would have shut him down. Claire could say more without speaking than anyone Jack had ever known.

At least, those were all things she would have done *before* Jack messed up their friendship. Jack's face burned just thinking about that night.

But Claire wasn't around to see any of this. Eight days earlier she had transferred, on scholarship, to finish the school year at a boarding school in New Hampshire. They had recruited her to help the girls' cross-country team make it to the state championship for years to come.

At the front of the classroom, Freddy charged ahead. "Elk Island is *invisible*, Mr. Robbins."

"Excuse me?"

Freddy held up a clarifying index finger. "No one has found it because it's hidden from satellite imagery—for security purposes."

"Ah." Mr. Robbins settled back into his seat and offered a solemn nod.

"What is it, some kind of wizard school?" Brandon's confidence was swelling.

"It's a military academy," Freddy explained. "You have to be thirteen to be selected. You're in the clear, Brandon, since you failed third grade. You're fourteen, right? Or is it fifteen?" That got Freddy a few laughs. "And they're not wizards—I don't think wizards even exist. The people recruited to the Hadley Academy have an improbable ability, a gift of some kind. But far more important than what those gifts are is what they *do* with them." Freddy cleared his throat and dropped his voice an octave. "They save the world."

For a moment the classroom was quiet. Mr. Robbins folded his arms. "From whom, exactly, does the world need saving?"

"From shadow reapers."

"As in the Grim Reaper?" said Sarah Murray in her are-you-really-this-dumb voice.

Freddy nodded vigorously. "Right. I mean, not *literally* the Grim Reaper. They don't wear black cloaks or anything. They look like humans. Unless they're coming for you. To their prey, shadow reapers look like some kind of . . ." Freddy's hands clenched the air around him as if physically grasping for the right word. "Ice demon, I guess. Anyway, if you see a reaper, you'd better run. If they touch you, they freeze your heart. Frozen solid. Kills you dead, just like that." He snapped his fingers.

"Why don't they just shoot people?" Brandon called out, drawing further cackles.

"Excellent question," Freddy said, pointing at Brandon. "Freezing internal organs shuts down the human body, making the cause of death a mystery. Bullets would draw too much attention. The police would have to open a murder case. This way it appears like a heart attack."

Mr. Robbins sighed. He clapped his hands on his knees and sat up. "Okay. Thank you, Freddy. Let's move on, shall we?" He took the notebook from his desk.

"Mr. Robbins, with all due respect, you didn't let me finish," Freddy protested.

"Does the latter part of your presentation contain evidence to support your claims?"

"You can find this stuff on the Internet," Freddy assured him. "You just have to know where to look."

Freddy lives in a different world than you and me, Jack. You can trust him without believing him." Jack's mom's words took on new meaning. Was it any surprise that Freddy would discover a supernatural explanation for the heartbreak he'd experienced?

Mr. Robbins did not share his mother's sentiment. "Your gullibility is a liability, Freddy. I'm frankly concerned that—"

"What about Carl?" Freddy interrupted.

Mr. Robbins paused. "The security guard? What does he have to do with anything?"

"Carl has been the security guard here for about a hundred years. But we haven't seen him in over a week. Why?"

"Carl has retired," Mr. Robbins said quickly. "The administration is currently searching for his replacement."

"Or he's being replaced by an operative from the Hadley Academy to recruit St. Paul's students." Freddy's arms were spread like a courtroom prosecutor who had just made the argument to end all arguments.

Mr. Robbins let the awkward silence permeate the classroom. Freddy's words hung in the air like a slowly deflating balloon until Freddy shuffled back to his seat.

"You will be receiving a failing grade for this project, Freddy," Mr. Robbins said, waving a pen in his direction. "It was, from beginning to end, a complete waste of our time."

"Sorry, man," Jack whispered. "I thought it was interesting."

Freddy swiveled around. "You believe me, right?"

Jack squirmed. "Uh . . . I have to go to the bathroom."

"Oh come on, man. Your mom understands this stuff way better than you do."

Jack already had his hand raised. He mouthed *bathroom* when Mr. Robbins made eye contact, and Mr. Robbins motioned him to go. He was still trying to get the class back on track after Freddy's presentation.

"Keep an eye out for that new security guard," Freddy whispered after him.

Jack scurried out. It was getting harder and harder to find creative ways to avoid telling Freddy that he was a lunatic.

Jack stepped out into the hallway and made a sharp left. He ran headlong into a man six and a half feet tall, nearly bursting out of a security guard uniform.

On his lapel hung a brand-new name badge: *Hans*.

"Jack Carlson?" The man had a vague European accent, cropped fair hair, and pale blue eyes. His jaw looked carved from a mountain. "Would you come with me, please?"

Jack's heart tumbled into his stomach. There was nothing good about a school security guard wanting to talk to you. He hurried to keep up as the man walked quickly down the hall. "Are we going to the main office? I'll need to tell Mr. Robbins."

"No."

"Then where—?"

Something on Hans's wrist buzzed. He pulled up his sleeve to reveal a band glowing bright red. An arrow pointed toward the window at the end of the corridor.

"What is that, an alarm clock?" Jack asked.

Hans strode to the window. They were three stories up, overlooking the street. Below, two police cars, sirens blaring, sped the wrong way up the one-way street toward St. Paul's.

Jack stepped back, staring up at the security guard's concerned expression. "Who are you?"

Hans turned from the window. "We have run out of time."

"Out of time for what?" Jack's heart beat wildly.

"Jack Keaton Carlson, you are hereby drafted into the Hadley Academy for the Improbably Gifted. We need to leave immediately."

"What?"

Hans furrowed his eyebrows, evidently unaccustomed to rhetorical questions. He repeated himself, but the wail of police sirens drowned out his words.

Hans hesitated only a moment. Then he grabbed Jack and threw him over his shoulder. "I am sorry, but there is not time to explain."

"Hey! Put me down! Hey!" Jack was a natural athlete with the narrow, strong build of a distance runner, but he had no chance in the grip of the much larger man.

Jack's stomach lurched as Hans carried him down the back stairs.

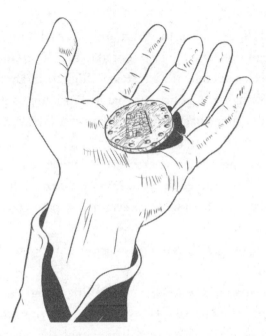

CHAPTER 2

THE COIN

Hans, with Jack still slung over his shoulder, burst out an emergency exit off the gym. He spun, scanning the line of cars in the gated faculty parking lot across the street. Then he loped across the road and tossed Jack in the open roof of a forest-green Jeep Wrangler.

"This is Mr. Robbins's car—are you kidnapping me?" Jack demanded.

"I am rescuing you."

"I don't need rescuing!"

"We need to keep you alive, Jack. You are the only one who can save them."

"Save who?"

Hans flipped down the visor and a key fell out. He jammed it into the ignition, and the Jeep roared to life. "Everyone."

He peeled out onto the street, smashing through the locked gate of the parking lot. A police car that had just zipped past screeched to a stop and arced back around in the narrow lane. Another police car sped from the left, blocking them in.

"Which way to your apartment?" Hans asked. "Without using these roads." Hans eyed the police cars and revved the Jeep's engine.

"How should I know? I've never had to plan an escape route to my apartment!"

Hans frowned. "I see. Please grip tightly onto the bar above your head."

Hans stomped the accelerator, heading straight for the cop cars. A moment before impact, Hans spun the steering wheel. The Jeep jumped the curb into a narrow alley, ripping the side mirrors off the vehicle. Jack yelped.

Hans hung a sharp left and an immediate hard right. They blasted across another street. Then Hans bullied Mr. Robbins's Jeep between two more houses, tearing off their aluminum siding. A police siren wailed on a parallel street.

A few minutes later, the Douglass Apartments rose straight ahead. Hans's wristband glowed scarlet. He peeled around Jack's apartment building, then skidded to a stop outside a heavily graffitied utility entrance between two dumpsters.

"What are we doing here?" Jack shouted.

But Hans was already out of the Jeep, pulling Jack after him like a rag doll. A rusted padlock hung on the utility door.

"That door doesn't open!"

Hans ran his fingers along the concrete wall, as if searching for a spare key. Behind them, two police cars skidded to a stop.

Jack turned, ready to explain his innocence. But then he saw them. A figure emerged from each car. They wore Jersey City police uniforms, but they weren't human. Their skin was tinted blue with an icy sheen; their violet eyes glowed with hate.

"Cursed shadow reapers," Hans muttered. They looked like ice demons.

The two shadow reapers lunged toward Jack with their hands outstretched. Just as one was about to reach him, a deafening pulse erupted from the roof. The shock wave blasted Jack into Hans and threw the shadow reapers back against their vehicles. A short figure in black landed on top of one of the police cars, its face hidden in the shadow of a hood. A second hooded figure leapt, whirling a blade with a short flame bursting out the tip. The reaper deflected the blade with its arm as if its skin were made of steel. Then the reaper attacked, reaching for its assailant's throat. The dark figure parried it back with the blade.

Amid the commotion, Hans continued to skim the wall with his fingertips. A square panel slid open under his fingers. Hans pressed his hand onto the pane of glass underneath, and it turned blue. Just then the second shadow reaper sprinted at Jack and Hans with inhuman speed.

"Hans!" Jack screamed.

Hans yanked Jack back by the collar. With his free arm, he pulled out a long, etched blade, the tip blazing with white fire. He swung it up with astonishing force. Sparks ripped across the reaper's abdomen like a match across a striker. Jack screamed again.

The reaper stumbled back. Then it charged once more.

A third warrior in black jumped between Jack and the reaper. The tip of the warrior's blade was an intense blue flame. The fighter thrust the flaming point straight and true at the center of the monster's chest. With a burst of violet, the reaper was gone.

Jack stumbled backward, and Hans caught him. Hans tucked something into Jack's pocket. "Give that to the Superior. He'll understand." Then Hans yanked open the door.

Jack was aware only of a rush of cool air, then darkness as Hans pushed him through. The door slammed shut.

———

Jack lay on smooth flagstones, their cracks filled with velvety moss. This was not the basement of the Douglass Apartments.

A gentle breeze flowed over him, then was still again. He was breathing the clean morning air of a forest, inhaling pine and earth and stone. He pushed himself up with a groan, and his voice echoed off the stones.

Jack was in a large outdoor courtyard, lit by lampposts and enclosed by a stone wall that stood two stories high. White-and-gray marble benches were scattered throughout the area. In the center of the courtyard stood a statue of a young man, crouched and gripping a blade in his hand. An illuminated inscription wrapped around the base: *One Life for Many.*

Jack had tumbled through what appeared to be, even on this side, an exact replica of the utility door from the Douglass Apartments, complete with rusted padlock and illegible graffiti. On either side of it, set in the stone wall, dozens of doors of various sizes and shapes encircled the courtyard: barn doors, paneled suburban front doors,

Middle Eastern doors with onion-shaped tops, intricately carved natural wood doors, and so on.

Footsteps echoed across the courtyard, and a man came into view. He was about fifty and wore a well-appointed charcoal suit and crimson tie. He had trimmed dark hair, sprinkled with gray, and looked like the curator of an art gallery.

The man stopped a short distance away and surveyed Jack suspiciously. "You're not my team of operatives."

Jack just stared at the man, unsure how to respond.

"Where. Are. My. Operatives?" the man pressed. "And who are you?"

"I'm Jack Carlson. What is this—?"

At that moment four individuals in black tumbled through the Douglass Apartments door. The leader lifted the hood, revealing spiked neon-blue hair and small black eyes. She stormed toward Jack, oblivious to the man in the suit.

"What do you think you're doing?" she barked. "Is this what recruits are doing these days? Trying to get a closer look at a reaper?" She let out a string of scorching words in what sounded like an Asian language and stomped toward Jack. She gripped him by the throat, lifting him off his feet. "We could have been—"

"That's enough, Operative Zhang," the man said, stepping into the dim light.

The woman turned, letting go of Jack. She and the other three in black gear came to attention. "Superior Blue. I didn't see you there."

"It's quite all right. You eliminated the reapers, I assume?"

"Yes. Flood blazed the first one. I blazed the second." She spoke in a chopped voice, staring straight ahead.

"Excellent work as always," Blue said. "I'm glad your team is safe."

Operative Zhang bowed her head slightly but didn't respond.

Then she glared at Jack, as if searing his face into her memory. The team of operatives left through a large gate, each swiping a wristband over a glass panel.

Superior Blue turned his attention to Jack. "How did you get in here?"

"I don't know where *here* is."

"Answer my question, please."

Jack rubbed the back of his head. "I was kidnapped. By my school security guard, Hans," he stammered. "We need to call the police."

"There are no recruiters named Hans." Superior Blue stared at Jack, as if trying to decode his words. "And our recruiting class is complete as of this morning," he said. "So let's start again. How did you get in here?"

Jack was turning in a small circle, trying to get his bearings. "Where am I?"

"The portal courtyard. This is the only way on and off Elk Island. It's the front door, the back door, and everything in between . . ."

"No," Jack interrupted. "This whole place. A second ago I was in Jersey City. Where am I now?"

The man squinted at Jack. "This is the Hadley Academy for the Improbably Gifted." He sounded unsure whether this information was too basic. It was not.

Before Jack could reply, the courtyard gate opened again, and a large chestnut-colored Labrador mutt barreled through. It bounded over to Superior Blue and sat at attention at the man's feet. The dog cocked its head at Jack.

The man didn't take his eyes off Jack as he addressed the dog. "Hello, Maggie. I imagine you're wondering who this young man is." The dog just stared at Jack in response. "Well, that makes two of us. But it's time for the Naming Ceremony, so we'll have to bring our young interloper with us for the moment. Open the gate, would you, Maggie?"

The dog twitched her head up to the man. The man raised his eyebrows at the dog. "Ah—worried that we are letting in an intruder? Good girl," he said. "But never you mind. Dr. Horn will mind-scrape him within the hour. *Hup*."

Mind-scrape. The term settled in Jack's stomach like a cannonball.

The retriever peeled off and leapt at the gate, her collar swiping across the glass panel. The gate swung open.

Superior Blue. The woman in black—Operative Zhang—had called him Superior Blue. Jack had almost forgotten. He reached into his pocket, fishing for whatever Hans had thrust upon him. He pulled out a small round object. It appeared to be an old coin and had an engraving of a stone silo on the front and a spiral of numbers on the back.

Whoever Hans was, there was no question that he had saved Jack's life. He was trustworthy. Jack handed the coin to Superior Blue. "That guy told me to give this to you."

The Superior took the coin from Jack tentatively and held it up to the light. "Somebody told you to give this to *me*? Who?"

"Hans. The guy who sent me through that door. He told me to give it to the Superior."

The Superior eyed Jack with new interest, then studied the coin. His eyes widened. "Follow me, please. We'll discuss this later."

Jack looked back at the graffitied Douglass Apartments door. Should he make a break for it? Or would there be more reapers on the other side?

Unsure what else to do, he followed Superior Blue through the gate.

CHAPTER 3

ER
REAPER
MENT

ESCAPES

EA

TRAMPOLINE GRASS AND STEEL TREES

Superior Blue was speed walking up the path. The dog, Maggie, trotted at his heels but peeked back often to make sure Jack was following.

They led Jack past castle-like ramparts that peeked through

thickets of slender, aged pine trees. Cobblestone paths divided the forest like dry creek beds, leading to all manner of clearings and structures. A bunker-like building sat off to his left. Its entrance resembled the open jaws of a crocodile that disappeared gradually into the ground. The black marble sign above it read Office of Reaper Engagement.

They crossed a flat wooden bridge over a narrow river. Far upriver, the bank rose into a long, rocky bluff. Atop that was a row of mismatched houses of widely varied architectural styles—from a simple thatched cottage of old Ireland to a traditional Japanese home with white screen doors.

Across the bridge, in the middle of the woods, stood an exact replica of a four-story tenement house, complete with a zigzagging rusted fire escape clinging to one side. Jack was about to look away when the top of the building burst into flames. The blaze exploded out the windows of the top floor.

Jack pointed dumbly and called to the Superior. "Uh, excuse me. Is that supposed to be . . . ?"

Superior Blue glanced over impatiently. "Yes, yes. It's fine. Lucent—the young woman sitting cross-legged there—will warn them when somebody needs to be caught. Hurry up now."

Jack kept up, but he couldn't look away. Two young people in black stood at the foot of the building, gazing up. A third, Lucent, sat on the ground with her eyes closed. A terrible crash echoed from inside, as if an entire floor was collapsing. The fire escape jerked off its bolts and smashed to the ground. Lucent turned to say something to her teammates, pointing to a fourth-floor window. A moment later, a teen girl plummeted out that very window, falling toward the twisted metal of the fire escape.

Jack swallowed a scream as one of the kids on the ground—a

girl with a green headband—stretched out her hand. Enormous vines erupted from the earth and ensnarled the ruins of the fire escape, yanking it out of the way of the falling girl. A boy with a blond surfer's haircut pressed his hand to the ground, and the earth shimmered.

The girl hit the grass. Then she bounced, unharmed, into the air.

"Escapes class," Superior Blue said over his shoulder. "Those old New York City tenement houses are terribly difficult to navigate. Firetraps, all of them."

"She fell . . . She bounced," Jack started.

"Because Bound there can turn any surface into an area of trampoline-like elasticity."

"And that other girl. She *made* vines."

"Ivy is what you dormants might call 'good with plants.' A green thumb, no?"

Maggie barked, drawing Superior Blue's attention forward. Up ahead, there was an enormous maple tree made entirely of steel. The detail of the leaves was extraordinary, and it glittered as if it had been newly polished.

"Boris Kleptov!" Superior Blue stormed up the path to the edge of a long clearing and shook a finger at a meaty-looking boy with dark hair matted to his head. "What have I told you? You want to destroy the entire ecosystem? You're supposed to be with your team, spotting for Escapes! Have you decided to shirk *every* responsibility?"

"Ivy won't let me use metallics on her vines," Boris mumbled in a Slavic accent. "She doesn't want the vines to get *hurt*. As if the plants can feel anything."

Superior Blue led Boris away from Jack, chiding him in a low voice. Boris eventually slunk past Jack toward the tenement house, his eyes fixed on his feet.

"Boris's spade is that he can turn organic matter into steel," Superior Blue informed Jack, motioning to the newly glittering maple tree.

"His spade?" Jack asked. He hurried to walk alongside the Superior, though he backed off when Maggie gave him a suspicious look.

"His gift," the Superior said. "Everyone is born with a gift, Jack, even a dormant—a civilian who hasn't discovered his or her gift. Someone like you." He eyeballed Jack up and down. "But more to the point, the problem is that nobody at Hadley has a spade that can turn metals back into organic material. Which means it is imperative to restrict where Boris practices."

"But that tree—it's beautiful."

"Yes, well, the next time he may try it on the grass, and we'll find ourselves walking on a field of needles."

Superior Blue stopped and considered Jack with a sparkle in his eye. "The only difference between Boris and you, Jack, is that Boris has broken through. Do you know how improbables tap into their gifts?"

Jack shook his head. Superior Blue leaned closer.

"They *believe* they have it!" Superior Blue spoke as if he were announcing ice cream for dinner. "Dormants listen to the world telling them, every day, that they can't have a gift. 'Be normal, like us!' the world says." Superior Blue waved his hand at their surroundings. "Improbables ignore what the world tells them. They risk looking different, looking strange, in order to explore their gifts. *That* is true courage."

There was a small explosion far ahead of them to the left, followed by a high-pitched, "WhooOOOOAAAHH!!" A boy surged above the treetops, arms flailing wildly.

Superior Blue didn't even react. "Come on now. No time to waste."

Along the way he called out to several more cadets. "Nice work!" He encouraged a slight-figured girl who had just hurled a throwing knife clean through the trunk of a tree. And he admonished a grinning boy reclining against a rock who was capturing random students in oversized bubbles and floating them high in the air until they were stuck in trees.

Only once did Superior Blue nod respectfully, to a group of four walking down the path. Or rather, three of them walked. A fourth leapt from one tree to the next, swinging impossibly from branch to branch. All four wore black uniforms, each with a different symbol on the chest. Jack fought an instinct to freeze, the way you might feel if you came across a bear in the woods or a stray dog baring its teeth.

"The one in the trees—she's impressive, no?" Blue whispered to Jack. "They call her Howler. Never seen her stand still. Try not to make eye contact with any of them. Operatives are not like you and me. They thrive on combat; they're bred for it. They see everything as a challenge."

Just as they were passing, Howler contorted her body and flung herself right at Jack. He flinched and collapsed into a crouch, hands covering his head.

But the operative had only come over to stroke Maggie's back as the dog passed by. In one smooth movement, Howler was back in the trees, catching up with the other operatives. Maggie barked happily.

"I know, girl," Superior Blue whispered to her. "Those operatives are hard characters, defending humanity as they do. But they love you, don't they?" Maggie barked again.

"Does your dog talk?" Jack asked.

The Superior stopped in his tracks. He turned to Jack and cocked an eyebrow. "Does Maggie *talk*?" he asked incredulously. "Margaret Thatcher here—she's a dog. Of course she doesn't talk."

"I didn't know . . . There's a lot of crazy stuff happening right now," Jack started, his cheeks growing warm.

Superior Blue's face softened. "Ah. You've never had a dog."

"No."

"A special bond develops between a dog and a human. It does not take an improbable gift. Now hurry, I'm late for the Naming Ceremony. We'll get you over to Dr. Horn immediately after. The mind-scrape won't hurt a bit."

Jack shuddered at the term but kept up.

As they walked through the island, the pine forest to the south grew denser. Only the occasional deer trail broke the darkness of the forest, and the sloping morning light stopped at the woods in a perfectly cut line. The entire place felt carved out of the woods. Even the path itself followed the natural contours of the land, winding around old trees. Notes of sea salt, too, were in the air, but Jack could neither see nor hear the water.

The dominant feature of the place, though, was the wall.

In the distance the wall rose two hundred feet in the air, above the tops of the tall pines. It was made of slate-gray stone, streaked with black metallic veins. The jagged and pockmarked face looked to be a single piece of stone, extending as far as Jack could see into the woods.

Soon the grounds became more manicured, with trees sculpted like oversized bonsais. The path divided, and they followed a darker stone trail leading off to the right and over a small rise. The path ran between two large boulders as tall as Jack. Inscribed on the stone to the left were the words *The Barracks*. On the boulder to the right was chiseled a relief of a boy with a blade, ready for battle. It was the same image as the statue in the portal courtyard, where Jack had entered. Beneath the boy, just as on the statue, were emblazoned the words *One Life for Many*.

"We're here," Superior Blue told him. Jack followed him between the boulders.

CHAPTER 4

HIDDEN NAMES

The Superior leaned toward Jack. "Just wait back here. The less you see, the less Dr. Horn has to mind-scrape."

They had arrived at a wide circle of a dozen grand residences of red brick and white pillars, each one with a slightly different design. Imposing Roman numerals hung in front of the pillars like pendants from a necklace, although Jack could not see what the numbers were actually attached to. The houses were marked from one to twelve around the circle, like elements of a giant clock. Soft pageantry music swelled across the green.

In the center of the circle, four dozen teenagers stood in formation, all in maroon tactical uniforms. Ahead of them, a podium sat next to an ancient wrought iron gate.

Superior Blue took a step toward the gate and then turned back to Jack, pulling out the coin again. "A man named Hans really gave this to you? He really sent you here?"

Jack nodded vigorously. "Yes. I didn't mean to come in here."

Superior Blue stared at Jack for a long moment, then looked back at the coin before he tucked it into his jacket pocket. Then he walked to the podium.

Waiting at the podium was a woman with short black hair that curled up as it touched her shoulders. Her narrow face ended in a sharp chin, and she wore a scowl of impatience. Thin dark eyebrows angled up like bolts of lightning. Superior Blue whispered something to her, and the woman squinted past the recruits to focus on Jack.

Then Superior Blue stepped to the podium, and the music faded out. "Congratulations, recruits. A week ago you came here with two hundred draftees. You are the last forty-eight standing, the most improbably gifted. I know this week has been exhausting and confusing. But you have passed every physical challenge, every mental examination, and every stress test. You are our finest."

The crowd murmured with anticipation.

"Your spade has defined you your entire life," he told them. "Your spade has shaped your personality and dictated your motivations. Understand your spade and you understand yourself."

Superior Blue paused. "But you are not here for a journey of self-discovery. You will learn to weaponize your gift, for the good of humankind. For that, I place you in the capable hands of our Director of the Office of Reaper Engagement: Director Iliana Darius."

The woman with the black bob stepped forward. "You now know of the shadow reapers and the war we fight," Director Darius announced. "Over the next three years, as you rise to the rank of cadet and graduate to become operatives, you will learn to blaze these reapers, and you will learn to survive."

Director Darius surveyed the recruits before she continued. "One Life for Many," she said. "It is inscribed on the statue in the portal courtyard. It was the first thing you saw when you entered Hadley. You will also find it inscribed on every one of your barracks. When you are hurt, when you are tired, when you are in pain, when you are afraid, repeat that mantra to yourself. Hadley stands between civilization and chaos. You will give your life to protect others if necessary. That is your calling."

Low, excited chatter spread through the crowd. Recruits rubbed sweaty palms against their uniforms, eyes darting to see how others were reacting. Jack wondered what they had learned over the last week to get them so ready to face the shadow reapers—the same reapers that had come inches from murdering Jack earlier that morning.

Director Darius motioned to the gate next to her. "This is the Spade Threshold. The Order of the Grays created it a thousand years ago. Since then, recruits have passed through to discover which spade classification they belong to: Kinetic, Theoric, Systemic, or Expathic."

Behind the podium a massive hologram appeared in the air: an orange square surrounding three strokes in a shape resembling the point of a sail and its connecting ropes. Jack recognized it as the badge on Howler's uniform.

"Kinetic," Darius said. "Kinetics are driven by physical activity. They are natural trackers and explorers. They are risk takers and thrill seekers. Their spades are often marked by strength, speed, or agility. They are restless, most comfortable in nature, and always seeking the next challenge."

The orange square blinked out and was replaced by a blue rectangle with an infinity sign in it. Jack noticed for the first time that Superior Blue wore the same icon on a patch on the breast pocket of his suit.

"Theoric," Darius continued. "Natural-born problem solvers and strategists. Theorics are highly curious and often extroverted. Above all, they are visionaries and leaders. They excel at finding solutions where none seem to exist."

Next, a green triangle with three parallel diagonal slashes, large to small, appeared in the hologram. "Systemic. Highly creative, they find patterns where others do not. Systemics are outstanding designers, architects, artists, and coders. They tend to be introverted, obsessed with reading, sketching, and creating."

The image faded and a fourth icon appeared, a slate-gray disc with four waved lines flowing outward—up, down, right, and left—from a small central circle.

"Expathics have a profound understanding of their environment, especially of nature and animals. They may be able to change the physical state of an object or even move it. Expathics are highly attuned to the emotions of others, allowing them to inspire and influence. They are exceptionally loyal and always looking to improve the world around them."

The hologram disappeared, and Jack studied the gate. Its

interwoven black iron beams rose out of the ground to form an arch that towered over Darius and Blue at the podium. Runes of the spade icons marked the three-foot-wide sides, two on each side. Across the arch stretched a single smooth sheet of metal.

Darius glanced over her shoulder. On the houses surrounding them, the Roman numerals on each residence lit up. "We will place you on twelve teams of four," she announced. "These teams are ranked from strongest to weakest, from one to twelve. Let your ranking motivate you, whether you are placed on Team Twelve or Team One."

Director Darius held up her band as if checking the time. A small holographic screen appeared above her wrist. She read four names, and four jittery recruits shuffled through the formation and came around to the other side of the iron gate.

"To hear your spade name is to hear your true identity spoken for the first time," explained Darius. "It is the name you have always had but have never known."

Director Darius and Superior Blue faced the gate and the four recruits. "Let the Naming Ceremony begin!" she called. The recruits behind her cheered.

Darius motioned for the first member of Team Twelve to pass through the Spade Threshold. A tall, tanned boy with green eyes stood straight and moved forward. As he stepped through, the blackened iron gate shone as if newly polished. On the left side of the gate, the iron rune in the shape of the Theoric rectangle glowed blue.

"Theoric," Darius announced.

The blank arch across the top of the gate dimmed, as if a cloud had passed over it. Then metal creaked, and a name stamped itself into relief across the arch.

"Maze!" Darius read the name triumphantly. The boy's face lit up, and the blue infinity patch appeared on his maroon uniform over his heart.

"Welcome to Hadley, Maze the Theoric." Director Darius said. She clenched a fist and pounded it against her own orange Kinetic badge. "One Life for Many."

"One Life for Many," Maze repeated, copying her gesture as well.

"One Life for Many!" the rest of the recruits shouted in unison.

The next recruit, a girl, wrung her hands before she stepped through. As she did, the orange rune glowed.

"Kinetic," Darius called.

Across the top of the gate, a word imprinted on the iron. "Spin!" Darius announced. The girl beamed.

"Welcome to Hadley, Spin the Kinetic!"

Spin was followed by the last two teammates, Turret the Systemic and Carbon the Expathic.

The names meant nothing to Jack. But it was clear each recruit had been deeply affected at hearing their names spoken.

After Team Eleven and Team Ten had completed the ceremony, Superior Blue whispered to Director Darius. She gave him a long look, then scanned over to pick out Jack from behind the remaining recruits.

"Instructor Suzuki, would you be so kind as to lead the rest of the Naming Ceremony?" Darius called over the invisible loudspeaker.

A tall woman in a black-and-white silk blazer left the front of the Barracks and came to the podium. Instructor Suzuki's long hair hung down to her waist in a perfect black braid. Only a slight quizzical glance from Instructor Suzuki to Superior Blue led Jack to believe the request was unusual. Suzuki tapped her band, and the hologram of names glided from Darius's band to hers. Instructor Suzuki read the names of Team Nine.

Director Darius and Superior Blue made their way past Jack, and Blue beckoned for him to follow them. They returned to the twin boulders marking the entrance to the Barracks, out of sight of the recruits and the Spade Threshold.

"You should have kept him in the portal courtyard," Darius told Blue. "Dr. Horn will have more to remove now that he's seen so much. The chances of brain damage are already increased."

Jack's stomach roiled. *Brain damage?*

"Except," Superior Blue answered. "I don't believe he should be mind-scraped. I believe Jack Carlson should join this recruiting class."

Iliana Darius's eyebrows raised. Her voice remained level, but she looked as though she'd just caught a whiff of something distasteful. "We have the Forty-Eight. Their cognitive access levels are exceptional. They had their breakthroughs long before they arrived here. They have spent years accepting that their gifts are real. This boy is a *dormant.*" She drew out the word, not disguising her scorn. "He has had no breakthrough. He believes himself to be completely normal. He is, in short, useless to us."

"No one accidentally stumbles into Hadley," Blue replied. "He claims he was brought by a man calling himself Hans who gave him this." Blue flipped the coin to Darius.

She caught the metal disc without taking her eyes off Superior Blue. Then her gaze fell to the coin and the etching of the stone silo. Her brow furrowed. She looked back up at Superior Blue. "Is this a joke, Superior?"

"It would be quite a joke, wouldn't it?"

Darius held up the coin to Jack. "Where did you get this?"

Jack swallowed hard. "It's like he said. This guy, Hans—the new school security guard—he told me I had been drafted. He told me to give that coin to the Superior. We were being chased by two reapers. He saved me."

Darius's expression clouded over. "What do you know about shadow reapers?"

"Nothing," Jack said quickly. "Hans called them that. And my friend at school . . ." Jack motioned weakly around him. "I need to get home. My mom is going to be worried."

Darius ignored Jack. She flipped the coin back to her colleague. "What exactly is your theory here, Superior Blue?"

"Jack Carlson is the Guardian." A long, awkward pause spread between them.

"Excuse me?"

Blue's expression remained even. "The Order of the Grays said that Wyeth—the Reaper King—can only be destroyed by the Guardian. The Guardian has arrived."

Director Darius took a step back and examined Jack. "Did he fall from the sky, as the Grays predicted?"

"Not literally, no. He came from New Jersey."

Darius rubbed her hands together in thought. "I am not sure where to begin, Superior Blue."

"Try the beginning, Director Darius."

Darius looked instead to Jack. "Jack Carlson, is it? Well, Jack. Superior Blue seems to believe that you are the one indicated by the Great Prophecy, the myth of an ancient order of monks. The Order of the Grays were the founders of Hadley, many centuries ago. Do you know anything about the Grays?"

"No, ma'am."

"Well, that is curious, since Superior Blue believes that you are the one they've been waiting on for a thousand years. Did you emerge from the Silo, by any chance?"

Jack was growing more confused by the moment. "Silo?"

"I'll take that as a no," Darius said. "More important than where you came from is who you are. Superior Blue believes that you have come to fulfill the prophecy by killing the Reaper King, Wyeth, and saving humanity."

Director Darius let that hang in the air for a moment. "Can you take a guess, Jack Carlson, as to why I believe you may be unable to kill the Reaper King?"

Jack gulped. "Because I don't know anything about reapers? And because this Reaper King could probably kill me pretty easily?"

"That is obvious and true, but it is not the reason I am thinking of." Darius tossed a look of annoyance at Superior Blue. "It is impossible because the Reaper King is already dead." A note of satisfaction shaded her voice. "Wyeth has been dead for thirteen years. Since then, not a single new shadow reaper has been created. Their numbers have dwindled, and we are on the verge of winning the Reaper War."

She turned back to Superior Blue. "Yet now you believe that the Guardian has arrived. Thirteen years too late."

"Wyeth is alive, Director Darius. Everything the Order of the Grays has ever predicted has come to pass. The Grays said that Wyeth could only be destroyed by the Guardian." Blue turned to Jack. "Did you ever kill a Reaper King, Jack?"

"No, sir."

"Then Wyeth cannot be dead," Superior Blue confirmed.

"The Bulgarian killed him, Superior Blue."

"The Bulgarian came to believe that he did not, Director Darius."

"Because he went insane." Darius's annoyance had soured into deep irritation.

"The Bulgarian came to believe the Grays were right," Superior Blue insisted. "They predicted that Wyeth would bring a darkness that would consume the world."

"For a thousand years we have fought the plague of shadow reapers. Was that not enough darkness for you?"

"The Great Prophecy predicts that in the final days, Wyeth will not merely have a reaper army. Rather, the world will *become* his reaper army," Superior Blue clarified. "Hadley operatives are trained to fight reapers. We are not trained to rescue a darkened world."

"But this boy, this dormant, *is* trained to rescue a darkened world?" she asked. They both turned back to Jack.

"You have the answers, Jack, even if you don't know it," said Blue.

"I don't even know what I'm doing here," Jack stammered. "I don't understand any of this. I need to get home."

Darius adopted a more practical tone. "Even if we wanted to keep him here, we don't have room. Would you propose we mind-scrape one of our skilled recruits?"

"No. We will create a thirteenth team."

Darius threw her hands up. "We have had twelve teams since the founding of Hadley," she pointed out. "We don't have extra recruits lying around with which to fashion a thirteenth team."

"I can find the rest of his team," Superior Blue said.

"The Dome identifies improbables from among millions of young men and women. It drafts a pool of two hundred to bring to Hadley each year. From this pool we select the Forty-Eight. You are proposing that you can find three other draftees out in the dormant world that the Dome somehow missed?"

"The rest of the team members are likely also dormants, so the Dome would not have identified them. This case requires that we use the ancient methods of the Grays."

Director Darius rubbed her forehead in frustration and took a deep breath. "I'm sorry, Superior Blue. I respect your gifts. And I have a deep reverence for what the Order of the Grays has given us—humanity owes them a great debt. But their time has passed," she said. "I will not support this radical idea of yours, and we both know that neither will the Council. This is their decision, not yours."

Superior Blue paused thoughtfully, staring off into the woods.

"I propose a compromise," he said at last. "Let Jack stay. Let me bring in the rest of a team. We give them three days. That's three simulations in the Dome. If Jack is truly the Guardian, they will easily complete a simulation within seventy-two hours."

"Three *days*? Superior Blue, you are talking about four dormants. It would take them three *years* just to discover their spades, let alone weaponize those spades, let alone defeat a shadow reaper in the simulation dome," she said. "It would be like gifting a boy his first pair of running shoes, then giving him three days to win an Olympic medal."

"You're saying it would take a miracle."

"A *literal* miracle, yes."

"Then we're in luck because that's *exactly* what stumbled through our portal this morning," Blue said, motioning to Jack.

She shook her head. "This would be pure folly. What happens when they fail?"

"If that happened, we would perform a mind-scrape on all four and send them back."

"Dr. Horn will have to go deep into the hippocampus to get all those memories out," Darius said. "Their potential brain damage doesn't concern you?"

"It doesn't concern me because we won't need to do it."

"Hey. It concerns *me*," Jack interrupted. "A lot."

Superior Blue raised his index finger. "It won't come to that, Jack. I've never been more sure of anything in my life."

"The Council will never agree," Darius said.

"Director Darius, I have a bargain to propose." Blue spread his hands as if he were presenting a ceremonial object. "Support my plan in the Council, and if in three days Jack's team has not completed a simulation, I will resign and you will become Superior."

Darius regarded Superior Blue coolly. "You're serious."

"I am."

Darius locked her hands behind her back and rocked back on her heels, staring at the ground. "It is my duty to express my deep concern to you, Superior Blue," she said quietly.

"Go on."

"You are the most powerful Theoric I have ever known, William, but you are ignoring your gift. Your iterative analysis spade should be presenting you with thousands of possibilities in an instant for you to calculate and assess . . ."

"I have sequenced the iterations, and this one is the most likely," said Blue. "Something is happening out there, Iliana. The Grays predicted it. The Bulgarian knew it. A darkness is coming. This is *precisely* when we need the Guardian."

"You are discarding logic for an absurd fantasy," Darius said. "Your friendship with the Bulgarian has compromised your judgment. You have not been the same since his death. You hope that, against all odds, the Bulgarian was right when he claimed he *didn't* kill Wyeth. You refuse to believe that he died pursuing an outlandish theory."

Superior Blue only smiled. "Thank you for your concern, but my offer stands."

Director Darius studied the Superior for a long moment. She nodded. "Very well. I accept the terms. Jack Carlson has three days."

"*I* don't accept the terms," Jack said angrily. "I don't agree to *any* of this. You have to let me go."

"You've been drafted, Jack," Superior Blue told him. "You are now a recruit. This is not your decision."

"But how will the Grays select the three additional recruits?" Darius asked, ignoring Jack.

Blue held up Hans's coin, the side with the spiral of tiny numbers toward Darius. "Twenty-seven numbers. Three sets of nine digits."

Darius squinted at the numbers.

"This spiral consists of three social security numbers," Blue explained. "The Grays have already selected the recruits. They sent this coin to me through Jack."

"You know that's impossible."

"Be that as it may, I need your help, Trail," Superior Blue said, calling Darius by her spade name. "You're the best tracker we have. I need you to help the recruiters locate the new recruits and have them back here in two hours. We have no time to waste."

"What makes you think these social security numbers will belong to living people? Or that they will be the proper age?"

"I believe the Grays. I am merely following their road map."

Darius took a long deep breath. "Very well. I will brief the recruiters. Then I will support your idea in the Council. And I hope you know what you're doing, Rook."

Jack wondered if that statement was sincere. In three days when he failed, she would be the new Superior.

"Excellent," Blue said, the bounce back in his voice.

Jack heard a low beep. Director Darius touched her ear. "Yes?"

She listened for a moment. "I see." She gave Superior Blue a severe look. "We have a situation at the Naming Ceremony. A situation we haven't seen in several years."

Superior Blue's expression dimmed. "Who?"

"The recruit's name is Miles Watt. Team One. I'll go now and test him myself."

"You know the protocol, Darius. Bring security with you."

She turned and walked backward. "That's ironic, given how you've handled it in the past," she called back to him. "I can deal with this myself. Have the recruiters meet me at the portal courtyard in ten minutes." She jogged back up the path to the Naming Ceremony.

Superior Blue put two fingers between his lips and whistled. A moment later, Maggie bounded from the Barracks and sat at attention at Blue's feet. Superior Blue squatted next to her.

"Take Jack to Requisition, would you, girl? Requisition. Go on now, *hup*."

Maggie barked at Jack before she took off down the path.

"I'll get the tech to meet you over at Requisition," Superior Blue told him. "Your team will meet you there as well." Superior Blue pointed to Maggie trotting down the path. "I'd keep up with her if I were you, Jack. You're not in uniform yet. An operative is less likely to vaporize you if you're with Maggie."

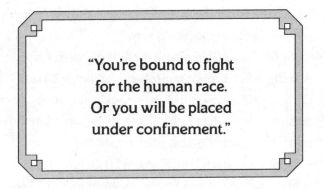

CHAPTER 5

"You're bound to fight
for the human race.
Or you will be placed
under confinement."

SUITING UP

Jack followed Maggie to a teak building, the size and shape of a tractor trailer. It was situated in a clearing enclosed by a knee-high brick wall. Maggie stopped at the entrance and sat at attention. Jack sat on the wall and waited. Finally a kid came walking up the path. He had slicked-back, widow-peaked hair and black eyebrows to match. His delicate cheekbones and slightly elongated nose gave him the appearance of a bird who had been magicked into a boy. He wore a black uniform two sizes too large.

Jack gave an awkward wave. "Hi—um, are you the guy I'm waiting for?"

The kid looked up. He must have seen something in Jack's expression because he pointed to four white stripes across his shoulder. "I'm an apprentice, you know," the boy said. "I outrank you. I outrank every cadet here, even."

Jack held up his hands in peace. "Sure, I didn't—Superior Blue sent me here to see the requisition guy."

"I'm not the 'requisition guy,'" he interrupted, his voice deepening. "I'm the lead tech, apprentice to Instructor Bakari. We're in charge of the simulation dome." Jack took a tentative step toward the apprentice. "Hey, listen, I don't even know what I'm doing here. If I offended you in some way, I didn't mean to."

The apprentice stretched to his full height for a moment, ready for an argument. Then he let his shoulders sag. "No, sorry," he mumbled. "It's just that I know I look young, but I'm sixteen. Sometimes even recruits think they can . . . You didn't do anything wrong." He rubbed his forearms, but when Jack didn't make fun of him, the apprentice seemed to relax a little.

"I'm Alexander." He stuck out his hand and Jack shook it. "Sorry you had to wait. I was setting up the Dome."

"I still don't get what the Dome *is*," said Jack.

"Really?" Alexander asked, eyebrows raised. "I thought Darius went over this on the first day. The Dome is the single most important thing at Hadley. It's the artificial intelligence that controls the simulations, the shadow map, the bands, everything." He raised his chin, his self-confidence returning. "That's why I work on it. I'm a Systemic. My primary spade is quantum adhesion. I can manipulate energy like glue. It sounds obscure, but for the physics of the portals, it's really important. I'm really good at making them."

Alexander studied Jack's shirt and jeans. "I received a message to meet a team of recruits here, so let's go ahead and get you set up. What happened? Did your uniforms malfunction?" he asked. "Doesn't usually happen to an entire team."

"I didn't get a uniform yet."

Alexander wasn't listening. He tapped his band and swiped through a series of holograms. While he was doing that, a raven landed a few feet away and hopped toward him.

"Don't mind him. I feed them sometimes," Alexander said, looking ruefully at the bird. "At least it's just one. A lot of times they come in . . ."

For the first time Alexander noticed that Jack was alone.

"Where are your teammates?" Alexander squinted as if he were trying to remember something. "Wait. Did you say you never *got* a uniform?"

"Right. I just got here today. And I don't know anything about my team except that they're out recruiting them now."

"You just finished the Naming Ceremony, didn't you?" Alexander asked.

"I didn't go through the Naming Ceremony. Like I said, I just got here a little while ago."

Alexander was paying attention now. "What team are you?"

"Thirteen."

"There is no Team Thirteen." Alexander cocked his head at Jack. "I'm not very good at getting jokes. If this is a joke, could you just tell me? Because I'm pretty busy."

"No *way*!" Running toward Jack, leaping and whooping like a kid trying to fly, was an ecstatic Freddy Sanchez.

"Jack!" Freddy threw his arms around Jack's waist and heaved him into the air, scaring the raven into flight. "You're *here*? When you never came back from the bathroom, Mr. Robbins sent me to search for you. But you were just gone. Then a woman came up to me at the water fountain and zapped me with some yellow laser thing. It said my name in this total robot voice, and she said I was drafted into the Hadley Academy for the Improbably Gifted. I thought it was a practical joke. But she took me through that utility door at Douglass and brought me here. And holy cow you're *here*, man! Whoa!"

Freddy did a little dance. Then he noticed Alexander and stuck his hand out. "Hey, man. I'm Freddy. What's *up*?"

Alexander held out his hand tentatively and Freddy slapped it backward and forward in a complicated ritual that Alexander just watched, bemused.

"So this is really a military academy that fights shadow reapers, right? Insane! Hey. What's with the pack of crows?" Freddy asked, pointing.

A dozen large black birds stood behind Alexander, watching the action. "They're ravens," Alexander corrected. "It's a conspiracy."

Freddy's eyes widened. "A conspiracy?"

"A flock of ravens. It's called a conspiracy." Alexander held up his hands as if trying to bring Freddy's chatter to a halt. "Forget the ravens." Alexander motioned between Jack and Freddy. "You guys know each other, and you're on the same team?" Alexander asked. "Because that would be a first."

Alexander suddenly stood at attention. Jack looked over to see Superior Blue walking toward them with two other kids.

"This is Team Thirteen, Alexander," Superior Blue said, motioning for Alexander to be at ease. "We're in an unusual situation. The Council's clearance has been sent to your band." The girl walking with the Superior wore a tight black ponytail and dark eyeliner winged out at the corners. Her skin glowed like sand catching the last of the evening sun's rays. The black guy walking behind her was sculpted like a linebacker, his head shaved completely smooth.

"Man, you can't keep us here like this," he said. "Is this some kind of prank? You can't just abduct people."

"Voss Winter," Superior Blue told Alexander. The Superior turned to face the new recruits. "You've all been drafted. By order of the Council of the Hadley Academy, you're bound to fight for the human race. Or you will be placed under confinement."

"Fight for *who*? What's going on?" Voss asked.

"Everything will be explained." Superior Blue motioned toward the girl. "This is Asha Hassan." He glanced at her. "Her recruiter reported that she had a little bit of a tough time coming through. But I believe she's okay now." He looked at her for confirmation, but she just stared blankly into space. He looked back at Alexander. "I trust you have this under control?"

"Sir—are they really Team Thirteen?" Alexander asked.

"They are, indeed. Which means they'll need their own door. The Council requests that you retrofit a thirteenth door onto the Dome."

"Yes, sir. By when?"

"Tomorrow."

"Tomorrow?" Alexander gulped. "With respect, sir, the process of creating a door can take weeks."

"You have a new portal door for Corpus Christi ready to be installed in the courtyard, as I understand," Superior Blue pointed out. "The Council has given permission to repurpose it for the thirteenth door. The same physics apply to the doors on the Dome as to the portals in the courtyard, do they not?"

Alexander cleared his throat. "Yes, sir, the door is the same. It's the chip that slots into the door that's different. But even just building a new chip will be extremely difficult on this timeline."

"Then we are fortunate that you are *improbably* gifted." Superior Blue cut him off, good-naturedly. "I have full faith in you, Edison."

Alexander straightened up at his spade name. From what Jack had gathered from the Naming Ceremony, a spade name was a sacred thing. To know it seemed to be to know something profound about the person, even if you didn't understand it.

"Alexander will take you to your barracks after you've been outfitted," Superior Blue told them. "I have to get back to the Council." He turned to Asha, who was still stony eyed. "I know you're still feeling a bit dizzy, Asha. Dr. Horn said that would be normal for another hour or so."

Asha started to topple, and Voss reached out to steady her. "You sure she's okay?" Voss asked. "She looks like she's about to pass out."

"She's fine, Recruit Winter," Superior Blue called back over his shoulder. "You'll take care of her. She's your teammate, after all."

"She's not 'fine.' You just drag people in here. How do you expect her to be? She needs to go home," Voss argued.

Alexander reached into a zippered pocket that ran up the side of his uniform. From it he pulled a glass screen and touched it to his band. The screen glowed for a moment, then chimed. Gingerly, he picked a small translucent disc off the tablet.

"Whoa, cool!" Freddy leaned forward. "Is that a tactile hologram?"

Alexander nodded to Freddy's question as he held the disc up between his thumb and forefinger like a monocle. "Okay. Who wants to go first?"

Freddy's hand shot up.

"For what?" Voss asked. "Nobody's explained what this is."

Alexander folded his arms. "You'll get all that information, Recruit Winter. And," he looked around at all of them, "we have outstanding protocols for explaining your absence to your families and schools, so you have nothing to worry about on that front," he explained. "All right, let's get you all in uniform, so I can get to work on that door."

"I want answers, man," Voss pressed.

Asha gazed up at Voss, who had at least six inches on her. "Voss, right? Listen, can we just get through this part? You're freaked out, and that's making you angry. I get that—"

"I'm not freaked out."

"Well, I *am* freaked out, so can you do me a favor and just let this guy do whatever he's supposed to do right now? He's not going to hurt us."

Asha's fingers were tapping the tip of her thumb as if she were hammering out complex Morse code messages. Voss glanced at the nervous tic. He gave only a short, irritated nod. Alexander waited to be sure the conversation was over and then pressed the disc into Freddy's palm.

The long, low Requisition building in front of them hummed to life. Alexander closed Freddy's fist around the disc.

"Hold on to this tight." Alexander gave Freddy's fist a shake. "Do you have any metal on you besides the band?" Superior Blue had given them all wristbands. They looked metallic, but Jack's molded to his skin like warm plastic.

Freddy shook his head. "No. But Jack has blackouts. Is it safe for him to go through?"

Jack groaned at his friend. "I haven't had a blackout in a while."

"You had that blackout when you wandered off and your mom couldn't even find you, just a few months back. And you had another one just over a week ago. Outside the diner. That's what caused all that trouble with Claire, remember?"

"I'm fine," Jack said.

"You sure?" Alexander asked. "If you want, Dr. Horn can check you out."

"I'm fine. Seriously."

"All right." Alexander shrugged. "Now everyone pay attention." He pointed at Freddy's hand.

"That disc you're holding is like a strong magnet. You're going to walk quickly through this door and straight out the other side. You'll feel the disc tugging to get out of your hand. *Do not let it go.* If you do, it'll twist everything up in there and I'll be up all night fixing it. It'll also give you a splitting headache."

"What's in there?" Freddy peered into the dark.

"When you get in there, don't stop walking," Alexander said, ignoring the question. "Don't slow down or speed up. Let the magnet do the work."

Alexander steered Freddy to the doorway and gave him a little push. He disappeared into the dark, and the door slid shut.

"Whoa!" Freddy came tumbling out the other side of the Requisition building thirty seconds later. He stumbled back toward them, arms and legs akimbo like a starfish learning to walk. He was wearing a maroon uniform, which he pointed to, delighted. "That was *awesome.*"

Alexander took the disc from Freddy and pressed it into Jack's palm. "Don't let this go, okay?" Alexander pushed Jack into the dark open doorway. The door whirred shut behind him.

Heat blasted at Jack. He focused on keeping his pace quick but steady and not running to the other end. The disc tugged at his hand like a puppy on a leash.

That's when it got really weird.

Jack's clothes were filled with such a gust of wind that he was almost slammed back against the door. For a brief, terrible moment it felt as though his clothes had been ripped off his body. Leaning into the scorching gale, Jack covered his face with his arms and charged forward.

He felt a new shirt settle on his torso. Then it expanded like a deployed parachute. He reached back and felt the new, smooth material and something like cardboard pressed against his back. There was also a zipper down his flank where none had been before. Jack tumbled out the other side of the Requisition building. He hadn't even seen the door open.

Jack blinked in the light. He peered down to find that now he, too, wore a maroon uniform. Jack held up his arms like a marionette to get a good look.

Alexander took the disc from him. "The zipper along your side is your pack. You can hold thirty pounds lying flat against your back without feeling it. It's already packed with the essentials. Everything in your pack is linked with the decision-making functions in your frontal lobe. When you reach in there, just focus on what you're looking for. It'll appear in your hand."

He nodded at their waists. "That steel baton magnetized to your hip is a Hadley blade. It's a training blade, used for recruits and cadets, but it functions the same as the rune blade used by the operatives. For now, don't even think about deploying your training blade outside of class. Darius will have you mind-scraped so fast you won't know what's happening. You don't want to wash out, believe me."

"Wash out?" Freddy asked.

"Get sent home. They scrape your memories out, so you can't tell anyone about Hadley. You keep your spade, but your breakthrough is undone."

"How can it be undone?" Freddy pressed.

"You'll just never remember that you have a gift. But being honorably discharged—like the recruits who didn't make the Forty-Eight—that isn't so bad. Honorably discharged improbables tend to be pretty successful. Systemics become famous musicians, prolific authors, video-game celebrities, or coding geniuses. Kinetics end up getting paid millions a year to play pro sports. Expathics show up as successful speakers or as one of those wackos who live with grizzly bears in the wild. Theorics turn into tech billionaires, successful politicians, brain surgeons. You get the idea."

"That sounds pretty good," Voss pointed out. "How about you wash me out right now?"

"I was referring to the *honorably* discharged. Quitting is treasonous. They say dishonorably discharged improbables disappear off the face of the earth. Only the top people at Hadley know what happens to them." Alexander paused. "Besides, you wouldn't ask to leave if you knew what was at stake here."

Voss clenched his jaw but said nothing else. He took the disc from Jack and marched into the door of Requisition, then came out the other side a half minute later. Asha went after him, walking with arms out to keep her balance. When she came out, she pulled the zipper on the side and rummaged around.

"Hang on," Alexander said. "I need to walk you through how to use your pack first."

But Asha had already pulled out a short, black throwing knife. They all took a step back.

"Whoa," Voss said, holding up his hands. "Put that thing down before you hurt yourself."

But Asha's eyes had sparked. "It just gives you whatever you're thinking about?"

"Not *whatever*," Alexander corrected, eyeing the weapon in her hand. "There is a wide range but still finite number of tools and such. But you need to learn how to—"

"Is this oxyacetylene?" Asha pulled out and twirled what looked like a short steel pen. "It's tiny!"

"Um, I think that's actually—" Alexander began.

Flame burst from the tip. Jack jumped back, but Asha was already torching the throwing knife. She shook it cool, then pulled out assorted bolts and pliers. A minute later, something whirred between her thumb and middle finger.

Freddy took a step closer and squinted. "Did you just make that?"

Even Alexander seemed stunned. "Okay, it's not normal that you could do that so quickly."

Asha wasn't listening. Her anxiety had melted away. She let out a long, quiet sigh of contentment.

Voss shook his head. "Man. You have control issues. My cousin was the same way—I can spot it a mile away."

Asha picked up her tools from the ground and slipped them into her pack, her creation still spinning like a propeller between her fingers. "Making things helps me relax," she said coolly. "You want to start labeling, go check the mirror. I'm sure you'll find lots of interesting stuff there."

Alexander pulled out his tablet. "Okay, let's get back to business, people." He scanned his screen. "I think we can skip the pack safety module. If any of you have any questions about your packs . . ." He motioned with his chin toward Asha. "Now. Did they tell you why you're here, why they've added a thirteenth team?"

"That's what I've been saying," Voss pointed out. "Nobody told us anything."

"Do you know your spades?" Another thought seemed to occur to Alexander. "Hang on—do you even know what spades are?"

Freddy's hand shot up. "I do." But Asha just slowly shook her head. Voss gave Alexander a blank stare.

Alexander rubbed his forehead. "Oh boy. You're dormants. So they just . . . what? Grabbed you from the street and brought you in?"

"Maybe they needed extra recruits," Freddy said confidently.

"That's the thing. The Reaper King was killed thirteen years ago. If anything we need fewer recruits."

"Maybe they think this Wyeth reaper guy came back to life," Freddy persisted. "The Shadow is a kind of reaper, right? Can't reapers do that?"

"No. Reapers can't do that," Alexander said dryly.

Freddy caught Voss's raised eyebrow. "What? I don't know."

"Then why are you talking?"

"Why are *you* talking, Voss?"

"Freddy," Jack interrupted. "Easy."

"I don't know what any of this is," Voss told Alexander. "The Shadow? The Reaper King? What's that supposed to be?"

"The Shadow isn't a reaper. It's a force that has always existed," Alexander said. "The Shadow became the Reaper King a thousand years ago. He was a man and a beast, a creator of killers. He did not die. He called himself Wyeth, and for centuries he rained terror down on the world. But thirteen years ago the Bulgarian found a way to kill him."

"Aren't there some people who think that Wyeth is still alive?" Jack asked.

Alexander gave him a suspicious look. "Wyeth is dead," he assured them. "But I suppose someone might believe that Wyeth is still alive if they follow the Grays' predictions too literally."

"Who are the Grays?" Asha asked.

"They're the monks who founded Hadley. They had this whole legend that the Guardian would fall from the sky and save the world by destroying Wyeth. They believed that the shadow reapers were only the beginning and that Wyeth would ultimately bring devastation to the world. They didn't believe that an operative could end the Reaper War. But that was before an operative actually *did* kill the Reaper King."

Freddy's eyes widened. "A guardian—that's awesome! When's that supposed to happen?"

"It's a myth, dummy," Voss said. "It doesn't happen."

"You just traveled instantly through a portal, and you can't believe this?" asked Freddy.

"The portal is science," Voss argued. "We just experienced it firsthand. A bunch of monks and a guardian falling from the sky? That's a fairy tale."

Freddy turned to Alexander. "Why don't we just ask the Grays?"

"We can't ask the Grays," Alexander said. "They were killed off in the Battle Beyond the Wall over a hundred years ago."

His band pinged. He looked down and scrolled around a new hologram that had popped up. "Now, you all have everything? I have to get you to your barracks."

"There's a Team Thirteen barracks?" Jack asked.

Alexander squinted at his hologram. "It looks like they improvised. Come on."

CHAPTER 6

THE WATCHTOWER

The path was unlike the well-tended cobblestone paths at Hadley. It was overgrown and partly obscured by knee-high switchgrass, as if they were following a long-forgotten trail. As they rounded a bend, an ancient stone building loomed ahead.

"This is the original Watchtower," Alexander said. "Most recruits don't even know it's here." The tower was four stories tall, with a round perch at the top. Weathered wooden shutters hung on windows scattered at intervals around the curved walls. Judging by the condition of the building and the vines that wrapped the walls, it had been unoccupied for a long time.

Alexander pulled his tablet from his pack and touched his band to it. After a moment, he picked up a shiny skeleton key right off the tablet. He jimmied it into the lock of the cathedral-like front door.

"This is the only building this close to the main gate." He nodded over his shoulder toward a massive gate, almost as high as the wall, barely visible through a grove of trees. "The Watchtower is a relic, from before the gate was reinforced."

Freddy looked up expectantly. "Reinforced against shadow reapers?"

"You're way too eager to fight a reaper," Alexander said. "And anyway, no. The wall is just for additional security."

"You don't need a wall that size for nothing," Freddy argued. He snapped his fingers and pointed at Alexander. "Dragons, right?"

Alexander cocked an eyebrow and turned to Jack. "Is he serious?"

"This ain't *The Lord of the Rings*, bro," Voss said.

"What's *The Lord of the Rings*?" Asha asked.

Freddy shot her a skeptical look. "You don't know *The Lord of the Rings*? The best trilogy in the history of the written word? The movies made, like, a billion dollars each."

Asha's face flushed. "I don't get out much. That's a crime now?"

"There's nothing on the other side," Alexander interrupted. "Nothing that can get through anyway. That gate has stood for a long time."

Voss folded his arms. "Hold up. 'Nothing that can get through' is way different from nothing."

"You're fine," Alexander assured him.

At that moment, something hit the other side of the gate so hard that it shook on its colossal hinges. Alexander flinched. The recruits ducked. Freddy yelped.

"What was *that*?" Jack demanded, pointing at the gate.

"There is *something*!" Voss said, backing away. "I knew it!"

Alexander paused. When nothing else happened, he forced a laugh and waved it off. "It's the wind. We're on an island here, you know. Jet streams."

"I know something about islands," Asha whispered. "That wasn't a jet stream."

"I promise, nothing can get through," Alexander insisted. "You're totally safe."

With a last apprehensive glance at the main gate, Alexander turned his attention back to the Watchtower door. The others watched the gate.

Frustrated, Alexander pulled the key out of the lock and held it up to the light. He touched his ear. "Hey, the new key isn't working . . . The original key may be in the lock on the other side . . . I can't hack the panel because there *is* no panel. It's a million years old . . . No . . . No, it's fine. I'll get the key from inside . . . Yeah, I'll figure it out."

Alexander stepped back and looked straight up the Watchtower. He sighed. Then he turned to the forest and whistled.

After a moment, cawing ravens swooped over the pines and down toward the clearing. They landed on the roof of the Watchtower and chattered among themselves. Then one disappeared through a space in the eaves of the tower. The rest followed.

A couple of minutes later, the ravens emerged from the same gap in the eaves. They dove down toward the door, ignoring Alexander.

The last raven held a key in its beak. After a couple of failed attempts, it managed to insert the key in the lock.

"Yeah, yeah, very impressive," Alexander murmured at the ravens. He turned the key. The lock clicked.

Openmouthed, Freddy pointed to the departing ravens, then back to the key.

"I thought your spade was manipulating energy," said Asha.

"It is." Alexander nodded. "But lots of improbables have minors too. I have a minor Expathic spade. I can communicate with ravens—just ravens. I don't know why."

Asha was wide-eyed. "That's amazing!"

"Not so amazing when you're out in the dormant world and you have ravens following you everywhere. They're messy." Alexander glanced at each shoulder. "I wasn't the most popular kid to begin with, and when other kids saw ravens seeming to attack me all the time, they thought it was hilarious. *Bird Boy*, they called me. I didn't understand my spade or know how to control it. I was just the weird kid."

"I feel you there, buddy," Freddy said under his breath.

Alexander shrugged. "Anyway. Quantum adhesion is actually useful. Having ravens follow me? Not exactly the stuff of a legendary warrior."

"I think it's awesome," Asha told him.

Alexander didn't respond, but Jack saw him flush slightly, and his mood brightened. He leaned into the door, popping it open. "Come on, I'll show you around."

Inside, the ground floor was a large, open round space that smelled like a rainy afternoon. When Jack craned his neck, he could see all the way up to the roof. Somewhere water dripped. Steps jutted out of the curved wall in a gradual spiral and led up to a landing about twenty feet up, where there appeared to be a wide room-sized loft.

They followed Alexander up the vertigo-inducing stairs. A draft swept down through large open windows high above them as they climbed. The loft—the common area, as Alexander called it—was as cozy as the ground floor was bare. A large crimson Persian carpet covered the floor. Overstuffed and well-worn leather couches and chairs faced a large fireplace already in full blaze. The team gravitated toward the heat.

"Man. They set stuff up fast," Freddy noted. "I bet that's somebody's spade."

"What, moving furniture?" Jack asked.

"A fireplace." Voss tapped his boot at a thick log. "That's supposed to be an amenity?"

"That's supposed to be a heat source. There's no electricity in this building," Alexander told him.

"You have portals through space, but you don't have electricity?" Freddy asked.

"*You* don't have electricity," Alexander corrected. "The rest of the grounds does. This place just has a few gas lamps."

"Where are we supposed to sleep?" Voss asked.

Alexander nodded at ladders attached to the wall. "They apparently converted the storage rooms into three bedrooms. Two of you guys will have to room together."

Freddy punched Jack's arm. "Nice! Wanna be roommates? Oh man, we're gonna have so much fun."

"Hang on," Alexander interrupted, touching his ear. "Yes, go ahead, sir . . . Okay, I'll send them immediately." He tapped his ear again and turned to the others.

"You're wanted at the Spade Threshold." Alexander led them

downstairs. "It's Naming Day, remember? You're about to figure out who you really are."

"Yo." Voss pointed ahead of them as they came out of the Watchtower. "There's a dog just sitting there."

Maggie was sitting patiently on the grass, to the side of the cobblestones. When they approached her, she barked once, then turned and ran up the path.

"That's Maggie, Superior Blue's dog," Jack said.

"Better keep up with her," Alexander said, closing the door behind him. "You don't have a lot of time."

Jack didn't need any encouragement. It felt good to run. Voss and Asha kept up with him. Freddy groaned and trailed behind.

When they arrived in the Barracks clearing, the podium was gone. The only evidence of the morning's ceremony was the trampled grass where the Forty-Eight had stood in formation. The Spade Threshold stood alone in the middle of the circle of residences, gleaming under the midday sun.

Director Darius, Superior Blue, and an older woman waited for them. The other woman was probably in her eighties with light-brown skin and a silver Afro. She wore a white lab coat, marked by a blue infinity rectangle over her heart. Her eyes glinted with youthful enthusiasm. Maggie ran up to her, wagging her tail madly. The woman squatted down to rub under Maggie's chin.

"Team Thirteen," Superior Blue greeted them. "This is Iliana Darius, Director for the Office of Reaper Engagement." Blue nodded to Darius. "And this is Dr. Horn, our chief medic."

Dr. Horn stood back up and smiled at Team Thirteen. "It's a pleasure to meet y'all." She spoke in a slow southern drawl. "I was standing right about here when Superior Blue was a pup, when he walked through this gate and learned his spade name, Rook." She patted Blue's shoulder. "I find spade names far more descriptive than the fancy titles like Superior and Director, don't you, Trail?" She aimed this last comment to Director Darius.

"We are grateful for your presence, Dr. Horn," Director Darius said, seeming unwilling to disappoint Dr. Horn with a negative response.

"Oh, it's no bother at all. I wanted to see how Miss Hassan was feeling anyway. Stepping through the Threshold is too important a moment for feeling poor." Dr. Horn nodded to Asha. "How is the dizziness, young lady?"

"It's gone, thanks," Asha said.

"Glad to hear it." Dr. Horn turned to face the rest of Team Thirteen. "The Threshold tells your spade classification and your spade name. But while other recruits learn their gifts through years of introspection, exploration, and ultimately, what we call the breakthrough, I am here to sweep your synapses and just tell you exactly what your spade is."

Superior Blue turned to the four recruits. "Who wants to go first?"

Freddy scurried around the iron gate and stood at the other side of the Threshold.

Darius faced Freddy through the Threshold. "Step through, Recruit Sanchez."

Freddy paused. Jack had never seen him nervous before. He squeezed his eyes closed and stepped through.

On the left side of the gate's broad vertical frame, the wrought-iron rectangle with the infinity sign glowed blue.

"Theoric." Darius announced.

There was a metallic creak, as if an invisible stamp was pressing through from the other side, and a name appeared.

"Your spade name is Link," Darius told him.

"Link," Freddy breathed. "Wow. Cool."

Dr. Horn walked over to Freddy. She held two fingers to his forehead and closed her eyes. "Link, your spade is incongruous logic. You are able to make connections that others cannot."

Darius stepped back up and pounded her fist against her badge. "One Life for Many."

Freddy, grinning broadly, repeated the gesture, pounding his fist on the blue Theoric icon that had appeared above his heart. "One Life for Many!"

Asha went next. She steadied herself, then walked through the Spade Threshold.

The circle on the right side of the gate glowed gray.

"Expathic." Darius announced. On the name arch, the word *Ice* appeared. "Your spade name is Ice."

Dr. Horn placed her fingers on Asha's forehead. "Ice, your spade is as your name says. You have an environmental manipulation gift: the ability to change water molecules to ice. You appear to have a minor spade as well, though the Threshold doesn't reveal minors."

Darius beat her fist against her badge. "One Life for Many."

Asha touched her fist over the new gray Expathic circle on her uniform. "One Life for Many," she said in a slight daze.

Voss walked up to the Threshold. Darius nodded to him, and he took one broad step through. On the left side of the gate, the orange square glowed.

"Kinetic," Darius announced. They all stared up at the name arch. "Your spade name is Torque."

Dr. Horn moved toward him, but Voss took a sudden step back. He spun around and stared at the name arch. He turned back to Dr. Horn. "How did it do that?"

"The Threshold is only a mirror," Dr. Horn said. "It reflects who you are. Does that name mean something to you?"

"No," Voss said quickly. "Nothing."

Dr. Horn studied him for a moment, then reached up and placed her fingers on his forehead. Her eyebrows furrowed. "You are especially gifted, Torque. You have the gift of strength. And you have a minor spade as well that feels as powerful as your primary spade. But it is buried deep. Do you know what it could be?"

Voss shook his head.

Darius pounded her fist against her badge. "One Life for Many."

Voss hesitated, then touched the orange square that had appeared on his chest. "One Life for Many."

Superior Blue looked at Jack. "Okay. You're up."

Jack walked around the gate. He paused, then quickly walked through without being bidden.

Nothing happened.

"It didn't work." Freddy frowned. "Is it out of power?"

"It doesn't run out of power," Dr. Horn said in a low voice. Blue and Darius looked at each other.

"Could it be another . . . ?" Blue started.

"No," Darius said. "When someone with a shadow spade passes through, the runes go black. The name arch goes dark." Darius motioned to the Threshold. "This is . . . nothing. It's as if nobody walked through."

"Maybe he has so many spades that they canceled out," Freddy suggested.

Dr. Horn approached Jack and gently put her fingers on his forehead. They felt like soft leather, and Jack felt a cool tingling where she made contact with his skin. She dropped her hand and turned to Superior Blue and Darius.

"He must have a gift; every child is born with one. But I can't detect anything. I can't explain it."

Superior Blue put his hand to his chin. "Well. That complicates things."

Iliana Darius turned to Blue. "Superior Blue, we can end this now. Dr. Horn can mind-scrape them, and we can have them off Elk Island immediately. You would retain the position of Superior."

Blue shook his head. "No, Director Darius. This only confirms what the Order of the Grays are trying to tell us. It all makes sense."

Dr. Horn gave a sidelong look at Darius. She put her hands in the air, disavowing any responsibility. "This is between y'all. I'm heading back to the clinic. Let me know if you need me."

Darius turned back to Blue. "What's the next move, Superior Blue?"

Blue seemed surprised at the question. "The same as all the other teams, of course. Team Thirteen will report to the Manifestation Room in the Kwei Library. Reapers 101 is about to begin, and Instructor Suzuki won't appreciate it if they're late."

———

Voss stared at Jack as they followed Maggie to the library.

"Why do they want you here?" Voss asked finally. "You were the first one they brought through. Superior Blue clearly thinks there's something different about you. He barely blinked when you walked through that Spade Threshold and didn't show up as anything. What's the deal?"

Asha turned to face Jack. "Voss has a point. It seems like all this started with you. You don't have any insight here?"

Freddy answered before Jack could speak. "Think about it. Blue probably figures Jack is that Guardian person. The one who will destroy the Reaper King."

Jack stared at Freddy. "Actually—yeah. How did you know that?"

Freddy shrugged. "Seemed obvious."

"So we're here because of you," Voss said, pointing at Jack. "Because they think you're some kind of mythical figure? And now if we fail, we get a dishonorable discharge. They're going to scrape our minds and disappear us—or worse, put us back where we came from with big gaps in our memories? I don't know about you, but I like my mind just the way it is."

"We can't fail," Freddy shot back. "Weren't you listening? We're the ones who are going to help Jack kill the Reaper King!"

"The Reaper King that's already dead? How does that make sense?" Voss asked. "And what happens when they find out Jack isn't the Guardian?"

"Listen, maybe we'll be okay, right?" Asha said hopefully. "Think about it, what if Jack really is this . . . whatever?"

"This what? Finish that sentence, Asha," Voss pressed. "A boy who fell from the sky to save the world? I got news for you: Jack didn't come from the sky. And we have no clue how to kill shadow reapers. These people train for years to do that. They're improbables, with crazy gifts—we're not!"

"Relax. We have time," Freddy pointed out. "It's only day one."

Jack cleared his throat. "Yeah. Um. We actually don't have long," he said. "In order to get the Council to agree to all this, Superior Blue guaranteed that we would complete a simulation—kill a reaper, or I think they say *blaze* a reaper—in . . ." He wiped his suddenly sweating palms on the legs of his uniform. "Well, in a shorter time frame."

Asha stopped walking. Voss stood in front of Jack. "Hang on. How long, exactly?"

Jack swallowed hard. "Three days."

Even Freddy did a double take.

"Okay, that's not going to happen," Asha said. "We need a new plan. How do we get to stay?" She chewed on a fingernail. "I can't go back to where I came from. I can't."

"We figure out how to use our spades, and we complete the simulation," Freddy said, his bravery returning. "Maybe we only come close to blazing the reaper in the simulation tonight. By tomorrow we'll complete a simulation. By day three we'll be reaper-destroying machines."

Asha just stared at the ground. Voss seethed.

Freddy ignored them, pointing up ahead. "Whoa. That must be where we're going."

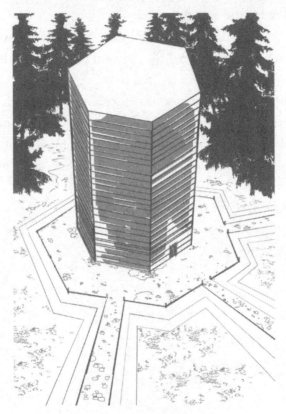

CHAPTER 7

REAPERS 101

The Kwei Library was a perfect hexagon. It looked like a modern art gallery—a three-story, windowless building. Horizontal stripes of alternating black and gunmetal stone, smooth as glass, formed the six walls. Inside, the walls were lined from floor to ceiling with books that appeared to be merely decorative. Glass terminals lined the hallway and several other smaller rooms that Team

Thirteen passed through before they crossed over a bronze plaque on the floor that indicated they were entering the Manifestation Room. The room contained a hexagonal ring forty feet in diameter, surrounded by low bleachers. The recruits took their seats, as if a show were about to start.

Instructor Suzuki walked in and stood before them. "Welcome, recruits. Today's demonstration will prepare you for your first engagement in the simulation dome, taking place this evening," Suzuki announced. "I will manifest a basic overview of the behavior and biology of shadow reapers before you see the real thing—or a simulation, at least—in the Dome. In the Dome you won't have time to study one up close; you'll be fighting for your life."

Instructor Suzuki strolled back and forth as she spoke, carefully arcing around the ring. "I'm an Expathic—my spade is tactile holographic manifestation," she said. "My spade name is Ghost. The holograms I manifest have a life span of only moments, yet they have physical properties. This ring is for your protection; it safely constrains the holograms. A hologram reaper is not real, but it can hurt you. So when the ring is lit, please do stay in your seats."

"I told you," Freddy whispered to Jack, then popped a large chunk of granola bar into his mouth. He had been delighted moments earlier to find it in his pack when he reached in.

"You told me what?"

"That reapers exist! In my presentation. But you didn't believe me."

Jack stared at him. "Yeah. We're beyond the point of 'I told you so' though, don't you think?"

Freddy shrugged and swallowed. "I'm just saying."

Voss turned around from the row in front of them, where he sat with Asha. "Be quiet."

"Sorry," Jack whispered.

"I'm allowed to talk," Freddy whispered to Jack. "We still have freedom of speech in this country. We're not communists."

Asha pressed her finger to her lips, which communism notwithstanding, silenced even Freddy. She had good reason: The ring around the center of the room glowed. And it was no longer empty.

Standing in the ring was an unremarkable-looking man in a button-down shirt and khakis. Only his blank expression made him seem unusual.

"The first challenge with reapers is that they resemble humans to everyone except their victim. This makes it impossible for anyone else to pick them out—including operatives. The reapers' prey will appear to be hallucinating. Let me give you a sense of what a victim would see."

Suddenly, the reaper was no longer a blank-faced human. It was the thing that had chased Jack in Jersey City: a terrifying creature, gleaming as if covered in a thin layer of ice, eyes glowing a violent purple. The audience of recruits recoiled. Just as quickly, the figure's features turned back into a human face.

"The shadow map in the Office of Reaper Engagement is able to detect a reaper because its organic makeup is decidedly nonhuman. When the shadow map detects a reaper in hunting mode, a team of operatives gets called in." Suzuki walked toward the reaper, and it tensed, like an animal sensing danger.

"Do not expect to identify reapers by outward appearance. The best operatives learn to sense them, as all reapers have one very small tell," Suzuki said. "I'll turn up the volume, so you can hear what I mean."

This time, when the reaper moved, Jack heard it crackle softly.

"That tiny sound is the unique biological makeup of a reaper,"

Suzuki said. "What looks like skin is actually a hardened icy exo-skeleton with a tensile strength of a little over two million KSI. That's about twenty times harder than tungsten carbide. You could bounce a Sidewinder missile off it. Watch."

Suzuki held up her hand. An Uzi submachine gun appeared in her hand, and Suzuki let fly a deafening round of ammunition at the reaper. The reaper crouched as bullets ricocheted off it, scattering and vaporizing as they hit the perimeter of the ring. Suzuki snapped her fingers, and the Uzi became a long knife.

"They're also exceptionally fast." Suzuki slashed at the reaper, which dodged her knife. "And strong." Suzuki added as the reaper lunged at her. A curtain of steel appeared between the instructor and the reaper. The reaper drove a fist hard into the metal, creating a round steel bulge just inches from Suzuki's face as she leaned backward.

They froze in that position as Suzuki gauged the recruits' reactions. She relaxed, and the reaper wandered back to the center of the circle. The steel curtain vanished.

"Reapers kill with one method. We call it *icing*."

Another human form appeared in the ring. He stood as still as a mannequin. The reaper sprung at him and pressed its open palm against the man's chest. The civilian stumbled back as if he had been shocked, then stiffened and clutched his chest. Finally, he fell over in a fetal position.

"Reapers blast-freeze your organs. They stop your heart and freeze the blood in your veins, just long enough to kill you. This method is silent and leaves no marks. Completely untraceable. It appears that the person has died of a heart attack or an aneurism. When fighting reapers, you must, by any means necessary, keep their hands away from your chest and throat."

Suzuki motioned at the civilian, who stood and walked to

the edge of the ring and out, disappearing. The instructor made a wide circle around the reaper, coming to a stop directly in front of it. "And just as they kill in only one way, there is only one way to destroy them." She took her rune blade from her hip. The hilt was marked with the charcoal-gray circle of the Expathic.

Suzuki twisted the handle. The blade sprung from the hilt. The very tip of the blade was an intense silvery-gray flame, short but powerful like a blowtorch. "The hilt acts as the striker, igniting what we call the blaze. The elements inside any Hadley blade create a blaze powerful enough to destroy a reaper's ice exoskeleton. But the blaze must strike the reaper at its weakest spot—between the rib cage. We call this area the bull's-eye."

Suzuki held her blade level and pressed it to the center of the reaper's chest. The reaper vaporized in a burst of violet dust.

"They disappear when blazed. That's another way they have managed to remain undetected for centuries." Suzuki held her blade straight up and nodded at the flame. "The blaze lasts just two minutes. When it expires . . ." The gray blaze flickered out. "You must re-strike the tip to light it again. Think of it as cocking a rifle. It is the same principle for training blades as well as for rune blades. You will learn to do it quickly in the heat of the battle." Suzuki twisted her wrist. The blade retracted in a split second and sprung back out, the blaze once again lit.

Instructor Suzuki checked her band. "That's all for today. You are dismissed, recruits." She blinked out the light of the manifestation ring.

Voss stood and pointed at the ring. "You see that reaper? She couldn't bring that thing down with an Uzi. You got something up your sleeve, Sky Boy? Because I ain't going back without my memories, bro."

"It's not Jack's fault, Voss," Asha interrupted. "What did you want him to do?"

"Tell them he's not some mythical guardian!" Voss said, throwing his hands up.

"I *did* tell them that!" Jack interjected.

"*How* did you tell them? Because one minute I'm out there, going about my day, and the next minute . . ."

But Jack wasn't listening anymore. He was staring past Voss, at a girl walking toward the door. Freddy followed his gaze to the recruits across the room.

"Whoa," Freddy breathed. "Is that who I think it is?"

Voss looked behind him. "Who?"

But Jack had already pushed past them. He followed the girl across the Hexagon. He stayed a couple steps back until he saw her face—the pale skin, the subtle freckles across her nose and cheeks. "Claire?"

Claire Lacoste was walking in a tight group with her team.

Jack hurried up to her. "Hey, Claire, it's me."

Before he reached her, he bumped up against a wall of air. It was like Claire had some kind of force field around her. Jack pushed, but he couldn't move through it.

Claire didn't slow her pace. But one of her teammates did. He blocked Jack's path.

"You need something?"

"I'm trying to talk to Claire. She's my friend."

"Your friend?"

"Yeah, our friend." Freddy pushed his way into the kid's face, despite the boy being about Voss's size.

"She doesn't want to talk," the boy said.

"How would you know?" asked Freddy.

"Because you couldn't get near her." The boy checked over his shoulder. "That girl is the second-ranked recruit in Hadley. Her spade name is Static. That negatively charged ion field you bumped into? That's because she wanted you away from her. She lets her team near her, that's it. We're Team One. If she wanted to talk to you, she would have let you in."

"Static?" Freddy asked. "Like static electricity? How does that—?" Freddy cut off, suddenly wincing and holding his head. He turned away from the boy, who was shooting an intense look at him.

"Hey! Are you doing that to him?" Asha barked. "Quit it!" She shoved the boy in the chest.

"Miles Watt!" Instructor Suzuki stormed over. Miles looked up. Freddy gasped for breath but seemed to be free of pain.

Miles Watt. That was the recruit who had caused such concern at the Naming Ceremony. The one Darius and Blue had been worried about. The first in several years to . . . what? They hadn't said.

"Don't you *ever* attack a recruit. Do you understand?" Suzuki's face flashed with anger, and she clutched her blade.

"Yes, ma'am," Miles answered, lowering his gaze. "I apologize, Instructor Suzuki."

Suzuki stared at her hand on her blade for a second, then quickly let it go. "Now out, all of you." The recruits that had paused to watch the confrontation filed quickly out of the room.

"She doesn't want to talk," Miles said again. "Plus, I heard you guys are washing out in three days." Miles leaned forward to whisper to Jack and Freddy. "Either of you try to distract my teammate again and I'll end you." He turned and followed Claire and the rest of Team One down the hallway to the library entrance.

Freddy was still rubbing his temples. He watched Miles walk away. "I've got a bad feeling about that guy."

Voss raised an eyebrow. "Yeah? That your spade at work, Link? Pretty bold observation."

Freddy spun and pointed at Voss. "At least Asha had our back. Some teammate you are."

"We get our own backs, bro. Get used to that."

Outside of the library, Freddy whapped Jack on the shoulder. "Dude, Claire Lacoste! She's not at boarding school at all; she's *here*. Aren't you happy I made you stay now?"

"You didn't make me stay, Freddy. They drafted us. We can't leave."

"I totally made you stay," Freddy said. "And she's clearly still mad at you. How crazy was that, her keeping you away with that static spade? That actually makes sense. She was alone a lot at St. Paul's."

"Lots of people like to be alone sometimes," Asha said.

"Not like that though." Freddy looked at Asha. "She hardly ever talks. I never understood how Jack could hang out with her for hours every day. What did you do when you guys hung out, Jack? Just sit there and stare at stuff? I mean, I get it, if you're hanging out with your cat or whatever, but—"

"Just because she doesn't talk incessantly doesn't mean she doesn't talk," Jack said. "We talked."

"Yeah, until she left without saying good-bye," Freddy said. "But I'll tell you what. When she finds out you're gonna save the world, she's going to be intrigued, dude. Girls love that stuff."

Asha gave him a look. "Girls love what stuff?"

Freddy waved her off dismissively. "You wouldn't understand."

"I wouldn't understand girls?" Asha rolled her eyes.

"No, I mean . . ." Freddy checked to make sure Jack wasn't paying attention. Then he whispered to Asha. "It's complicated."

"I can hear you," Jack said. "And it's not complicated."

"Perfect," Voss mumbled. "A distraction. Because we were already doing so well."

Freddy clapped Jack on the shoulder. "Come on, man. We'll see Team One at the Dome. You can talk to her then."

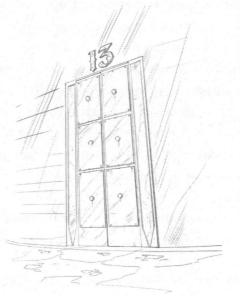

CHAPTER 8

THIRTEEN DOORS

The simulation dome will either mold you into an operative," Instructor Bakari announced, "or it will break you." He spoke with an accent that made his words round, hard, and rhythmic, like bullets hitting a target. "There is nothing in between."

Instructor Bakari stood with the bearing of a general on the grassy floor of a large outdoor amphitheater. The recruits sat above him on stone benches secured to stair-stepping terraces that formed a half-moon. The instructor wore a flowing hunter-green tunic with a traditional African print, round glasses, a long gold chain around his neck, and a severe look that suggested he had never laughed in his life. Behind Bakari stood the Dome.

The curved steel walls shone in the low evening sun. The roof swelled in a shallow dome of tight mesh. The entire structure wasn't much larger than a one-story house. Built into the walls were thirteen doors, each marked with its number. The first twelve doors were smooth polished steel, matching the mesh of the roof. The thirteenth door was brushed copper with exposed bolts running along the edge, as if a facade were going to be installed on it but never was. This must have been the Corpus Christi door Alexander had repurposed.

Instructor Bakari checked his band and barked for his apprentice. Alexander, rubbing at his nose with a handkerchief, hurried over to manipulate a small screen on the front of the Dome. He stumbled as he returned to his place, drawing Bakari's exasperated glare. In Bakari's presence, Alexander reminded Jack of a dog accustomed to being beaten.

"You are charged with identifying and blazing the reaper in your simulation," Bakari continued. "The threat level of the reaper will be matched to the skill level of your team. Team One's reaper will be closest to what an operative would face in combat, but each reaper is different," he said. "You have one chance to identify the reaper correctly. You won't have time to recover from a mistake."

Team One's bands glowed yellow and vibrated. "That's your signal, Team One," Bakari said. "Good luck."

Team One lined up in front of the first door. Claire stood calmly behind Miles, staring forward at the Dome.

She was so focused, it was aggravating. Jack had waited at the front of the amphitheater before they arrived. Claire had walked past him as if he didn't exist. When Jack leaned forward to try to catch her eye, he experienced an uncomfortable jolt, the same feeling you got touching a doorknob after walking across the carpet in your socks. He noticed others around him leaning back as she passed. They all seemed to know that you don't try to get close to Claire Lacoste.

Jack had spent a lot of time with Claire over the last two years. He knew her face as well as his own. But her expression now was unlike anything Jack had seen on her before. It was as if he were watching a humanoid Claire, one that hadn't yet had an emotional motherboard installed.

The first door slid open, and Team One disappeared into the Dome. Immediately the world around Jack changed. At first he thought he had merely gotten something in his eye. But it was more than that. Everything got hazy, like heat rising off a parking lot in summer. The murky air filled the amphitheater, thickening until they were no longer looking at the Dome; they were looking at a farm on a bright sunny day.

Jack felt the wind blowing and could smell the harvest. The wide door on a red barn swung open and out walked the four members of Team One. They wore old jeans, boots, and T-shirts or button-down flannel shirts with the sleeves rolled up. Besides Miles and Claire, the team was made up of Kasun Banda, a kid with long limbs who seemed to be constantly talking to himself under his breath, and Janelle Moreau, a girl with the gait of a ballerina who barely left a footprint in the dusty landscape.

"The farm is the standard recruit simulation." Bakari's voice came to them like an announcer in a dark theater. "There are up to twenty-four characters in the farm. One of them is the reaper. Which one will change every time."

A woman and her two grown sons stood on the wide porch

of a cream-colored house with black shutters. They were typical white Midwesterners, their skin tanned from years of outdoor work. Surveying the house from the bottom of the porch steps were three individuals in crisp gray suits, two men and a woman holding a clipboard. A For Sale sign hung in the yard. The word *Foreclosure* had been added to the sign's top.

In an adjacent field, a farmer sat on a rumbling tractor. Four workers crouched on the roof of a faded red barn, repairing an area that had been torn off. Walking up the long driveway from the dirt road were a half-dozen farmhands lugging carpentry tools, talking and laughing as they came.

Claire wore a snug white T-shirt, scuffed working jeans, and a faded blue baseball cap. She had on a pair of large gray work gloves. She and the others blinked in the glare of the cloudless day, shading their eyes.

Bakari motioned vaguely at Team One, who could not hear him. "You will notice that the recruits are no longer in their uniforms but rather in typical farm gear," he pointed out. "Recruit uniforms are made from fabric that adapts to the setting. It saves operatives from worrying about the appropriate clothing for an engagement."

The recruits in the amphitheater looked down at their own uniforms with new appreciation.

Miles, in a red flannel shirt with pushed-up sleeves, was barking orders at his team through earpiece communication monitors. The four of them fanned out, each moving toward a different group on the farm.

"You cannot rely on your eyes to identify the reaper," Bakari reminded them. "You must learn to sense it. You've learned that reapers have a skin that crackles slightly. The best operatives can almost feel the vibrations of it, even from a distance."

"Don't our bands glow red when a reaper is present?" asked a kid from the front row.

"Operatives use bands as a last resort only," Bakari answered. "Wait for the band to turn crimson and you'll find the reaper may be too close to its prey for you to stop it."

"How is Claire supposed to fight a reaper with static?" Freddy whispered to Jack.

"I don't know. How are you supposed to fight a reaper with conspiracy theories?" Jack asked.

"Hmm. Fair point."

Claire was now tracking the farmer, jogging toward his tractor in the field. Miles Watt and Janelle approached the workers on the roof of the barn, calling out something to them. Kasun walked up to the farmhouse.

Before Kasun arrived, the farmhouse porch broke into chaos. The two sons were shouting at the visitors in suits about how many generations the family had lived on the farm. Then one of the sons lifted a rifle that Jack hadn't noticed before and pointed it at the agents, still yelling. The agents backed away. The mother shouted desperately at her son to lower the gun.

As Kasun ran closer, he touched his ear and called over the monitor that one of the brothers was the reaper.

Janelle Moreau broke into a run toward the farmhouse. After a few strides, she squatted down and sprung through the air, over about twenty feet. She landed soundlessly like a grasshopper and continued springing in huge bounds.

On the porch, the son cocked the rifle and aimed at the terrified agents. The other son picked up a baseball bat just as Kasun reached the steps. Jack wondered which man he would go for. But a moment later the recruit physically split into two identical Kasuns. One

Kasun tackled the son with the bat, and the second Kasun pinned the son with the shotgun against the wall. The mother screamed while the brother with the gun, his back pressed flat against the house, shouted for help. Kasun snatched his blade off his hip and deployed the long sword with a quick twist of his wrist.

Kasun hesitated, his knee pressed against the chest of the brother. "He's not fighting back!" The brothers and the agents were all shouting, bewildered and terrified.

Instructor Bakari's accent filled the amphitheater. "Recruit Banda has mistaken human anger for the behavior of a reaper. It is a common recruit mistake. A disappointing start for Team One."

Jack's attention was drawn far from the house, to the group of construction workers approaching the farm from the long driveway. He sensed something from the group. A vibration of some kind. Or a crackling sensation.

Then he spotted him. A small man in a blue plaid button-down and torn jeans. His face was blank, like a wax mask.

Jack grabbed Freddy's arm. Freddy jumped. "What?"

"The reaper is in that pack of men coming down the—"

Jack didn't finish his sentence. The bands on Team One flashed crimson and buzzed madly.

"There!" Miles screamed over the monitor.

But his teammates were too far away. The shadow reaper was now running toward the day laborers. One of the laborers turned to look at it and screamed. He saw the monster for what it was. Team One members deployed their blades and sprinted toward the driveway.

From the other side of the farm, Miles ran at the reaper. He had no hope of reaching it. Then Miles stopped and put his hand to his forehead. The workers fell to the ground in agony, gripping their heads. The reaper stumbled too, flinching as if he had taken a physical blow to the skull. But the beast recovered quickly.

"A strong effort by Miles Watt," Bakari said. "But his spade is not yet powerful enough to work on reapers, and certainly not from that distance—"

Bakari stopped speaking. Something was happening. The hair on Jack's arm stood on end. Moisture seemed to be sucked from the air, like the moments before a storm.

Claire ran with the grace of a gazelle, toward the reaper. She peeled off her gloves and tossed them aside. Then she rubbed her hands together as if to warm them.

In a full sprint Claire clapped her hands together and then swept them apart. A single, colossal bolt of lightning torpedoed from the sky like a javelin. It struck the reaper with a deafening thunderclap. The reaper careened a hundred yards through the air and slammed against the wall of the barn.

Claire pulled her blade from off her hip. The tip exploded with blue fire as she drove straight toward the center of the beast's chest. The blaze met the reaper's icy exoskeleton, and the reaper vanished in a puff of violet smoke.

The world they had been in—the immersive hologram of the farm—blinked out. They were back in the amphitheater. The Dome stood before them. Not a single recruit breathed.

A green light illuminated Team One's silver door as it slid open. Out tumbled Claire, followed by Miles, Janelle, and Kasun. They staggered into the open space of the amphitheater, checking themselves for wounds that weren't there.

Kasun and Janelle leapt on Miles in jubilation. All of them, Jack noticed, were careful not to touch Claire, who remained expressionless.

"Congratulations, Team One," Bakari announced. "You've just completed your first simulation."

The bands of Team Two glowed yellow and buzzed. They looked more nervous than Team One had, having just watched the events of the past few minutes.

"Learn from what you saw," Bakari advised them. "Claire Lacoste has never used static to affect the troposphere before today. She relied on her instincts. Trust your spade. And be ready. The reaper will be different every time."

The second door opened and Team Two disappeared inside.

By the time Team Twelve staggered out of the Dome, Jack had given up hope. Instructor Bakari had continually reminded them that the reapers were matched with the team's skill set and that the Dome would never give them something they couldn't handle. But to Jack's eye there didn't seem to be a great deal of difference between the reapers in any of the simulations.

"Team Thirteen." Instructor Bakari's tone dripped with contempt. As they approached their door, Bakari looked them over as he might look at a mutt that had wandered into the Westminster Dog Show. "Don't worry too much about being unprepared, Team Thirteen," Bakari said absentmindedly, checking a hologram that hovered over his wrist. He peered over his glasses and picked out Jack. "I expect your reaper will cower before the mythical Guardian."

Jack felt his face burning. He knew Claire was watching.

"Let's just get this over with," Voss said under his breath.

Bakari heard him. "I don't control the Dome, recruit, and neither do you. The Dome decides when you enter."

The moments passed achingly slowly as they stared at their bands, waiting for them to turn the canary yellow and vibrate. Jack's chest constricted so tightly that his lungs had difficulty inflating.

Then, with a single tone, the Dome's golden light blinked off. The entire structure whirred as it powered down.

Bakari looked at Alexander. "What's happening here, Edison?" he asked angrily. "You told me the installation was complete."

Alexander shrunk, furiously flipping through holograms, tapping out codes. "It was, sir. The door is functioning properly."

"Then why did the Dome not call Team Thirteen in? It's programmed specifically so that an improbable can . . ."

Bakari paused, as if coming to a realization. He walked over to Team Thirteen. "But you're not, are you? You're not improbables."

Asha took a breath. "Not yet, sir."

"The Dome is programmed for improbables. The Dome does not give access to dormants." Bakari practically spat the last word. "When Director Darius and Superior Blue convinced the Council to accept a Team Thirteen based on the Great Prophecy of the Order of the Grays, I was skeptical. Still, I thought perhaps there was some reasoning behind it. But no." He pushed his glasses up his nose. "And while I have the highest respect for the Order of the Grays, the Great Prophecy was never—*never*—meant to be taken *literally*."

He shook his head, a mix of disgust and pity. "There is no way for you to simply manifest your spades overnight," he said. "If we must go through this charade for two more nights, then so be it. But I recommend you search for a way to be honorably discharged before that time."

Bakari turned to the crowded amphitheater. "That concludes the Dome session for today. Excellent work, the rest of you. You are released for dinner."

The twelve teams filed past them. Jack watched Claire go, her face still expressionless. He felt defeated and hopeless and utterly alone.

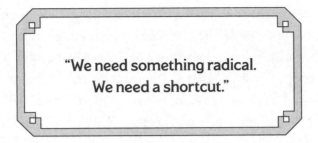

CHAPTER 9

"We need something radical.
We need a shortcut."

THE INCIDENT

It's only day one," Freddy said as he reached for a dinner roll from a basket in the center of the table. "Of course, the Dome didn't let us in yet." They sat across from each other in Prophecy Hall. Jack had never been in such a beautiful building in his life. The dining hall was named for the thirteen prophecies of the Order of the Grays. The walls, wooden pillars, and rafters were covered in intricate symbols, hand carved by the Grays centuries ago.

Recruits and cadets filled the center of the hall, laughter echoing around the high ceilings. Between tables, recruits pushed butcher block carts piled high with grilled steaks, rotisserie chicken, and thick pork chops, sautéed green beans, roasted carrots, and massive bowls of salad. Instructors and apprentices like Alexander sat together at long tables that ran along the west side of the hall. They were served by cadets rather than recruits.

Jack's team, along with Team One, had been on setup duty, lugging a couple hundred plates and bowls to the tables from the industrial-sized kitchen in the back of the hall and setting the tables. Voss had physically carried the heavy carts from the kitchen into the hall without breaking a sweat. Kasun split in two to cut his work in half. And Janelle leapt across the hall with silverware and cloth napkins. Now they were finished and could relax. For the first time since he'd arrived at Hadley, Jack found he had an appetite.

"The Dome probably just forgot we were there," Freddy went on. "It's had twelve teams to deal with forever. It'll be different tomorrow." He leaned back as a recruit from Team Five served them. He poured multiple drinks simultaneously, controlling the pitchers of water as if they were on invisible wires.

"You should try turning that into iced tea." Freddy pointed toward a steaming glass of apple tea in front of Asha.

"But I want it hot."

"I mean to practice manifesting your spade," Freddy clarified. "Freezing your tea would definitely be a breakthrough. Try it."

"The Dome tracks all of us through our bands," Voss conceded, motioning with a cup of coffee toward Asha's tea. "He could be right—it could help us get into the Dome."

Freddy beamed at Voss's validation. "See that?" He waggled a finger between himself and Voss. "Same wavelength, man."

Asha hesitated. Then she placed a hand on each side of her cup, so just her fingertips touched the glass.

"You can do this," Freddy said.

Asha closed her eyes and sat perfectly still.

Her eyes snapped open. "I can't do it when everyone's staring."

She started chewing her thumbnail. "It took everyone else here years to break through. You think you can just say 'do it,' and I'll be able to do it? It's hard!"

"Freddy," Jack said. "You've been using your spade since I've known you. How come you haven't broken through?"

Voss frowned. "What do you mean?"

"His spade is conspiracy theory. He never shuts up about these crazy ideas."

"Incongruous logic," Freddy corrected. "And my ideas aren't crazy. Everyone just refuses to see what's right in front of them."

"He hasn't figured out how to control the ideas he's spouting off," Asha said. "It's like stray voltage. I read that Theorics like Freddy have a harder time breaking through than the other classifications because they aren't even aware they're thinking differently than everyone else."

Freddy wrinkled his nose. "How do you know all that stuff?"

Asha held up her band. "Alexander showed me how to remotely access the Kwei Library. They have tons of training manuals and information about spade classifications." She looked at them curiously. "What were you all doing with your downtime when all those teams were failing in the Dome?"

Freddy shrugged. "Watching them fail, I guess." Then he perked up. "Does the library have stuff on the Guardian?"

"Yeah, but it was mostly just versions of what we already know," she said. "I ran into restricted archives, but for that you need permission from the Hadley historian. So I looked him up. But the cadet forums say he's some crazy old man who never leaves his house. So that was a dead end."

"We haven't broken through, and we're not going to." Voss skewered a massive seared rib-eye steak from a cart rolling past.

He dropped it on his plate. "Not this fast anyway. The Dome isn't going to accept us in the next two days. We need to get out of here soon with an honorable discharge. A mind-scrape after three days of memories is gonna mess with our brains."

Asha slammed her cloth napkin on the table and glared at Voss. "You want to run away? They brought us here to protect people who can't protect themselves! That includes little kids, and old people, and everyone walking around every day with these monsters just waiting to attack."

Voss's vast forehead wrinkled. "This morning you could barely stand up straight, man. Now you're all committed to the cause?"

"I'm not a *man*, Voss. I have a name. Use it," Asha snapped. "And I was having a bad morning when they brought me in."

"Fine, *Asha*. Just remember that the only person who thinks we're supposed to be here is delusional. Nobody else thinks we're qualified. Because we aren't. The Dome just confirmed it."

"You're avoiding the question: How can you want to quit? They save lives here. They protect people. I want to do that too." She nodded at the large crest above the door. "One Life for Many. You see anything up there that says, 'Unless you're Voss Winter?'"

"You show me one person who's ever fought for me, and I'll sign up," Voss said through a clenched jaw. "Until then, don't give me that greeting card junk."

Asha jabbed a finger at him. "My father fought in the marines to protect everyone—even the people who called him a terrorist when he wore a turban. He fought for them right up to the moment he was killed by a suicide bomber in Kandahar. So don't talk to *me* about what's greeting card junk. You're selfish and stupid, and you don't know what you're talking about." She crossed her arms and jolted back in her chair, shifting her gaze away.

"They can't make me stay," Voss said finally.

"Then sneak away," Asha said, pushing her plate away. "You'll become one of the Many everyone here is willing to die for. My father protected cowards like you every day of his service. You go ahead and run. I'm staying as long as they let me. Even if that's only two more days. Even if they lobotomize me afterward." She began chomping angrily on her fingernails.

Freddy glanced back and forth between them. "Asha makes a lot of good points."

"Nobody asked you, bro." Voss scowled at him. Then he gave Asha a long look. "Sorry about your dad."

Asha sat back, the anger draining from her. She stared at her chewed fingernails and tucked her hand under her thigh. "I don't even remember him," she said. "He died before I was born."

"I'm still sorry."

A scuffle and a clatter echoed from across Prophecy Hall. A small redheaded boy sprawled on the floor in the midst of a broken plate and a pile of food. "Oops." Miles stood over the boy. "You should be more careful." Miles and Janelle erupted with laughter.

Miles reminded Jack of Brandon Jordan back at St. Paul's. They were both used to the hearty guffaws of a fan club. Freddy leapt up and ran across the hall to help the kid to his feet. He glared at Miles as he helped wipe food off the redheaded recruit's uniform. Jack watched Claire, who was pretending not to notice the commotion.

"That guy's a jerk," Jack said, high-fiving Freddy as he returned. "That was cool of you." Jack turned back to his table to find his team watching him. "What?"

Asha nodded at Claire, seated at the Team One table. "I thought you were friends with that girl, but she won't even talk to you. What's up with that?"

Jack shrugged.

Freddy grimaced. "Sensitive issue."

"So what's up?" she pressed.

"Jack's an idiot," Freddy answered.

"I coulda told you that," Voss said through a mouthful of fried potatoes.

Freddy pointed a finger at him. "Don't call my friend an idiot, or I'll kick your butt. Only I can call him that."

Asha rolled her eyes. "You can't kick his butt, Freddy. His gift is strength."

"He hasn't even tested it out yet." Freddy looked at Voss. "Can you twist an iron bar with your bare hands?"

"No, of course not," Voss stammered.

"But you haven't tried, right?"

"Why would I have tried to twist an iron bar?"

Freddy intercepted a nearby food cart and pushed it toward Voss. "No time like the present," he challenged. "Try to bend that bar on the side."

Voss shot a glance at it and turned back to his plate. "Nah. I'm good."

"Don't you want to know?" Freddy asked. "Or maybe you're afraid to fail in front of everyone? Don't be! Who cares if you fail? Fail all you want, we won't care."

Voss glared at Freddy, then spun on the bench to face the cart. He placed both hands on the metal bar that formed the side brace of the cart. His muscles tightened. But the bar remained straight.

"Told you," Voss grumbled as he turned back to the table and stuffed his mouth with a forkful of steak.

"You barely gave it any effort!" Freddy protested, throwing his hands up. "I know you're stronger than that."

Asha turned to Jack. "So what happened with that girl?"

Jack shrugged again. "Nothing. We're friends. We were, anyway."

Asha looked to Freddy.

"Let's just say Jack made a couple of bad choices."

"Will you please stop talking, Freddy?"

"What? This is good therapy. That's part of my spade."

"No it isn't," Jack said.

Freddy ignored him. "So Jack and Claire were, like, super close since sixth grade. They were both on the track team."

"Cross-country," Jack corrected him.

"You want to tell this?" Freddy asked. Jack just snorted at him, and Freddy turned back to Asha. "Jack was city champ for middle school. The guy can fly. And Claire was the junior New Jersey state champ in the girl's division. So they used to go on long runs together, like ten miles long."

"You seriously ran ten miles a day?" Voss sounded reluctantly impressed.

"See, the doctor told him to take up exercising," Freddy continued. "So Jack starts doing three hundred sit-ups and a hundred push-ups before bed. Ran ten miles every morning."

It had turned out that running came naturally to Jack. In fifth grade he started running through Jersey City, early in the morning. But when he blacked out and woke up on a random park bench, his mother forbade him from running alone. The cross-country team at St. Paul's started at eighth grade, but Jack's mom called the coach anyway. Coach told her Jack was welcome to run with the team during practice, but he pointed out that Jack wouldn't be able to keep up with the older kids. He would need a running partner.

Then one afternoon in early September, Coach introduced Jack to a transfer student, a girl who was also going to be in sixth grade.

She was looking for a running partner. Coach told them to meet him the next morning at five thirty in the St. Paul's parking lot.

They didn't talk at all that first morning, he and Claire. They sat in the front row of Coach's large van. Six older kids flopped in the rows behind them, snoring on the twenty-five-minute drive to the running trails at Glen Ridge. When they arrived, Coach opened the doors and the older kids rose like zombies, out into the cool air, jogging to warm up. *"Back here in an hour,"* Coach told the two sixth graders. *"You're not here, I leave you."*

They ran together, still not saying a word. Claire was a natural. Jack felt clumsy next to her, but at least his lungs and muscles were in good enough condition to keep up with her. They made it back in under an hour.

It took them a full week to say more than two words to each other, but it was the beginning of a strong friendship. They were a team within a team. And he never blacked out when he ran with her. Not once.

That friendship lasted until eighth grade. That's when Brandon Jordan, the football star and unrepentant bully, asked Claire out. The news flashed through the middle school. Nobody had ever seen them talk before. The girls thought he was out of her league. Jack thought Brandon was a jerk.

Inexplicably, Claire had said yes. And to Jack's own dismay, the news struck him like a wrecking ball to the stomach.

Toward the end of the school year, Jack found himself telling Claire, in the middle of a crowded diner on Kennedy Boulevard, that he had feelings for her.

"She got upset," Freddy narrated.

Asha sat back, twirling a teaspoon between her fingers. "That must be hard to lose a friend like that. You were just being honest."

"Right, but that wasn't the bad choice," Freddy said.

Jack knew that for all Freddy's transparency, for all his lack of filters, he wouldn't tell them about the Incident. That was Jack's alone to tell.

Asha and Voss looked at Jack. Freddy elbowed him. "Therapy, man," he said. "Besides, if we get our minds wiped, they won't remember it anyway."

Jack sighed and began to talk.

―――――

Claire was upset when Jack told her he liked her. But a couple of weeks later she asked if they could meet up. He kept putting her off. He didn't want to be vulnerable in front of her again, and he was incapable of faking it—at least with Claire. She was smart enough to see that.

Then Claire did something very un-Claire: She didn't let it go. She texted him again. She asked if they could meet up at the diner on Kennedy Boulevard that Friday, just like they used to. She wanted to be friends, and she wouldn't take no for an answer.

Jack stood outside the diner that night, trying to muster the courage to go inside. He saw her sitting in a booth near the far window, in a midnight-blue dress.

He wasn't ready yet. But he didn't want to stand there like an idiot, so he took a brisk walk around the block. He practiced saying "Hey, Claire" in a breezy way. He practiced his casual wave. He and Claire had been close, but she wasn't a hugger, or even a high-fiver. Claire was a waver. Come to think of it, Jack had never so much as seen her holding hands with Brandon.

Jack quickened his pace around the block. It was now or never.

But then he slipped away.

One minute he was walking up to the diner door. The next he was standing in the parking lot, leaning against his bike. Jack had blacked out.

Panicked, he looked at his phone. 10:40 p.m. Two texts from Claire.

9:20 p.m.
Ur coming, right?
9:55 p.m.
Guess not. Thx a lot.

He sprinted to the diner and yanked open the door. Claire wasn't there. He texted her once, then twice, then called three times in a row. Nothing.

Claire never answered any of his texts. He counted down the hours until Monday when he could see her in class and apologize. But Claire wasn't in class on Monday.

Freddy overheard Brandon telling his friends that Claire had transferred. Typical Claire, she hadn't told anyone. Freddy reported that Brandon actually seemed upset—an emotion Jack didn't know he had.

That's probably why she wanted to meet at the diner, Jack had thought. She had wanted to tell him she was leaving. For a while it was the great mystery of the school. Claire had just up and left, dropping everything in her life.

Only Freddy had trouble believing it. "She wouldn't just leave," he insisted. "Maybe she was kidnapped."

"If she was kidnapped it would be all over the news, Freddy," Jack had said.

But a few days later, Freddy found a website that transcribed police scanners and showed Jack a printout.

At 10:09 p.m. on Friday night, police were called by an elderly woman at 62 Highland Avenue. She had heard screaming. Out her bedroom window she had seen a girl, Caucasian, long brown hair pulled back in a ponytail, in a midnight-blue dress. The girl was crouched on the sidewalk. She was the one screaming. A man in black was walking away from her.

"That's six blocks from the diner," Freddy told him. "What was Claire wearing that night? Did you see her?"

"Just tell me what happened," Jack demanded, his heart beating out of his chest.

Freddy placed a second printout in front of him. Police had arrived at the scene. But there was no girl and no man in black. They searched the neighborhood and found no trace of them. There was no evidence that anything had happened. The police concluded that the elderly woman had either imagined it or that whatever happened would remain a mystery.

Frustrated and shaken, Jack held up the printout. "What am I supposed to do with this, Freddy?"

Freddy didn't know. Jack didn't know. They contacted the school she was attending up in New Hampshire. They assured them that Claire was fine. That was the last piece of information Jack had about Claire—until he saw her across the library's Manifestation Room at the Hadley Academy for the Improbably Gifted.

Jack pushed green beans around his plate. Around him, kids talked and laughed and shoveled food in their mouths. The activity made the cavity in Jack's chest that much worse.

"She's okay now," Freddy assured him, gripping his shoulder.

"Is she? I haven't talked to her. I don't know what happened. She won't let me apologize. I can't even get near her."

"They really create a fake school like that?" Voss asked. "They answered the phone and everything?"

Asha sighed. "You're missing the point, Voss." She turned to face Jack. "No wonder she's not talking to you. But you have to let it go and focus on what we need to do now." She waved a hand in the air. "You make eighth grade sound so dramatic. Somebody dated somebody else. Who cares? Why couldn't you just act like normal human beings?"

Voss cocked an eyebrow at her. "What kind of middle school did you go to?"

Freddy had picked a roasted chicken drumstick off a serving tray and dropped it on his plate. "None. She was homeschooled. Right?"

Asha's face reddened. "What makes you say that?"

Freddy wiped his hands on his napkin. "It's not an insult. Homeschooling is a totally underrated form of education. You just have no idea what middle school is like. You're sheltered."

"I'm not sheltered."

"Okay. What's *Star Wars*?" Freddy asked.

Asha's fingernail was back in her mouth. "What, because I don't know some dumb TV show I'm sheltered?"

"What's Facebook? What's Instagram? You ever heard of those?" Freddy continued.

"We're not talking about me right now, Freddy. This is about a distraction that we can't afford."

"Wait. You've never heard of *Star Wars*?" Jack asked.

"Were you held in some tower, like Rapunzel?" Freddy asked.

He snapped and pointed at Asha. "Wait. Maybe a desert island? Was there an evil mom involved? Keeping you away from the world?"

"Do you just spew out whatever comes into your head?" Asha demanded.

"She's homeschooled. Who cares?" Voss said. "In three days we won't even know each other. And Jack here won't remember that girl he's so in love with," Voss said, pointing across Prophecy Hall. "We got two more chances in the Dome, and bro, I am *not* going back with my memories scraped out. Who knows what else they might take by accident? So if Jack is the Guardian, he better come up with a new way of breaking through or whatever. Because the way everyone else here broke through ain't gonna work for us."

Freddy sat up, a gleam in his eyes. "Hey. This big meathead is right."

"What did you say to me?" Voss demanded.

"I said you're right," said Freddy. "Superior Blue has set us up to do the impossible. And it is impossible—*if* we try to follow the same path as everyone else. These guys took years to break through." He looked around the hall. "We need something radical. We need a shortcut."

Asha was nodding now. "But no dormant has ever even made it into Hadley. Every other draftee has already broken through."

"That's what the official record says," Freddy said, pinching his lip. Jack knew the look. "But what about the archives? Surely it's happened once since the Dome has existed? We're talking about thousands of recruits who have come through. You said somebody had access to that?"

"An old man who doesn't leave his house," Voss reminded them. "That ain't gonna work."

Asha was already poking and twisting through hologram

screens hovering above her band. "Alistair Rufus, instructor emeritus," Asha read. "He maintains the residence he's had for seventy years, on the Bluffs with the other instructor housing."

Freddy rubbed his hands together. "Let's go talk to him."

"What, now?" Voss asked, glancing around to see if anyone else thought this was a dumb idea.

"This was your idea, Voss." Freddy clapped him on the back. "You said we needed to find a radically new way of breaking through. We're gonna find out if it's been done before."

"I didn't really say that."

Freddy pushed back his chair. "Come on. It's the best plan we have. Let's get going before this old dude falls asleep." Freddy grabbed a handful of cookies off a tray as they passed. "Jack, grab me some cookies."

"You have cookies."

"Grab me *extra* cookies. I don't want to look greedy."

Jack took Freddy by the shoulder and steered him out, following Voss and Asha. "Let's go see if we can find out something about dormants at Hadley."

Freddy grinned and let himself be pushed out. "I think this is the first time you've ever agreed to one of my plans."

"Don't get used to it."

CHAPTER 10

INSTRUCTOR HOUSING

THE BLUFFS

THE HISTORIAN

Team Thirteen took two wrong paths on the way to the Bluffs. Freddy had insisted he had a minor spade in knowing which way to go. Finally Asha asked directions from a team of cadets training in the fading daylight. The team was arguing around a gleaming steel beanstalk that wrapped its way up a rocky outcropping just off the path. A freckled girl wearing a green headband was shouting at a thick boy with bedhead. *Boris Kleptov*, Jack recalled.

"I told you not to kill my plants, Alchemy!" the girl snapped at Boris.

Jack recognized Ivy. She had created the vines that yanked the fire escape out of the other girl's way.

"I'm making them beautiful," Alchemy protested in a Russian accent.

"They're not beautiful; they're dead!"

"You know how she feels, Alchemy," the other boy said. *Bound*, Jack recalled Superior Blue calling him. The boy was gently bouncing on a shimmering patch of earth.

The fourth teammate, a small girl with a shaved head, was sitting cross-legged and wearing a broad smile. "Hi! My name's Lucent. I already know your names. You're looking for the Bluffs," she called out in a singsong voice. "It's back the way you came. First path on the left, down through the glen, then cross over the Tangled Bridge. Then left, following the river."

Asha stopped and rattled her head. "Wait. How did you know . . . ? Never mind." She waved a thank-you. "Come on," she said to the team. "It's back the way we came. And Freddy's not leading anymore."

A few minutes later they crossed the river and made a left along the rocky bluffs. They passed the residences of other instructors: a thatched cottage, a Japanese-style home, a long, low modern bungalow that looked lifted from the Scandinavian countryside. At the end was the home of Instructor Rufus. His house was a sprawling, unkempt Gothic mansion. It teetered at the end of the row, closest to the edge of the Long Woods.

Asha rang the bell. A cadet opened the door partway. "Can I help you?"

Asha cleared her throat. "Yes, we're here to see Instructor Rufus."

"He's resting." The cadet moved to shut the door.

"Got it. Thanks," Voss said, turning away.

"For Pete's sake, Barney, let them in!" a voice bellowed from inside, followed by the clack of a cane rapping the floor and labored breathing.

The door swung wide open. Inside stood a portly old man, balding but for the wild goose-gray patches around the back of his head.

"Out of my way, Barney!" He pushed his much taller apprentice in the shoulder with his cane. Instructor Rufus's walnut-brown wool jacket with tan elbow patches and matching corduroy pants looked like they'd been lifted from a small-town museum. A strange smell came from inside, as if something was boiling that was not meant to be eaten.

"It's Barnabas, sir. And Dr. Horn specifically said you were to be resting in the evening."

"I *am* resting!" Rufus cried. "This is me resting. I'm walking with a cane, which uses only half my legs, and I'm talking to you, which uses only half my brain. How much more rest do I need? Now, if you want to be of service, Barney—"

"I do, sir, that's why—"

"Go get me one of those blueberry tarts from Prophecy Hall." He waved his cane toward the main grounds. "And don't give me that look. Would you have me waste away? Get some for our young friends as well."

"We already ate, sir," Asha told him.

"What's that? Speak up, young woman!"

"I said we already ate, sir."

Barnabas muttered to himself and walked off toward the central grounds.

"Well, what are you waiting for?" Rufus said. "Come in, come in! You're no doubt seeking some guidance from Hadley's fount of wisdom. Well, let me offer you some tea, and you sit down and tell me your problems."

They followed him through the foyer and down the black-and-white marble hall into his study, where a fire blazed. Rufus disappeared and returned with an odd-smelling kettle. They politely refused, but Rufus poured himself a large cup.

"You'll need something to eat." Instructor Rufus strained to turn around in his chair. "Where's Barney?"

"You sent him out for tarts, Instructor," Asha said.

Rufus stared at Asha as if she had made a profound discovery. "So I did! Well, have a seat." He made himself comfortable in a wide armchair that looked reinforced to support his weight. "You too," he said, motioning to Voss. "I can already see that you need a specific invitation." He studied Voss for a moment. "You look like an outside linebacker."

"Why's that?" Voss asked defensively.

"Because of the way you're standing. Played the left side, did you?"

"I played defensive end," Voss grumbled. "And yeah, left side."

"In my day I was a three-sport athlete; I can spot it a mile away. I was more of a baseball player myself, though. I can still swing a bat, believe it or not." He stood and shakily held up his cane, leaning it on his shoulder and staring down an imaginary pitcher. Then he pointed the cane at Freddy and Jack and let the stick fall. "You two, sit over there on that couch."

Rufus settled back into his seat. "Now. Ask away. How can I help?

I suppose you went to your mentor, some pretty boy like Santori, and found he didn't have the answers you were searching for."

"Instructor Santori is Team Three's mentor, sir," Asha said. "Our mentor is Superior Blue."

"Superior Blue doesn't mentor teams. What team are you?"

"Team Thirteen, sir," Freddy announced with pride.

Instructor Rufus belted out a loud, barking laugh that deteriorated into coughing. "Impossible, lad, there's no such thing." He wiped the tears from his eyes and leaned forward to shout out the door. "Barney, bring my files in here."

"You sent him out, sir," Jack reminded him.

"Ah yes. I'm afraid you'll have to do it yourself, then. Would you be so kind as to hand me the files on my desk, the ones with the red mark on them?"

Jack found the files labeled *Recruits* and brought them to Rufus.

"No Team Thirteen. Normal forty-eight recruits, as usual." Rufus flipped through the documents. "Wait a moment." He squinted at them. "You're the ones they were speaking about in the Council this morning. Something about the Guardian." He sat up in his chair and rubbed his eyes. "My goodness, I swore that I dreamed that. I tend to nod off during those sessions, frightfully dull."

Rufus looked at each one of them in turn, his eyes coming to rest on Jack. "It's true, isn't it? Superior Blue believes you to be the Guardian."

Jack shifted in his chair. "Yes, sir."

Rufus sat back. "Well, well." He gave a low whistle. "The Guardian. Come to us at last. And here in my sitting room."

Voss watched him with a skeptical look. "Hang on. You actually believe this?"

Rufus's eyebrows shot up. "Of course I believe it. The thirteenth prophecy? The *Great* Prophecy! Every other prophecy of the Grays has come true. What reason would I have to doubt the last one?"

"Because . . ." Voss started.

"Yep, Jack's the Guardian," Freddy interjected loudly, giving Voss a look to stop talking. "We're the team that's joined him. And we have a problem we could really use your help with, sir. Surely nobody possesses the kind of information and data you have access to as the Hadley historian."

Rufus puffed out his chest. "You're right about that, young man. I have unrestricted access. How can I be of service?"

"Actually, sir," Asha said. "We need any information on how a dormant could become an improbable."

Instructor Rufus nodded slowly. "Well, yes, of course. We do have many documented cases of dormants realizing their spades later in life. Of course, by that time they are too old to be drafted into Hadley."

Jack raised a finger. "She means, sir, whether there have been any cases of a dormant becoming an improbable on an extremely fast timeline. Like, in two days."

Rufus stroked his chin. "Hmm. You *are* dormants, aren't you? All four of you," he said. "And still Superior Blue believes you can complete a simulation in three days. That was this morning, which means you have two days left." He shook his head sadly. "I'm sorry. I genuinely wish I could help. But we have never had anything like that. We've never even had a single dormant in Hadley before, let alone four on the same team. The very notion is absurd."

Team Thirteen glanced at each other. "Okay, well, thank you for your time, sir," Jack said, standing up along with the others. "Sorry to have bothered you."

"Can we please get out of here now?" Voss whispered, opening the door into the hallway.

"Of course, that's not to say it's impossible," Rufus said.

One by one, they turned around. One by one, they sat back down in their chairs.

"There have been cases of dormants having rapid breakthroughs, without the years of introspection typically required," Rufus began. "Their spades have emerged under, let's say, *unusual* circumstances."

"Unusual how?" Voss asked.

"They have found themselves in situations of extreme stress, mortal combat, or impossible dilemmas," Rufus told them. "It is in this moment of great desperation that a spade may, theoretically, spontaneously emerge."

Asha had pulled her spinner from her pack and was nervously whirling it between her fingers. "So you're saying we would have to put ourselves either in extreme stress, mortal combat, or face an impossible situation?"

"No, no. Experiencing one of those highly uncomfortable situations would merely create a breakthrough. You don't need just a breakthrough. You need a breakthrough *and* a mastery of your spade *and* a weaponization of your spade, all with a skill level high enough that you can defeat a reaper in a simulation."

Rufus leaned forward. "In order to have any hope at all, you couldn't possibly experience one of those things. You would have to experience all three simultaneously."

Jack gulped. Then he asked the question nobody wanted to ask.

"And how would we put ourselves in that situation all at once, Instructor Rufus?"

"Extreme stress, mortal combat, impossible yet desperate situation," Rufus said thoughtfully, squinting at the ceiling. "All by tomorrow?"

Jack, Freddy, and Asha forced themselves to nod. Voss just stared at the old man.

Rufus breathed deeply and pursed his lips together, as if reluctant to give the answer. "I'm afraid there's only one way. It could be highly effective, but it's absurdly dangerous," he said. "You'll have to pick a fight. One that you have no hope of winning. One that will almost certainly end in your death."

Jack felt light-headed. But Voss narrowed his eyes. "And what kind of fight is that, exactly?"

"Why, against a team of operatives, of course!" Rufus exclaimed. "In the Pit. It's in the restricted zone, but I can grant you access. And I'm afraid it will be a fight to the death. Operatives don't fight any other way."

There was a long silence. Jack glanced at the others, then back at Instructor Rufus. "You can't be serious."

Freddy looked ill. "That can't be a real thing."

"Stressful, isn't it?" Rufus seemed encouraged.

"They don't *actually* fight to the death, do they?" Asha asked, her breathing shallow.

"They most certainly do," Rufus assured her. "But it's temporary. Usually. Every team has to challenge another team in a fight to the death—only once every five years, thankfully. It's horribly bloody."

"Instructor Rufus, you can't be serious," Jack repeated. "Why would Hadley operatives fight each other to the death?"

"They need to know that they *can*," Rufus told him. "The stakes in the dormant world are too high. If the reapers win, humanity will pay too high a price. So the operatives practice fighting to the death." He must have noticed the horror on their faces because he softened his tone. "Dr. Horn is always on-site. Her job is to get to a dead operative immediately and revive them with minimal long-term damage. She is excellent. And her techniques are quite successful."

"Has she ever failed?" Freddy asked.

Rufus shrugged. "Nobody's perfect. But the truth is that I have no idea. They don't keep records at the Pit. No surveillance is allowed, no spectators, nothing. This is the operatives' territory alone. They run it themselves. They are a unique group, operatives, borderline psychopaths. The training and what they go through to save humanity on a daily basis—all very intense."

Rufus eased himself up and hobbled to his desk, his cane bearing his weight. He scribbled something on a piece of paper, rolled it up, and slipped it into a plastic tube. He placed the tube inside a small door in the wall. There was a brief sucking sound, and the tube and paper were gone.

Rufus limped to his chair. "I don't like using bands and holograms for communication. Don't trust them. But that note will get there just fine, don't worry."

Jack felt a growing sense of alarm. "What note will get where just fine?"

Rufus looked surprised. "I challenged Operative Zhang's team to a death match on your behalf. At dawn tomorrow. My goodness boy, you just *asked* me to."

"*What*? No I didn't!"

Rufus frowned. "Are you sure?"

Asha jumped up and ran to the tube, sticking her fingers in it. "Get it back!"

"Oh, a challenge can't be revoked, any more than an insult hurled at somebody can be unsaid. Operative Zhang and her team would simply hunt you down. It is highly insulting to be challenged, you see, even by another team of operatives. To be challenged by a team of recruits?" Rufus laughed until he coughed. "I can't even imagine the level of humiliation they are feeling right now. I chose Zhang's team because they were on an engagement yesterday. With any luck, they'll be marginally more tired than any other team. At any rate, if this doesn't spark a breakthrough, nothing will."

He craned his neck to peer into the hallway. "Barney! I'm sending you out for blueberry tarts."

"You already sent him out, sir," Jack said in a flat voice.

"Hmm. So I did. Well." Rufus tapped his cane against the floor. "Off you go then, and no thanks needed, my young recruits. Excuse me for not getting up again, my knees aren't what they used to be."

CHAPTER 11

DEATH MATCH

eam Thirteen followed the trail south from the portal courtyard. The morning sky had lightened just enough that they could find their way without flashlights. Ahead of them was a long stone wall topped with ramparts, with large open archways every few yards. An identical hologram filled each archway with a sheer red haze. On each one, stamped black lettering declared *Restricted Zone*. As they passed through the archways, twice as tall as Voss, their bands chimed. Rufus had indeed granted them access. They took the wide, well-beaten trail to the left.

Before them, a low, wide hill crested at a height of perhaps thirty feet. It was clearly man-made: a long rectangle of a mound with rounded edges. An arched dark tunnel led directly underground.

Dr. Horn was waiting for them outside the tunnel, arms crossed. "Are y'all completely out of your ever-lovin' minds?" Dr. Horn's southern drawl had lost its leisurely pace. "Y'all challenged a team of operatives to a death match? Have you ever met an operative? They aren't like normal people. The fear processors in their brains have become practically numb. Their sense of honor has been cranked up as if on steroids."

"It wasn't our decision," Jack told her, the panic rising in him. "We went to see Instructor Rufus about how to speed up the process of breaking through. Next thing we knew he had sent the challenge."

"Oh my, child, why did you go see *him*? Alistair Rufus is senile! He probably doesn't remember he even did this."

Voss gritted his teeth. "Let's just get this over with." He peered into the dark tunnel. "When do they arrive?"

"They're already here, son. You'll see a light at the end of this tunnel when it's time to meet them in the Pit," she said, grabbing his uniform to pull him back. "But first—the rules of engagement. When you walk in there, the stone door seals behind you. That's the signal to begin. Remember that you *do not* have to fight them. You just have to survive. Death matches are two minutes exactly. Believe me, that's more than enough time for them to kill you all."

"So we can just run?" Freddy asked hopefully.

"Of course you can run. But the Pit has thirty-foot walls and is only slightly larger than a basketball court. So there's nowhere to go." She turned to see the first rays of sun coming over the trees and turned back to them quickly. "If you remember nothing else, remember this." Team Thirteen leaned toward her. "You *must* try to get killed close to the access point. It's at the far side of the Pit. I have already summoned more medics. We will be waiting there. The moment the two minutes is up, the door will slide open, and we will revive you as quickly as we can. And protect your chest and head at all cost. It will be much harder to revive you if essential organs are destroyed."

A light appeared at the far end of the tunnel. The door had slid open.

"It's time." Dr. Horn sounded mournful. "Remember, get to the far side of the Pit, and stay alive as long as you can."

The Pit felt like pure claustrophobia.

They stood with their backs to the open door, at the short side of the rounded rectangle. Across the Pit were four operatives in black. Jack immediately recognized Zhang: short, spiked neon-blue hair. Her uniform bore a blue rectangle with the infinity sign. He also recognized the saucer-eyed French woman with oversized round glasses and cropped brown hair. That was Operative Chandle. The other two operatives had been in the portal courtyard the morning he had tumbled into Hadley, but he hadn't gotten a look at them. Their expressions were blank, as calm as if they were waiting for an elevator.

"What's the plan here?" Jack asked the others.

"Survive for two minutes," Voss said, his voice dull.

"Getting to the other side is going to be difficult," Freddy whispered. "We'll have to go through them."

"Can't help that now," Asha said. "Voss is right. We survive—that's it. Don't pull your blades; we have no chance of engaging them in combat. Keep your hands free. But don't make it easy for them either. When that door closes behind us, scatter."

There was a creaking noise behind them. They turned around to see the stone door slowly sliding shut. It sealed with an echo of stone hitting stone. Jack's heart pounded. He turned back to face the operatives.

There were only three of them.

"Look out!" Asha shouted. An operative with an orange patch on his chest was sprinting almost faster than Jack could see, running on the side of the wall itself. By the time Jack's eye caught up to him, the operative was already on the wall behind him, his rune blade drawn with an orange blaze erupting from the tip. Jack felt a searing pain in the back of his ankle. He howled and dropped to his knees. Freddy fell next to him.

Asha and Voss rolled away from the wall and into the middle of the Pit. Asha drew her blade despite her own advice.

Voss charged at Operative Chandle, who was walking calmly toward him. She flicked her wrist, and what looked like a clicker appeared in her hand. She squeezed it. A deafening pulse echoed off the walls, knocking Jack back against the wall behind him. Voss hit the wall a split second later, but he pulled himself up again, shaking his head.

He sprinted toward Chandle, noticeably weaker this time. Asha's head had slammed against the wall from the force of the pulse, which had somehow left the operatives unaffected. She forced herself up too.

Jack watched Zhang walk out to meet Voss. Voss drew his blade. With seemingly no effort, Zhang deployed her rune blade and disarmed him instantly. Then she slashed Voss across the arm, scorching his uniform with a blue blaze. She kicked him square in the chest, sending him tumbling back again. Zhang turned in time to meet Asha, who had picked up her blade.

Zhang flicked Asha's blade out of her hand with a swift movement. All at once, the cold steel of Zhang's blade was against Asha's throat.

"No!" Voss screamed, struggling to his feet.

Zhang looked at all of them, almost amused. She turned to the last operative still against the far wall, a small Expathic.

"Flood," she called back to him. "Drown them."

Zhang sprinted to the side wall and leapt, where she was caught by the Kinetic and pulled up. Operative Chandle climbed up the opposite wall.

Jack glanced back toward the operative on the far wall. But he saw only the wall of water coming at him. The tidal wave engulfed him, and water filled his lungs.

Then everything went dark.

Jack opened his eyes. He was lying on a firm mattress covered with a kind of leather material that molded to his body. He realized he was nestled in the bottom half of a clamshell-style bed that resembled a tanning bed. He was comfortably warm.

He sat up. Voss sat in a chair across from him, a silver thermal blanket over his shoulders. "You're up," he said. "Your buddy's just waking up too."

Jack looked to his left. Freddy was sitting up and blinking. He, too, examined the clamshell bed he found himself in. "Where are we?"

"Hypothermia beds. In the clinic," Voss explained.

"Dr. Horn brought us back to life," Freddy said dumbly.

Voss shook his head. "She didn't have to. We never died."

Dr. Horn came in. "Welcome back, boys. How are you feeling? Warming up at last, I hope?"

Jack felt down to his ankle. Nothing. Not even a scar. "You fixed . . ." He stopped and whipped his gaze around. "Where's Asha?"

"She's speaking with Superior Blue in the other room. I'll go on and fetch them."

"Is she okay?" Freddy called after her.

"You don't remember, do you?" Voss answered.

Jack and Freddy just stared back. Voss leaned forward. "You and Freddy went down at the start, with your tendons slashed. Asha and I dodged that operative, but the Systemic developed some kind of localized pulse that practically paralyzed us. We managed to get up, but we had no chance against Zhang," Voss said. "That's when the flood hit."

"That's the last thing I remember," Freddy said. "The water hitting me, knocking my head against the back wall. I couldn't swim against the wave, and I knew I was going to drown. Then I must have passed out."

"I was fighting to get to the surface," Voss said. "But that pulse made it almost impossible to move. Then I saw Asha." Voss shook his head at the recollection. "She was on the ground on one knee—completely dry. It was like she was in a tiny invisible room that the water couldn't get to."

Jack was confused. "How?"

Voss almost smiled. "Ice. She must have instinctively frozen the water around her, all in that split second it took the flood to rush over us. A perfect cube, underwater. She looked stunned. That's when she saw me," Voss said. "She put her hand to the ice wall and it became a wedge, like a plow. The ice wall pushed the water out of the way until it got to me. Somehow, I tumbled into the air lock she had made. I was covered in a sheet of ice, freezing but alive."

"She did the same for you both." Voss nodded at Freddy and Jack. "It must have taken her less than a minute. Then she pressed the water out of your lungs with CPR." He shrugged. "When the water receded, Dr. Horn came running in. She had to smash through the ice to get us out." He checked his band. "That was about an hour ago."

Asha and Superior Blue walked in.

"Hey!" Freddy leapt up from the bed and took her by her shoulders. "You're a rock star. You saved our lives!"

"Seriously, Asha—holy cow," Jack said. "Voss just told us. Are you okay?"

She nodded. "I'm as surprised as you are. But yeah, I'm fine, Dr. Horn fixed me up."

"She's better than fine," Superior Blue interjected, beaming. "She broke through! She's an improbable. They said it was impossible." He turned to Jack and Freddy. "I'm sorry. I should have stopped you. If I had known you were going to talk to Rufus . . . The man is not in his right mind. What happened was unacceptable."

"It worked," Freddy said, full of relief and joy. "That's all that matters."

"It worked for Ice," Voss corrected.

Superior Blue shook his head. "It doesn't matter. Don't you see? This will get you into the Dome tonight. There is only one essential component of breaking through—you *believe* it." He motioned to Asha excitedly. "Nobody has ever gone from dormant to fully weaponized spade in an instant. Asha's breakthrough can only be because the Grays have chosen you. And it's only day two. The Great Prophecy is being fulfilled!"

There was an awkward pause.

"That's the thing, sir," Voss said slowly. "All I know is that everyone, except you, believes the Bulgarian killed Wyeth. I don't see any evidence that this prophecy is real or that the four of us have been chosen by monks. You're saying all we need to do is believe, but I can't believe something that has no evidence."

Superior Blue nodded thoughtfully. "You're right, Torque. I've been naive thinking you could just accept all this." He clapped his hands together. "Dr. Horn," he called into the other room, "I'm checking your patients out." He turned back to them. "Get up, Thirteen. We're going on a field trip."

The sign hanging askew on the door identified the cottage: The Workshop. What type of workshop, Jack couldn't imagine. It looked like some rustic abode you might find in *Town & Country* magazine, a simple dwelling in the woods where some famous author spent a bitter winter writing the great American novel. They had reached the cottage down winding paths no wider than deer trails. Superior Blue rapped on the door.

From inside came a yelp of surprise and a clatter of metal. Then the door swung open. Standing there, seeming bewildered, was Alexander. Maggie bounded in past him, and a half dozen ravens ricocheted around the room before flying out and into the sky with Maggie leaping joyfully after them.

"Superior Blue!" Alexander said, eyebrows raised. He glanced at Team Thirteen behind him. "Is anything wrong?"

"Not at all, Edison," Superior Blue said. "I was hoping you could help me with a little show-and-tell for our new recruits."

Alexander rubbed his forearms. He was a few inches shorter than Jack and so skinny it was a wonder he didn't sway when he stood upright. He cocked his head but stepped aside for everyone to enter. "Of course. However I can help."

A pair of ravens that had withstood the canine invasion perched behind Alexander, peering up at the visitors. They cawed loudly before hopping and flapping out of the way.

The inside of the Workshop resembled what Jack imagined the International Space Station might look like if it were inhabited by a disorganized auto mechanic. In the main room a large glass table dominated the center of the space like a formal dining room table would. The glass top was actually a screen, and it displayed an image of a full-sized copper door.

Asha immediately went to check out the odd objects stacked on the shelves on the wall next to the fireplace. A small silver tripod with a mounted laser scope began crawling away from her when she reached for it, scurrying up the wall like a spider. She snatched it.

"Hey! Don't touch anything, please!" Alexander said, peering over Superior Blue's shoulder.

Asha already had a pin-sized screwdriver in her hand. She also pulled from her pack a pair of glasses that Jack realized, when she looked up at them with gigantic eyeballs, was a portable microscope. "One of the gimbals is misaligned," she called back. "It's going to throw the laser off. I can hear you from in here."

"I built that myself."

"You built it wrong, then." Asha didn't look up. "But it does have an awesome intel chip. If I find another one around here, can I borrow it?"

"Let her take it, Edison," Superior Blue said. "She's a Systemic minor. You must have noticed that she's a natural engineer. She'll find something interesting to do with it."

Asha frowned. "I'm not a Systemic minor. I just like to tinker with things."

"You're correcting the work of Hadley's tech," Superior Blue informed her. "Trust me. You're a Systemic minor." Blue turned back to the image on the table. "That's the Corpus Christi door that you reprogrammed, Alexander?"

"Yes, sir." Alexander snatched a tissue from a nearby box and blew his nose before he rubbed it vigorously. "That was the model I built off of. I just took out the portal chip and installed a new simulation dome program. See?"

Alexander swiped at the screen and the door image turned ninety degrees. Where a dead bolt would be in a normal door, there was a narrow slot for a large chip.

"Excellent work there, Edison," Blue said. "Now. I need your assistance to log in to the shadow map. I'd like to give Team Thirteen a little demonstration. Just to catch them up, you understand."

Alexander hesitated. "You want me to hack into the Bunker, sir?"

"It's not hacking if I'm giving you permission. I just don't want to waste valuable time marching Team Thirteen all the way to the Bunker, getting clearance from Director Darius, et cetera, et cetera."

"You are authorizing this yourself," Alexander confirmed. "As the Superior."

"Absolutely. And no need to bother Director Darius with this."

"No, of course not," Alexander agreed. He took a small breath and turned back to the glass table. He swiped over it, and the door flew offscreen. Then Alexander tapped his band, and a hologram hovered above his wrist. The sphere-shaped object was covered in symbols.

Voss leaned in for a better look. "What is that thing?"

"It's a different interface I came up with. I use it to hack into . . . to *access* certain systems." Alexander took the spherical hologram in his hands and began spinning it into different combinations, the way you might spin the sides of a Rubik's Cube. "I call it a spin cipher. It's easier and quicker to manipulate than working through endless stacks of code. This way allows me to create hundreds of combinations simultaneously. And it's portable and it interfaces with anything. It's actually kind of fun to just mess with. Here, I'll send it to you."

Alexander flicked the hologram and it scattered into four separate spheres, each landing above the band of a member of Team Thirteen.

"Check it out." Freddy started spinning his cipher, reorganizing the pattern of symbols on the sphere. "I'm hacking the mainframe. Hack, hack. Hackity-hack-hack."

"That's not what hacking sounds like, dude," Voss interrupted.

"Oh, so you're the big hacking expert now?"

Alexander continued trying combinations of symbols. After a couple minutes, a virtual map filled the screen.

"You got into that really fast," Asha pointed out. She placed the tripod on the wall next to her, and it scurried back to its place. "Also, I found an intel chip like the one in that little spider tripod thing. I'm borrowing it."

Alexander started to protest again, but Superior Blue cut him off. "I'm guessing this was not Edison's first time logging in to the Bunker," Superior Blue said. Alexander turned red.

Blue called up a floating holographic keyboard and opened a

dialogue window on the screen. "I'll use the training demonstration program. No need to further breach security by giving you a real-time look."

"*Further* breach security?" Alexander asked.

The satellite view zoomed in on a crowd in a generic public park. Just behind the crowd, a purple flare hovered, the same size and shape as the humans. Blue pointed. "When a reaper chooses its target, something changes in its chemical makeup. The map is able to detect that change. That's the purple flare you see."

"And the reapers just hunt random people?" Asha asked.

"Random? Quite the opposite. Target selection is highly sophisticated," Blue said. "The Shadow's single-minded goal is to be the most powerful force in the world. That requires stripping people of the power to control their lives. In order to do that, however, the Shadow has to first break down human civilization as we know it. So what keeps our civilization from descending into darkness?"

He didn't wait for an answer. "It's simple: civilians themselves! More specifically, the remarkable individuals who keep our society standing and intact. At Hadley we call these individuals *roots*. Roots come from many different walks of life, but they all have two core characteristics."

Blue held up a finger. "First, they put others before themselves. This is not simply a moral decision. It is one that creates a culture and protects a society that benefits all, including the poor, the sick, and those who have suffered discrimination."

Another finger went up. "Second, roots are gifted speakers, leaders, writers, or activists—or all four—from across the political and socioeconomic spectrum. Roots do not simply *believe* in the principle of putting others first and strengthening society. They *act* on these beliefs. They use their power of influence. These individuals are the foundation of any civilization, and every civilization has them."

Superior Blue pointed at the shadow map. "Reapers hunt these individuals and attempt to kill them. This is how the Shadow seeks to destroy our civilization."

Freddy was soaking this all in. "Hadley must be great at beating reapers before they can kill these people. Civilization hasn't fallen yet."

Superior Blue raised his eyebrows. "Consider world history, Link. How many dictators have led their countries to ruin?" He shook his head. "Hadley has saved a great number of civilians and civilizations alike. But make no mistake, Wyeth is responsible for the deaths of millions. Countless dictators, vicious empires, kingdoms, fiefdoms, going back a thousand years—civilizations have fallen over and over again. All of those could have been prevented if the roots of that society hadn't been killed off."

"You're only tracking reapers," Voss said. "Couldn't you track down Wyeth himself?"

"Wyeth changes not just his appearance but his actual genetic composition. Without that, the shadow map has nothing to hold on to, so to speak."

"How did the Bulgarian track him down, then?" Freddy asked.

Superior Blue sat down in one of the high stools surrounding the table and motioned for the others to do the same.

"Listen carefully, Thirteen," he said. "Whether you believe the story I'm about to share may very well determine the fate of humanity itself."

"Vladimir Petkov was a most gifted improbable. In addition to animating objects into creatures, he was the best tech in Hadley history," Superior Blue began. "He created the program that saved the world—the Signature Algorithm."

"The Bulgarian," Blue explained, "knew that the only way to track Wyeth was to find something consistent in him. Then he realized one obvious fact: The one thing Wyeth couldn't alter was his own consciousness. He couldn't change the fact that he knew he was Wyeth.

"The Bulgarian spent years developing an algorithm to detect the brainwave that determined a person's consciousness of themselves. He became a recluse and relocated the Workshop from the central grounds to this abandoned cottage in the Long Woods." Superior Blue motioned around them. "This was where the Bulgarian spent all his time, right here.

"When he finally completed it, Petkov hacked into the shadow map. In the map's digital archives, he searched for instances where the shadow map had momentarily detected Wyeth before it lost him again. He used the Algorithm to map the pattern of Wyeth's consciousness.

"Then Vladimir Petkov set his trap. He overlaid the Signature Algorithm to the shadow map, and he waited.

"And one winter's day thirteen years ago, the Bulgarian saw him. It was from a satellite passing over southern Norway. That very instant he ran to the portal courtyard. And in the back streets of Oslo, Norway, the Bulgarian killed Wyeth.

"The shadow map flashed an alert, as it always does when a reaper is killed. But that day the map displayed a different message than usual. For the first time in Hadley's history, the map named the dead: David Wyeth. The Reaper King was dead. Those working in the Bunker that day still talk about that moment, the message that changed everything. The celebrations went on for weeks, and the Bulgarian was a hero."

Asha looked puzzled. "So the Bulgarian did kill him. What would make him think Wyeth was still alive after that?"

"Petkov could not let go of his obsession with Wyeth. He became consumed with the Shadow's origins, then with the thirteen prophesies of the Grays. Ultimately, he came to believe that he could *not* have killed Wyeth, despite what his rational mind told him because it's not what the Great Prophecy said would happen," Superior Blue said.

"So he became a fanatic?" Voss asked.

"Some might call him that. But Petkov considered the evidence. He concluded that if the Grays had been right about the other twelve prophecies, then it stood to reason that the thirteenth prophecy must be true as well. When the Bulgarian killed Wyeth, it was supposed to end the Reaper War. But the reapers hadn't died. They shouldn't have been able to live without their host," Blue explained.

"The Bulgarian once again took to the Workshop to study the shadow map. He had missed something. Everybody had."

A raven cawed so loudly from across the room that Freddy jumped. Jack spun to see the bird in a territorial scuffle on the mantel with the tripod-spider. Alexander stormed over, shouting at both of them. "Sorry about that," Alexander mumbled when he returned to the group.

"So what happened with the Bulgarian?" Voss asked Blue. "What did he miss?"

"He was likely standing where you are right now, Torque," Blue replied, nodding at Voss's position at the end of the table. "It was just six short months ago. He detected an anomaly. He called it a dead zone on the shadow map. It looked like a black spot on the map, as if nothing existed there. Something was, impossibly, shutting off all surveillance in that tiny area, killing the power, hiding from all satellites, and blocking any surveillance cameras in the area.

"At that exact moment Petkov's Signature Algorithm blipped for the first time in twelve years.

"The Bulgarian ran to the portal courtyard, just as he had done thirteen years earlier. He transported into the dead zone."

Superior Blue turned to Alexander. "You know what happened next, don't you, Edison? You have all Petkov's research here in the Workshop; you must have studied it. Why don't you tell our friends?"

Alexander looked hesitant, but he turned to Team Thirteen. "In that dead zone the Bulgarian discovered a new kind of reaper."

"*What?*" Jack asked, stunned.

"The first one created in thirteen years," Alexander told them. "It was proof, the Bulgarian said, that Wyeth was back. Hadley's surveillance was unable to pick up anything because of the dead zone, so Darius immediately deployed a team of operatives to investigate the scene."

"So Wyeth *is* alive?" Asha asked. "He must be if there are new reapers."

Alexander shook his head. "The operatives went through the portal to investigate. They didn't find anything," he said grimly. "The Bulgarian had either gotten rid of the body, or he hadn't killed anyone and was going crazy."

Freddy recoiled. "Did they ever figure out what happened?"

"The Bulgarian claimed that Wyeth had turned a man into a kind of reaper," Alexander said. "Petkov called it *darkening* because the man's eyes went black and his skin froze, just like a reaper. He believed the dead zone occurred because Wyeth had used so much energy in darkening the civilian. He said when he blazed the darkened man, the icy exoskeleton shattered and vaporized, leaving no trace." Alexander stood taller. "But it's just not possible. The Shadow creates reapers; he can't corrupt humans, or he would have done it a long time ago."

"The Council didn't believe Petkov," Superior Blue added. "They thought he was mentally unstable to begin with. A single occurrence with no evidence was simply too much for them to believe, especially after there were no further instances of this so-called darkening."

"So there were no more dead zones?" Jack asked.

"The Office of Reaper Engagement determined the dead zone to be a satellite malfunction," Blue said. "Our researchers concluded that nobody, not even the world's greatest hacker, could simultaneously block a Hadley satellite and shut down all power and cameras in such a focused area."

Superior Blue slapped the table, sending static signals rippling through it. "But you must see—that is the proof itself! No hacker alive had the ability to do that. And a malfunction in the satellite didn't account for the power outage in that area. It was Wyeth—it's the only explanation. But the Council refused to accept it. They wanted the Bulgarian locked up. Some even called for him to be sent to the Asylum, where they believed he should have been all along."

Freddy's eyes widened. "What's the Asylum?"

Alexander gave Superior Blue a strange look. "The Asylum? Even I've never heard of that."

Superior Blue cleared his throat and smoothed his suit jacket and tie. "It's irrelevant. And more importantly, it's classified. The point here is that Vladimir Petkov escaped, out a portal. Two months ago he was reported dead. Killed by a reaper."

The Superior took a deep breath and studied the team. "And that is the evidence, Thirteen," he said. "You may have difficulty believing the Great Prophecy, but remember that Vladimir Petkov was not a monk but a data scientist. Consider that as you decide what to believe."

Superior Blue let that sit with them for a moment, then pushed himself up from his stool and walked to the door. He checked his band. "You've already missed Escapes. The Forty-Eight are about to start their first blade agility training with Instructor Santori at the Bridge. You'll need to run to make it on time. Your life may one day depend on how well you do in that class."

CHAPTER 12

BRIDGE

ПО RETREAT

The wooden platform the recruits stood on was seven stories above the ground with no guardrails. It was broad enough to fit them all comfortably, but at that height, nothing would stop you from accidentally walking off the ledge. Even climbing the rope ladders to get up to it had made Jack sick with nerves.

An identical platform at the same height was positioned fifty feet away. On it stood Instructor Santori, who looked like a European soccer star, complete with short scruff on his chin and dark hair pulled back in a short ponytail. There seemed to be little, if anything, holding the twin platforms up; they were impossibly cantilevered off the tall pines. Linking the two platforms was a flat wooden walkway that reminded Jack of a dock.

Santori walked toward them, the hilt of his blade in his hand. He stopped at a black line that marked the middle point of the bridge. He flicked his wrist and the blade sprung from the hilt, igniting the short but brilliant blue blaze at the tip.

"For the purposes of our lessons, I will be using a training blade like the one you use rather than my rune blade," he announced. "Now, there are four things you need to know about the Hadley blade." Santori held the blaze toward the recruits. "The first is that the blaze at the tip of your blade is the *only* way to destroy a shadow reaper. It is powerful enough to combust the ice-based exoskeleton of the reaper.

"Second. The reaper has only one weak point: the bull's-eye. The blaze must make direct contact with the bull's-eye. Here." Santori tapped the center of his chest. A round metal shield the size of a dinner plate had appeared on his uniform. At the center of the shield, an indented red point marked the vulnerable point. Jack noticed that his uniform had adopted a similar round steel plate over his own chest.

"Next," Santori continued. "The blaze will stay lit for only two minutes; after that you have to cock it to reignite." He flicked his wrist again and the blade disappeared for a split second into the hilt and sprung back out.

"And last, the Hadley blade is linked directly to your band, which is linked to your mind. The blade goes where you want it to go, with minimal effort," he told them. "The challenge, then, is to *know* where you want it to go. The blade requires one thing from you: instruction. To give it that instruction, you must have vision. You must have confidence. You must have, above all, imagination."

Jack wondered whether Santori had translated that word into English correctly. How could a Hadley blade rely on his imagination?

"You cannot learn this. You must feel it." Santori drew his blade straight up. "Who will be first? Choose a member of your team to come out."

When nobody stepped forward, Santori pointed his blade at the short red-haired boy closest to the bridge. "Team Four's representative. Step up, please."

Jack recognized the boy as the one Miles had tripped in Prophecy Hall the day before. The kid's shoulders sagged for an instant, but then he stood up straight and crept out to Santori. The bridge was only five feet wide and, like the platform, had no railings.

"Blade agility is not about the movement of your body. It is about your control of the blade. When your hand controls your blade in harmony with your mind, the rest of your body needs to move very little," Santori informed them.

"But . . . what if we fall?" the boy asked, peering down at the open air.

"Ah yes, thank you for reminding me." Santori momentarily lowered his blade to address the recruits. "Please stay on the bridge. If you flail your body around, you are not using your blade correctly, and you risk falling off. If you do fall, please remember to relax your body and land on your legs, with your knees bent slightly, like this." Santori lowered into a squat. "It will protect your essential organs and limit broken bones to below the pelvis. Okay. Team Four. If you please."

The redheaded kid from Team Four took his blade from his hip, his hand trembling. Somehow, he managed to twist his wrist, and the blade sprung from the handle.

Santori tapped his band. A small holographic screen appeared on the recruits' platform, in the place where a doorbell might appear if the platform were the front step of a house. The hologram spun in a spectrum of color until settling on the words *Recruit Training*.

Santori held out his blade and tapped the boy's blade. "Spade name?"

"Core, sir."

"Push me back to my platform, or I will push you back to yours," Santori announced. And suddenly his blade slashed through the air in complex patterns. Core barely got his blade up in time to parry. Santori paused.

"You are relying on your skill, Core, of which you have none. *Tell* your blade where to go!"

Santori came at him again. Core quickly retreated, though his blade managed to at least defend himself against Santori's attack.

"I am moving at only a fraction of my potential speed, Core," Santori barked at him. He slapped the steel plate on his chest. "I am a reaper—strike me! You cannot defend forever."

Santori's onslaught continued. Core swung his blade more quickly now, his eyes fixed on his opponent's weapon. But still, within moments, Santori drove him back to the other recruits. The screen buzzed as Core stepped back on the platform.

"A weak display." Santori walked back to the center of the bridge. "Core's mind was linked to his blade, but the best he could do was to imagine how to defend himself. The blade followed his commands, though awkwardly, because he had no vision. No imagination. His mind was consumed with fear, and thus he stayed on the defensive. If I had wanted to, I could have slashed him a dozen times before he knew what had hit him." He reached the center of the bridge and spun around. "Who's next?"

Miles Watt approached the bridge, pausing to touch the

hologram. He spun it right then left. Then he returned it to *Recruit Training* and walked onto the bridge.

Instructor Santori raised his eyebrows as Miles drew closer. "Recruit Watt, isn't it?"

"Yes, sir."

Santori studied him a moment before raising his blade. "Very well. Come."

Miles drew his blade. Before Santori could make a move, Miles came at him. Santori's blade swung up to parry Miles's first strike. For a few seconds Miles actually held Santori to his side of the bridge, the exertion visible on his face. Then Santori sped up his movements. His blade moved far quicker than it had against Core. He drove Miles backward to his platform so rapidly that Miles lost his footing. The other recruits gasped as Miles slipped off the bridge.

Santori's reflexes were quick. He reached down and snatched Miles by the wrist. For a moment he held him there, dangling, eyes locked. Then Santori pulled Miles up.

"A strong showing, Recruit Watt," Santori said over his shoulder, walking back to the center of the bridge. "But you relied on anger, not on imagination. Your anger is powerful." He turned and pointed at Miles. "But I warn you—put this anger aside. Test it no further."

Santori and Miles stared at each other for a long moment. There was something strange happening. Jack sensed it in how Santori spoke to Miles. And how Instructor Suzuki had looked alarmed back in the Hexagon when she admonished Miles. And how Darius's face had fallen when she heard whatever had happened to Miles at the Naming Ceremony.

Miles Watt was different. Jack just didn't know how.

"Team Thirteen." Santori called. "Step up, please."

Freddy pushed his curly black hair out of his face. He turned to the rest of the team. "Okay. I got this."

Voss grabbed his arm. "I'll go. Or Asha. She's already broken through."

Miles Watt smirked. "He's right, Curly. No need to humiliate yourself out there."

Freddy spun to face Miles. "The way you just humiliated yourself, you mean?"

Freddy pushed past Miles and strode out to meet Santori. Santori watched him with interest.

"Spade name?"

"Link, sir."

With a deep breath, Freddy pulled his blade from his hip and deployed it. He waved the blade around helplessly. It did nothing. Santori walked toward him, his blade almost touching the plate on Freddy's chest. Freddy backed up instinctively.

"Fight, Link! Get through me! The object is to force me back to my platform, not to retreat to yours."

Freddy swung the blade back and forth awkwardly. It refused to obey any commands, even as Freddy muttered at it under his breath.

Santori looked surprised, lowering his blade. His eyes narrowed. "You're a dormant."

Freddy lowered his blade but stood up straighter. "Not for long, Instructor Santori."

"You are not able to use a blade. It will only connect to the mind of an improbable. Thus, you have no use for it, and you do not deserve to have it." With a quick motion Santori flicked at Freddy's blade.

Freddy flinched, and Santori slashed him across the hand, drawing blood. Freddy yelped and dropped the blade. It retracted and fell over the side of the bridge, clattering on the flagstones far below.

Santori retracted his blade. "You should never have been allowed into this academy," he said. "Back to the platform, dormant. You have no concept for how improbables fight."

Freddy seethed, staring at his blade seven stories down. His face flushed with embarrassment as he turned to walk back to the platform.

But Miles Watt stood at the front of the platform, blocking Freddy's way. With a smirk, Miles lifted a finger to the hologram and swiped. *Recruit Training* spun away. The dial continued past *Cadet* and past *Operative*. It landed on a red setting: *No Retreat*.

The planks of the bridge between Freddy and the recruits' platform began to fall away, one after another, like tumbling dominoes. Freddy's face was pure panic as he now backed toward Santori.

"Freddy!" Jack screamed. "You're an improbable. You've always known it. Go through him!"

Freddy locked eyes with Jack as the boards a few feet from him tumbled away. His expression hardened, and he spun to face Santori. He let out a piercing war cry and stretched out his arm over the side of the bridge, palm open. His blade flew up from below and slapped into his hand. He twisted his wrist, and the blade deployed.

Then he was on Santori, who raised his blade just in time to parry Freddy's onslaught. As boards continued falling behind him, Freddy's blade was a blur. He drove Santori back so quickly that Santori stumbled and tumbled all the way back to his own platform, landing on his back.

Freddy leapt onto Santori's platform just as the last boards fell away under him. He stood above the instructor, the tip of his blade pressed to Santori's bull's-eye. The blood from Freddy's hand dripped slowly down his blade and sizzled on the blaze.

A small smile crept across the instructor's face. "*That* is how an improbable fights," Santori said. "Welcome to Hadley, Link."

CHAPTER 13

THE THIRTEEN PROPHECIES

Superior Blue met them on the way to the Dome wearing a wide smile. "Link, the improbable," he declared, walking up to them. "My theory continues to be validated. Two dormants spontaneously becoming improbables in the same day. If that isn't evidence, I don't know what is." He winked at Voss.

"Most believe that Kinetics are the best swordsmen and women, but Theorics are by far the most powerful with the blade." Superior Blue tapped the blue rectangle over his heart. "Theorics are visionaries. We can imagine an idea, no matter how radical, and our minds find a path to reach that goal. Once Freddy was encouraged by Miles Watt's stunt, the blade movement came instinctively. And impressively, from the report I received."

"It was amazing," Asha said, wide-eyed. "You should have seen it."

"I will, in the Dome. Half of you are now improbables. You are more than qualified to engage in a simulation."

In the amphitheater, the Dome wasted no time in calling Team One. Team Thirteen watched from the back of the amphitheater as the farm simulation settled over them. It was early evening on the farm. Folding chairs and long tables filled the front yard. White lights hung from poles outlining the area. Dozens of people chatted and ate barbecue from paper plates, couples sat on picnic blankets, and classic rock wafted from speakers on the front porch. It seemed the whole town was gathered to celebrate the end of the work week. Team One mingled among the guests.

"Hunting a reaper in a crowd requires quick identification," Bakari informed the recruits in the amphitheater. "You must blaze it without harming nearby civilians."

"There. That's the reaper," Jack whispered to Freddy, nodding at the cook working the barbeque smoker.

"How can you tell?" Freddy squinted at the man. Jack didn't know how he knew. He just knew.

A moment later the cook turned from the smoker and began stalking a woman walking past the tables. Miles finally saw the reaper from across the yard and touched his ear. "The cook!"

The reaper reached for the woman. Miles touched his temple

and the woman collapsed in pain, causing the reaper to miss her. Janelle leapt like a grasshopper, landing next to the woman. Janelle grabbed the woman around the waist and leapt again, out of reach of the reaper. Civilians nearby screamed and ran. Kasun split into two and flanked the reaper, aiming his blade at the reaper's chest. The reaper snatched both Kasuns' blades and threw the twins across the yard, where he landed as one person. That left Claire, who stood twenty feet away. The reaper came at her. Claire snapped her fingers.

Behind the reaper the propane tank of the smoker exploded, sending the reaper flying toward her. Claire's blade was already out and braced against her shoulder. The reaper smashed into the blazing tip and combusted in a purple vapor.

Claire was downright lethal.

It was almost six o'clock as Team Twelve stumbled out of the Dome, looking relieved to be finished. Asha stood. "All right. Let's do this." The rest of Team Thirteen followed her down the broad shallow steps. The assembled recruits stared at them in silence. Jack felt suddenly ridiculous in his uniform, like a kid playing dress up as a soldier.

"Confidence, man," Freddy whispered to Jack. "Believe that we can do this, and we can do it. We've watched two dozen simulations now."

"It's not that simple, Freddy."

"It's exactly that simple. You saw me on the Bridge. If I can do it, you can do it."

They walked past Team One. Miles sneered at them. Jack wanted to punch him. Freddy lifted his chin in greeting at Claire.

"Hey, Claire. How's it going?"

Jack looked up to catch her expression. Nothing. She watched them as if they were complete strangers.

"Good to see you too," Freddy whispered to himself in a high voice, pretending to be Claire. "Good luck, guys! And I totally forgive you, Jack. St. Paul's Pride forever. Go Panthers!"

Asha stopped in front of the Team Thirteen door. They lined up behind her. Alexander, off to the side, gave them a subtle thumbs-up. Instructor Bakari stared at the light that usually illuminated a door when the Dome called a team. Then he stared at their bands, waiting.

A long, quiet minute passed. Jack could hear his own heartbeat.

Then the same clear tone rang out. The Dome powered down. This time Bakari didn't even look at them. He turned to address the Forty-Eight. "Recruits, you are dismissed. See you tomorrow."

Prophecy Hall was empty and quiet following another noisy dinner of teenagers stuffing their faces. Jack loaded dirty plates onto a counter next to the kitchen where an oversized yellow vacuum silently sucked up plates and silverware and transported them to the industrial-sized dishwashers. Across the hall, Asha swept as Freddy held a dustpan. Jack listened to them brainstorm how to get Voss to break through.

"Voss already knows his spade is strength," Asha said. "He's just being stubborn—will you quit moving the dustpan?"

"I'm moving it to where it needs to be." Freddy argued. "And he's not being stubborn. He's afraid to try because he's afraid to fail in front of other people. He's got way too much pride. Why do you think he left early from cleanup and didn't tell us where he was going? He's probably out in the Long Woods right now trying to break a tree in half, out of sight from anyone else. Hey. You missed those french fries. Under the chair."

Nobody brainstormed how Jack could break through. What would be the point? Nobody even knew where to begin. Everyone else was getting a sign: Asha in the Pit, Freddy on the Bridge. Voss would get his sooner or later. It was as if their spades were calling to them, forcing their way to the surface.

Jack's steps echoed across the cavernous hall as he went back to clear more tables. He walked slowly, staring at the walls around him. The carvings were spectacular, if indecipherable, covering every inch of surface on the pillars, rafters, and walls.

Jack stopped in the middle of the hall. Something seemed different.

He put down the trays and turned in a slow circle, studying the great hall. Asha and Freddy were still sweeping and debating. The yellow vacuum was still cleaning plates. But he had seen other movement. Then his eyes were drawn to the walls. He was beginning to see a pattern forming. For the first time, he realized the carvings seemed to be ordered, progressing like the numbers of a clock face. At the one o'clock position a story of carvings proceeded from top to bottom.

It was the first prophecy: the coming of the Shadow.

A dark mist covered the world. Cascading down the wall, the mist funneled like a tornado and formed into a faceless beast. The carvings flowed from one to the next as Jack watched. As he tracked them downward, the beast took the shape of a man.

Jack stepped to the two o'clock position. Where before he had seen only random carvings, he now saw the second prophecy: a village by the sea in ancient Ireland. The flagstone walls and sloping roofs of the primitive houses formed one continuous arch, with a small entryway as the only opening. Jack followed the story down to the orphan boy who had been found by the Order of the Grays.

This was Jacob Hadley, the boy with the gift, a new kind of warrior. The Grays adopted him and raised him as their own.

The third prophecy: The Grays traveled the ocean to Elk Island, where they built a world inside the world. The carvings told of the building of the Silo and the forging of the Spade Threshold.

And on they went, every prophecy. The tenth: The Battle Beyond the Wall. The eleventh: The creation of the Dome. Jack felt like he was understanding a new language for the first time.

Finally, Jack made his way back to the front of the room, where the carvings told the twelfth prophecy. It was the only one Jack didn't understand. The symbols appeared to show two people facing each other. Each of their hearts was made from charred wood.

There was something about it, something important. Jack had heard bits and pieces of the other prophecies, but nobody ever spoke of the twelfth one.

And then another question occurred to him. "Where's the thirteenth?" Jack asked aloud.

Freddy and Asha paused their clean up. "The thirteenth what?" Freddy asked.

"The thirteenth prophecy," Jack clarified. "The other twelve are here but not the thirteenth."

Freddy and Asha looked around at the walls. Asha crinkled her nose. "What prophecies? I just see a bunch of abstract carvings."

Jack kept turning slowly. The thirteenth prophecy had to be up there. Unless . . .

He ran over to one of the enormous wooden pillars. Using the carvings as handholds, he scaled the beam.

"Dude, what are you doing?" Freddy called up.

"Move the tables," Jack called back, carefully pulling himself onto the broad rafters. "Just move them from the center of the room."

The other two shrugged at each other. Strange requests at Hadley were becoming part of everyday life. They put down the broom and dustpan and pulled tables from the center of the room.

The floor of Prophecy Hall was a dark mahogany. Jack had assumed the light marks were scratches from the years of shifting tables and chairs. But now he saw it: a towering silo, a black sky with a black sun, and between the sky and the earth, a figure. It was falling from the heavens. The Great Prophecy.

Jack stared at the figure plunging through the sky. *That's not me,* Jack thought. He was not gifted. He definitely didn't fall from the sky. It was day two. In twenty-four hours they would mind-scrape him, and he wouldn't remember any of this.

He wouldn't remember Claire.

A switch flipped inside him. He had no purpose at Hadley. Tonight, though, he was still Jack Carlson. Jack Carlson, thirteen-year-old kid from St. Paul's Prep School in Jersey City. There was one thing that he could still do.

Jack climbed down. For the first time since he had arrived at Hadley, he knew exactly what he was going to do next.

"What were you looking at?" Freddy asked.

But Jack was already pushing through the main door. "I'll meet you back at the Watchtower," he called back.

Jack walked outside into the fresh night air. The last forty-eight hours had been the most difficult and painful and strange of his life. So why couldn't he stop thinking about Claire? What was wrong with him that his emotions controlled him in a way his rational brain couldn't?

The day that Brandon had asked out Claire was the day Jack realized he had feelings for her. As ridiculous as it sounded now, that had been the worst day of his life. His mother had seen it on his face the moment he stepped in the door.

"Hard day," she had said. It hadn't been a question.

"Please don't give me the it-gets-better talk," Jack mumbled, opening the fridge.

"I won't because it doesn't," his mother told him. "This is what it feels like to have your heart in somebody else's hands. Helpless, isn't it?"

"I'll get over it."

"Not too quickly, I hope. It's good practice, realizing that you have very little control over this life. It teaches you to make good decisions in the moments you *can* control."

Then his mom had pulled out the ingredients for chocolate chip cookies, as she had done since he was a little boy coming home with scraped knees.

Jack broke into a jog toward the Barracks. He needed to try to talk to Claire. This was a moment he could control. This was his decision.

The lights were on in all twelve barracks when Jack arrived in the quad where the Spade Threshold stood, eerily lit in the dark. He walked up to the brick and white-pillar mansion with the colossal number one hanging from it. But before he reached it, the door opened. Miles Watt came striding out.

"You don't belong around here."

"I just want to talk to my friend," Jack said.

"She doesn't want to talk to you." Miles crossed his huge arms.

"I want to make sure she's okay."

Miles got closer. "You're nobody. You know that, right? You're the mistake of a deluded Superior."

"You worry about yourself, Miles," Jack shot back. "I'll be fine."

"But you're not fine, are you?" He narrowed his eyes at Jack.

Jack felt like a vise was tightening around his mind, squeezing out his thoughts. He gritted his teeth. "Get out of my head, Miles."

"That blackout you had outside the diner, when you were supposed to meet Claire—it happens a lot, doesn't it? You lose time." Miles's hot breath hovered on the top of Jack's head. "It happened to you last night, even, didn't it? You didn't tell anyone. You woke up outside Requisition? What were you doing there?"

It was true. Jack had blacked out, or sleepwalked, or something. He didn't remember anything after going to bed until he had woken up slumped against the stone wall outside Requisition. He had tried to forget about it; he didn't want to freak anyone out.

Jack fought to get Miles out of his head. "You're the one with a secret, Miles."

"You let Claire walk home, alone, in that neighborhood." Miles seemed to savor Jack's discomfort. "But something happened to her, didn't it? She screamed, and you weren't there to help her."

"Whatever you're thinking, you're wrong," Jack growled. But Miles wasn't wrong. Miles was dead right.

"This has nothing to do with what *I'm* thinking," Miles hissed. "I'm just a mirror." Jack felt a searing pain in his head, as if a hot iron pressed against his brain. He clutched his head and stumbled backward.

The pain stopped suddenly. Jack looked up to see Voss standing over Miles, whom he'd just tossed to the ground. Miles sprung back up like a cat and leapt at Voss. For a moment, they had each other by the throat. Miles was incredibly strong, but Voss was in another league.

"Get off my teammate," Voss snarled at him.

"Found him!" Freddy called from behind, where he and Asha were approaching. "Boy, you're lucky Voss got here first, Miles. I would have really kicked your butt."

Kasun and Janelle stormed out of the Team One residence. Kasun split into two and flanked Voss and Freddy. Janelle crouched slightly, ready to attack. Upstairs, a figure appeared at the window.

Miles held up his hand, halting his teammates. A smile drew across his face as he studied Voss. "You *are* desperate, aren't you, Torque? I didn't realize how bad it was back home for you. What sort of trouble are you in, exactly? Because—"

Miles stopped. Then he squinted thoughtfully at Voss. "Wait. You went to go see her, didn't you?" Miles asked. "I knew you were a coward."

"Went to go see who?" Freddy asked.

Miles's eyebrows went up, and he looked back at Voss. "You didn't tell them you were going? You put on a show for your teammates here, but you're just going to abandon them, aren't you?"

Voss picked Miles up by the front of his uniform. Miles swung hard and hit Voss across his bare skull, but Voss barely flinched. The twin Kasuns grabbed him. Janelle leapt at him and held him in a headlock. Voss carried them all as if they weighed nothing. He took two steps and catapulted Miles, Kasun, and Janelle across the entire quad. They landed on Team Seven's porch in a stunned heap.

Freddy pointed at him, slack-jawed. "Dude. You just threw three people about a hundred feet."

"Leave me alone, Sanchez," Voss growled, turning and stomping off toward the Watchtower.

"That's not just strong, man," Freddy called after him. "That's improbably strong. That's what they call a breakthrough."

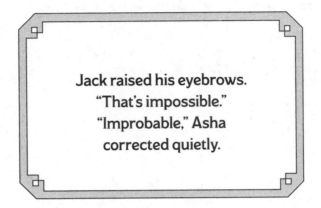

CHAPTER 14

Jack raised his eyebrows.
"That's impossible."
"Improbable," Asha
corrected quietly.

TORQUE'S STRENGTH

Jack looked back at the Team One barracks. Claire wasn't at the window anymore. He cursed under his breath and ran to catch up with the others.

Asha was already walking backward in front of Voss. "Who did you go see? Spill it."

Freddy, speed walking alongside them, suddenly had a thought. "You were coming from the Bunker. You went to see Darius, didn't you?"

"Get outta my way, bro."

"Or what? You'll toss me over the wall with your new super strength?"

"Don't tempt me."

A fog was forming around Voss. He batted it away. "You making this fog, Asha? You trying to slow me down?"

"I'm trying to get you to answer my question!"

"You know why I went to see Darius," he said. "We have twenty-four hours before we're dishonorably discharged: memories wiped."

Asha stood in front of Voss with her hand out like a traffic cop. Finally, he stopped. The fog dissipated.

"You asked Darius for something. What was it, Voss?" she asked.

He stared around at them before finally speaking. "I asked her for help. And she *agreed*. We can get an honorable discharge if we leave tonight. She wants us out of here too. This whole guardian theory is becoming a distraction that could split the Council," he told them. "We leave, she benefits."

"She told you this?" Freddy asked, incredulous.

"We're getting our memories of this place wiped out, don't you get it?" Voss asked. "It doesn't matter anymore what she tells us. We get our lives back."

"What if the Bulgarian was right?" Asha demanded. "What if we can make a difference here? This is bigger than your wanting to go home, you selfish jerk!"

"You don't know what I was dealing with back at home." Voss's words came flooding out. "If we get a dishonorable discharge, they scrape our memories of way more than just Hadley. It will change us. I have a little sister. What if she gets in trouble? What if I forget how to protect her? Call that selfish if you want." He glanced at Asha, already anticipating her protests. "But we all listened to Superior Blue. That whole dead zone thing isn't evidence. It's nothing!"

"Voss, listen to me," Jack said. "I'm as skeptical about all this as you are. But Superior Blue and Alexander both said that no hacker could have created that kind of power and surveillance outage. What if that really was Wyeth?"

"Blue and Alexander are wrong about this one. That dead zone wasn't unique to Wyeth."

"How can you know that?" Jack insisted, feeling more desperate by the second.

"He knows because he made one," Freddy interrupted. He nodded at Voss. "Right Voss? You've created a dead zone like that before. Haven't you?"

Voss stood, tense, like a statue. "What do you know?"

"What do I know," Freddy repeated thoughtfully. He hopped up on a boulder to the side of the path and gazed off into the woods. "What do I know . . . ?" He cracked his knuckles before he hopped back down and walked straight up to Voss. "I know you're not the type to give up. You care more than you let people know. And though it pains me to say it—and it does pain me—you are way, way smarter than you let on. Which means if you *are* giving up, then you've figured out that Wyeth can't be alive and that all this guardian stuff is a ridiculous myth."

Freddy paused. "How am I doing so far?"

Voss didn't say a word.

"To come to the conclusion that Wyeth can't be alive, you'd have to debunk the existing evidence that Wyeth *is* alive—or at least debunk the existing hypothesis," Freddy continued. "And there's really only one piece of evidence that the Bulgarian relied on, outside the prophecies of the Grays: the dead zone."

Freddy turned to Jack and Asha. "But how could Voss debunk that? What would make him certain that the dead zone wasn't unique to Wyeth?" he asked.

Freddy glanced at Voss. "You want to tell them . . . ? Or should I?"

Freddy waved to somebody behind Voss. "Hey, Core! You guys heading to the library?"

Team Four was coming up the path. Three of the recruits passed them, but Core, the small redheaded kid, slowed down. "The lab, actually. Weaponized Chem officially starts tomorrow, but I already drew up a new compound for this awesome paralytic. Instructor Vishnarama's letting me mix it tonight. You wanna come? I'll make you a batch."

"Can't right now," Freddy apologized. "But you keep doing your chemistry thing. You'll be a reaper-destroying machine, bro."

Core sniffed. "Tell that to Santori next time I humiliate myself on the Bridge." He glanced at Voss. "Hey. I saw you toss Miles across the Barracks. That was pretty cool."

Voss just grunted. Freddy waved as Core hurried to catch up to his team up the path.

Freddy turned back to Voss. "So? You gonna tell everyone what you are or not?"

Voss just glared. Freddy shrugged. "My guess is that you're a hacker," Freddy said. "A closet-genius, military-grade super hacker. You've figured out, theoretically, how to create a dead zone. And if you could do it, you figure somebody else has figured it out too. Right?"

"Voss is a Kinetic," Asha said, confused. "His spade is strength."

"His spade name isn't about brute strength, though, is it?" Freddy held a finger up in discovery. "His spade name is Torque. And I finally remembered where else I'd heard that name. *Torque.* Ring any bells, Jack?"

Jack had a moment of clarity. "The Torque Syndicate."

"The Torque Syndicate," Freddy said, pointing at him. "Exactly."

"What's that?" Asha asked.

Of course Asha had missed the sensational headlines about the Torque Syndicate over the past year. The world's most nefarious hacker syndicate had destroyed corporate mainframes they'd deemed to be evil. They had manipulated elections in corrupt countries, handing unlikely victories to young opponents bent on change and empowerment. The Torque Syndicate and its members were viewed as heroes by many.

"You worked for the Torque Syndicate?" Jack asked, still confused.

"You guys stole 280 million." Freddy whistled. Public opinion had soured when the Torque Syndicate stole 280 million dollars from Global Trust. At first it seemed like a prank. But the money disappeared, along with all traces of the Torque Syndicate.

"Not a bad payday," Freddy noted. "So what did you do for them, Voss? What was your specialty?"

Voss chewed his bottom lip before he finally spoke. "It was just me," he said slowly. "I was the Torque Syndicate. I did it alone."

Jack raised his eyebrows. "That's impossible."

"Improbable," Asha corrected quietly.

"Improbable," Voss repeated, as if trying on the word. He rubbed his chin, reliving some memory, before he looked up at Freddy. "You're right," he said. "About everything. Except I didn't actually create a surveillance dead zone. I got close, but I never figured it out. But I figured somebody must've done it. There must be a better hacker than me out there. And that's a whole lot more believable than a dead Reaper King coming back to life."

"What if there *isn't* a better hacker out there?" Freddy asked earnestly. "What if nobody can do what you can do? Doesn't that leave some doubt in your mind? Maybe Wyeth *did* create it."

"Wait. You have 280 million dollars?" Jack asked.

"It wasn't for me." Voss slumped down on the boulder by the side of the path. "I was blackmailed. Somebody found out who I was. They threatened my little sister. I had no choice, man. Those sickos made me steal it, then they turned me in to the FBI."

"They threatened your little sister?" Asha asked angrily. "People who threaten kids should be jailed for life. No parole. I'm serious."

"Why did they turn you in to the FBI?" Jack asked. "You helped them."

"Because they knew I'd come after them," Voss growled. "They knew if I had access to a laptop I'd hunt them down and launch a missile at them. For two months, I didn't even go online, bro. But the FBI tracked me down a couple of days ago. The SWAT team stormed the apartment, cuffed me, threw me in the back of a van. Then the van stopped, and I heard this scuffle. The door swung open, a recruiter pulled me out, and next thing I know we're stepping through a portal."

"So if you go back . . ." Asha started.

"I go to prison for funding a terrorist organization. Which I'm actually guilty of. Life in prison. *Life.*" He looked up at Freddy. "You wanna know why I cut a deal with Darius? 'Cause if we get mind-scraped and I get sent back home, the FBI will have me locked up in twenty-four hours. I won't even remember that I gotta run from them. Man, I won't even know why they're locking me up."

"Voss," Asha said. "There's a chance—a small chance but a chance—that Wyeth is alive, and he made the dead zone. Isn't it worth it to—?"

"Risk my life? To you maybe. It sure ain't worth it to me." Voss pushed himself up and tried a different tack. "Listen, all this, getting drafted in here, everything—it's all based on Wyeth being alive. But if he were alive, Director Darius would be on to him. She's brilliant. And she's completely rejected the idea."

Voss turned to Asha. "Darius's deal is simple. We can go back to our lives. I get a new identity. We all come out okay."

"You have any idea what happens if I get sent back to my life, Voss?" Asha asked coldly.

"I ain't saying you had a great life, Asha."

"You're so consumed with poor Voss. With where your recruiter found you. With how you can't possibly go back," Asha said, shoving Voss in the chest. "You never even asked where my recruiter found me."

"You were homeschooled, I get it."

"I wasn't homeschooled. You have your labels for everyone, and that's all you need. 'Asha is sheltered. Asha has anxiety.' Well, I don't care about your opinion of me, Voss." Asha was angrier than Jack had ever seen her. "I spent years trying to escape. I finally did, and still I would have been caught if the recruiter hadn't gotten to me first. This place saved my life."

"Escaped what?" Freddy asked.

Asha's jaw muscles squeezed like a vise as she bit down on her thumbnail. "I'm not going back. Do I need to tell you more than that?"

Voss was quiet for a long moment. He shook his head. "Nah." He turned to Freddy and Jack. "All right, forget it. Forget Darius."

Asha took a subtle, deep breath, as if she was calming herself down.

"So you're staying?" Freddy asked Voss. "I give you all these brilliant theories and reasons to stay, and Asha just asks you to stay, and you stay?"

"Your theories are crazy."

"You're not answering the question."

"I'm going back to the Watchtower, and I'm going to bed," Voss said. "Tomorrow is day three. It's our last shot at the Dome. And this time we're not going to fail."

Jack stared at the thirteenth door. Its copper construction stood out from the other twelve doors of polished steel.

Team Thirteen had completed their third day of classes. In Weaponized Chemistry they manufactured a temporary-blindness chemical as a nonlethal weapon against hostile civilians. The delivery system for the chemical resembled a miniature pan flute. Core had been excused from the lesson to work with Boris Kleptov, who was on the other side of the lab turning houseplants into steel. Core, who clearly had some kind of chemistry spade, appeared close to developing a concoction to turn the steel back into plant life. Team Thirteen had spent the rest of the day learning to navigate a crumbling, exploding apartment building in Escapes; completing another harrowing blade-agility lesson with Santori on the Bridge; and visiting the library's manifestation ring for Reapers 101, where Suzuki taught them how reapers attacked.

Between classes they had brainstormed and hypothesized about what Jack's spade could be. Freddy had made Jack try everything: lifting stones, cutting through walls with his mind, turning a roll into a donut. Jack had humored Freddy for most of it, but he didn't have any idea what his breakthrough was supposed to look like. Dr. Horn couldn't even find a spade inside him. What chance did he have?

And now they stood in front of the thirteenth door of the Dome. The third and final day. Their last chance.

Behind them, the Forty-Eight and a few stray faculty members murmured indistinctly. Jack wondered if crowds sounded the same across cultures and languages. As he stared at the back of Voss's head, he wondered whether he could pick out individual voices if he listened hard enough. But he didn't want to hear what anyone was saying. He focused on the cawing of Alexander's ravens in the trees surrounding the amphitheater.

Jack liked Alexander's ravens. It was nuts that he could talk to them, but it was wonderful, like so many things at Hadley. If the door didn't open, if Dr. Horn scraped his memories, he wouldn't remember the ravens or Alexander. He wouldn't recognize Voss on the street, or Asha either. Or even Freddy.

And he wouldn't remember Claire.

Jack snatched the thought back. He wouldn't think about her. He wouldn't think about how she was less than thirty feet behind him. Watching. Was she hoping the door opened? Or was she hoping he would wash out?

Jack stared at his band. It *would* glow yellow. It *would* vibrate. They'd come so far—it had to.

He stared at it. He tried to think only of the band. But it was Claire in his head. *For her*, he thought. He squeezed his eyes shut and focused all his energy on the door before them. *Open for her.*

Then, a chime. Jack's eyes popped open.

The Dome had sounded its tone. The golden light blinked off. The Dome powered down. There was no other sound in the amphitheater.

Instructor Bakari approached. He clasped his hands behind his back, then looked past Team Thirteen into the amphitheater. Superior Blue walked slowly down the steps. He reached the bottom and stopped to stare at each of them in turn.

"I'm sorry, Team Thirteen. By the binding order of the Council, you are dismissed from the Hadley Academy," Superior Blue announced. "Please report to my office so we can arrange your mind-scrape and your reentry into your lives in the dormant world. I wish you the best of luck in your futures."

CHAPTER 15

OFFICE OF THE
SUPERIOR

THE GIRL IN THE
BLUE DRESS

Asha sat cross-legged on the floor of Superior Blue's office.
Balanced on her left knee, her homemade spinner whirred so
fast that it appeared to be moving backward. Tiny sparks flew and
singed the thick carpet as she gingerly soldered closed what looked

like the shell of a softball-sized robotic ladybug. She inserted the intel chip she had borrowed from Alexander, then sat back as it took off, buzzing lazily around Superior Blue's wall of bookshelves. The creation circled higher and higher with a rapid clicking of metal against metal. Asha wrung her hands, shaking them out before picking her spinner back up.

The door opened, and Voss stormed back in, twisting his band nervously. One by one they were escorted out of Superior Blue's office and into a small room off the hallway, where a woman in white sat at a desk. She instructed Jack to place his band on a dark marble slab on the desk. Then she studied a glass tablet in front of her. Jack asked if this was part of the mind-scrape.

"The mind-scrape will happen tomorrow morning," the woman informed him. "This is to determine how to best reintegrate you into your former life." She reached out and patted his arm. "Don't worry. Your case is quite straightforward. I'll have you out of here in a couple of minutes."

Sure enough, a few minutes later Jack was back in Superior Blue's office. Asha took almost half an hour. Voss, the last of them to go, also was in with the woman for what seemed like an eternity. Now he paced the room.

"Maybe I tattoo myself a note onto my skin to remind me who I am and who I'm running from," he said. "Or I could brand myself—"

"I would do that in a second if it would help me," Asha mumbled. "But it won't. It's over. We're going back."

This is my fault, Jack thought, over and over. He was the only dormant. He was the reason the Dome didn't let them in. Everyone else had shouldered their burden.

Jack thought about Claire. He couldn't leave her with Miles. He had to do something. But what? He was useless to the Hadley

Academy. He was not the hero that Superior Blue had believed him to be. He had been unable to offer any proof that he was special in any way.

Jack sat up. "What if I prove that I'm the Guardian?" he asked suddenly. "When Superior Blue walks in here, what if I give him actual evidence that he can take to the Council? They would have to give us another chance."

Voss just snorted. But Freddy jumped up. "Yes. Great idea. How are you going to do that?"

Jack cleared his throat. "That's where you come in, Freddy. You're the Theoric with incongruous logic. You're the idea guy."

Freddy's eyes widened. "Wait. *Are* you the Guardian?"

"Of course not. I'm asking how we make them think I am."

"Okay. Not a problem." Freddy paced back and forth, crossing paths with Voss. He scratched his chin, pursed his lips, and squinted at the ceiling. Voss stopped to watch Freddy.

Freddy screeched to a halt and pointed at Jack. "You have to know something that you couldn't possibly know unless you really are the Guardian."

Jack nodded. "That's not a bad idea. Like what?"

Freddy squeezed his eyes shut and vigorously scratched his scalp, as if trying to jump-start his brain. Then his eyes popped open. "The dead zone. That's what they've been trying to figure out, right? That's the evidence that Wyeth is back. You have to give them something about the dead zone."

Voss crossed his arms. "You can't just make something up. They'll know you're lying."

"Not make it up," Jack said thoughtfully. "We'll tell Superior Blue something that only he would know."

"Director Darius," Asha corrected, putting down the spinner.

"Blue already believes us. If we tell Darius something only she would know, she will have to let us stay. It would at least indicate that Jack is someone special."

Jack spied something on the Superior's desk. A glass tablet. "This must be a terminal," Jack said, walking over. "He's gotta have access to everything on here. Including stuff that could convince Darius." He swiped his band across it. The screen glowed red.

"Of course, it's encrypted," Voss said.

One by one, they all looked at him.

"So get us in. Alexander gave you the spin cipher," Asha said. "It's not like we have anything to lose."

Voss hesitated for a moment. Then he strode over, tapping his band. The spin cipher hovered over his wrist. Voss took the sphere and spun the symbols in different directions. The others sat back to watch.

In just a couple of minutes, the tablet dinged and turned from red to a clear blue. Jack expected to see a screen pop up before them. But he had underestimated the technology in the Superior's office.

Suddenly, Team Thirteen was sitting in a white room with every Hadley instructor sitting in chairs in front of them. For a sickening moment, Jack thought they had just connected into a council meeting as Superior Blue. But no—Superior Blue was one of the seated people. This was some kind of immersive hologram, like the one used by the Dome.

"What is this?" Asha asked, puzzled.

"It looks like a program," Freddy said in wonder. "The Dome records everything through people's bands. It must record conversations too."

Jack leaned forward, remembering that the terminal would

think he was Superior Blue. "Computer, replay a conversation I had with Darius about the dead zone."

In the immersive hologram, Darius and Blue stood up from their chairs, but they didn't speak. A synthesized female voice said, "Please narrow your search."

Jack altered the command. "Play the conversation we had about the dead zone when it appeared in the shadow map."

"To which dead zone are you referring, Superior Blue?" asked the voice. "The first or the second?"

Voss looked at the others. "There was a second one? Superior Blue said there was only one, six months ago, when the Bulgarian killed the civilian."

"Maybe the other one was classified," Freddy said, excited. "When did the second dead zone happen?" he asked the program.

"Ten days ago," the voice responded.

"Play the conversation about the second dead zone," Freddy instructed.

"Filtering by most relevant," the voice said. "Conversation between Director Darius and Superior Blue, taking place three days ago. Playing now."

Darius and Blue faced each other, as if they were having an actual conversation. It was eerie.

"You cannot deny what is happening, Iliana," Superior Blue said, walking after her. "It's happened again, and it's exactly as the Bulgarian described. *Exactly*. A dead zone and a darkened in the precise area."

"This event is not proof that Wyeth is alive, let alone that he darkened a civilian, William."

"The girl is an improbable!" Blue shot back. "The event is too similar to the Bulgarian's encounter for it to be a coincidence."

"None of this can be verified because the girl won't talk." Darius argued. "We cannot rely on a police report based on what an old woman witnessed out her window."

"Pause!" Freddy shouted, and Blue and Darius froze in the hologram. "They're talking about Claire!" Freddy bounced on the balls of his feet. "Ten days ago was the day Jack was supposed to meet Claire at the diner. I knew something happened to her."

Jack felt sick again. He had felt bad enough about not meeting Claire that night. But this was horrific.

"We're running out of time," Voss reminded them.

"Play," Asha commanded the program.

"She has to speak to somebody," Superior Blue said. "She's the only witness. She's the only one who can prove that Wyeth is back."

Darius cut him off. "Or prove that this is all a fantasy. She could prove that these dead zones have nothing to do with Wyeth," she said passionately. "I don't doubt the girl was traumatized that night. But that is not evidence. You must stop pushing this irresponsible theory that Wyeth is back and turning humankind into a race of darkened. It distracts from Hadley's true mission!"

Darius held out her hands to try to calm the situation. "Listen, Rook. I'm taking care of it. You were distracted with the Jack Carlson boy. I was the one dealing with the Naming Ceremony. But now you know what Miles Watt is. We have decided to allow him to stay for this very reason. He will get the answers that she refuses to give. He will clear this up once and for all."

"Miles Watt should never have been allowed to remain. The boy is not an improbable; he is a Psionic, Darius," Blue said angrily. "He has one of the ancient shadow spades. We should have given him a deep mind-scrape immediately and sent him to the Hadley Asylum with the other ancient spades and the dishonorably discharged."

"The Asylum exists to keep dangerous improbables away from the rest of the world. Miles is too valuable. He may be our only hope of finding out what happened to that girl," Darius countered.

"He will snap her mind in two," Blue warned. "I will *not* sacrifice Claire Lacoste's life."

"Pause," Jack barked. He was shaking.

"That explains why Claire isn't talking," Asha said softly.

Voss swiped away the hologram. "I don't get it. Did Claire kill a man, like the Bulgarian did?" he asked, incredulous. They were back in the Office of the Superior.

"Not a man—a darkened," Freddy urged. "At least that's what Blue thinks. Claire must have witnessed Wyeth darkening a civilian."

"And Darius has sent Miles to crack her mind." Asha fumed. "He's dangerous!"

Pure fury rose inside Jack. He stood up. "I'm not going to let him hurt her."

Voss looked up, suddenly interested. "What are you going to do, break into the Barracks?"

"That's exactly what I'm going to do," Jack said.

"I'm coming too," Freddy said.

"Me too," said Asha.

Voss nodded. "What else can they do to us, right? It's about time we broke some stuff around here."

Asha, Voss, and Freddy threw themselves into rapid strategizing. They would break into the Team One barracks—everyone would be back from Prophecy Hall by now. Everyone would also be awake, so it would have to be a blitzkrieg that could catch Miles, Kasun, and Janelle off guard. Voss and Asha—who had just constructed a makeshift Taser and was weighing it in her hand—would contain the others long enough for Jack and Freddy to get to Claire. The risk was that she would use her spade to keep them at bay. But they had to try. Jack had to talk to her. He had to tell her what Miles was doing.

"You have very little control over this life," Jack's mother had told him. *"Make good decisions in the moments you can control."*

Jack had control over this decision. They were never going to complete a simulation, but they were going to do everything in their power to save Claire.

They walked down the steps from Superior Blue's office. By the time anyone noticed they were missing, they would be at the Barracks. Voss stretched his neck. "You all ready for this? It's gonna be a fight."

Asha nodded. Freddy cracked his knuckles, resolute. Voss motioned for Jack to lead them out. "All right, man. Let's go get your friend."

Jack swung open the door. Standing outside was Claire Lacoste.

"Hello, Jack." Claire's voice was weak. She looked over Jack's shoulder at the rest of the team and offered a small wave. She looked back at Jack nervously. "Maybe . . ." She swallowed and tried again. "We could talk?"

CHAPTER 16

THE WITNESS

Jack and Claire walked away from the Office of the Superior. Freddy asked to come along, but Voss took him in a gentle head-lock and dragged him back inside.

"Miles is trying to break into your mind, Claire." Jack spoke quickly, afraid that this moment would somehow slip away or that he would be physically repelled by whatever ionic forces she controlled. "He can really harm you—"

"I know, Jack."

Jack stopped. "You do? But then . . . why won't you talk to anyone?"

Claire kept walking across the East Clearing. Jack followed her to the striking steel tree that Boris Kleptov had created. She reached up to brush her fingers along the still leaves of a low-hanging branch. "I couldn't relive what I saw that night," she finally answered. "Not to Director Darius, not to Dr. Horn, not to anyone. By their urgency I could tell they needed to know, immediately. But"—her gaze fell to the ground—"I couldn't. I don't know how to explain, exactly."

"You experienced something unspeakable," Jack said. Claire looked up quickly. "Voss hacked into Superior Blue's records," Jack explained. "I know some of what happened to you that night."

Claire's shoulders softened a little, as if Jack's knowledge helped somehow. Then she turned and placed her palm on the smooth trunk of the steel tree. "Think of this tree as a brain, Jack," she told him. "I can control static electricity, and there's a lot of electricity running through a brain." The entire tree buzzed with a billion tiny blue sparks, lighting up every centimeter. Jack stepped away from the tree, unable to take his eyes off the exploding beauty around him.

"I created a synaptic fence around my memories of that night," Claire said. "I buried the memories deep." The current shifted to the outer branches and leaves, leaving a small dark space in the middle of the tree. "I wasn't sure I could access them myself, even if I wanted to."

"But you're talking now."

She dropped her hands, and the tree went dark again. "When your door didn't open back at the Dome, I knew you were washing out. I was afraid you'd try to come talk to me again. That changed everything." She looked at him seriously. "Miles would have killed you if you had come. I mean literally. He's different, Jack. He's not like everyone else here."

"They call him a Psionic. It's apparently a different kind of spade. Blue called it a shadow spade," Jack told her. "I don't know anything else about it."

Claire nodded. She seemed tired.

Jack summoned the courage to say what he needed to. "I'm really, really sorry, Claire. I never meant to leave you alone that night. I had a blackout. I'm just . . . I'm sorry."

"I forgive you, Jack," she said. "I believe that you didn't mean to. And yes, it was a horrible, horrible night." She looked at him. "I want to tell you. But you'll think I'm crazy."

Jack indicated the world around them. "I have a much higher bar for crazy these days."

Claire gave a weak smile that quickly faded. "Can we walk?"

They took one of the small beaten trails through the forest, crossing over cobblestone paths until they reached the river, where they turned upstream. The slow-moving water lapped against the rocks.

"I was angry when I left the diner," she began. "I thought you stood me up. I was walking home." She paused.

"There was a man at the corner, across the street from me, leaning against a brick wall. He was big and had on a red coat with a fur-lined hood. He seemed drunk." Claire stood still for a moment, as if the memory of the night had arrested her movement. Jack waited.

"I pass guys like that all the time in the city. I wouldn't have given him another thought, except for what happened next. Another man came up the street, same side as the drunk guy. He was walking from the direction of the diner, and for a second I thought it might be you."

Her expression hardened. "But it wasn't you. He was dressed in black clothes and he was hard to see. He stayed in the shadows, away from every light."

Claire swallowed hard. "The man in black walked straight up to the drunk guy in the red coat. He put his hand on the man's shoulder. Then everything went dark: streetlights, lights in windows, everything," Claire said. "The man in the red coat wasn't leaning against the wall anymore. He was standing straight up, shaking, practically vibrating. It was as if he'd been electrocuted."

Claire squatted down and picked up a rock, then skimmed it into the river, staring out at it, as if summoning the strength to divulge the entire story. "Then he came at me," she said softly. "The drunk guy—but he wasn't drunk anymore. He ran at me like a charging rhinoceros, like he was going to kill me with his bare hands. I screamed and dropped to the ground."

"But . . . he didn't? What happened?" Jack stuttered.

"I looked up just in time to see it," she said, her voice edged with effort. "The other man—the man in black—grabbed the man in the red coat from behind in a bear hug, ripping open his coat and shirt and pressing something like a butane lighter to the man's chest. The man screamed, and I heard ice shattering. Then the guy just . . . vaporized. Gone. The man in black turned and walked away."

"You're saying . . . ?" Jack started.

"The man in black turned that guy into something. Something like a reaper." Claire stood up straight and faced Jack for the first time. "The man in black was Wyeth, Jack." Claire's tone pleaded to be believed. "Wyeth touched that drunk guy, and he turned him into something awful, something that wanted to kill me. Then Wyeth destroyed it, before it could harm me."

Claire continued upstream. Jack followed her. "Have you ever seen someone right after they die, Jack?"

He shook his head.

"I have," Claire said. "Just once. I was in the hospital room when Nana passed. When she died, this complete stillness came over her body. I knew my grandmother's face as well as I knew my own parents—I spent every weekend with her. I knew the instant she passed away. I could see the peace settle over her. It might sound weird, but I knew just by looking at her that her soul was gone, that it had been freed from the physical world. It actually gave me peace."

Claire turned to face Jack. "The thing that attacked me was dead, but it wasn't empty. It was filled with rage. Its eyes were pitch black. It was like its soul was being tortured, trapped in a prison. But when it was destroyed, in that split second before it vaporized, its eyes went back to normal and it let out this sigh. It was like its soul had been . . . freed."

She winced. "Trust me, I know how that sounds. But I didn't imagine it. I think Wyeth has found a way to trap people's souls inside their bodies after he kills them."

"I believe you," Jack said. "But—"

"Don't say *but*," Claire interrupted. "It makes me feel like I'm going insane."

"Sorry, I didn't mean it like that. And I believe you. I'm just thinking, if Wyeth is alive, he's found a way to somehow hide his identity from himself. That's why the Bulgarian's Signature Algorithm hasn't been able to track him except for tiny pings, like when he emerged in the first dead zone," Jack said. "So why did he come out now? Why come after you?"

"The question that scares me isn't why he decided to kill me, Jack," she said. "It's why he decided to save me."

They walked until they reached the next bridge over the river, at the edge of the woods. Upriver Jack could see the rocky bluffs with the odd assortment of instructor housing. The path to the east forked in several directions. One path would lead back to Claire's barracks. Another would take Jack back to the Office of the Superior, back to his team. Jack didn't want the night to end.

"How long do you have left?" she asked him.

Jack checked his band. "Five hours until the procedure. It takes some time to arrange the integration back into our old lives. I'm still not sure where everyone's going to end up. I guess I'll be back at St. Paul's tomorrow, not remembering any of this."

"And there's no alternative? You can't stay?"

"I don't even have a spade. The others on my team, they weren't selected by the Dome," he said. "Superior Blue was right about Wyeth being alive, but he was wrong about everything else. We don't serve any purpose. It's up to the operatives now. And up to you, I guess."

Claire looked up at the stars above this small island that nobody knew existed. "I don't understand this place," she said. "But I didn't understand the dormant world either." She seemed like she wanted to say something else, but she didn't. "I'm going to go now."

He wanted her to stay. But he wouldn't ask her. "Be safe, Claire," he said. "Keep breathing, okay?"

She smiled at the expression they said to each other during every long run, when one of them was almost gassed. It was the thing that kept them going, together, always.

"Keep breathing, Jack." She walked off into the night along the edge of the Long Woods, back toward the Barracks.

Jack watched her until she was out of sight. Then he turned to head back to the Office of the Superior. He wanted to be with his team until the end.

A voice from the woods made him jump. "Well done, Jack."

Superior Blue walked out. He put a hand on Jack's shoulder. He looked behind him. "Are you convinced now, Iliana?"

Director Darius walked from the trees with her hands locked behind her back, staring at the ground in thought. "You were right, William. The boy was able to get her to talk. What Claire described can only have been Wyeth's doing. He must have discovered a new weapon or gained some kind of new power. He is turning humans into something like reapers."

"It's even more sinister than that, Darius," Blue told her. "Wyeth has found a way to trap his victim's soul inside a reaper-like exo-skeleton. That is the source of their rage and their black eyes. The Bulgarian called them 'the darkened' for this reason." Blue turned to look in the direction Claire had gone.

"But how is he doing this?" Darius asked. "It must be some kind of virus. But who could create a virus that powerful?" Director Darius suddenly glanced at Jack, as if she'd forgotten he was there. "Well done, Jack Carlson. I admit that Superior Blue's faith in you was well placed." She turned to Superior Blue. "You knew that only her closest friend could get her to talk."

"I ran thousands of iterations, Darius. Miles Watt may have eventually gotten the information out of her, but not without destroying her mind. The only person who had a chance of getting her to reveal what happened to her that night was her best friend, Jack. She trusted him more than anyone."

"And this whole nonsense about the Order of the Grays and the Guardian?" Darius asked.

Superior Blue held up his hands. "I confess it was dramatic. But I had no plausible reason to bring in a dormant like Jack Carlson. So I created the fiction that I believed he was the Guardian, and I convinced you to indulge me."

"So there is no Hans?" Darius asked. "I have to say that the name of the Gray who led the monks to Elk Island was a powerful element of your story."

"No, there is no Hans. Or rather, there was somebody pretending to be Hans," Blue said. "James Halloway."

"Your former teammate," Darius said thoughtfully. "And Vladimir's too."

"It was his idea to use the coin to add to the mystery of it all. He was the one who put the social security numbers on the back: Voss, Asha, and Freddy. They were all close to their breakthroughs; the Dome had been monitoring them for months. I knew they would at least have a chance of discovering their spades. It was pure luck that they actually did."

Darius cocked her head at Blue, as if replaying the events in her mind. At last she said, "I understand why you kept me in the dark, though I wish you had trusted me with it. We will bring all this information to the Council together."

"Of course. I imagine they will sanction me for lying to them. I'll take the consequences," Blue said. "More importantly, we have a new way of tracking Wyeth: the dead zone."

"Yes, of course!" Darius said. "We will begin work on coding an early detection system for dead zones in the shadow map. It will take some time, but if we're lucky, the next time a dead zone appears, we'll know that Wyeth himself is present. It is only a matter of time before we trap him!"

"We can still win the Reaper War, Darius."

Jack was listening to all of this, incredulous. "Wait. This was all a setup?"

"You may not agree with the methods, Jack, but this is bigger than you," Superior Blue said. "Our civilization faces a grave new danger now that we know Wyeth is alive. He has darkened at least two civilians with whatever virus he has gotten his hands on."

Blue turned back to Darius. "With this behind us, I will issue two orders, effective immediately. First: Miles Watt is to be mind-scraped right away and sent to the Hadley Asylum. He may be young now, but he is one of the most dangerous shadow spades we've seen. He presents a threat, not just to his fellow recruits, but to the entire world. He must be contained."

"He'll resist," Darius said.

"Do whatever is necessary," Blue answered in a low voice.

Darius glanced at Jack and back to Blue, then cleared her throat. "The existence of the Hadley Asylum is *classified*, Superior Blue."

"It's okay, Trail. Jack will be mind-scraped in the morning. That's the second order. But he will be given an honorable discharge, with every courtesy extended to him," Blue said. "As for the other three, they are strong improbables. I propose we find a way to keep them here."

Darius nodded. "I wish we could harness Miles's abilities. He is only the second shadow spade we ever let remain in Hadley beyond the Naming Ceremony. But I have come to share your opinion of him. He is a Psionic, which is rare, and a powerful one at that. He will be sent to the Asylum at once. As for Jack, I agree wholeheartedly." She looked at Jack. "You've done Hadley and the dormant world a great service, Jack. I wish you the best of luck."

With that, Director Darius turned and strode back off into the night. Superior Blue and Jack now stood alone on the border of the Long Woods. Maggie came running up.

"Yes, I know we're late for your walk, Ms. Thatcher." Blue patted her head and eyed Jack. "Can we walk you to the Watchtower, Jack? Your teammates are being escorted back there. And Maggie has taken a liking to you."

They crossed over the bridge and walked in silence for a long time, Jack processing everything from the night. "Did we ever have a chance in the Dome?" he asked the Superior.

"The Dome never even registered you, Jack. It wasn't your fault. You simply were not a full team of improbables."

Jack shook his head in disbelief. "You saw all the possibilities that nobody else saw. And you pulled it all off. You got Claire to talk. It seems impossible."

"Improbable," Blue corrected. "Don't forget, Jack, this kind of thing is my gift."

They were approaching the Watchtower, and Superior Blue stopped. Maggie wiggled her way between Jack's legs, allowing him to scratch her back.

Blue smiled at him with Maggie. "If you have any final questions, this is the time to ask. You're about to be mind-scraped, so I can tell you just about anything. You've earned it."

Jack thought for a moment. "What killed off the Grays?"

"The Grays died protecting this academy in the Battle Beyond the Wall."

Jack peered through the dark at the imposing main gate. "But what killed them? What's outside the wall?"

Blue raised an eyebrow. "You won't sleep well."

"I won't sleep anyway."

Blue stared at the main gate in the distance for a long time before answering. "Dragons."

"You're kidding, right?" Jack asked.

"I am not kidding, no."

"Freddy said there were probably dragons out there."

"I'm surprised you haven't given him a little more credit by now," Superior Blue said.

"But *dragons*? There's no such thing."

"They were the creation of one of our operatives, a long time ago," Blue explained. "She could transform local fauna—squirrels, chipmunks, that sort of thing—into ferocious beasts. Bright, angry red, large as a bull, and exceptionally dangerous. Very difficult to kill. Harder than reapers in some ways."

"Why did she make them?" Jack asked.

"She created the dragons to kill the Reaper King. They are exceptional hunters."

"But it didn't work."

"No. When that operative was killed by a reaper, the dragons went wild and turned on the improbables, killing almost a dozen. The Grays emerged from the Long Woods and fought the dragons."

Superior Blue motioned to the wall. "That was when the wall was created. An operative named Isabella Kwei had a masonry spade, and she erected the entire wall in a matter of minutes, under tremendous stress. The wall ripped right through the Long Woods and encircled the entire academy. She saved hundreds of lives. The Kwei Library is named for her. The Grays drove the dragons out the gate. Hadley operatives searched for weeks for survivors. There were none."

"And the dragons are still out there?"

"The wall keeps them out," Blue assured him.

"So the Grays gave their lives to save this place."

"They did, yes. And you're doing your part too, Jack, in your own way." Blue gave him a thoughtful look, then he glanced at his watch. "We have a few hours left. Can I show you something?"

CHAPTER 17

THE SILO

Superior Blue and Jack climbed up and over rock formations, pushing their way south and east through a mass of undergrowth. They were deeper in the Long Woods than Jack had ever been, crossing back over the river by leaping from boulder to boulder. Just when he was about to ask where they were going, he realized that Maggie had disappeared. One moment she was in front of them, the next moment she had vanished.

After a few more steps weaving through the dense trees and overgrown grass, the lattice of trunks and branches in front of him dissipated like a mirage. Jack stepped through a curtain of leaves and air and found himself in a clearing. Maggie ran to him and barked with delight.

In the center of the clearing, a stone silo rose into the sky. It was about fifty feet tall and fifteen feet in diameter. The stonework was rough and imperfect, unlike many of the other carefully masoned buildings on the central grounds.

"This is the Silo," Jack said in wonder.

"Yes. To keep it safe from the scrabble and commotion of recruits, we cloak it with the same technology that makes Elk Island invisible," Superior Blue said. "It's a matter of turning certain surfaces reflective."

Superior Blue walked up to the monolith, staring straight up. "Before the creation of the Dome, the Grays were Hadley's intelligence. They sensed and tracked reaper activity and sent improbable warriors out into the dormant world to destroy them. Many Grays were warriors themselves."

Superior Blue patted the Silo. "This was their first structure on Elk Island. For the Grays, this was the most important thing they ever built."

"What's inside?" Jack asked, noticing a low archway that came up to his chest.

"See for yourself."

Jack peered inside. The air whistled gently across the open top like a breeze across an empty bottle. He took a step into the darkness. Inside, the Silo was a small round room. A soft, thin layer of straw covered the dirt floor. Otherwise it was completely empty.

Jack looked up. The early night sky was visible through the top. The Silo gave the effect of peering up a tunnel to a perfect circle filled with stars. But there was something odd about the sky from inside the Silo. It was blurry, as if Jack was looking through prescription glasses he didn't need.

"There's something up there," Jack said, ducking back out.

"The effect is from several hundred strands of transparent netting, all the way to the top of the Silo," Blue said. "The strands refract light."

"Of course. This is where the Order of the Grays believed the Guardian would fall," Jack said. "They built the Silo to catch him. I saw it carved on the floor of Prophecy Hall."

Superior Blue reached in through the low entry and pulled out a few pieces of straw, compressing them between his fingers. "The superiors of Hadley no longer tend to the Silo. We honor the Grays by improving our technology to better protect the dormant world from reapers. The story is a myth, but the Silo meant everything to the Order of the Grays. I believe there is some truth to it."

"Do you believe the Guardian is coming?" Jack asked.

"I believe ending the Reaper War and killing Wyeth requires something unlike anything we've ever seen," Blue said. "The Bulgarian was not the Guardian, but I believe that someone will come. The question is whether we can defeat Wyeth in time."

"In time?" Jack asked.

"Thanks to Claire, we now have a better idea of how Wyeth darkens," Blue said. "I just can't imagine where he got such a virus. But now he knows it works."

Blue turned to face Jack. "A virus this powerful, once released, cannot be contained. We must find a way to stop Wyeth before he releases this into the masses. The last dead zone may have been the final test. We may have only days. It is why getting Claire to talk was so critical."

Jack felt his palms sweat. In a few hours he would be mind-scraped, and he wouldn't know about this war going on between Hadley and the Shadow. He wouldn't know how close humanity was to the brink of destruction.

Blue stared up at the Silo for a moment, then turned back to Jack. "You mentioned the thirteenth prophecy carved on the floor of Prophecy Hall. How did you find that?"

"I noticed the first twelve prophecies going around the walls, and I wondered where the thirteenth was. I climbed a support beam, and there it was under me."

Blue cocked his head at Jack. "I believe you are the second recruit in forty years to be able to read the carvings. They seem like unintelligible symbols to most. Did you understand them all?"

"I think so—all except the twelfth prophecy," Jack said. "The two figures with dark hearts facing each other. Has that already come to pass?"

Blue nodded. "It has, yes," he said quietly.

"What did it represent?"

Blue looked at him, his eyes betraying an unexpected sadness. "I told you I could answer almost any question," he said. "This is one I choose not to answer, Jack."

Blue turned toward the trees and waved for Jack to follow him. "This isn't your fight anymore, Jack. You'll be home tomorrow. And don't worry. Your mother was told you were away on a class field trip that she had forgotten to mark on her calendar. She is your adoptive mother, I believe?" Jack nodded.

"Well, she loves you very much. And don't worry, she's fine. We can be very persuasive in convincing parents of their child's safety."

"Thanks. I wouldn't want her to worry." Jack took one last look at the Silo before he entered the woods. "You'll take care of Claire. You promise?"

"You have my word," he said.

On the walk back, Jack realized he was ready to have his memory wiped. Claire had forgiven him. And the fate of the world was in the hands of those who had protected it for a thousand years.

Back at the Watchtower, he sat with his friends, who had waited up for him. As Asha's robotic ladybug buzzed around the ceiling of the Watchtower, Jack told them everything, so they would remember it all even as his own memories were removed. Team Thirteen would be disbanded, but Darius and Blue would find a place for Asha, Voss, and Freddy at Hadley. Jack went to bed content for the first time since stepping foot in the portal courtyard. The instant his head hit the pillow he fell into a deep sleep.

In Jack's dream, he was falling. He fell endlessly through darkness, out of control, spinning. He felt nothing but dread. The world was made of it.

But in this dream, he wasn't Jack. He was the Guardian. *This is how it ends,* Jack thought.

His eyes snapped opened. He was in his bunk, on Elk Island, in the Watchtower. Freddy's soft snoring rose from the bunk below him.

But there was another sound too. Jack sat up. His wrist glowed pale yellow in the dark. The band was vibrating. The Dome was calling Team Thirteen.

The door exploded open, splintering as it hit the wall. Voss, shirtless, held up his wrist and pointed to his glowing band. "What's *this* supposed to mean?"

An air horn blasted behind him. He spun around to see Asha's ladybug hovering with a tiny trumpet retracting back inside its shell. It turned and zipped through the air toward the spiraling staircase. Jack jumped from the bunk bed.

"Thirteen! Dressed and downstairs." Asha shouted up the steps. "Now!"

Freddy popped out of his bunk, colliding with Jack. They pulled on their uniforms like firemen. A minute later they stood on the cold stone ground floor of the Watchtower.

"Let's go." Asha unzipped her pack and let her ladybug fly in.

"It's a mistake." Freddy's voice was hoarse from sleep. "We're not even a team anymore. And the Dome doesn't run simulations at night."

"Freddy! Don't choose now to start thinking logically," Asha said. "Right now we have to get there before the Dome closes the door. Maybe it changed its mind. Move!"

They ran—through the dark, toward the Dome.

When they arrived, a dim light illuminated the exterior of the Dome. The thirteenth door was open. They stood staring into the darkness.

"Can we even go in if nobody is here?" Jack asked. "Don't we need to wait for somebody?"

Asha checked her band. "If we wait, the door might close. This is our chance to prove ourselves. We go now."

They lined up behind Asha. Jack felt a cool rush of air. Then they ran single file into the dark.

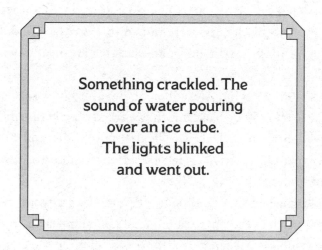

CHAPTER 18

Something crackled. The
sound of water pouring
over an ice cube.
The lights blinked
and went out.

UNTIL DEATH

Something was wrong.

Jack faced a wall of exposed brick. It was not the inside of the weathered red barn he had become familiar with from other teams' simulations. Where had the Dome sent them?

"This isn't the farm," Freddy said.

Team Thirteen stood in a tall passageway, empty except for a single wooden door and a ladder that led to a hatch high in the ceiling. Asha held up her arms, examining the black tactical uniform she was suddenly wearing. Voss, on the other hand, looked like a model for Versace, in a black tux. Jack caught Asha doing a double take at him while Voss examined his mirror-shined shoes.

The adaptive fabric of the three boys' Hadley uniforms had morphed into expensive dark suits, perfectly tailored to each boy's build. Freddy's black curls were tamed in a way Jack hadn't seen since picture day in sixth grade, and Jack felt his own brown locks slicked back.

Jack's suit felt tight. Alexander, at Superior Blue's request, had given Jack a prototype blast suit that worked exactly like the other adaptive-fabric suits. Jack wasn't an improbable, and Superior Blue wanted him to have extra protection. Right now it was just uncomfortable.

Asha touched the monitor in her ear. "Can anyone hear us? There's a glitch in the simulation. We're not on the farm."

No response. All communication was cut off in the Dome.

Jack stared at the lone door. "I think I hear people out there. A lot of them."

"This must be an advanced simulation," Asha said. "It's probably an error. The Dome brought us in at the wrong time, after all. Recruit simulations don't run at night."

"What's the Dome doing bringing us in at all?" Voss asked, stretching his arms in the stiff suit. "Jack said it didn't even know we existed."

"I said it was never going to call us in because we weren't a team," Jack corrected.

"So what changed?"

Nobody knew.

Asha faced them. "Okay. Blades ready to deploy the instant you see a threat." She glanced down at herself again. "I'm clearly the odd one out. I think I'm supposed to go up that ladder, to get a view of whatever is out there."

"You sure?" Voss's gaze followed the rickety ladder to the top.

"I'm not *sure*, Voss! But that's the plan, okay?"

"Yeah. All right. Just be careful."

"Hoods up, everyone," Asha directed. Team Thirteen took a collective breath.

They pulled up the thin, transparent hoods from the back of their uniforms. Jack watched as their faces disappeared into shadow, then became visible again. "It's not working."

"Your face is visible to your team," Asha answered. "We're still in shadow to everyone else." She grabbed the first rung of the ladder. "You go first, Voss. The shadow reaper is in there somewhere. If it's on the other side of the door, the simulation will be over quickly."

Voss leaned into the door, hand on the knob. The three boys crouched together. Jack gripped the hilt of his blade as Voss mouthed *one . . . two . . . three!*

They slammed into a mass of humanity. Blood rushed through Jack's ears like whitewater, and the hilt of his Hadley blade slipped from his hand. He dropped to his knees and patted the ground among a forest of moving legs.

"Excuse me. Did you drop this?" A soft, unfamiliar accent. Female.

Jack rose slowly. Holding out the six-inch handle was an elegant older woman in a light green gown and an impossibly ornate hat. Jack took the hilt from her, wondering if this was a trap.

"I was just wondering where you got that gorgeous eyeglasses case," the woman said. "My husband would love one."

Her voice was replaced by Asha in his ear. "Jack! Move!"

179

Jack mumbled a response to the woman and pushed through the crowd, running into the base of an angel statue.

"It's a wedding," Asha said over the monitor.

"Do you have a visual, Asha?" Voss was already cutting through the crowd.

"I'm in the rafters," Asha said, breathing heavily. "There's a balcony. Jack, get up there. We need you spotting."

Freddy's voice cut in. "I'm already heading up. Jack, stairs in the back, through double doors, west side."

Jack squeezed past coattails, glossy gowns, and shimmering jewels. Then he pushed through the doors, climbed a back staircase, and emerged into a wide balcony where a hundred or so people were already seated.

Freddy waved to him from a front-row seat reserved for somebody else. Below was the great hall of a grand cathedral, every inch of every pew occupied. Oversized vases of lilies lined the aisle, and the smell of bouquets and candles wafted up. The altar at the front was a bed of white flowers. Jack stepped over several seated wedding guests and perched next to Freddy.

"Voss is crowd control," Asha said. "Jack, you're always the quickest to spot the shadow reaper. You think you can pick it out?"

"Of course he can," Freddy said, elbowing Jack. "He's gonna rock it. He's gonna rock it like a . . . pocket." He grimaced.

"What's that supposed to mean?" Voss whispered over the monitor.

"It doesn't mean anything," Jack answered. "He said it because it rhymes."

"Focus." Asha urged as Jack scanned the crowd below.

"We're in Belgium," Freddy whispered.

"Huh?"

"Belgium." Freddy motioned around him.

"You know that speed metal band, Geit Hoofd? I made that playlist for you."

"No."

"You said you liked it." Freddy exhaled. "Anyway, the band is Belgian. I recognize some of the Flemish words on the signs. The prince must be Belgian."

"What prince?"

Freddy motioned to the man in military dress uniform at the side of the cathedral. "The groom—he's royalty." Freddy pointed out the security detail posted around the cathedral. "Those are the visible security. But you see the others?" Freddy began picking out seemingly random people in the crowd, all on the aisles. "Those are the real security. Undercover. Professionals."

Jack shifted to face Freddy.

"If you . . ." Freddy stopped. The woman next to him was eyeing Freddy's hand at the hilt of his retracted blade.

Freddy gave her a reassuring smile. "My lucky pen." He held up the hilt. "For signing the guest book."

The woman squinted at his shadowed face. Then she gave up and smiled back. "That is very sweet," she said with a thick accent. "You are English?"

"American." He leaned back so she could see Jack. "This is my brother Panther."

The woman gave a little wave. "Hello, Panther," she whispered loudly. "Are you enjoying your time in our country?"

"Oh, he loves it here," Freddy assured her.

"Freddy!" Asha hissed in their ears.

"There's no reaper here," Jack whispered.

"There's gotta be," Voss said. "That's the whole point of the simulation."

"You're sure?" Freddy asked.

"Positive," Jack said.

The prince made his way to the altar and the crowd hushed. Jack stood. "I'm going to look around." He squeezed out of the pew and back down the stairs. Instead of going into the main hall or back into the entryway, he tried a door to his right. Locked.

He reached into his Hadley pack and focused on needing a key. His suit was really just his academy uniform, adapted for the occasion. He retrieved something like a short, flat screwdriver with a forked end. He pressed it into the lock. The door popped open.

Jack stepped into a small room, where a woman in an angel-white dress stood facing a second door. She hummed to the music, awaiting her cue. Jack's heart beat loudly in his chest. He needed to back out quietly, but his feet wouldn't budge. It was stuffy in the room, and he felt a little faint. Blackness gathered at the edges of his vision.

"You're not supposed to be back here," she whispered.

Jack flushed and started to apologize. But she wasn't talking to him.

"I'm a friend," said a man on the far side of the room.

The man approached her confidently. He was slender, with dark hair, about Jack's height. There was something strange about him and also something familiar. "I want to offer my congratulations. This will be a historic day."

He extended his hand. Reluctantly, she took it. He bent and kissed it, then stepped back. The bride froze. Something crackled. The sound of water pouring over an ice cube.

The lights blinked and went out.

Through the door the wedding march began. The bride seemed to wake from a trance. Then she glided out of the room, which opened next to the main hall's entrance doors.

Through the doorway Jack could only see her back. As he watched, the first guests turned. The room glowed with the midday sun filtering through the vaulted stained-glass windows and with candles flickering. The electric lights were off.

The bride faced the hundreds before her. Then she took a practiced step into the aisle.

The man turned slowly and faced Jack. A deep cold penetrated Jack's organs. Wyeth smiled. "You recognize me, don't you? Interesting. I didn't know if you would."

Jack, with cold sweat dripping into his eyes, grabbed his blade hilt. An unseen force yanked the weapon from his hand, and it smashed against the brick wall behind Wyeth.

"Oh, it's too late for that, Jack. But watch if you like." Wyeth nodded toward the main hall.

"What did you do?" Jack forced his voice out.

"IImm. You're not fighting me," Wyeth said. "You're weaker than I thought."

Then he walked past Jack, who was still paralyzed, out the back door that Jack had come in. The door shut, and Jack could move again. He grabbed his blade and followed, but Wyeth had vanished.

Jack ran back through the room and to the gaping doors of the cathedral hall. "Wyeth," he hissed over the monitor.

"Jack! I've been calling you," Freddy whispered. "I was afraid you'd blacked out."

"The bride," Jack said. "Wyeth touched the bride and darkened her. He gave her the virus. Get to her before she kills somebody."

Voss's voice came over the monitor. "Taking out the princess bride on the altar? No way, Jack."

Jack stared up the aisle. The bride wasn't attacking anyone. She was standing at the altar, across from the prince. Could he have imagined it? He sprinted back to the stairs and up to Freddy to get a better view, drawing the grumbles of those around him.

"There's something wrong with her eyes," Asha whispered. "They're completely black."

The bride clasped the prince's hands. The prince seized up and twitched. His head snapped to the side as if he had been electrocuted. The bride let go. The prince stood perfectly still.

The bride wandered down the steps. Murmurs rose from the audience. A few in the front pew stood to catch her.

Then the prince jerked again. Even from a distance Jack knew his eyes would be black. The royal groom grabbed the bishop by the chest and slammed him to the ground. The bishop convulsed, eyes squeezed shut. Guests screamed.

"The bride darkened the prince!" Jack yelled over the monitor.

"Wait. The bride is Wyeth?" Voss asked.

"The darkening is spreading!" Jack shouted. "Don't let the bride touch anyone. Voss, get to her. Now!"

But it was too late.

In the front pews, the family reached for the bride, trying to help her, to steady her. Others ran to get the prince off the bishop. But the bishop was already rising to his feet.

"The prince and bishop have black eyes now!" Asha shouted over the monitor.

One after another, the bride touched the guests in the front pew. The crackling echoed through the cathedral like an iceberg splitting in half. The sound of skin hardening. The sound of darkening.

"Get to the prince, Voss," Asha shouted. "I'm going for the bride. And watch out for anyone with black eyes. Those are the darkened!"

A massive pillar of ice exploded from the rafters. Asha slid down into the fray accompanied by a hail of hard ice pellets. Jack checked his band. A bright crimson arrow stretched toward the front of the cathedral. Then more arrows appeared, fanning out as if they were filling a clock. "The darkened are everywhere!" he said.

"I can't get to the prince," Voss panted. "I just tried to tackle one of the security team members, and he threw me off. Who are these guys?"

Jack heard a scuffle and a clash of metal over the monitor. "I can't get past security either," Asha called.

Freddy turned to the woman next to him in the now-dim light of the balcony. "Don't go down there!" He flicked his wrist, deploying his blade. The woman's jaw went slack in the light of the blue blaze.

Freddy and Jack ran the length of the balcony. Below, Voss wrenched an entire pew from the floor. He smashed it down on the darkened, which were multiplying through the cathedral, tearing at the panicked civilians. Jack and Freddy ran down the wide back staircase. Crowds of the darkened raged forward, still in suits and gowns.

Freddy yanked Jack out of the way and spun his blade in a blurry figure eight. He held the pack off just long enough to cock his blade and reignite the flame.

He blazed the closest of the darkened coming at him. Jack managed to blaze a second one. Both darkened shattered and vaporized. But in the split second before they disappeared, the whites of their eyes reappeared. Jack thought he heard a high-pitched exhale.

There was no time for thinking—Freddy and Jack leapt over the bannister together. They dropped onto the landing several feet below, then jumped down the last few steps and pushed through the swinging doors into the entryway.

They ran into a wall of darkened. Jack and Freddy stood back-to-back, blades drawn, blue flames reflecting off pitch-black eyes.

Suddenly Jack felt like his body was being sucked through a garden hose. Then he was stumbling out the door of the Dome. He landed in a heap with the rest of Team Thirteen in the predawn morning glow. The green light, the one that lit when a simulation had been completed, remained dark. It looked as if the Dome had never turned on.

Instructor Bakari marched over. "What were you doing in there?" Bakari's hair was pillow-squished, and his tunic hung crooked.

Team Thirteen pulled themselves from the floor.

"You can't just wander into the Dome," Bakari shouted. "It has to signal you. How did you get the door open?"

"It was open when we got here, sir," Freddy stammered.

"You realize you could have damaged the AI?" he barked back. "It's not a playground! You can only go in when there's a simulation."

"There *was* a simulation, sir." Asha struggled to catch her breath. "We were signaled."

Bakari stalked over to the glass podium, traced a passcode on it, and tapped. The hologram display of the amphitheater glowed white, then gray, then faded to black. "If you completed a simulation, why isn't it playing back?"

"Maybe there's something wrong . . ." Asha started, but Bakari was staring out past the amphitheater. "Instructor Bakari?"

He shushed her. A siren swelled, filling the amphitheater like water rushing into a sinking ship.

"What's that?" Voss asked.

"That's the portal siren." Bakari didn't look at them. "Something has happened out in the dormant world."

CHAPTER 19

INTERROGATION

Team Thirteen stood next to an old stone well in the center of a large circle of well-spaced trees. They faced an operative, sitting in a simple wooden chair just outside the circle. She scribbled with a pen on an actual legal pad, although she also wore a band.

"Welcome to the Focus Atrium," the woman called. "My name is Operative Sanders-Watson. I'll be interviewing you about the events of the past couple hours. The Focus Atrium is simply a tool to help you recall the facts of your experience in the simulation dome."

The woman spoke in an elegant English accent. She took off her glasses and placed them on the notepad. "Please place your right foot—or whichever is your dominant foot—on the short, round post behind you. There should be four of them. I'll wait until you get your balance."

The wooden post was the diameter of a large fence post, wide enough for Jack to balance on one foot, but small enough that he had to concentrate. It rose a little more than a foot off the ground.

"Everyone ready?"

The well next to them began to overflow, and their posts rose as the water level increased. Jack concentrated to keep his balance. Before the water reached Sanders-Watson, it stopped at a transparent wall that stretched between the trees.

"Hey! We're in a tank," Voss said.

"Well observed," Sanders-Watson said. "A former instructor drew the transparent sap out of the trees and stretched it between the trunks. Beautiful, really." The water was now fifteen feet deep, their posts two feet above the surface. "There, that's high enough, I think," she said.

"High enough for what?" Asha asked. But a moment later, three tiger sharks swam up and out of the well. They circled the poles.

Voss yelped and almost fell, maintaining his balance at the last moment. Jack felt like he was going to throw up. He looked up at the woman. "What are you doing?!"

"I will be conducting your interview, of course."

"Why are there sharks below us?" Freddy demanded, breathing heavily.

Sanders-Watson crossed her legs and repositioned her notepad. "I have learned that it is extremely difficult for a person to tell lies when their mind is singularly focused on a physical task, for example, maintaining one's balance."

She motioned to the four of them. "Just as importantly, when one of you is speaking, I will read the faces of the others. At a place like Hadley, it is always possible that one of you is a gifted liar. But you will not all be good liars," she said.

"I can't deal with sharks." Voss sucked air in short gulps.

"Well then let's conclude this quickly. The use of spades in this session will result in your immediate dishonorable discharge. And I recommend not looking down for the duration of our time together."

Jack looked down. The tiger sharks slalomed between the posts and circled the tank. He had never wanted to be home so badly.

Operative Sanders-Watson read from her notepad. "You told Instructor Bakari that the Dome called you in. Yet there is no record of the Dome summoning you. More importantly, there is no record whatsoever of the simulation you say you completed. Instructor Bakari informs me the Dome has never run a simulation without recording it." She looked up. "Ice. How do you account for any of this?"

"I can't," Asha said quickly, her arms out like a tightrope walker. Her ladybug circled Asha frantically, seemingly unsure how to help. "But we went in. We all experienced it."

"Link. Did you encounter a reaper?"

Freddy started to nod but realized that it messed with his balance. "Yes."

"Torque, did you engage the reaper?"

"Yes! There were a lot of them." Voss spoke in a loud whisper, as if to avoid drawing attention from the sharks below. "Wait. They were darkened, not reapers."

Operative Sanders-Watson dropped her hands to her lap. "I'm sorry. Did you say *darkened*? Hadley operatives received a briefing on the darkened less than six hours ago. The Dome has already incorporated the darkened into the farm simulation?"

"We weren't in the farm simulation," Jack said. He stared straight out to the horizon to keep his balance. "It was a completely different simulation—a Belgian cathedral, during a royal wedding. Wyeth was there. I saw him myself."

The operative had been watching the faces of the others as Jack spoke. Now she stopped and focused back on Jack.

"A Belgian cathedral with a royal wedding?" she demanded. "That can't possibly be accurate." She quickly scanned the faces of the others.

"It is!" Freddy insisted. The rest of the team howled that it was true.

"Lose the sharks," Voss demanded.

"You are all absolutely positive?" she asked carefully. "You have those details correct: a Belgian cathedral and a royal wedding?"

Freddy nodded vigorously. And in that moment, he lost his balance. He tried to recover, but his foot went out from under him. He screamed as he hit the water.

The operative was already standing up and speaking into her band, her back turned. "Central, this is Operative Sanders-Watson at the Focus Atrium with Team Thirteen. Requesting immediate emergency Council manifestation here." She turned back around, eyes down on her notebook.

Freddy splashed helplessly as the others reached desperately for him. Asha's ladybug pinched at his fingers when they came above water, tiny wings beating upward but unable to lift him. The sharks circled.

"Empty the Atrium," Sanders-Watson said absently. The water rushed back into the well, sucking the sharks back with it. Asha leapt off the post and grabbed Freddy, who was caught in the outward flow. Together they stood on the wet ground, panting.

Voss was on one knee, warily eyeing the well. Operative Sanders-Watson walked into the grove. The sheen of the air around her shifted as the sap melted away to form an archway. Then the wall sealed back up behind her.

"Why are you calling the Council?" Jack asked. "We're not lying."

The operative reached into her pack and pulled out a small black cube, the size of a die. "You haven't seen a news feed in the last few hours?"

"We haven't seen a news feed since we've gotten to Elk Island," Freddy said, whisking his wet hair with his fingers. The ladybug fluttered over and blew hot air from a tiny funnel onto his head. Freddy mumbled his thanks to the little drone.

Sanders-Watson pinched the cube by the corners and flicked it into a spin. A wide holographic screen sprung into the air. The image was blurry before sharpening into high definition. Two anchors sat behind a desk with the BBC logo.

"If you are just joining us, we're looking at what are being called the Belgian Riots," said one anchor. Behind the desk a live feed from a helicopter showed a street filled with rioters. Houses burned in the background.

"At least 260 are confirmed missing from St. Michael's Cathedral in central Brussels, where they were attending the morning wedding ceremony of Prince Verhoeven of Belgium. According to early reports, Prince Verhoeven and his bride themselves attacked and incited the crowd." An image of the prince flashed on the screen, alongside the bride Jack had seen in the back. The one Wyeth touched. The darkened bride.

"We stress that these reports are early and unconfirmed," the anchor continued. "The search for the missing who were inside the cathedral has been severely hampered by rapidly escalating violence spreading across Belgium this afternoon."

The BBC image minimized. Then it was joined by one telecast after another on the floating screen. Each one focused on the Belgian Riots.

". . . authorities are refusing to speculate what would cause civilians in Brussels to turn on each other with such astonishing murderous rage . . ."

". . . What would have compelled royalty to incite a violent riot . . . ?"

Voss rose to his feet and pointed dumbly at the image. "What is all that?"

"That's what we are going to find out," Operative Sanders-Watson said.

In that moment, the faces of the Council appeared on the glassy sap walls surrounding them. "What's so urgent, Discern," asked Superior Blue. "We are extremely busy."

"The Council needs to hear this, sir."

———

"And you have found their statements to be completely accurate, Discern?" Director Darius asked the operative. Thirteen had just relayed every detail of the simulation that they could recall. Jack noticed that Darius stood in a dark command station. *The Bunker,*

Jack thought. He could see a corner of a large screen behind her, which he assumed was the shadow map.

"Completely, Director Darius," Sanders-Watson replied. "They all experienced the same simulation."

"What does the shadow map tell us, Iliana?" Superior Blue asked. "The AI of the Dome powers the map. Surely we had surveillance in the vicinity?"

"The map gave its usual alert of reaper activity," Darius responded. "We received no warning that this was another dead zone. We have not yet been able to create an algorithm that allows the shadow map to detect a dead zone. We couldn't have known in advance that it would happen . . . One moment."

Darius's feed muted as she listened to somebody offscreen. "I need to step away," she said when she came back online. "We're tracking a team of operatives that went missing a few hours ago." Her image blinked out.

"Instructor Bakari, how would you explain what happened this morning?" Superior Blue asked.

Bakari shook his head. "I am as bewildered as you," he said. "There is absolutely no evidence that anyone entered the Dome. And yet, in tracking the events in Belgium, it seems the Dome mirrored, in real time, the events in this Belgian cathedral."

Instructor Suzuki chimed in. "Is that even possible? A dead zone shuts off all surveillance. How would the Dome know what was happening in the cathedral?"

Bakari hesitated. "You're right. The moment the dead zone occurred, the Dome would have been blind, so to speak. Theoretically, however, the Dome could have gone back to collect data from that area the instant before the dead zone occurred. With that vast amount of data and the power of the Dome's AI, the Dome could have possibly predicted and recreated what the Dome believed was happening inside the dead zone. If it did that, it could create something of a simulation of those events."

There was a moment of stunned silence.

"I knew the Dome was intelligent," Instructor Santori said, awed. "I had no idea it would be capable of such a thing."

"And yet I have no idea why the Dome would do it," Instructor Bakari admitted. "And why it would bring in a team to witness it in real time."

"I think I do," Superior Blue offered. "The Dome knew that it would be blocked from gathering data inside the dead zone. It also knew how critical surveillance was, given the presence of Wyeth. So it not only created a simulation of what was happening, it introduced a key element: a real team of improbables that could interact with the simulation it had created and report back what happened. At least, what happened in theory."

"But if that is the case, why choose Team Thirteen? Why not bring in operatives?" asked Instructor Vishnarama. The question hung in the air unanswered.

Darius reappeared in her holographic window, looking disturbed. "Superior Blue. Council. We have tracked down the missing team. They were the team of operatives deployed to Brussels when we believed we were facing a standard reaper engagement. They were inside the cathedral at the time of the darkening."

"What did they see?" Suzuki asked, leaning forward.

"You misunderstand," Darius said, her voice heavy. "They are gone. Missing. They were caught in the riots, overrun by the darkened. Our team of operatives were darkened."

Instructor Santori sat up. "That's impossible. An entire team killed and turned into these monsters?"

Darius nodded gravely. "I am still getting information. We've never lost an entire team in one engagement."

There was a long silence as the Council and Thirteen absorbed the news. Superior Blue rubbed his forehead. "The Dome sent in Team Thirteen. They must have experienced something along the lines of what our lost team experienced." A notion seemed to occur to him. He turned to Voss. "Torque. You and Ice both said you were fighting to get to the prince and his bride. You said you couldn't get past one of the members of the security team."

"Yes, sir," Voss said. "He met me blow for blow. It was weird. I know I'm just a recruit, but I shoulda been way stronger than a dormant."

Asha nodded in agreement.

"Did you get a good look at him?" Blue asked.

Voss considered that. "Actually, no. I couldn't really see him well, now that you say it."

"*Hoods,*" Freddy said under his breath. He gazed at Jack, wide-eyed, then at the images of the Council members. "Hoods! They were hooded. I saw the security team too. Or rather, I didn't see them. I couldn't get a look at their faces either, even though I had a good angle on them. They were wearing hoods. Like this!" Freddy pulled up his hood. His face fell into shadow, his features became indistinguishable. He whipped his hood back off.

"Civilians don't have access to Hadley uniform hoods," Darius replied.

"Operatives are fighters. They're survivors." Freddy's two hands shot up in apology for interrupting. "But maybe the operatives couldn't survive fighting off a cathedral full of darkened *and* being ambushed by the security detail. Whoever that security detail was, they stopped a team of operatives. Who could do that?"

"That's the question before us," Superior Blue said thoughtfully.

Someone in the Bunker handed Director Darius a piece of paper. "This was found in the cathedral. It's in the handwriting of one of our operatives," Darius explained. The paper appeared to be a bloodstained wedding program. "She scrawled it, knowing she would not make it out alive."

Darius held it up to the camera, so everyone could see it.

Prince's security = traitors

The Council erupted.

"Wyeth has recruited one of our own teams to protect himself," Director Darius declared above the noise, her voice dripping with fury. "We will identify this Rogue Team. We will take them out."

CHAPTER 20

BREAKING NEWS

A t least we've got TV now." Voss hung over an armchair in front of the Watchtower's fireplace.

"It's not TV, Voss. It's a media feed." Freddy lay on the rug, turning the small black cube over in his hand. "I thought you were supposed to be some kind of computer genius."

"You gonna turn it on, or are you just gonna play with it?" Voss said.

"Blue didn't tell me how to turn it on. He said our new teammate would know," Freddy said.

"What new teammate?" Jack asked.

"Me." Claire Lacoste stood in the doorway.

"The quiet girl," Voss mumbled. "She speaks."

"Don't be a jerk, Voss." Asha pushed herself up from a chair and walked to Claire, extending a hand. "Hey—I'm Asha."

Claire held up a hand rather than taking Asha's. "I'm fighting a cold . . ." She stopped herself. "Actually, that's not true. That's just what I've always told people. The truth is, I don't really like to shake hands. Is that okay?"

Asha dropped her hand. "Totally. It's a no-judgment zone here. Anyway, I've seen you in the Dome, and we've heard a lot about you. From Jack, I mean."

Claire glanced at Jack. "Oh yeah?"

Jack fought back the blood rising to his cheeks. "Short on people skills much, Asha?"

"It's fine. I know people talk," Claire said. She shot Voss a cool look. "And yeah, I'm quiet. I don't take that as an insult. Did you mean it as one?"

"Nah. I'm good with quiet. Not enough of that around here."

"Then we'll be fine." She nodded at Freddy. "Hey, Freddy."

"Hey, Claire."

"Sorry I didn't say hi when I saw you."

Asha's ladybug picked up the cube. The drone flew the tiny box over to Claire and dropped it in her hand. "Can you work that?" Asha asked.

Claire held the cube but stared at the ladybug. "Where did you get that?"

"I made it. I make things when I'm anxious. Which is all the time." She exhaled and her shoulders relaxed. "I like this honesty thing."

"This thing is awesome," Claire said, watching the hovering ladybug. "How did it know to bring me the cube?"

Asha bit her lower lip in thought. "Huh. I don't know."

"Oh, yeah. I messed around with its intel chip last night," Voss told Asha. "I tweaked the learning code in its processer and uploaded a facial recognition program, specific to you, so it'll follow basic commands without you giving it verbal orders. Sorry, probably shoulda asked. I couldn't sleep."

"I love it!" Asha exclaimed.

"It's like a pet," Freddy said happily. "You need to name it. I've got some ideas."

"Lady," Asha interrupted. "Short for *ladybird*. I already call her that."

Freddy rolled his eyes. "Seriously? You name your dog *Dog* too?"

"She built that thing herself, man," Voss said. "She can name it whatever she wants."

Jack nodded at the cube in Claire's hands. "So can you work that thing?"

Claire held the cube between her thumb and forefinger and spun it. A matrix of news feeds projected into the air. The cube, Claire told them, aggregated data about ongoing reaper engagements. It collected any media reports from the dormant world about operatives in battles into one resource for Hadley operatives. The cube also pulled from surveillance footage, video cameras, and social media feeds.

Almost all of the current news feeds centered on Brussels and the surrounding areas. Most showed helicopter footage of a bright sunny morning on the streets of Brussels, capturing the moment civilians and darkened flooded from the cathedral into the streets.

The darkened attacked the spectators waiting in the street for the bride and groom's exit procession. Jack's body shuddered.

The darkened had been even worse than the shadow reapers in Jersey City. While the reapers were mindless extensions of the Shadow, the darkened were rage incarnate, attacking everyone who wasn't another darkened.

"Jack? You okay?" Asha was watching him.

"Yeah . . . Yeah, I'm fine."

The cube switched to a feed from CNN. "It's day three of the Belgian Riots, with no end in sight," the anchor said. "There is still no confirmed inciting event for the riots, which began at the wedding of Prince Verhoeven and his bride. But images have confirmed a physical change in those that were in the cathedral. Their eyes seem to have gone completely black. By comparing footage we are able to confirm that most or all of the missing have been afflicted with this change. It is accompanied by a kind of rage-filled psychosis that is thus far unexplained."

Scenes of the carnage flashed in a montage across the screen: smoke billowing from stores as civilians stepped through smashed windows with arms full of canned food and water, injured people huddled outside full hospitals, a makeshift morgue in a parking lot, police stations with doors torn off their hinges. A still image from a video was the most haunting though: a close-up of a woman with pitch-black eyes.

Claire spun the cube. French troops waited at the Belgian border. Cars trying to leave the city jammed highways in Brussels. Planes lined up far down the tarmac.

Freddy pointed at one small box in the matrix of live images: a woman with jet-black hair in a dark blue suit being interviewed. "Who's she?"

Claire manipulated the cube through the programs until they were watching the interview. A local news reporter in Santa Barbara, California, sat opposite the woman in the navy suit. The broadcast banner identified the guest: *Dr. Cynthia Thayer, President, Pacifica Institute.*

"This is what the Pacifica Institute has been warning the public about for years, Julie," Dr. Thayer said. "We have spent millions of dollars on this research, research that the world has ignored."

The anchorwoman peered at her interview subject. "Just so I understand, Dr. Thayer, your institute claims these riots in Belgium are, in actuality, a virus spreading?"

"You're seeing the footage. Dignitaries at a royal wedding turning into bloodthirsty monsters? Their eyes completely black? They were in close quarters when the Dark Virus was released," Thayer said. "Read the reports from the few people inside St. Michael's Cathedral who survived. The stories tell of normal citizens having some kind of seizure, followed by manic, hyper-violent behavior. This is a bona fide medical emergency. We call it the Dark Virus."

"Do you have any evidence that this is an actual virus?" Julie asked.

"Yes. More importantly, the Dark Virus was created in the labs of the United States government. They are to blame," Thayer asserted.

"I've heard that name before," Voss said, "Pacifica Institute." He sounded it out.

"Who is this woman?" Freddy asked. "How is she figuring all this out?"

"She's a conspiracy theorist," Jack said. "She's on a tiny local news outlet in Santa Barbara."

"Maybe, but her assessment of the virus is pretty accurate, even if it wasn't created by the government," Claire started.

"She's insane. Turn it off," Asha snapped.

Freddy shushed her, staring at the projection. On the screen, the anchorwoman sat back in her chair with a tired sigh. "And why, Dr. Thayer, would the government want to create the Dark Virus, as you call it?"

Thayer laughed. "Surely you are not that naive, Julie."

"Pretend for a moment that I am, Dr. Thayer."

"The US government wants to enslave our population," Thayer said.

Asha snatched up her books, shoving them in her pack. "Fine. Watch this stupid garbage. I'm going to bed." She stomped off up the stairs, calling over her shoulder, "Glad you're here, Claire. I guess you're bunking with me; make yourself at home."

Freddy thumbed at her. "What's up with her?"

"She doesn't feel like filling her head with junk," Voss said.

"Belgium was just a test," the blue-suited woman said. "As you can see, it was a success. They will unleash it here next."

The anchorwoman's thin eyebrows raised.

"Wouldn't that be suicide? Leaders themselves would be in danger of the virus."

"The government has teams of special ops who serve as bodyguards to keep the infected at bay," Thayer insisted. "They are highly skilled."

"Mmm." The anchorwoman was pretending to listen, glancing at someone offscreen. "And your organization." The anchor glanced at her notes. "The Pacifica Institute. You have a way of stopping this?"

"The Pacifica Institute has been preparing a contingency plan for a decade." Thayer stared into the camera. "We can keep people safe. But people must follow my directions before it's too—"

"I'm afraid that's all the time we have, Dr. Thayer," Julie said with a practiced smile. "We turn now to events . . ." She faded out as the cube switched to another feed.

"Man, that's crazy," Voss said. "Woman's probably trying to sell a book or something."

Freddy perked up. "That's right," he said, turning to Voss.

"She's trying to sell a book?" Jack asked.

"No, Voss is right that everyone has an agenda, an endgame. So, what is Wyeth's goal?"

"He's been creating reapers for thousands of years," Jack said. "He's about killing people."

"That's all he wants? To kill people?" Freddy asked skeptically. "That makes no sense. Why would somebody fight for centuries just to kill people?"

"Maybe he wants to wipe humans off the planet," Voss said. "Like an exterminator."

"No, Freddy's right," Claire said.

Freddy seemed surprised. "I am?"

"If Wyeth's goal was to kill people," Claire continued, "why would he disappear for thirteen years? Plus, the darkened are different from reapers. His strategy has evolved. He must have found somebody with the ability to create a virus like that." Claire looked at Jack. "You said the simulation of Wyeth spoke to you. What did he say?"

"He didn't say much," Jack admitted. "Just that I was weak, stuff like that. Taunting me, almost."

"Say that Freddy is right," Voss said. "That Wyeth is trying to accomplish something. How are we supposed to figure out what that is?"

"Same way you figure it out about anyone," Freddy said. "Figure out who he is and where he came from. Find out who he is at his core, and you'll find out what he wants."

"That actually kinda makes sense, Freddy," Jack said.

Claire was already tapping her band, pulling up holograms. "Seems like reaper origin records are classified." She turned to Voss. "But I bet you could get into them. I heard you can hack anything."

Voss shrugged. "Worth a shot." He pulled up a similar hologram on his band. Then he pulled up his spin cipher. He twisted the cipher around for a few minutes before he swiped it away.

"I can't get it," he said, frustrated. "It's not hackable."

Freddy hooted. "Big, bad hackerman! What, you finally discovered the perfect online security system?"

Voss shot him a sour look. "Yeah, as a matter of fact I did. It's called a book." He focused on Claire. "These files are kept by the historian. In actual books. The only way to access them is to ask him if we can read them."

"Then what are we waiting for?" Claire asked. "Go get Asha. We're going to visit Instructor Rufus."

Rufus answered his own door. Apparently, Barnabas had served his time and managed to transfer out of the historian's apprenticeship.

"A history project? And you need my help?" Rufus asked.

"Yes, sir," Freddy said.

"Well, you've come to the right place!" Rufus walked back to a large bookshelf with seemingly no organization. "As you know, I happen to be the Hadley Academy historian. And your project is on . . .?"

Freddy cleared his throat. "The Reaper King, actually. On his motives and what he's trying to accomplish."

"Well, I am afraid that the information on Wyeth is classified. You knew that, perhaps?"

Freddy's face fell.

"Of course," Claire interjected. "But now that they know Wyeth is back, they've declassified everything on him. They want everyone working on gathering information, even recruits. I'm sure they told you first, as the Hadley historian?"

Jack tensed. Rufus's eyes clouded momentarily. Then he relaxed with a smile. "Ah yes. The declassification memo. I was involved in that decision, in fact."

Freddy shot Claire an impressed look. "I didn't know you had that in you," he whispered.

"You're rubbing off on me."

"Is that, like, a static electricity joke?"

"No."

"Because it was pretty good. You should take credit for it." Freddy turned back to Rufus. "So. You have files on him, right?"

"All of them! But these are the files on reaper activity," he said, motioning to the messy bookshelf. "We'll want the history of Hadley." He waved at them to follow him into another room.

Voss frowned. "The Reaper King data isn't under reapers?"

Rufus hesitated. "Wyeth wasn't a type of reaper, dear boy. David Wyeth was an improbable. The first, as a matter of fact."

Instructor Rufus dropped a dusty book onto the desk. It was the sixth book he had brought from the back room, but each time he had completely forgotten what book they wanted. Scattered over the table were books on outdated recruit training techniques, honorably discharged improbables who had done amazing things in the dormant world, and a handwritten cookbook of the Maliseet Indian tribe. Finally, they had found the relevant book.

Rufus opened the large tome and flipped through the pages. "David Wyeth, let's see . . . Move that lamp closer, would you dear?" he asked Claire. "Ah, here. David Wyeth was born in Scotland in the early eleventh century. Wyeth's birth was foretold in the first prophecy of the Order of the Grays. He was the first human born with what we now call an improbable gift. Wyeth has often been mistaken as an immortal, but that isn't technically accurate. He could shift his cells and DNA so that he would never age. He could still be killed, but this gift made him extremely powerful and gave him unnaturally long life. For this reason, the Shadow chose Wyeth and entered him when Wyeth was a baby."

Freddy looked at the others, confused. "But where did the Shadow come from?"

"The Shadow is a spirit, my young improbables. It is a mist, an ancient force. The Shadow chooses a human to inhabit."

"What about the ability to create reapers?" Jack asked. "Wyeth was born with that?"

"Wyeth was not born with one of the four spades of the Grays. Instead, Wyeth was born with one of the three ancient shadow spades." Rufus counted off on three fingers. "Creator. Psionic. Viral. Wyeth was a Creator. You've seen his creation: the shadow reapers."

"I thought Jacob Hadley was the first improbable," Voss pointed out.

Rufus slapped Voss on the back. "That's public relations for you, young man! How inspired would you be to be part of the Hadley legacy if you knew the first improbable was Wyeth himself?" Rufus hacked out a laugh that descended into a cough.

"Jacob Hadley was the second improbable, as foretold in the second prophecy." Rufus continued after taking a sip from a mug of tea. "The Grays found the boy in a village in ancient Ireland. He was the first person to manifest one of the four spades of the Grays. He was a Theoric, a leader." Rufus flipped past several pages. "Jacob Hadley also had the ability to identify other improbables, and he was a natural general. He led his recruits into battle against Wyeth and the earliest shadow reapers. He established the Hadley Academy for the Improbably Gifted on Elk Island. Jacob Hadley and David Wyeth, the first improbables, represent not just the two kinds of spades, but indeed the two sides of the struggle for the human soul."

"The struggle for the human soul?" Asha asked.

"You came here wanting to know what Wyeth wants, which is the same as what the Shadow wants," Rufus reminded them. "The Shadow wants a world he can control. The Shadow knows, just as the Order of the Grays knew, that each one of us has both good and evil inside us. Every day is a battle for our soul. Will we be other-centered or self-centered? Will we sacrifice ourselves or our neighbors? Which voices do we choose to listen to: those that tell us the world is here to serve us? Or the voices that tell us that we are here to serve the world?"

Rufus tapped his chest. "Every day we choose. Our soul chooses," he said. "Wyeth knows that the human race is far easier to control when people choose self above others."

"So the shadow reapers prey on people who can lead others to the self-sacrificial side. Roots, right?" Freddy interjected.

Rufus closed the book, producing a small dust cloud. "Throughout history we've seen the impact of taking down a single leader—one who stands out, one who inspires others to make a difference in the world," Rufus confirmed. "Yes, we call them roots. The reapers prey on those roots." He grunted as he lifted the book to carry it back to the other room. "Help me with this book, won't you, young man?"

Voss took the book and they all followed Rufus to the back room of the archives. It was literally a gigantic pile of books, as if they were about to be lit in a bonfire. "Just toss it with the others, thank you."

Voss set the book down gently and wiped his hands. "So why did he create the darkened? Why now?"

Rufus pressed a handkerchief to his nose and trumpeted into it. He wiped vigorously before he pocketed it in his jacket. "The Shadow wants to remake the entire human race. For a thousand years he's tried to break civilization using reapers. But he has discovered a far more effective way—to turn the civilians of the world into reapers."

"So why didn't he do that from the beginning?" Claire asked.

"He never had the power before," Rufus told her. "Wyeth has one very powerful shadow spade. He is a Creator. But he does not have the ability to affect the souls of civilians. For that he would need somebody with another shadow spade. Wyeth would have needed a Viral to join him, a maker of viruses. One who could create a virus capable of enslaving the very soul of a person. For that, he would need a very powerful Viral indeed."

"And now he's found one," Jack said grimly.

"It seems that he has, yes," Rufus said. "Just thinking about it all is exhausting, don't you think?"

Rufus yawned, and his eyes began to close. Voss caught him as he started to list to the side. The old man woke with a start and looked around at Team Thirteen.

"Ah. You must be from Prophecy Hall. Come seeking the famous broiled mackerel recipe of the Maliseet tribe, have you?" He chuckled. "I have it here somewhere."

"No thank you, sir." Freddy eased Rufus into his chair and glanced up at the others. "I think we have what we need," he whispered. "Let's let the old guy rest."

They stepped outside onto the Bluffs. The river just below them rushed past in the dark.

"Wyeth is an improbable," Asha said. "In a way it's good. If he's not immortal, then he really can be killed."

Claire shook her head. "It makes me more worried. He's turned a team of operatives against Hadley. And somehow he's found this Viral to create this Dark Virus."

Freddy checked his band. "We can talk about this later. Right now we're on cleanup duty again at Prophecy Hall."

"It only really takes two of us," Claire said. "I can go. Jack, you wanna join?"

Jack nodded. "Yeah. I'd like to."

Freddy gave them a cautious look. "You guys sure?"

"Yeah." Claire headed down the path, back toward the bridge. "Hurry up, Jack. I'm not starting without you."

CHAPTER 21

PROPHECY HALL

A GIANT PROBLEM

Claire speared a bite of apple pie. "They just leave all this dessert out. It's dangerous."

"It's motivation to do cleanup duty," Jack replied, pushing himself up from his chair. "We should get started."

Claire took a last bite of pie and wiped her mouth with a napkin. "You know you want to ask."

"Ask what?"

"Why I dated Brandon." She stood, gathering up their dishes.

Jack stacked the plates left on the table next to them and considered how honest he wanted to be. "Okay. Fine. Why did you? The guy is a jerk."

"He wasn't a jerk to me," Claire said. "And he didn't need me to be chatty or chirpy or whatever. He didn't need me to constantly tell him he was great. He didn't need any of that. He planned everything, and he did all the talking. I could just relax with him. And I liked that."

She put her plates on a rolling cart and added Jack's to the stack. "He didn't have anyone in his life he could talk to. Not about the real stuff. So he talked, and I listened. He was the loneliest person I've ever met."

"Lonely?" Jack asked. "I never saw him alone. He was surrounded by a dozen friends all the time."

"Being alone isn't the same as being lonely," Claire said. "Everyone wanted to brag that Brandon was their best friend. Being close to him made them look good. You think anyone actually cared who he was as a human being?"

"Okay, fine. But . . ." Jack shifted uncomfortably. "Why did you *date* him?"

"He kept his hands to himself, Jack," Claire said firmly. "He just wanted a connection with somebody where he could be himself."

"What could Brandon have to hide?" Jack asked. "He was the king of St. Paul's—the star athlete, son of a famous billionaire defense contractor. What more does he want?"

Claire rolled her eyes. "Can you even hear yourself? Think how hard it must be for him to live up to that stupid, unrealistic image! It's exactly that attitude that makes people like Brandon hide his real self from the world. His father is in the news all the time, getting interviewed about whatever new weapons systems he's created. That kind of fame is just more pressure piled on. Everyone is watching Brandon, waiting for him to fail."

"So he has the right to be a jerk?"

Claire turned around and stretched out a hand. Three more metal carts, piled with the dirty plates they had gathered, came rumbling toward her. Jack caught two of them and pulled them toward the kitchen. Claire took the remaining two carts and followed him between the tables.

"He has the right to keep people away from him," she corrected. "He did that by being a jerk. Everyone hides part of themselves."

Jack stopped and turned around, leaning on one of the carts. "So what are you hiding?"

Claire stopped short. Jack wished he could suck the question out of the air and back into his lungs.

But he didn't take it back. He didn't change the subject. This wasn't eighth grade, not anymore. This was the Hadley Academy, where quirks turned into weapons—but only if you had the courage to explore the good and the bad of your strange gift, the weakness with the strength. Hide your vulnerability and you would never discover what you were truly capable of.

"My dad," Claire began quietly. She leaned against one of the heavy wooden tables and stared up at the tall ceiling. "Everyone liked him. He was so charming. But Dad would start drinking before dinner. I can remember him dancing with my mother in the kitchen, holding her tenderly and singing to her. Then something would set him off. He'd bump into a chair or spill his drink, and he would snap. Every night. He was an abusive drunk. That's what love looked like to me: a swinging pendulum of violence and charm, never coming to rest."

Jack had never heard Claire talk about her parents. She had told him about her grandmother, who she visited every weekend, and an aunt, who was like a big sister to her, and friends at her old school. Jack had thought she didn't bring up her parents because they were divorced, and she didn't want to talk about it.

"One night when my father came in to say good night, he bent over to kiss my forehead and apologized for 'disagreeing with Mommy'—that's how he said it. His breath stank of alcohol. He mumbled that he would never hurt me, as if it was okay to hurt my mom." Claire scratched at a stain on the side of the table. "That's when I discovered my spade. The spark was so loud. It threw my father against the wall."

"I went out for a run the next morning before he woke up. I started doing that every morning, and I tried to come home after he had passed out." She looked up at Jack. "That's why I never wanted to be touched. Because that's how it starts, that's how they manipulate you. They pretend they care. Then they own you. Then you're my mother."

"And you discovered you could keep people away."

"When I was little, I thought everyone could do it. I wasn't sure exactly what I was doing, even, just that I could control the energy around me and control my personal space," she said. "That was important to me."

Jack thought about the countless hours in Coach's van. Coach picked them up in front of their apartments, Jack first, then Claire sliding in next to him ten minutes later. Coach kept his window cracked open, even in the winter, and one day Claire brought a thick red flannel blanket under her arm. She threw it over the two of them and jokingly patted it down on him like a mother. But they had never touched skin to skin.

Jack and Claire said almost nothing on those drives. Then they ran, working their way up in distance. By eighth grade they ran ten miles in silence, pace matching each other. They ran through the woods, over roots and puddles, with their milk-white breath chugging out like steam trains. They would end up back at the gray St. Paul's Prep van, where Coach would click the stopwatch like a proud father. Claire would hold up her hand and Jack would mirror it. That remote hand slap was as close to a secret handshake as he had with anyone.

Then in the van, Claire would put her knees up and talk. She told Jack about her old school, her grandmother's house that was next to a playground, some test they had coming up, all that she had been processing over the run. Jack would just listen. It was his favorite part of the day.

"Fine, I admit it. I didn't like that you dated Brandon."

"And you took it out on me," Claire added.

"Yeah. I guess I did."

"But you've changed, right?" Claire said slowly. Jack looked up to see her smile flicker.

Jack laid his palms flat on the cart and stared Claire in the eye. "I was a jerk. And judgmental. And I've changed. You're my best friend."

"After Freddy."

"Freddy is more like my brother." Jack squirmed. "You're really making me work for this."

"It means a lot to me."

"I really am sorry I had a hard time being friends over the last year. It was dumb. I don't know what else I can say. You believe me?"

"I know you, Jack. I don't get close to many people, but I trust you. That's more powerful than believing you."

Jack froze. "You trust me," he repeated.

"Yeah?"

"Wyeth . . ." Jack lowered his voice, even though there was nobody else in the dining hall. "He has this Rogue Team, right? This team of operatives?" He leaned forward. "How did he recruit them?"

Claire started to answer, then stopped. "I don't know."

"My mom used to say the same thing that you just did," Jack said. "That trusting someone is more important than believing them. But what about Wyeth? How did he get an entire team to come to his side and betray Hadley? He was here so long ago; nobody actually knows him now. And they sure don't trust him."

Claire was beginning to follow. "You're saying somebody else recruited the team."

"Somebody they knew. Somebody they trusted."

"Who? Superior Blue? Darius?"

Jack shook his head. "Whoever recruited them had to have contact with Wyeth, right?"

"Which isn't possible," Claire pointed out. "Everyone here is on the grid. Somebody of that stature couldn't just sneak off the radar of everyone. The Dome would have picked it up."

"But there's one person who wasn't on the grid," Jack said. "Somebody the operatives would have trusted."

"The Bulgarian." Claire stared at him. "Except the Bulgarian killed Wyeth. Or he thought he did. The Bulgarian was on our side."

"Freddy said that people don't change. But he meant that what they want deep down doesn't change. They might change allegiances if they think it's a better way to get what they want."

"You think Wyeth and the Bulgarian wanted the same thing?"

"I don't know," Jack admitted. "But think about it—the Bulgarian would be pretty terrifying if he had joined Wyeth. The guy was a technical genius. He had that animation spade, where he could make monsters out of stuff."

"He also died two months ago. You think he secretly recruited for Wyeth, then he just let himself be killed like that? It's strange." Claire squinted at Jack. "I know that look. You have an idea, but you're afraid to say it."

Jack hesitated. "You'll think I sound like Freddy."

"Try me."

"Maybe the Bulgarian wanted people to think he was dead."

"He was reported dead, remember?" Claire asked.

"By who? Who found his body? Is it possible it was the wrong body?"

Claire stared at him for a moment, then took the two carts and pulled them past Jack, toward the kitchen. Jack kept up with her. They reached the yellow vacuum next to the kitchen and offloaded the dishes and silverware onto the counter, letting the vacuum suck them up a few at a time.

"So the Bulgarian's been in hiding this whole time pretending to be dead?" Claire asked, methodically loading plates into the vacuum. "Why?"

"So he could be off the grid to serve Wyeth. Wyeth must have convinced the Bulgarian that he was on the right side and Hadley was on the wrong side. Or—" Jack snapped his fingers. "Now you're really going to think I sound like Freddy. What if Wyeth convinced the Bulgarian that he, Wyeth, really was the Guardian? The Bulgarian was obsessed with the Gray mythology, remember?"

"You're right. You sound like Freddy."

"Yeah, I know."

"So, Wyeth recruits the Bulgarian," Claire said. "The Bulgarian recruits a team of operatives to Wyeth's side. The only problem with all this is if the Bulgarian really is dead."

"Right." Jack loaded in the last of the plates and grabbed a fresh kitchen towel hanging from a bar to wipe his hands. He tossed it to Claire. "It's a lot easier if he is dead. I doubt we'd live very long if he was trying to keep us quiet."

Claire caught it and slowly wiped her hands. "You're freaking me out, Jack."

"I'm freaking myself out. I think we need to tell Superior Blue about this."

"No, we need to check the archives again first," Claire said. She tossed the towel onto the counter. "Rufus won't even remember we were there earlier tonight. Come on."

Jack followed her to the side door. At the last minute he reached around her to open the door for her. Except it didn't open.

"Locked. Come on, we'll go out the kitchen." Jack walked ahead of her, holding open the swinging door for Claire. They walked through the industrial kitchen toward the exit.

But at the back exit, they found a long-handled metal spatula tied around the handles of the double doors, impossibly twisted like string.

Claire furrowed her eyebrows. "How did . . . ?"

She was interrupted by metal clattering and hinges groaning. Everything that was not attached to the floor was flying together, as if magnetized. The ovens were wrenched from the floor. Cutlery and cutting boards, knives and plates, everything gathered and assembled into a humanlike shape. The kitchen was coming to life.

Not coming to life. Jack felt a cold stab of fear pierce his chest. *Animating.*

"Run!" Claire yelled.

They sprinted in different directions. The monstrosity charged Jack, and he leapt away just in time. It had legs made of ovens, ranges for feet, a rippling stream of plates for arms, and long metal skewers for fingers. Its hands spun steak-sawing butcher knives. Cups crunched and forks screeched against the floor.

The creature groaned and lunged for Claire, who slipped trying to get out of the way. Jack ran at an oven, drawing his blade and swinging wildly through the monster's leg. Several plates shattered, and the thing stumbled just long enough for Claire to roll to safety.

The monster reconstituted as it turned back to Jack. It cornered him, sharpened knives glinting in the half-lit kitchen. Jack ran at full speed and slid through the creature's legs as it struggled to turn around. Its head clanged against a now-empty pot rack on the ceiling. Jack raced out the door that led into the main hall.

The doors cracked behind him as the thing tore them from their hinges. The monster contorted its body and angled through the doorway. The knives slashed against the old oak walls. The creature's feet scarred the floorboards.

Jack dove under a table. The monstrosity flung it aside and raised a colossal fist. Jack held up his blade, helpless. But the fist didn't come down—it was wrenched away, torn right off the monster in a hail of sparks. Claire was standing behind it, hands outstretched. The monster roared and tilted its head. Then it kicked a table at Claire, sending her flying back against the wall.

Jack ran at the locked door, throwing himself at it. The door groaned but Jack fell back on the floor. He pulled out his blade to try to blaze through it, but he wasn't fast enough. He had to throw himself out of the way as the monster swung at him. The breeze created by the flying industrial dishwasher lifted his hair. The punch blasted the double door off its hinges and left a hole. Jack leapt for it, scraping and forcing himself through the jagged wood.

Behind him the monster swung his other fist at Claire. She jumped out of the way, and he missed her. This time, the rest of the door exploded off its frame. They ran.

A few strides out of Prophecy Hall, Claire's foot caught a root, and she tumbled so hard that her hands didn't even catch her fall. Jack skidded back to her, his blade held over his head.

The realization that they would not survive engulfed him. The Bulgarian was alive. He was working with Wyeth. And that secret would die with Claire and Jack. Their mangled bodies would be found outside Prophecy Hall.

The monster raised a massive fist, a hideous mess of blades and steel. The small bottle caps that formed his mouth swept into a crazed grin.

In the dim light of the lamppost behind the monster, a large pine tree uprooted itself with a tremendous noise of dirt and rocks falling from the huge roots. The tree lifted itself straight up in the air. It was twirling slightly, almost, it occurred to Jack, like a baseball bat in the hands of a slugger.

The upper body of the monster exploded as the tree made contact. Pine needles and branches, plate shards and silverware bits flew through the air.

Jack and Claire huddled near each other as the shrapnel rained down. Then there, walking toward them through the settling dust, holding his cane on his shoulder like an old-time ballplayer, was the portly silhouette of Instructor Rufus.

He stopped a few feet away and looked around, surveying the Long Woods. His eyes shone clear and intelligent.

The old instructor leaned on his cane and gazed down at the recruits. "Jack. Claire." He sighed. "It's time we had a talk."

———

"You're lucky it was me out there." Rufus handed Jack and Claire cups of foul-smelling tea and settled into a chair in his living room. "Some instructors' skills would have been a poor match for that junk giant. Drink that up, young ones—it does wonders."

Jack ignored the tea. "You've pretended to be a senile old man this whole time."

"Interesting choice of words, Jack." Rufus blew on the surface of his tea, sending ripples out to the edges. "You may want to reserve judgment on how senile I am until you get to know me better."

"You've been lying about who you are," Claire insisted.

"We all put forth a set of traits to best serve our interests," Rufus corrected. "You saw in me an old instructor nobody took seriously. You assumed I have no real power. That was useful to me. Assumptions discourage exploration."

"How did you know we would be attacked?" Jack demanded. "You were ready for it—you must have known the Bulgarian was still alive!"

Rufus sighed. "I knew he was alive, yes. I was the one who reported him killed in the first place."

"What? Why did you do that?" Jack asked.

"Because he asked me to."

"He asked you to?" Jack felt his blood boiling. "You're on his side?"

"I was," Rufus admitted. "Or, rather, I gave him the benefit of the doubt when everyone wanted to destroy him, from the moment he stepped through the Threshold as a thirteen-year-old boy."

"Why did everyone want to destroy him?" Claire asked.

The answer came to Jack suddenly. "Because when the Bulgarian stepped through the Threshold, the runes turned black. Didn't they, Instructor?"

Rufus nodded. "The Bulgarian has a shadow spade. He's a Creator, like Wyeth. That may be what bonded them."

"Why was he allowed to stay, if he had a shadow spade?" Jack asked. "Why didn't they send him to the Asylum?"

"Superior Blue—Petkov's teammate—convinced the Council not to. The first time in history a shadow spade was allowed to stay."

"Why would anyone listen to a thirteen-year-old recruit?" Claire asked, her voice shaking a little.

"William Blue was no ordinary recruit. He claimed Vladimir would fulfill the twelfth prophecy of the Order of the Grays. You have to understand that very few recruits in history have ever been able to even discern the carvings, let alone interpret them," Rufus told them. "William was one of them. He saw it in the carvings: two men with black hearts, facing each other. Two improbables with shadow spades. He calculated that they were the Bulgarian and Wyeth. The prophecy predicted the showdown between them, and the Bulgarian did supposedly kill Wyeth."

Rufus carefully set down his tea. "It was William Blue that gave Vladimir the name 'The Bulgarian,' you know. The Threshold does not convey spade names on those with a shadow spade. That is why Miles Watt did not have a spade name."

"Just like I have no spade name," Jack pointed out, feeling suddenly cold.

Rufus shook his head. "You do not have a shadow spade, Jack. The runes did not turn black when you walked through the Threshold. You may not be an improbable the way we think of them, but you do not belong with those who possess the shadow spades," he said. "I thought the Bulgarian was a hero when he killed Wyeth. Now I see he was like a pet tiger cub. It was only a matter of time before he turned against us."

"Do you think the Bulgarian recruited the Rogue Team of operatives?" Claire asked.

"I do, yes," Rufus said. "The Bulgarian was a mythic figure for the operatives. Many would follow him anywhere. I believe he joined the Shadow because Wyeth convinced him that he, Wyeth, was the Guardian who could save the world. Remember, the Bulgarian saw Wyeth die. To see him come back to life must have had a profound impact on him. And they were bonded by the shadow spade. It was, perhaps, inevitable . . . Ah, good evening, William."

"Hello, Alistair. Thank you for calling me." Superior Blue filled the doorway. "Jack. Claire."

Rufus was lifting his cup of tea to his lips, when he paused and pointed it at Claire and Jack. "These two must be important if the Bulgarian risked breaking into Hadley to kill them."

"These two are the only living people at Hadley who've had meaningful interactions with Wyeth himself, don't forget," Blue said.

"How could we?" Claire asked with a shiver.

"We don't know who the Rogue Team is, if that's what you're getting at," Jack said quickly.

"You'll have a chance to discover their identity when Wyeth strikes again, assuming the Dome calls you in again," Blue told them.

"Why us?" Jack asked. "Why not a team of operatives? Why not anyone else?"

Superior Blue shook his head. "The Dome must know something we don't. But be prepared. Wyeth's Dark Virus has already worked. He knows our operatives are struggling to contain the darkened in Belgium," Superior Blue told them. "He will not wait to strike us again. Our next chance is almost certainly our last."

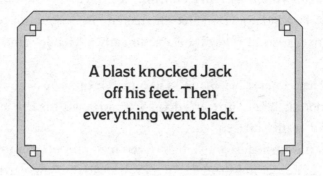

A blast knocked Jack
off his feet. Then
everything went black.

OUTBREAK

Team Thirteen jogged down the amphitheater steps. Their wristbands vibrated and glowed yellow.

"Is this a normal simulation or another mirrored engagement?" Darius demanded of Bakari. Asha had alerted Blue, Darius, and Bakari as soon as their bands went off. Blue, who hadn't arrived yet, had been right. Wyeth wouldn't wait.

"We'll know soon," said Bakari, squinting into the noon sun. "The Dome still has no way of predicting the dead zone. Our only indication that Wyeth may be active is that the Dome is calling them in."

"But we need to know where it's taking place. We need our operatives there," Darius said.

"If it is a mirrored engagement, Team Thirteen will witness

Wyeth's attack and bring back intel," Bakari said. "But we won't know where the event is taking place until they go inside."

Darius stared at Thirteen, fuming in frustration. She spun back to face Bakari. "Don't let Thirteen in. Let's send in a team of operatives instead. They'll be able to gather reliable information quickly."

"That's impossible, Iliana." The Superior came up behind them. "The door is Team Thirteen's door. You can't trick the Dome. It has selected Team Thirteen."

Darius turned back to a half dozen men and women from the Office of Reaper Engagement. "Report back to the Bunker. Have all operatives on standby at the portal courtyard." Darius pointed at Team Thirteen. "Get us something useful, recruits: a face, a spade, anything to identify the traitors. Understood?"

———

The world inside the Dome went dark. Then sunlight hit a large stage. They were in a field packed with people lolling against each other in temporary suspension of the laws of personal space. The place smelled of sunscreen and sweat. A voice echoed through the crowd from gigantic speakers mounted above the stage. Jack stood next to Claire, both of them in jeans and T-shirts.

"Washington, DC," she said, nodding toward the White House in the distance.

"Okay, Jack, we need you to identify Wyeth." Asha's voice came over the monitor. "The rest of us will draw out the Rogue Team. Their spades will identify them. Get them to use their gifts. Got it?"

"Awesome," Freddy mumbled.

"Okay, hoods up," Asha said.

"And don't get killed," Voss added. "You're useless if you get killed in a simulation, remember."

Jack gulped, then pulled his thin hood over his head. The others did the same.

"I'm heading to the stage," Claire said.

"Be careful," Jack urged.

"I'm an improbable, remember? You're the one needing that blast suit Alexander gave you. You be careful."

"The woman onstage," Freddy called over the monitor. "It's what's-her-name from the cube."

Jack peered through the heads of the taller men standing in front of him. Dr. Cynthia Thayer was taller than she appeared on TV. Dressed in an elegant gray suit, she reminded Jack of a presidential candidate. The look was even made complete by the large navy-blue banner hanging behind her.

The Pacifica Institute, it read. Three white stars underlined the words. Thayer, freed from the confines of a news studio, was animated up onstage.

". . . Which is what they want you to think," Thayer bellowed into the microphone. "But our government—the United States federal government—they created the Dark Virus! They claim to protect you, but they want to cull the poor and the weak and the powerless. They are creating a new nation, one that will serve them. Our civilization is on the brink!"

"This woman is a nut bar," Freddy muttered.

"Jack, you picking anything up?" Asha asked.

"Nothing."

". . . I have been challenged to produce evidence that the government knows about the Dark Virus," Thayer said. "And that they have special forces to control the infected." Thayer's voice dropped dramatically. "I will let you decide for yourselves."

Two large screens on either side of the stage glowed to life. Security camera footage of the Belgian Riots rolled. A river of darkened flooded the street, smashing through windows. Glass shards shrieked as they scraped against their hardened skin. The security camera panned up. Four figures, their faces in shadow, stood, bracing for the mob.

"Operatives," Voss said.

There was no sound to the video, and the crowd of hundreds went silent. The operatives, thankfully, were subtle with any spades they had—that was protocol when operating in heavily populated areas. One operative gave a slight hand motion as a group of darkened suddenly had difficulty lifting their feet. The other three pulled Hadley blades.

The crowd was shouting now. This was Thayer's moment.

"They've already taken Belgium. They've come for Europe. And now they are coming for you!" The vibrations of her amplified voice rattled Jack's rib cage. "The Pacifica Institute has a vaccine for the Dark Virus. We have our own trained forces that can protect you. But our government wants to silence us. They call us traitors. I say *they* are the traitors!"

The crowd roared in approval.

"We must end this genocidal regime. We must oust them before they exterminate us!" Onstage, men and women bearing navy-blue flags with three white stars joined Thayer.

"Together we will march to the White House—and take back our government!"

Are you still hoping to stop me, Jack?

Jack spun around. The crowd surrounded him, but no one was paying him any attention.

Hadley is on the wrong side of history, Jack. But you know that. You could have stopped me already. But you won't.

Jack jolted. For a second, he thought Wyeth had darkened him. But no. Had he blacked out?

The crowd around him stirred. Someone near him yelled, "We can't hear you!" The sound system had gone silent.

". . . Jack?" Freddy's voice sounded in Jack's ear.

"I'm here."

"You disappeared for a second—"

"I think we all did," Jack said over the monitor. "It's a dead zone—Wyeth's here."

Jack's band lit up red. An arrow pointed into the crowd. He looked up. A man in a baseball cap jolted. Then slowly, the man walked away. Wyeth had darkened him. Jack didn't need the arrow on his band. He felt it, as clearly as he had heard Wyeth's voice in his head. But the man was now out of reach.

"Dark blue cap." Jack shouted. "He's been darkened."

"Voss—blue hat, at your six." Asha said over the monitor. "Don't let him touch anyone. Jack, where's Wyeth?"

The crowd chanted, fists raised. Jack pushed his way toward the man in the cap. Voss's voice came over the monitor, breathless.

"What is—?" He clipped out.

The crowd's frenzy increased as Jack fought his way through. Asha shouted for Voss to respond. Jack was in a forest of humanity, arms and backs and shouting.

Jack's hair blew back as something flew past him with the force of a train. Jack craned his neck to the left to see. It was a body, thrown as if shot out of a cannon. Jack looked back through the path cut through the crowd. Voss stood there, hands on his knees.

"An operative just cut me off. The Rogue Team is here!" he managed to get out. "Get down! That guy has some kind of jet propulsion."

A blast knocked Jack off his feet. Then everything went black. He felt legs and torsos and shoulders pile on top of him. He struggled to push his way out of the pile. The weight squeezed the air from his lungs. He couldn't move. He couldn't cry for help.

Then somebody grabbed his wrist and yanked. He was pulled through the sweat and flesh. He gasped.

Voss held him up by the shoulders, checking his eyes. "You okay, man? Still with us?"

Jack weakly patted his chest. "Alexander's blast suit. It absorbed the impact. Saved my life, I think."

Voss steadied him. "I lost that rogue operative. Wyeth has to be nearby."

Jack looked up in time to see the man in the blue hat at the base of the stage. The man placed his arm around a young woman in braids who seemed surprised at the gesture. Her chin snapped up. Her friends, wearing matching orange T-shirts, shifted away from her. But it was too late; she reached out to one of them. The Dark Virus crackled and spread.

The crowd immediately sensed that something was terribly wrong. Those closest to the girls in orange pushed away but not quickly enough. Jack pulled his blade. He was caught in a tidal wave of darkening as it spread through the crowd.

The first darkened came at him, black eyes filled with rage. The monster lunged at his throat. Jack got his blade up in time to strike him across the chest with the blaze. The darkened's exoskeleton crackled. Its eyes instantly fluttered back to normal, the rage vanishing just as the thing shattered into dust and was blown away by the wind. Another darkened leapt toward Jack.

On the other side of the stage, a narrow tornado of snow formed, right in the center of a mob of darkened. The tornado jerked as Asha gripped the end of the funnel in her fist. She cracked it like a whip through the darkened, sending them flying. But more swelled toward her.

"Asha needs help!" Jack shouted over the monitor.

"On it!" Claire sprinted through the darkened crowd, clearing them out of her way like dead leaves blasted by a leaf blower. They catapulted straight into the mob attacking Asha. She flicked her fingers, and the darkened, now all in a heap, ricocheted off each other like popcorn popping. Tiny sparks flew as she manipulated the ionic charges. Only Freddy, ably swinging his blade through the fray, seemed immune to Claire's static.

Dr. Thayer's voice shoved through the commotion. "The government has unleashed the Dark Virus on you!"

The darkened climbed onto the stage. Thayer scaled one of the speaker towers, still clutching a dead megaphone. "Get to the airports!" she shouted into the crowd. "Pacifica can save you. Get to the airports to receive the vaccine!"

The speaker tower creaked, listing for a sickening moment, before it crashed into the mob. Thayer leapt off and landed on the stage. Then she stopped in her tracks. "Asha!"

Asha was in front of the stage. She looked pale, staring up at Thayer.

Thayer ran to the front of the stage and reached down. "Come with me, Asha!"

Asha shook her head and stepped backward. The tornado melted away. A dark cloud swirled above her.

"I won't let them take you," Thayer shouted, leaning farther over. "I can save you, Asha. Come with me!"

Claire grabbed Asha and pulled her away. "We're getting out of here."

The world around Jack shrunk into a pinhole. Then the feeling of being sucked through a tube. Finally, Jack staggered out of the Dome and landed on the grass. The amphitheater roared to life at their reappearance. It was now full of instructors, recruits, and cadets.

Darius yanked Jack to his feet. Her face hovered inches above his. "What happened in there?" she shouted. "Where were you?"

"Washington, DC," Jack gasped. "A rally near the White House. Pacifica Institute was there. And Wyeth. The Rogue Team stopped us from reaching him. The whole crowd is infected."

Darius didn't let him continue. She touched her ear. "All operatives to DC, Portal 4960," Darius barked. "Send *everyone*."

Behind her, Bakari frantically tapped and swiped and waved at the Dome console. "Impossible!" he cursed. "Where is the recording?"

Superior Blue stepped forward. "What did you see?"

"One of the guys on the Rogue Team," Voss answered, "had a spade like a localized propulsion."

The Superior turned to Alexander. "Get everyone you can find into the archives, including the files classified as special operations. If someone doesn't have access, give it to them. Search for operatives killed in action in the last five years. The Rogue Team may have faked their deaths, planning for this. We have to consider all possibilities." Alexander left to get others started on the database.

Jack looked down to find Asha on the ground, holding her ankle. "Asha?" Jack asked.

"That woman, Cynthia Thayer," Freddy said, bewildered. "She knew you."

Lady buzzed around Asha's ankle.

Voss moved Freddy out of the way. "She's in pain, man." He eased her up. "I'm taking her to the clinic. Come on, Lady." Lady flew next to them as Voss carried Asha.

Darius shouted orders into her monitor. "I don't care what you *think*. I care about what you *know*." She listened for a moment. "Yes. Understood."

Darius looked at Blue. Jack had never seen that expression on her face before. "They're gone."

Superior Blue rubbed his temple.

"Who's gone?" Freddy asked, glancing between them.

"The operatives," Claire answered quietly. "The team that was sent to the rally when the map sounded the reaper alarm. They must have been darkened, right?"

"They were ambushed by the Rogue Team," Superior Blue said, his voice flat.

"If we hadn't been extracted, we would have been overrun too," Jack said. "We saw what the operatives saw. We were fighting that Rogue Team. You can't fight operatives and the darkened at the same time."

"Everyone will go to the airports," Freddy said.

Darius and Blue turned to Freddy. "What are you talking about? Why?" Darius asked.

"The rally was for the Pacifica Institute," Freddy told them. "Their leader is Cynthia Thayer; we've seen her before on the cube. She was talking about the Dark Virus and how the government was killing its own people. She told the crowd that Pacifica could save everyone if they went to the airports."

Blue and Darius looked at each other. They knew something. Darius touched her ear again. "Get surveillance up on Reagan National Airport. And find out what in the world the Pacifica Institute is."

CHAPTER 23

THE ASYLUM

Underground in the Bunker, the Office of Reaper Engagement was dark and tight. From black padded benches, Jack, Claire, and Freddy watched surveillance footage of the rally on a hologram. The operator sped through the setup of the stage, the gathering crowd, and the beginning of Thayer's speech. Then everything went dark.

"That's when Wyeth darkened that civilian in the baseball cap," Freddy said. "The power went off. Speakers, lights, everything."

"That's his signature," Blue confirmed. "That's the dead zone. You were inside it."

"I heard him," Jack told them. "I heard his voice in my head again."

Superior Blue looked at Jack. "What did he say?"

"That I was on the wrong side of history. That I couldn't stop him."

"That was the Dome. It wasn't actually Wyeth," Freddy pointed out.

"It sure felt like him."

Alexander entered, his expression somber. "They asked me to inform you, sir. It's been confirmed," he said. "We've lost contact with all four operatives. They must have been darkened at the DC rally. None of them were extracted. It seems they were ambushed by the Rogue Team, then overwhelmed by the darkened."

Blue's jaw tightened. "You have their files for me?"

"On your band now, sir."

Blue tapped his band. Jack watched as Blue flipped through the dossiers of four different operatives. It was hard to look at their photos, knowing what they must have gone through.

"You said you were hit with a propulsion of some kind, Jack," Blue said.

"It felt like getting punched in the chest," he confirmed. "Alexander's blast suit protected me."

"One of the operatives we sent in had that spade," Blue said. "Which means the Expathic on the Rogue Team must have a mimic spade. I'll examine the archives myself to see if I can identify an operative with that ability. Edison, give me a hand in the archives, will you?"

As Blue and Alexander left the room, Freddy pointed at one of the cube screens. "She's back."

A close-up showed Cynthia Thayer, her face scratched and bruised, her eyes hard. She was standing in front of a banner of the Pacifica Institute. "Pacifica has been preparing for this moment. We have established a safe zone at Reagan Airport. If you are in DC, make your way to the airport, and you will be safe. Do not heed government warnings. If you stay in the city, you will be infected."

"What's at the airport? How are they doing all this?" Jack asked, confused. "I thought Pacifica was a research institute."

"She seemed to know all this would happen. How were they ready for it?" Freddy asked. Claire just shook her head, staring at the screen. They turned when Lady buzzed in. Asha followed, walking with only a slight limp and wearing a brace around her ankle. Voss came in last.

"Hey, how you feeling?" Jack asked, getting up.

"Dr. Horn mended my ankle. It was broken," she said. "It'll be fine tomorrow." Asha's gaze drifted to the screen, to Cynthia Thayer speaking.

Freddy watched her reaction. "That woman, Asha. She knew you."

Asha eased herself down into a chair and took a deep breath. "She should. She's my mother."

"The Pacifica Institute isn't a research facility," Asha told them. "It's a prison. My mother was an inmate there. That's where I was born."

Asha smiled grimly. "I didn't know it was a prison until I was older. There were no cages or anything. My mom used to tell me we never went on trips because we had everything we needed right there on that beautiful tropical island. She said that we lived in paradise, so why would we ever leave? I believed her." Asha rubbed the brace covering her ankle. She didn't look up at them.

"My mom and a handful of others, they were kept separate. We got 'special treatment,' my mom used to tell me. Pacifica was a whole community of maybe 150 inmates of all ages, from teenagers on up. The only time we were allowed together with the other inmates was for meals, in this spectacular cafeteria overlooking the ocean."

"I've never heard of any prison like that," Claire said.

"Me neither. The first time I ever had access to the Internet was here at Hadley. I spent all night looking for any information about Pacifica. There's no record of it." Asha swallowed hard.

"My mom met my dad, Omar Hassan, at Pacifica. My mother told me he was a marine and that he was killed in Afghanistan before I was born. But as I got older I questioned that, since nobody was ever allowed off the island," Asha said. "Nobody ever told me what happened to him."

She glanced up at Voss. "I guess I just wanted to believe that lie about him. And there was something very wrong with my mother."

"Did she hurt you?" Voss asked.

Asha shook her head. "No, but the people who ran Pacifica feared her. I could tell. It's why they kept her confined. She told me she preferred to be in her room. It had an entire open wall overlooking the ocean," she said. "I could leave that room whenever I wanted, though. I used to hang out in the metal shop with the mechanics who worked on the generators that powered the island. I learned how to build boats down at the dock with the mariners."

"Why were the others afraid of her?" Jack asked.

"I'm not exactly sure, but she was brilliant," Asha said. "When she did go to the cafeteria, she gave these fiery speeches to the other inmates. She would tell them that they, the ones at Pacifica, had been betrayed. That they were the only sane ones, the only ones who saw the truth."

"What truth?" Freddy asked.

Asha paused. "That reapers were real."

Jack rattled his head. "Wait—what?"

"That's what she said. Reapers," Asha said. "And the entire place would go crazy. Not just the ones they kept in solitary confinement like my mom, but everyone. They all believed her. They believed in these monsters that appeared out of nowhere, that killed people."

"She knew about reapers?" Voss asked.

"They all did," Asha said. "I thought they were crazy. But now, I wonder what they knew." Asha spoke through her fingers as she bit her nails. "How much they knew."

"So you ran away," Freddy said. "How did you get off the island?"

Asha pulled her fingers out of her mouth. "Sorry. I didn't know that was a gross habit until I met you guys."

She tucked her hand under her thigh self-consciously. "The mariners were building this super-fast boat—narrow hull, carbon fiber and Kevlar, jet engine. They let me work on it with them. I stole the boat and headed straight for the mainland. I didn't know what I was going to do when I got there. I hadn't brought anything with me." Asha paused, recalling the memory. "But then there he was—a Hadley operative, waiting right there on the dock. I was still in a daze from escaping. Next thing I knew we were going through the portal to Elk Island and I was meeting you guys."

Asha had been talking into her lap without making eye contact with the others. But now she looked up. "The night before I left, my mother told me she was starting a revolution. That's why I ran."

Freddy leaned forward in his chair. "Asha, your mother and the other inmates at Pacifica, how do you think they found out about reapers?"

"They didn't find out." Superior Blue stood in the doorway. "They remembered."

Superior Blue walked to the hologram terminal and entered a long code. The images of Thayer were replaced with the words *Highly Classified* outlined in red. Then a series of mug shots populated the screen.

"Your mother and the rest of the community—they named their institution *Pacifica*. But we have a different name for it."

He walked up to the hologram and pointed out a photo of a thirteen-year-old Cynthia Thayer, same eyes and expression. He looked back at Asha.

"Your mother is the Viral that Wyeth recruited to create the Dark Virus," he told her. "And Pacifica isn't a prison. Pacifica is the Hadley Asylum. And their revolution has only just begun."

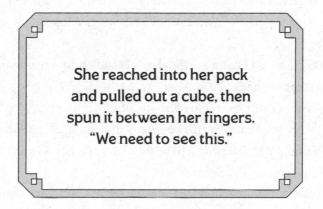

CHAPTER 24

She reached into her pack
and pulled out a cube, then
spun it between her fingers.
"We need to see this."

CONFESSIONS

Team Thirteen was surrounded by three dozen ferocious dogs, growling and snapping from only a few feet away.

"Pull your halcyon glove from your pack," Sushila Patel shouted over the barking. Her voice echoed around the concrete walls of the large open room. "Quickly, before the dogs attack."

Jack reached into his pack, forcing himself to concentrate on what he needed. When he pulled his hand out, he was wearing the black glove. The others already had their gloved hands outstretched toward the dogs. Claire shrieked and yanked her hand away as a pit bull snapped at her.

"I've had bad experiences with dogs," she said, her voice shaking. "I thought Animal Empathy was supposed to be a second-year class."

"We have orders to accelerate your training," Sushila called from across the room. "You cannot let an angry dog keep you from a reaper. Focus."

"The glove isn't calming the dog!" Freddy said, breathing heavily and stepping back.

"The glove isn't meant to calm the dog," Sushila corrected. "The glove is meant to calm you. The dog is just being a dog. The glove gives you empathy. The dog will sense that. Feel the connection with the animal through the glove."

As the five of them huddled closer together, the three dogs nearest Voss suddenly stopped barking. They stood up straight, staring into his eyes. Then one by one, they nosed his hand and jumped up on him, licking his face. More dogs piled over to Voss, who was quickly overwhelmed with happy canines.

Freddy turned to Sushila, pointing at the stripes on her shoulder. "You're a cadet. What are you teaching this class for?" A dog barking at Freddy suddenly relaxed and began sniffing his hand. He turned to it, cautiously delighted.

"My gift is animal empathy; my spade name is Bond. And I'm teaching you because I'm the best," she said matter-of-factly. "Also I'm the one who convinced them to create the Den here in the lower level of Kwei Library." She nodded at Voss. "You're a natural. You have an Expathic minor or something?"

Voss was sitting cross-legged on the floor, holding a massive Rottweiler that had climbed into his lap. He shook his head. "I just know what it's like to be misunderstood," he said under his breath. He looked up at her. "Where did you get all these guys?"

"Superior Blue lets me rescue them." Sushila scratched the thick neck of a pit bull. "These are the dogs that get abandoned, the ones who usually get put down because nobody adopts them from shelters. I rescue them and bring them here."

Sushila touched her ear. "Yes, sir. Turning it on now." She shouted a command, and the dogs all immediately ran to the other side of the room and sat in formation. She reached into her pack and pulled out a cube, then spun it between her fingers. "We need to see this."

A hovering screen appeared to their left. On the cube, the secretary of Homeland Security didn't bother hiding his fury. He labeled the Pacifica Institute as a bastion for treasonous fearmongers. An institute, he added, that was unsanctioned and that had no known history whatsoever.

"And just so we're clear," the anchorwoman said, "the United States government is asking people to wait in their homes for the National Guard. Is that right, Mr. Secretary?"

"Precisely, Jane." He spoke through gritted teeth. It had been thirty-six hours since the DC rally, and the secretary looked like he had been awake that entire time. "People must remain calm. Your local National Guard will be moving systematically through neighborhoods to make sure families are safe."

"I'm told we have footage of the National Guard now," said the anchorwoman.

The footage showed uniformed members of the National Guard storming down a street in a pack, out of formation. One stormed up the steps of a town house and kicked repeatedly until the door exploded inward. Others flooded in behind him.

"Mr. Secretary, this footage was taken twenty minutes ago," said the anchor, visibly shaken. "Does that seem like normal behavior to

you? Is the National Guard infected with this so-called Dark Virus?
Do you actually have any control over this situation?"

The secretary stuttered and cleared his throat several times.
"Where did you get this footage?"

"Is the US government able to stop the spread of the virus,
Mr. Secretary?" the anchor demanded. "Can the government protect its citizens or not?"

A familiar voice came over the cube. Along the bottom of the
broadcast flashed *Voice of Dr. Cynthia Thayer, Pacifica Institute.* She
didn't wait to be introduced.

"Protect us, Jane?" Thayer's voice asked over a bad phone line.
"The United States government is behind the Dark Virus!" A stock
image of Dr. Thayer flashed on the screen.

"Who's that supposed to be?" Sushila asked nobody in particular. Jack glanced at Asha, who had sat on the floor. A pit bull
padded over and nuzzled her.

"You have seen the carnage for yourselves," Dr. Thayer said. "All
civilians must make their way to the closest airport immediately.
We have commandeered all airports as Pacifica safe zones."

Footage came up of men and women in navy-blue Pacifica uniforms, three stars across their chests. They had automatic weapons
strapped over their shoulders with telescopic lenses to spot the black-
eyed darkened. Others had infrared scanners. Thayer explained that
the darkened had low body temperatures, detectable from a distance
by the scanners. Immediately in front of the gates were a line of
flamethrowers. Pacifica had figured out the only way to defeat the
darkened was through direct flame.

Frightened civilians flooded through the gates of the airports
in the Washington, DC, area.

"Everyone who makes it to a safe zone will be inoculated," Thayer said. "We have been preparing the vaccine for years, preparing for the time we would need it to save this country from its government."

The video showed Pacifica nurses injecting men, women, and children. Interviews with grateful civilians told their harrowing stories of barely escaping the infected. They told of how Pacifica had taken them in and provided food, shelter, and protection.

The broadcast showed a series of clips from around the world. Civilians speaking in different languages pleaded for Pacifica to come to their country and help them. The virus was spreading.

"Where did they get all these weapons? And mercenaries?" Jack asked. "Where did she get millions of dollars to secretly build an army?"

Voss froze. "Two hundred and eighty million dollars," he said softly. He turned to the team, making sure Sushila was out of earshot. They huddled closer to him. "She got it from me."

"What?" Asha asked, puzzled.

"That's where I've seen the name *Pacifica*," Voss said, more quickly now. "Embedded in the programming. That's where the money got wired to—the money I stole: two hundred and eighty million. When I researched the name, nothing came up. So I ignored it." Voss slammed a fist into the palm of his other hand. "But it was her. I funded this."

Freddy looked at Jack. "I know you don't like my theories . . ."

"I'm a lot more open to them these days."

"Superior Blue told you he brought the three of us in to fill out Team Thirteen, all in this elaborate ruse to fool Darius," Freddy said. "He said he chose random recruits to fill out this team, just so you could stay in Hadley, so you could get Claire to talk."

Freddy waved his hand at Voss and Asha. "Does this seem random to you?"

"Jack. Did something happen?" Superior Blue answered his door in black workout attire.

Jack was relieved that he was still up. Maggie bounded over to him from behind the Superior. Jack squatted down to give Maggie a scratch behind the ear. "You told Darius that your old teammate, James Halloway, brought me in. That he was pretending to be a member of the Order of the Grays named Hans."

"Yes, I did."

"You're, what, fifty years old?"

"Fifty-four."

"The man who drafted me couldn't have been more than twenty-nine or thirty. He couldn't have been James Halloway." Superior Blue didn't say anything. Jack stood up. "Superior Blue, who brought me in here?"

"I have no idea." Blue looked more tired than he had a moment ago. "I kept up the lie about Halloway, even to Darius, because I didn't want anything to distract from the true threat—Wyeth is back. But the truth is I have not yet solved the mystery of who brought you here."

"What about the coin?" Jack exploded. "The silo coin you invented? You said it was an 'especially convincing detail.'"

"I don't know where you got that coin, Jack," Blue said. "I don't know who Hans is. I don't have any of those answers. Though the numbers on the back of that coin really did correspond to the social security numbers of Asha Hassan, Voss Winter, and Freddy Sanchez."

"But, you can check surveillance footage around St. Paul's. You can see who Hans is."

"I did check. It's the first thing I did, even as I listened to Darius begin the Naming Ceremony. I accessed anything I could, and I calculated every possibility," Blue told him. "But none of them turned out to be correct. Whoever Hans was, he did an extraordinary job of staying out of sight. I caught you a few times talking to somebody, but Hans must have known the location of every camera in the city. He stayed hidden."

Jack searched his memories of Hans for anything that might identify him. All Jack knew for sure was that Hans protected him and had sent Jack into Hadley.

"Whoever he is," Blue said. "He named himself after the founder of the Order of the Grays, and he's done us a service to match the name. We wouldn't have figured any of this out without him. I can't solve every mystery at once, Jack. For now, I am merely grateful for him."

CHAPTER 25

WORKSHOP

SHUTDOWN

Just five weeks after the DC Massacre, Cynthia Thayer's message was routinely carried on all media, more extensively even than that of the president of the United States. The public didn't know whom to trust. Thayer urged citizens not to leave the country. The Dark Virus had gone global, and Pacifica couldn't protect them if they left. The Pacifica Institute and their mysterious army now controlled every major airport in the country.

As they ate granola and pancakes in Prophecy Hall, the team watched the cube in case there had been any developments. "What do you tell people who say that Pacifica is prohibiting people from leaving?" The questioner was Julie something, the news anchor who first interviewed Dr. Thayer months earlier.

Dr. Thayer, answering from a remote location, scoffed. "The citizens of this country are coming to us, Julie," she insisted. "We are protecting them from the virus. We have enough of the vaccine for every citizen, and our security teams are able to fight off the infected. The only rules we have are the ones that keep our citizens safe."

"So why not let them leave the country?" Julie pressed. "Reports are that virtually every airport in the country is controlled by Pacifica's security teams and that international flights are banned."

"They are banned from entering the country, certainly. This is not a time to try to process immigrants, nor is it safe. We don't know what kind of contagions may be carried into the US right now."

"So you *are* banning flights?"

"We are exercising caution in an unprecedented time," Dr. Thayer corrected. "People are free to come and go from the safe zones. You have interviewed them yourself, Julie. The people have lost faith in the government. They trust us. We are the only reason there are citizens left to protect in this country!"

"Hey!" Claire crossed Prophecy Hall. "You guys gotta see this. They're doing an Engagement Ceremony."

Team Thirteen followed her outside, down the trail, and all the way to the East Clearing in front of the Office of the Superior where they found Director Darius facing a team. They stopped beside the steel tree. Then the rumbling began, like an earthquake. The East Clearing had always been an open field, manicured like the fairway of a golf course. But now the grass and ground were opening up, sliding apart behind Darius. Rising out of the ground was a wide stone monolith, the size of a garage door.

"Cadets," Darius announced, "you have learned to fight, and you have learned to die. Today you are no longer students. Today you are operatives. We are entrusting you with the fate of our civilization. You are casting aside your training blade. Today you will receive the blade of an operative: your rune blade. Please approach the Forge."

The cadets stepped closer to the monolith. Four panels slid open, one in front of each of them. Each panel revealed the hilt of a blade.

"The Forge begins crafting your rune blade the day you step foot on Elk Island," Darius told them. "Your rune blade is embedded with an AI chip. It learns your strengths, your weaknesses, what you fear, and what drives you into battle. Your new blade will anticipate what you will do before you know yourself."

Darius took the first blade and turned to the first new operative. The hilt was beautiful, steel with a thin flat strap of fine leather crisscrossing up the handle. The base of the hilt was emblazoned with the green Systemic rune, matching the insignia on the new operative's chest.

"One Life for Many, Lumin." She handed the new operative the blade.

"Why are they graduating? I recognize them; they're second-year cadets," Freddy pointed out. "They have another full year of training."

"They ran out of operatives," Claire said. At the Forge, Darius handed each new operative their rune blade. They received it, repeated the Hadley mantra, then examined the new blade in wonder. "They need fighters. They'll start graduating them more quickly now."

"How does this all end?" Jack asked.

"The reapers die when Wyeth dies," Freddy said. "Because he's the host. But Wyeth didn't create the darkened. What happens to them is a mystery."

Boom boom boom! A knock echoing through the Watchtower snatched Jack out of a deep sleep. When he arrived downstairs, Claire had already opened the door for Alexander, who stood just inside, rubbing his forearms and looking jumpy.

"Superior Blue asked me to bring you to the Workshop."

Claire looked back to see Team Thirteen standing above in the loft, staring down at them.

"What are we doing?" she asked him.

Alexander glanced into the Long Woods behind him. "It's safer if I tell you when we get there."

Inside the Workshop, Alexander shooed a raven out of the way. "Here, you should all sit." White stools rose out of the floor, pushing aside an assortment of multicolored cables and a half-designed prototype that lay in pieces on the table. Alexander hurriedly tried to get it all out of the way.

"Well, don't just sit there; get this stuff out of here," he mumbled to the two ravens who had perched on the back of one of the stools. The large black birds hopped onto the table, grabbed the cables in their claws, and flapped awkwardly into the other room, dragging the cables behind them. Then they returned to rest on the fireplace mantel. Alexander stuffed the prototype pieces in a milk crate and slid it out of the way. He went back to the table and swiped it. It glowed to life.

"We've located the Bulgarian," Alexander told them. "I intercepted a message coming out of the Center for Disease Control. It was from Petkov himself to Thayer. I passed it on to Superior Blue. He's overseeing the operation from the Bunker. He ordered the teams immediately to the CDC, based in Atlanta."

Freddy sat on a stool. "What's he doing at the CDC?"

"Whatever Thayer's vaccine is, Pacifica needed to mass-produce it. Apparently, they've taken over the CDC and are using the facility to mass-manufacture it now. They've already injected millions of civilians at this point," Alexander surmised.

"So are they going after him?" Asha demanded. "What are they waiting for?"

"Operatives are already on the scene. Instructor Santori himself is leading two full teams. They're not taking any chances." Alexander looked up from manipulating the code streaming across the table. "They think the Bulgarian will lead them to the Rogue Team, possibly even to Wyeth. They brought Discern—Operative Sanders-Watson—with them to get the truth out of anyone they find." Alexander motioned at the table. "Superior Blue wanted you to have a front-row seat."

Voss squinted at the table. "You can't watch live engagements on the cube. They're encrypted."

"Who do you think does the encryption? I'm already in," Alexander said, though his boast was dampened by a rapid succession of sneezes and a fumbling for a nearby box of tissues. "Sorry," he mumbled.

On the screen, the code faded and was replaced by a feed from a uniform cam on an operative. They heard Giovanni Santori giving commands to two teams. Then the operatives took up positions outside the CDC complex. Two Systemics tossed a half dozen discs into the air, where they hovered for a second before zipping off to surround the large glass building. An Expathic rounded the side of the building. Then for a second, it seemed as though the CDC had disappeared, but a second later it was there again. A Kinetic on the other side of the building was silently scaling its glass facade.

"They went through the portal to Atlanta within minutes of getting the intel," Alexander explained. "They're only now getting structural maps of the CDC to plan their attack, so they'll be doing recon for a while. There's no rush. They're containing anyone inside. But once they breach the building, they'll have to navigate bunker-like conditions on the lower level. Everything has to go perfectly."

Alexander stood and stretched. "It may be a while before anything happens. You guys should get comfortable. Feel free to keep an eye on the feed. I've got more work to do."

Alexander grumbled from a holographic terminal in the corner, sitting back and rubbing his forehead in frustration. Jack wandered over, his anxiety from watching the feed from the CDC had turned to boredom after an hour with no development. "What are you doing?"

Alexander spun around in his chair. "Darius just sent me a message," he said. "She's had me shutting down military systems in unstable nations as a precaution for the last hour." Alexander tapped the hologram, his finger poking through it. "She just sent me another message about this particular power grid. I don't know what it is; it's protected by some insane 4096-bit encryption. But we need to shut it down. It must be guarding something unbelievably important, something that requires a lot of power."

"Maybe a missile system?" Jack asked.

"What else could it be? It doesn't matter. It only matters that we get it shut down. I know encryptions, but this one is beyond me."

Jack turned to Voss, who was staring at the hologram. Lady emerged from Asha's pack and buzzed over to him. The little drone hovered right in front of Voss's face, causing him to snap out of it. He turned around. "What?"

"Can you do it?" Asha asked him.

"I'm not a missile-systems expert, Asha."

"Voss. It's a massive power grid that clearly powers something very important that Darius needs shut down. Can you break the encryption or not?"

Voss opened his mouth to protest. Asha cut him off. "I know you're afraid to fail, Voss. I'm afraid of that too. But you won't. So you can't say no."

Voss scratched his head. He gave her a sly half smile. "Fine. You keep your fingernails out of your mouth; I work on it. Deal?"

Asha pulled her pinky from her mouth and held up both palms. "Happy?"

Voss took Alexander's seat at the terminal. "Yeah," he said without looking up as he tapped on his band to pull up his spin cipher. He held it between the fingers of both hands and studied it a moment.

They left him spinning the sphere in multiple directions, like someone rapidly solving a Rubik's Cube. Code streamed across the terminal faster than Jack could follow. Alexander lay on a couch, and a few seconds later he was snoring. Lady, meanwhile, zipped off and came buzzing back shakily gripping a mug of coffee with her six robotic legs. She set the drink down next to Voss.

"That from you?" he asked Asha, nodding at the coffee.

"Nope. Lady did that herself. Guess she's learning your grumpy expressions."

Voss grunted and peeked over at the metallic ladybug, which had zipped off and was coming back with creamer. Voss waved her off. "I'm good. I take it black."

Lady alighted on Voss's broad shoulder. He seemed about to rebuke her but instead shrugged and turned back to the hologram.

A half hour later, Voss leaned back. The spin cipher shone green.

"Voss, the super hacker!" Freddy said. "Don't worry, big guy, your nerd secret is safe with me." Freddy put his feet up on a box of parts and grinned. "It's cool to be a nerd, you know. All the tech billionaires probably start off as unpopular nerds. It's not like I knew you when you were hacking into global banking networks."

"I can be thankful for that," Voss muttered. "That you didn't know me, I mean. I don't think we'd have been friends."

"I would have been friends with you," Freddy corrected. "You wouldn't have given me the time of day."

Voss looked at him. "You think you know me, Sanchez. You don't."

"So tell me."

"I'm busy."

"You already shut down the power grid."

"I want to see if Alexander got any other instructions on that. He's still resting; I can take care of anything else."

Voss scrolled back to Darius's last message to Alexander. He swiped at the screen, and the entire message flipped over like a baseball card to reveal a thick block of code. He squinted at it, scrolling through it carefully, then flipped the screen back to the message. "This ain't from Darius."

"Darius. Right there." Freddy pointed at the signature.

"I know it says Darius, dummy. I'm saying that the code ain't from Darius. It's forged. It came from . . ." He flipped back to the code and peered at it for a long time. Then he sat back, confused. "It came from here," he said. "Somebody sent this message from right here, inside the Workshop. Right after we got here."

"Who sent it?"

"I don't know. I only know the location."

"Jack disappeared for a while," Freddy said. "Maybe he did it by accident when he was in the bathroom."

Jack gave him a look. "I don't even know—"

"I'm joking," Freddy interrupted.

At that moment Alexander charged in, holding a tablet and pointing at it. "Did you guys turn off the feed?"

"Just the visual," Freddy said. "Audio is still on."

"No, it's gone. What did you do, exactly?"

"We didn't do anything. Must have done it by itself." Voss turned in his chair to face Alexander. "Yo. That message from Darius. It wasn't from Darius."

Alexander was checking the cube's feed from the CDC operation. It was black. The audio was off.

"What do you mean, it wasn't from Darius?" Alexander asked absently.

"It was somebody making it look like it was from Darius. It was sent from somewhere in the Workshop."

Alexander was still staring at the dead feed. "It's okay; they may be saving power or something." He checked his band. It was one in the morning. "I should be able to get a satellite over them, so we can pick up sound and visual. It won't be as good a source, but it'll work."

He eyed Voss. "What were you saying? Somebody mimicked Darius's message signature?"

"Is anyone else here?" Claire asked.

Alexander motioned to the cramped surroundings. "This whole place is three rooms. Nobody is hiding here. And I'm pretty sure the ravens don't know how to code."

"What about outside?" Freddy asked. "If someone sent a message remotely it might appear like it came from in here."

"Um, guys," Asha interrupted, pointing at the screen projected up by the cube. Nothing was there, not even network news stations. All communications had gone dark.

Then the lights flickered out.

"This is a lot like what happens when Wyeth darkens somebody," Claire said, her voice trembling.

"It's not Wyeth. Hold on," Alexander said. After a moment of scuffling and tapping, the lights popped back on. "There. Now let's see if we can view the engagement."

Alexander located the recording and sped through from the beginning. When they finally got to the last several minutes of the feed, Instructor Santori and several operatives were in position outside a large double door.

Alexander turned up the sound. Everyone jumped up and gathered around the screen.

Suddenly a bright spark flashed over the screen, accompanied by an explosion. Then tornado-strength wind tossed debris in the air and ripped the building partly off its foundations, twisting it like a rag. The doors melted away. The operatives charged in.

Then there was a full minute of shouting, but no shots. Then nothing.

Now Santori was on his monitor, his voice thick with static that drowned out most of the words.

". . . No sign . . . Rogue Team isn't . . ." Santori spun to face his team. "Trap!" he shouted, still breaking up. ". . . drawn us out . . . Hadley . . . Rogue." The feed cut off.

"It sounds like the Bulgarian and Rogue Team aren't there," Asha said, staring at the screen.

"And Instructor Santori thinks the Bulgarian lured the operatives away from Hadley," Claire said.

"I've got a bad feeling." Freddy rubbed his forehead. Something caught his attention in the other room. "What's with your birds, Alexander?"

The ravens were hopping around the mantel. Then with a loud cawing, they dropped down into the hearth of the fireplace, and one after another, flew up the chimney, their complaining echoing up and out of the Workshop.

Asha looked at Alexander. "What was that all about?"

An explosion sent Thirteen careening against the back wall. The door to the Workshop was torn off by a monster made of stone and rock. It let out a deafening roar. The Bulgarian had come for them.

"Run!" Alexander screamed.

Team Thirteen was out of the Workshop, scattering, running. Jack sprinted next to Claire. Behind him the Workshop exploded into kindling as the Bulgarian's monster shredded it to pieces with a series of grunts and moans.

Jack and Claire raced into the dark woods. They scrambled over a rock formation and lay flat on their stomachs, faces in the dirt. They tried to catch their breath while they listened. There was no sign of the rest of the team or Alexander. No sign if they had made it out.

Then they heard it. Two sets of footsteps. One man. One monster.

Claire's face was close to his. "We're about to find out how long the Long Woods really is," she whispered. "Keep breathing, okay, Jack?"

He nodded. "Keep breathing, Claire."

They ran.

———

There seemed to be no end to the Long Woods.

They sprinted at first, desperate to get away. Then Claire came alongside him and gave him a look he had come to know so well. It meant a change in pace. Just as they had always done, she slowed her breathing and he matched her, breath for breath. They took turns leading, finding the route, saving the person behind from the mental energy of picking out the safest footing.

At some point, Jack glanced at his band. They had run for almost an hour.

Then Jack saw it: the wall, green-gray and streaked with black, one single piece of rock rising up two hundred feet. Claire came to a stop, bent over, hands on her knees.

"It's the southern wall," she panted.

Jack felt fear setting in. In the dense woods, it had not occurred to him there would be a dead end.

Claire looked back. "We're gonna have to try to break back through, toward the main grounds."

"We'd never get past him," Jack said. "We can climb it. Anything this tall has to be wide at the top. We'll lie flat up there. The Bulgarian will think we're still in the woods."

"He'll see us climbing."

"It's dark. And he won't be looking up."

Claire stared back at the woods. They were facing two terrible options, and she knew it. "Okay, go."

The forest grew right against the wall, providing cover. The wall was pockmarked with narrow but manageable handholds, allowing them to climb quickly. They made it halfway up before they were exposed.

Below, they heard the Bulgarian's monster bullying its way through the forest. Jack's heart thumped louder as he focused on making it to the top, on getting off the face of the wall.

The monster had stopped. It was rustling around, searching the undergrowth. Jack hoped it wouldn't look up.

Claire reached the rim of the wall first and pulled herself up. Far below, Jack heard a scraping noise. He glanced down, and his stomach dropped. The Bulgarian had spotted them. He was scaling the wall.

Next to him, the rock monster's hands morphed into dozens of tiny stone-shard fingers, and the beast began to climb. But then it slipped and crashed to the ground, unable to pull itself up the narrow holds. The monster bellowed in frustration.

Jack scrambled to the top of the wall. It was impossibly narrow for such an enormous wall—maybe eighteen inches wide. "You think you can keep your balance up here, Jack?"

The wall stretched for miles ahead and behind, a stone balance beam in the sky that could take them back to the central grounds. A rock broke loose from the wall below and tumbled past the Bulgarian who was still climbing. "Go!" Jack answered.

Claire and Jack ran down the wall, focusing on picking their steps. Jack tried not to think about the breeze against his face, realizing that a strong gust of wind could push them off. And he tried to ignore the fact that over the other side of the wall, several dozen man-eating dragons lurked.

Jack glanced over the trees. The stars filled the sky, ending in a sharp line at the horizon—the Atlantic Ocean. Jack had almost forgotten it existed.

Something crashed against the wall just below them and the structure shook. Claire yelped, but somehow, they kept their balance and continued running. Just behind them on the ground, the Bulgarian's monster wrenched an immense boulder from the earth and readied to try again.

Jack heard a low whistle and ducked, squeezing his eyes closed. The boulder pulverized the top of the wall, inches in front of them, and suddenly, his feet felt only air beneath them. Jack gripped frantically at rubble and dust. They tumbled—not toward the Bulgarian but over the other side of the wall.

CHAPTER 26

HUNTED

The trees grew high against the wall on the other side. Jack and Claire tumbled into them, jerking and twisting as their weight snapped through the branches and vines. Jack hit the ground hard enough to feel the vibration in his bones.

Jack's right shoulder burned. He got to his feet and steadied himself next to a tree. Then he did something Voss had taught him that he had hoped he would never have to do: he gritted his teeth and slammed against the tree, popping his shoulder back into place. For a long time, Jack squeezed his eyes shut against the pain, trying not to scream.

The air here was thick, like a cold, wet blanket. The forest floor was wild with thorn bushes and tangled with vines. A heavy rain started to fall.

He could hear Claire breathing rapidly, but he couldn't see her through the gloom and rain. Jack found her holding her ankle. "You okay?"

She used a tree to push herself up, then fell to the ground again. Jack squatted beside her under the tree, trying to escape the rain. "Is it broken?"

"I think it's just a sprain." She pointed at Jack's wrist. "You're holding your wrist."

She was right. He touched his left wrist and pain shot through his arm. He grimaced.

"Broken," she said. "Which won't make climbing back over easy. And I can't use my spade on whatever mineral this rock is. It doesn't conduct electricity."

"We can't go back up anyway. The Bulgarian will be waiting for us," Jack said. "But he'll think we died from the fall. Or that we were killed by the dragons."

"He'll be right."

"The main gate is our only way back in, on the far side of the wall, right?" Jack asked, his voice dropping to a whisper. "If we had a boat we could get to the mainland, and maybe locate a portal."

"I didn't bring a boat, Jack."

"No . . . me neither."

"How far do you think the main gate is?" Claire asked.

Jack looked down the wall. "Maybe ten miles?"

"President of the Cartography Club, right?" she said. "Okay. We'll need to stay close to the wall and stay invisible for ten miles." Claire pulled herself up, holding onto one of the lower branches of the tree. "Let's get this over with."

"Put your arm around me," Jack said.

"I don't need your help."

"I'm not asking you to hold hands," Jack said. "Hold on to my uniform."

She smiled grimly and leaned on him. Her wet brown hair fell on his shoulder. Jack took her weight and wrapped his good arm around her waist. "This okay?"

"Yeah, thanks. Just make sure—"

"*Shhh!*" They crouched.

Claire stared at Jack, eyes wide. *Dragon?* She mouthed.

Jack nodded and gulped. He motioned to the west, along the wall.

Jack focused every ounce of attention through the rain and tried not to breathe. He could see them just through the grove of trees: three large reptiles, larger than the rhinos at the Bronx Zoo. Their tails dragged the ground behind them like whips, their jaws gaped like a crocodile's.

Jack and Claire remained deathly still, not breathing, rain dripping down their faces.

The trees exploded as the three dragons crashed through the forest. Jack lifted Claire over his good shoulder, fireman style. He slipped for a moment in the mud, then hurtled away from the predators.

Tree trunks snapped behind them like rifle shots. Branches tore at his face, arms, and legs. He barely felt them. A split-second image of one of the dragons behind them had locked in his mind: a mass of muscle with fire-engine-red scales.

Jack hurdled over a fallen tree. But he didn't clear it. His uniform caught, and they went down. Jack gripped Claire and braced for a fall. He tried to turn his body before he hit the slippery ground, so he could at least get one good kick at a dragon before it tore into him. Maybe he could give Claire a chance to run.

But he didn't hit the ground, or not flat ground anyway. They tumbled down a slope, through the underbrush as if the world itself had tilted. Gaining speed, they plowed through brambles and vines, bouncing off thick trunks and sliding off mossy, wet rocks.

Jack's face plunged underwater, a shock of cold. For a moment he thought he was in the sea. But it was only a creek, swollen to the size of a river from the heavy rain. The rocks brought a painful end to their tumbling. Jack's head pounded.

He was about to pick up Claire and run again when he saw something across the black water: the mouth of a cave in a tall rock wall. Jack helped Claire into and across the cold water, fighting to keep their balance in the current. He reached up to grab the lip of the cave mouth, then pulled himself and Claire up.

Jack's cheek rested on hard, cool dirt in the dark. Claire was nearby, her labored breathing echoing in the silence. Outside, rushing water filled the space with white noise.

Slowly, carefully, Jack sat up and pulled his flashlight out of the pack of his torn uniform. He switched on the narrow beam and scanned the cave behind them. His head came about two feet from the roof of the cave. It was deeper than he first thought, maybe sixty feet from the mouth of the cave to a sharp curve. Along the cave wall, as it narrowed, lay what looked like long branches of bleached driftwood. Jack kicked at it. Bones from a large animal, deer or moose.

Claire had followed him to the back of the cave, where they were out of view of the mouth. She tapped her flashlight, making it light without using the battery. Then she stood it up to create a dim glow reflecting off the ceiling. A narrow chimney let in a fresh breeze, though no light. Jack guessed it was near morning now.

Claire gingerly probed her ankle and lower leg with her fingers. "I think we're stuck here for a while."

They were alive. But their situation was bleak. Elk Island, outside the wall, was a death trap. They would be exposed as soon as they left the cave. They wouldn't last ten miles; they wouldn't even last ten minutes. If they were healthy, they might be able to hold off one dragon for a few minutes. If he didn't have a broken wrist. If Claire's ankle wasn't badly sprained.

Only the single dim circle of light on the ceiling of the cave from the flashlight kept the cave from complete blackness. Claire stared into space.

"What is it?" Jack asked.

She came out of her trance. "You had quick instincts, picking me up like that. You saved my life."

"I didn't want you to get hurt."

"I've faced death three times now, Jack. In Jersey City, then in DC, and now." She shivered. "I'm not sure I'm built for this."

"I've seen you in the Dome. You're the most lethal recruit at Hadley. This is exactly what you're built for," he said. "But you need rest." He retrieved a packet of pain pills from his pack and swallowed one to ease the sting in his wrist. "Sleep will help." He held the packet out to Claire, but she shook her head.

"I'll wake you up in an hour. We'll take turns on watch."

She hesitated, then stretched out. "Can I lean on you?"

"Sure."

Claire put her head on Jack's shoulder. For a minute he thought she had already fallen asleep.

"Why did you like me, Jack?" Her eyes were still closed. "You did, right? Why?"

"Why are you bringing it up?"

"Because I know why Brandon liked me. I already told you. He needed a friend not a girlfriend, somebody who would listen. He could trust me."

Jack hadn't really thought about *why* he liked Claire. Not clinically, not like that. He considered it in silence for the first time. And even when it came to him, he wasn't sure how to say it in a way that would make sense.

"I don't usually feel in control, I guess. Blackouts will do that to you. I thought if I did all those sit-ups and push-ups every night, I could muscle through it. It's why I started running. When I ran, I felt like everything in that moment was in my control. It felt like . . . freedom. I was happy when I was doing that, which is maybe more like the absence of dread and anxiety, but whatever. It counted as happiness for me."

"You're avoiding the question."

Jack cleared his throat. "I guess I'm saying I realized that it wasn't the running that made me feel that way. It was running with you," he said. "You made me feel like everything was going to be okay. I don't know how, but you did."

Claire didn't react at first. Her hand was near his, just an inch away. Jack could feel the energy off of it, a tingling.

Then she reached a little farther and took his hand, pressing her palm to his palm, her skin to his. A river of soft energy flowed into Jack, warmth flooded his entire being. Then her hand gently slipped away.

Claire looked up at him. "Wake me in an hour?"

"Yeah, okay."

Claire's eyes closed before he'd finished answering. Her breath slowed, and her neck and body relaxed against him. Her flashlight powered down as she fell asleep. Jack leaned against the wall of the cave and stared into the dark, resting in the lingering warmth that flowed from that touch.

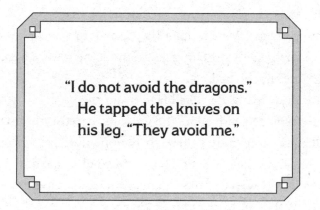

CHAPTER 27

"I do not avoid the dragons."
He tapped the knives on
his leg. "They avoid me."

THE BOY IN THE WOODS

Jack opened his eyes. Glancing at his band, he realized with a
start that he had fallen asleep. It was three hours later and still
dark toward the cave's mouth.

He looked around frantically. But they were safe. Claire was still
fast asleep against him. They had made it through the night.

Jack eased Claire's head to one side. His wrist wasn't as painful—
the pain pills he had taken were strong. He stretched out his fingers
to see how much movement he could handle with his broken wrist.
Then he pushed himself up and turned on his light. He couldn't see
the mouth of the cave from where they were. He followed the curve
of the cave toward the front, shining his light around the walls.

Something rustled at the end of the cave, right at the mouth. He thought it was the creek, which should have gone down by now after the night's rain. He shone his light toward it.

He shrieked.

Three dragons were forcing their way into the narrow arch of the cave, razor teeth glistening, jaws stretching toward him.

"Claire!" he shouted.

Jack drew his blade. The blaze lit up the cave. His wrist and shoulder exploded with pain. The dragons roared as they struggled to pull their large bodies through the opening. Jack gripped his blade, blocking their way to Claire. He tried to channel Freddy's imagination. It was a Hadley blade; if he could envision what he could do with it, he might stand a chance.

Thock. The first dragon's head jerked forward. Its eyes rolled backward in its sockets. The second dragon was yanked from behind, legs flying out from under it. *Thock.* The third dragon screamed. Then it turned and attacked whatever was behind it. It disappeared for a moment, followed by a mad scuffle and two more shrieks before it, too, went silent.

Jack stood frozen at the back of the cave, blade drawn.

A pair of legs appeared. The figure squatted down and peered into the cave. Jack's blaze illuminated chiseled features and cropped blond hair. The man held a long blade.

"Hello, Jack," Hans whispered. "I am sorry. I did not mean to wake you."

Jack tore across the cave and threw his arms around Hans's waist. Hans patted Jack awkwardly on the back. When Jack didn't let go, Hans put his substantial arms around the boy and did his best impression of a hug in return.

Jack let go. "You came back."

Hans frowned. "Yes. Did you think I would not?"

"Nobody knows who you are," he said. "You disappeared."

"I have been very busy. There is much happening."

Jack gazed around at the dragons, frightening even in death. "I didn't know you could kill dragons."

"I also did not know. I had never tried before." Hans shrugged. "They were distracted. I perhaps had an unfair advantage."

"How did you know we were here?"

"I found you out of seven billion people in the world, Jack. You think I could not find you on one small island?" He studied Jack. "I know this look. You have questions. Go wake Claire and come out. There are no dragons outside."

Claire was still fast asleep. But when Jack nudged her, she opened her eyes as if she had been merely resting.

"What time is it? You didn't wake me." She didn't even sound groggy.

"How did you not hear me? I screamed your name."

She was up like a shot. "What happened?"

"Everything's okay." Had he only imagined shouting her name? "Come on, we have to go. And I want you to meet somebody."

But Hans wasn't outside. Claire blinked in the early morning light. "You sure he said to meet you out here?" She winced in pain. Her ankle was swollen.

Jack knelt down and pulled a stiff bandage and spray from his pack. He wrapped the cloth around Claire's ankle and sprayed it to harden it into a cast. He pulled out two tablets. "Hadley painkillers," he said. "You're not walking without them."

Claire hesitated, but she then grabbed them and swallowed them down. She froze as she saw something.

"What?"

271

Claire pointed past him. Jack turned. A boy stood there, alone in the forest. For a long moment, they just stared at each other.

The boy spoke at last. "You are from the other side of the wall." It was a statement rather than a question. "You came just as he said you would."

The boy wore slim-fitted pants, footwear that seemed molded to the skin, and a long coat that buttoned up to his neck. His face was slender and child-like, his head shaved down to stubble. Four short throwing knives ran down his leg in sheaths. Behind him, on the ground, were the wet remains of a campfire and a small shelter.

"Yes, we're from the other side of the wall," Jack said slowly, looking around for Hans. "Have you been waiting for us for a while?"

"I have been waiting for eight months." The boy picked up a thin leather backpack and put it on.

"Eight *months*?" Jack said, puzzled. "I thought Hans brought you here."

"He did," the boy answered. "Just as he brought you here."

"Hans didn't bring us here." Claire started. "Wait. How did you avoid the dragons? There were three of them, right out there."

"I do not avoid the dragons." He tapped the knives on his leg. "They avoid me." The boy stamped out the fire. "Hans told me that you would be searching for answers."

Jack nodded.

"Then come with me." The boy started walking.

Claire looked at Jack skeptically. "You trust this kid?"

"I trust Hans. He saved my life twice. And now yours too."

Claire cracked her knuckles. "Then I guess we follow the kid."

For two hours they pushed their way through the dense forest, moving slowly through the thick underbrush on their injured limbs. They climbed over a large fallen log, and the boy slowed down.

He put his hand in front of him, as if he were feeling his way through a dark room. The air rippled before him. The forest in front of them distorted, as if it were just a vast painting on a curtain the boy was pushing on.

"When we walk through, you must remain calm and keep in a straight line," he instructed them.

"When we walk through what?" Claire asked, looking around. "We're still in the forest."

"It's like the Silo," Jack said in wonder.

"Are you able to remain calm and keep in a straight line?" the boy repeated. "If you panic and move out of line, I don't know if I can keep you safe."

Jack gulped. "Yes. We'll remain calm. And in a straight line."

The boy pushed through the invisible curtain of the forest. They were suddenly in a vast clearing. Not far ahead of them was a heavy wooden wall of uncut horizontal logs stacked two stories high. A simple iron gate created the only break in the wood structure. Surrounding the wall, and standing between them and the gate, must have been thirty dragons.

Jack's heartbeat stuttered at the sight. Claire gasped and stumbled backward. Jack caught her and held her in front of him, directly behind the boy. Jack grabbed his blade hilt. But the boy reached back and snatched Jack's hand before he could deploy the weapon.

"Remain calm," the boy said firmly.

The dragons ranged in size from a wolf to a dump truck, all blood-red and scaled. Their bodies also had different shapes. Some were long-jawed reptilian monsters while others reminded Jack of jaguars, sleek and angular.

"They're going to kill us," Claire whispered, panicked.

"They will not kill you," the boy said evenly. He drew his four knives from their sheaths and stacked them in one hand. "I will not let them."

The boy hurled the knives high into the air. They rose like magnets attracted to something high in the sky until they disappeared from view.

"Okay. We can go." The boy walked toward the compound. Claire and Jack followed right behind. Jack stared straight ahead into Claire's hair. He could feel the volcanic breath of the dragons closing in around them. Then one of the beasts sprung at him from his left. Jack flinched and cried out. Something above whistled.

Hundreds of knives fell from the sky, like sleet, a gray sheet of them. Dragons roared and yelped and let out high-pitched screams. Jack felt the hail of metal pressing in around him, but nothing touched him. Around him the dragons fled, daggers stuck in them like steel quills.

When the metal had stopped falling, the boy held out his hand. The hundreds of knives had vanished. Only his four knives fell from the clouds, landing in a perfect stack in his palm. He sheathed each of them in turn. Then they continued to the gate.

Claire stared at him. "You're an improbable."

"I am human, and every human is born with a gift," the boy told her. "I have chosen to use mine." He pushed open the iron gate.

Inside the large compound was an open grassy field. The wall that surrounded the community formed the backs of simple wooden huts that lined the clearing with no space between them. It reminded Jack of the wagons he'd seen circled up on documentaries of the Old West. Men, women, and children stood by their open doors or squatted on flat roofs.

"She's been waiting for you," the boy said.

Seated cross-legged and serene in the clearing was a woman in a coat and pants that matched the boy's clothing. She rose and walked toward Claire and Jack.

"Who is she?" Claire asked as the woman approached.

But Jack was speechless. The woman stopped a few feet away from him.

"Hi, honey."

Jack's mother embraced him. Tears streamed down his cheeks and soaked into the shoulder of her coat. He stepped back. "What are you doing here?" Jack asked, his mouth dry. "What is this place?"

"This is where our people live." She took his hands in hers, as she used to when he was a boy. "We're the Order of the Grays. Our people have been on Elk Island for a thousand years."

"The Order of the Grays died out a hundred years ago," Claire said.

But Jack was still trying to grasp his mother's presence. "What do you mean, your people?"

"I'll try to answer your questions, my sweet boy. But first, you need to eat." She was still just his mom. Food came first.

The monks brought them plates of freshly stewed rabbit and venison with potatoes and vegetables and charred corn on the cob. The food all came from a large fire pit in the center of the circle of log huts. Families of Grays sat on the ground near the fire, eating their midday meal together. Across the field, a young brother and sister, identical twins, sat on either side of the large fire. They took turns shaping the rising smoke into perfect images of animals while smaller children gathered around them, laughing and clapping. As Claire and Jack ate, Jack's mother told them her story.

"Thirteen years ago, the Supreme One, the greatest of the Order of the Grays, summoned me."

"He was born last night." The Supreme One sat cross-legged, across from Sarah, inside his wooden hut.

"Who?" she asked.

"The Guardian," said the Supreme One. "You will raise him until he is ready."

"I was dumbfounded," Jack's mom told him and Claire. "Every Gray knows they have a role to play, but I was thirty-three years old, single, and had never been off Elk Island. I was unremarkable in every way. I'd assumed I would live out my days here." She touched Jack's cheek for just a moment, then continued. "Grays are not supposed to be afraid. Not ever. But I was terrified."

"You were the one in Hans's vision," the Supreme One told her. Sarah could not argue with a vision.

"You know why the Order of the Grays exists, Sarah."

"We exist to protect civilization. We exist to fight the Shadow. We exist to bring the Guardian safely into the world."

"This boy—he is the Guardian," said the Supreme One. "The one who will end the Reaper War."

The visions of the Grays were never clear. But even by that standard, Sarah was confused. "I am not qualified to raise a warrior," she said.

"Hans is only asking you to raise a boy."

"What if I fail?" Sarah asked. "What if I cannot protect him?"

The Supreme One placed his hand on hers and squeezed like a reassuring parent. His skin was tough, like a hide. "He will be your son, and you will be his mother. You have been chosen."

"I don't understand any of this," Jack said. "I can't do the things you say I'm supposed to do."

Jack's mother took his hand in hers, as the Supreme One had done for her years before. Jack realized he had been gripping her wrist, afraid she would somehow vanish before she could answer.

"You can do more than you know, Jack. We've been tracking your progress at Hadley. You sense the presence of reapers faster than anyone. You understand Wyeth in a way that nobody else can. Can you hear him? Does he speak to you?"

Jack hesitated, then nodded. "I've heard him. But it's my imagination. Or the Dome. I don't know which."

"Jack, you are powerful. You are linked to Wyeth; you can learn to control him," she said.

"I can't control Wyeth," he said, startled.

"The Order can teach you all of this," she said. "We have been waiting for you. You were destined to come over the wall, destined to come out of that cave. That's why the boy was waiting."

"Hadley is losing operatives every day. We're fighting a war. I have to go back!" Jack pleaded.

"No, Jack. There is only death inside the wall."

"If the Grays believe I'm the Guardian, then the Great Prophecy says that somehow I'll win the war," Jack said. "I don't understand that. But right now I belong with my friends, at Hadley."

"The prophecy says that you will *end* the Reaper War, Jack," his mother said slowly. "It does not say that you will *win* it."

"It's the same thing."

"It is not," she said earnestly. "Listen to me. The prophecy says you will be a light in a darkened world. *A darkened world*, Jack. Wyeth will win the war."

Jack slowly shook his head. "That can't be true."

"The Guardian will rebuild our civilization. The outcome of the Reaper War has been decided for a millennium. This is only the beginning of the darkness. Stay with us, Jack." Tears gathered in her eyes. "This is where we will rebuild, together."

"I have to go back," Jack repeated. "I have to."

She stared at him for a long moment before she spoke again. "I'm afraid to let you go through that gate." Her voice was soft now. "I know you are the Guardian. Because of that, I know what going back will cost you. I don't know if I'm strong enough to bear that."

———

Claire rested inside one of the huts that afternoon, only rising for a small meal in the early evening. Jack and his mother walked through the compound and then stayed up in the evening talking. The boy would bring Jack and Claire back to the main gate the next morning.

"You never introduced me to her," Jack's mother said.

"Who, Claire?" Jack asked, lying on his back in the grass and looking up at the stars. "You just met her."

"I mean when you started hanging out together in sixth grade. You never brought her to the apartment."

"We didn't live in a great neighborhood, Mom. I didn't want to freak her out."

"I really am sorry about that," she replied. "But that's where Freddy lived, so that's where we went."

Jack sat up next to her. "What does Freddy have to do with this?"

She seemed surprised. "Why do you think Hans called him in?"

"Because he was my friend and close to his breakthrough?" he guessed.

Jack's mom squeezed his shoulder and rocked him slightly. "Oh Jack, you're sweet. Freddy is a Gray. How did you not see that?"

Jack furrowed his eyebrows. "What do you mean?"

"And not just any Gray. Freddy is a great prophet. He is the first of the next generation. One day Freddy Sanchez will help found the next Hadley Academy. In the rebuilt world."

Jack stared at her. "You're messing with me."

She cocked her head at him. "How did you think he knew all those things? He used to come over to our apartment every night with his visions. We talked for hours."

"I thought you were humoring him."

"I love that boy, but I wasn't humoring him," she said. "Didn't he do a presentation on the Hadley Academy?"

"He said he researched all of that on the Dark Web."

She laughed. "How would Freddy gain access to the Dark Web? He didn't even have Internet access in his apartment. And I doubt the public library or St. Paul's had access to the Dark Web. No, dear. Freddy has a gift."

"So it wasn't a coincidence that we were both brought into Hadley." Jack thought about that for a while. "I don't think I'll tell him that yet. About how he's destined to lead the next generation."

"I think that's very wise." She took his face in her hands and planted a kiss on his cheek before she rose to her feet. "I love you, my sweet boy. Get some sleep."

CHAPTER 28

LAST ONES OUT

Jack and Claire approached the main gate, unsure how to make it open. They didn't have to wonder very long. As Jack reached for it, the gate groaned open on colossal hinges. They were met by a startling sight: a two-story semicircle of gigantic steel vines, riddled with metal thorns the size of traffic cones. It looked like an enormous bear trap ready to slam shut on them.

"Hey!" Jack shouted, panicked. "It's us! What is this thing?"

Lady's little bug face appeared, having zipped over the steel vines and down to greet them. The drone beeped happily and zipped back up and over the bear trap. Freddy's voice came from the other side. "Jack! Awesome! Lucent told us to open the door for you."

The steel in front of them began to soften, then slowly turned green. The vines peeled back to create an entrance. Ivy and Lucent pushed their way through, followed by Boris Kleptov and Core. Bound leapt over the vines, landing and bouncing slightly on the ground next to Claire.

Claire motioned to the vines that Voss was pulling apart to create a wider entrance. "What was all that for?"

"Precaution," Ivy told her. "Ice told us you'd gone over the wall. Lucent said you'd be coming through the main gate. So we built an extra line of defense in case any dragons tried to get through. I provided the vines and thorns, and Alchemy here toughened it up a bit."

"It was very beautiful, no?" Boris asked, beaming.

Freddy came running up and slapped Core on the back. "And Core figured out how to change metal back to organic matter," he hooted. "In his first few days at Hadley! That's talent."

"Welcome back you guys," Asha said, striding up with an excited wave. "We were worried about you, even Voss." She nodded back at Voss, who was busy tearing down the vines.

Ivy and her team left with Core after many thanks from Thirteen. When they were out of earshot, Voss looked at Jack and pointed back to the gate. "I thought I saw a kid behind you."

"He's probably just one of the Grays. I bet they've been living out there all along, right?" Freddy offered. "But I'm just glad you guys are back!"

"Actually, yeah," Jack said. "That's crazy that you know that."

Jack thought of all the ridiculous things Freddy had told him over the years, all the things he had been so quick to dismiss. Like the family of yetis living in northern Canada. What was he supposed to do with that information?

Voss stared past them at the closed gate. "The Grays are still alive," he said thoughtfully. He turned to Jack and Claire. "But forget the Grays, how are *you* guys still alive?"

"Seriously!" Asha exclaimed. "We found the trail—the Bulgarian's monster left a wide one—all the way to the wall. From the scratch marks, we figured you went over. How did you survive the dragons?"

Jack and Claire told them everything. When Jack relayed how Hans had saved them from the dragons, Freddy jumped up. "That's the guy who brought you in here, right? I gotta meet him."

Then Claire explained that the Order of the Grays weren't extinct after all. "And," Jack continued. "My mom was there. She's a Gray."

Asha's jaw fell.

"Wait. The Grays have your mom?" Voss asked, completely lost.

Freddy, though, merely squinted thoughtfully. "Yeah . . . that makes sense," he said. "I miss her. She totally gets me. And those chocolate chip cookies she makes are genius."

"What's happening with Pacifica?" Claire asked when they had finished updating the rest of the team.

"Nothing good," Voss muttered.

Asha turned to Jack and Claire. "You remember that before the Bulgarian attacked we lost communication with Instructor Santori and his team?" she asked.

"Yeah, our communications went offline," Jack finished. "What about it?"

"Our communications haven't come back," Voss answered.

"That was nearly forty-eight hours ago. And it wasn't just that satellite over the CDC in Atlanta. It's everything: audio and visual from all surveillance equipment in the dormant world. I tried to bring stuff online, but we've lost power to a ton of systems too. Something happened out there. But we've got zero idea what it is."

"It's actually worse than that," Freddy said. "Nobody has come back through since you left."

"Alexander says the reentry function on the portal is on a separate power structure," Asha explained. "And that structure seems like it's been permanently disabled. But how, Alexander doesn't know."

"It happened simultaneously to the communications system going down," Voss added.

"So Santori and the others—they can't get back?" Claire asked. "And we can't even talk to them?"

Voss shook his head. "It's bad. Hadley's got almost no manpower left," he said. "Two days ago they started sending out recruits, starting with Team One. They let Ivy's team and Core stay behind to help us get you guys back inside the wall, but that's it. The Council announced that we aren't doing any good keeping our warriors here on Elk Island when the world outside must be falling to the darkened. One Life for Many, right? This is the time for sacrifice. We all have to be ready to go fight."

"We're the last team of recruits left at Hadley, Jack," Freddy told him. "We get sent out in a couple days. We just have one more thing to do. Alexander is going to tell us about it tonight."

"You'll be shipped out right after the final simulation," Alexander told them that evening in the Watchtower.

"What are we supposed to learn from a final simulation?" Voss asked. "We're about to go out and fight the real thing."

"This isn't a physical simulation," Alexander said. "It's a mental one: the Death Simulation."

"The *Death* Simulation?" Voss asked.

"Every operative must learn to die before they go out on an engagement," Alexander explained. "The Dome gives you a simulation with no solution. You have to die to complete it. Operatives must to be willing to sacrifice themselves if the time comes. That doesn't come naturally to most people. You have to learn it."

"How can it teach us how to die?" Asha asked.

"Well, *practice* is probably the better way to say it," Alexander said. "It's the final test. The simulation prepares you to do the right thing when the time comes. That's why there's a twenty-minute time limit. You can't hesitate."

Freddy whistled under his breath. "You think it works?"

"I know it does. We've all been through it. But every Death Simulation is different. You'll find out for yourselves tomorrow night."

Jack couldn't sleep. For one thing, the dragons were trying to get in the main gate. Jack had gotten used to the slamming. But now that he had seen them, he wasn't sure whether the sound was more or less frightening. Probably more.

Freddy snored on the bunk below. How could he sleep? Tomorrow they would face the Death Simulation. Then they would be sent through the portals, with no idea what they would find.

Jack couldn't lay still any longer. He got dressed and went outside.

He had no particular destination in mind. He only wanted to breathe some fresh air and not go crazy lying in his bunk bed. If he could have found a way through the gate and the dragons, he would have gone to visit his mother beyond the wall. His mother, the Gray.

Jack passed the portal courtyard. It was the first thing he had seen of Hadley, and now it would be the last thing when they went out. He put his hands on the gate that led into the courtyard. Then he turned to head back to the Watchtower. He would see enough of this soon.

A voice came from inside the portal courtyard. Jack froze. The voice was weak, as if the person was injured.

Jack pressed his ear to the gate. A man was calling Jack's name.

The portal courtyard was all shadows, only dimly lit by the lamps that ran along the wall. Something moved near the statue.

A man about the age of Superior Blue slumped on the ground. His broad back rested against a bench and his arms hung limp at his sides. His shirt was torn and bloody, and under rough stubble, his face was thatched with deep scratches.

The gate closed behind Jack with a soft ding. Jack and the man studied each other. Then Jack's chest seized up as he recognized the face. He was alone in the courtyard with the Bulgarian. Jack backed up. He reached behind him for the panel to open the gate.

The Bulgarian let out a labored breath and spoke with a voice like gravel. "I've got to hand it to you, Jack Carlson—you're difficult to kill." He looked half dead.

"How did you get in here?" Jack asked. "Nobody's been able to reenter the portals. They're an exit only."

"I did not use the portals." He reached into his pocket and pulled out something small and silver, like a thin deck of cards. "An instant portal." Pride cracked through his exhaustion. "My own invention, back when I was a cadet. It takes you anywhere and doesn't need a linked portal on the other side."

He shifted his weight and groaned. "The tech at the time confiscated my first one. She hid it in the Requisition building with so many other promising prototypes. But I was able to make a second one." He turned it over in his hand. "It's almost out of power. Useless now. Like me, I suppose."

Jack stayed where he was at the edge of the courtyard. He peered around the empty area; it was the first time he had been here since he had arrived. This didn't feel like a trick or an ambush.

Jack took one step toward the Bulgarian, his sudden rage defeating his fear. So many people darkened and operatives missing.

"What made you do it?" Jack asked angrily. "Do you know how many people have suffered because you joined Wyeth?"

The Bulgarian lifted his head. "What?"

"You swore an oath to fight the Reaper King!" Jack continued.

"And I have never broken it." The Bulgarian stared at Jack suspiciously. "This is a trick," the Bulgarian said. "This is what you do."

"What trick?" Jack's blood surged in his ears.

The Bulgarian sat up. "I have never broken my oath. I have risked my life again and again to stop you. You are the traitor, Jack. You have beaten me, but you have not deceived me as you have the others."

"I haven't deceived anyone." Jack stiffened.

"I should have seen it earlier," the Bulgarian went on. "I should have known it when a dormant bypassed the Dome and talked his way into Hadley. I should have seen it when, that same day, the Hadley Asylum staged a rebellion. I should have understood it when you brought in Thayer's daughter, and the hacker who funded Pacifica, and the prophet who would follow you blindly."

The Bulgarian shook his head vigorously. "But I only realized it when Cynthia Thayer went public. Everything led back to you: the boy with no biological parents. The boy with no spade. The boy who broke into Hadley to deceive us all."

Jack listened in stunned disbelief. He didn't know if it was the ramblings of a crazy person or a trap. The Bulgarian could be trying to get him to lower his guard. He was a master manipulator. He had recruited an entire team of operatives to Wyeth's side.

Jack's hand went to his blade hilt. "We're under surveillance here, you know," Jack said. "The systems may be down in the dormant world, but communications inside Hadley are functional. All of this is being projected back to Darius in the Bunker. They'll be here any second."

"Another distraction." The Bulgarian sounded tired. "Just like the silo coin you created. Like the story of the legendary Gray, Hans, personally recruiting you. Like the illusion of a team of operatives who had turned against Hadley to fight for Wyeth."

"Hans did recruit me," Jack said. "And you recruited the Rogue Team. You're denying even that?"

The Bulgarian squinted at him. "You're serious?"

"You gained the operatives' trust. You turned them to Wyeth's side."

The Bulgarian stared at him for a long moment, as if trying to read Jack's mind. "There is no Rogue Team, Jack."

"I've seen them myself, in the mirrored engagements," Jack said.

"Then how has Hadley not unmasked them? Hadley can't identify one of their own teams of operatives with all their resources? Is the Rogue Team made up of ghosts?" The Bulgarian closed his eyes.

"No. You, Jack, invented the Rogue Team to keep people looking away from you."

Jack shook his head. "I don't know if you're crazy or a liar, Vladimir. But I don't believe you."

"Do your teammates suspect you? Does Link know you brought him in because he would trust you implicitly? Does Ice know she is a hostage, used to blackmail and control Cynthia Thayer? Does Torque know he was brought here because he is the only one who could shut down the power grid?"

"You belong in the Asylum. They never should have let you stay on Elk Island."

"If they had sent me to the Asylum, I would have stopped Thayer," he spat out. "Instead Wyeth found Thayer, and she handed him the Dark Virus. And that is not even the greatest threat."

Jack didn't know what were lies and what was the truth. But the Bulgarian knew something. Jack waited for it.

"The vaccine!" the Bulgarian said passionately. "The darkened are herding millions of civilians into the arms of Pacifica. Dormants are begging for the vaccine—a vaccine created by Cynthia Thayer can only be disastrous. And you have orchestrated it all."

The Bulgarian pushed himself to his feet. A gleam flashed in his eyes. He moved toward Jack. Jack backed away, instinctively deploying his blade.

"You have been in the center of everything, Jack. You invented the myth of a Rogue Team. You distracted Hadley just enough to allow Wyeth to unleash the Dark Virus, to allow Pacifica to rise to power. Everything points back to you."

Jack stopped. The Bulgarian's words sparked something in him.

"Wait . . . You're right. Everything points to me." Jack retracted his blade. His arm dangled by his side. "Somebody has set me up."

The Bulgarian was still walking toward him. "You're lying."

"No, listen to me." Jack talked quickly. He reattached the blade to his uniform. "Everything does point to me, but Wyeth or Thayer or someone set me up."

"Why would they—?"

"So you would kill me."

The Bulgarian stared at him for a long time. "You said Hans brought you here," the Bulgarian said quietly.

"He did," Jack said.

"What did he say to you?"

"He said I was the Guardian and that I would save everyone." Jack looked directly in the Bulgarian's eyes. "Somebody thinks I am a threat to Wyeth, Vladimir. And whoever that person is, they want you to kill me. This is the setup. This moment, right here."

"Why should I believe you? Why shouldn't I kill you right now?" Vladimir stared back at Jack with equal force in his gaze.

Behind Jack the courtyard gate opened. Darius marched in, flanked by Alexander and several instructors. Darius's face contorted in fury. "Vladimir Petkov," she hissed. "You should not have come back here."

Jack turned to the Bulgarian. "You don't have to believe me, Vladimir. You just need to trust me."

"I don't trust you."

"Then I'll trust you first," Jack said. "Go. Now." Jack pulled his blade and stood between Darius and the Bulgarian. Darius hesitated for just an instant. Vladimir leapt for the nearest portal.

"Don't let him go!" Darius shouted.

Alexander lunged for the Bulgarian, but he was already out. No one followed through the portal. They had seen too many operatives leave and disappear. With the reentry function down, going through a portal was a one-way ticket out. With the darkening world, it may well be a death sentence.

Darius walked up to Jack and loomed over him, furious. "You fool! You've cost us our last chance to stop Wyeth."

———

As the sun settled below the horizon, Team Thirteen made their way to the Dome. It was a full three days after Jack had encountered the Bulgarian. Darius had delayed sending Team Thirteen out after Jack's stunt of letting the Bulgarian escape. But now it was time. The Dome summoned Thirteen for their final simulation.

Maggie padded along next to them as they left the Watchtower. But when they approached the fork in the path, she took the path away from the Dome, toward the Office of the Superior. She turned and barked at them.

Voss stopped. "She wants us to follow her."

"We gotta get to the Dome." Claire held up her band, glowing yellow.

"Yeah, I know. But has this dog ever taken us the wrong way?"

They looked at each other. Claire nodded. "Okay, but let's hurry."

They followed Maggie around a bend. The steel tree marked the edge of the East Clearing. From the other side of the field, Superior Blue and Alexander walked quickly toward them from the Office of the Superior. They met in the middle of the field.

"Thank you for coming, Thirteen. I apologize for the lack of notice." Blue greeted them. "But tomorrow you will be sent out the portals. We are in an unpredictable time, and this may be the last moment we have together. I wanted to be the one to present these to you."

The ground beneath them shook. A wide circle in the field slid open, revealing a rising platform carrying a stone monolith. The Forge locked into place. Five panels scraped open in the stone.

"Today the five of you become operatives," Blue told them.

Thirteen looked at each other with a mix of bewilderment and excitement. The moment had arrived, three years early—now.

They followed Blue up to the Forge. He reached into the far-left panel and took the hilt of the first blade. "Ice." He held out her rune blade. The hilt was marked by the gray symbol of the Expathic. Asha took it carefully and rubbed her thumb over the rune. "One Life for Many, Ice." She looked up at him and nodded. "One Life for Many, sir."

Superior Blue handed Voss his rune blade, marked with the green Systemic symbol. Voss raised his eyebrows. "The Spade Threshold identified me as a Kinetic."

"And so you are," Blue said. "But the AI in your rune blade has studied you from the moment you came through the portal. It knows you. To your blade, you are Torque the Systemic. One Life for Many, Torque."

Voss took the blade. "One Life for Many."

Freddy was next, claiming his Theoric rune blade from Superior Blue. Claire took her rune blade after him, repeating the mantra.

"And finally you, Jack Carlson." Superior Blue took the last hilt from the Forge and turned back to face Jack. "You must be wondering what symbol is on your rune blade."

Jack's heart pounded. "Yes, sir."

"I had my ideas, but I never expected to see this." Blue held out the hilt to Jack. The blade didn't look like any of the others. It was ancient, like a relic you might find in a museum of medieval swords.

Jack took the blade gingerly. The leather was somehow still soft, easy to grip. It was as if it was molding to his closed fist. Jack looked up at Blue. "Where did this come from?"

Blue shook his head. "That was my question as well. The Forge didn't create this. There is only one in existence, and it was located in the vault," Blue told him. "You are holding the first Hadley blade ever made."

Jack felt the weight of it in his hand. At the base of the ancient hilt was an engraving. Jack had to turn it over to recognize the image: a silo.

"The Silo Blade, they called it: the blade of the Guardian," Blue said. "The alchemists of the Order of the Grays created that blade. Every blade in the last thousand years was modeled on this. It should fit you perfectly. One Life for Many, Jack."

Jack gulped. He let the blade magnetize to his hip, then looked back up at Blue. "One Life for Many, sir."

Freddy was staring at Jack's blade. "So lucky, man."

"This is traditionally a day of celebration for new operatives," Blue announced. "It is a moment for the Hadley community to come together to celebrate your achievement. I regret that you will not have that experience. So you'll have to settle for some old friends congratulating you." Blue looked past them and nodded. "Okay, Bond. Let them come."

Before Thirteen could turn around, they were pounced on by a few dozen dogs. Voss's Rottweiler knocked him to the grass and licked his face. It was the happiest Jack had ever seen Voss. Sushila Patel sat with Maggie off to the side, watching with a broad smile on her face.

Claire scratched behind the ears of a charcoal mastiff who was nuzzling closer to her. She looked up at Jack. "I'm glad I got to celebrate this moment with you, Jack."

Jack felt his cheeks burn. "Yeah. Me too."

After only a few minutes, Alexander clapped loudly. "Team Thirteen. Make sure you have your rune blades, and follow me. We need to get to the Dome immediately."

The Death Simulation would be twenty minutes of mental torture, Alexander told them on their jog to the Dome. If they didn't complete it, they would have to start the torture all over again. At any other time, the idea of a virtual death would have terrified them. Now they had the additional prospect of actually going out through the one-way portals the next day. They walked down the amphitheater steps and stood before the Dome.

Asha rubbed her hands on the pants of her uniform, then clapped nervously. "Okay. Are we ready for this, operatives?"

Voss grinned at her. "Nice ring to that."

The team lined up behind Asha. One by one, they ran into the ink-black emptiness of the Dome.

CHAPTER 29

DEATH SIMULATION

Jack peered into the darkness inside the Dome. The ground moved beneath him, causing him to stumble. Voss caught him.

"We're on a boat." Freddy's voice sounded in stereo, over the monitor and from two feet away. Jack stared up into a sky full of stars.

"We're on a boat," Asha confirmed.

"Sharks again," Voss mumbled.

"We can do this, Voss." Freddy encouraged him. "We just have to focus. Let's try to think about something . . . that's not sharks."

"Not helpful, man," Voss said, irritated. "I don't like sharks, okay? Which means I don't like the ocean. Which means I hate boats."

"Good," said Asha. "Focus on that boat-hatred. Because our mission right now is to sink it."

Voss's balance wavered. This time Jack steadied him.

"Our mission is to die," Asha reminded them. "If we just jump off, one of us might try to climb back on the boat. We have to sink this thing."

Jack glanced around at the wooden yacht. It was maybe forty feet long with a full sail catching the wind and carrying them through the dark water.

"So we're just gonna drown?" Voss looked queasy. "I can't get eaten by sharks. I can't."

Asha took him by the arm. "Hey, it's okay. It's freaky, but it's okay. This is a simulation. It'll be over in a few minutes."

"I don't want to get torn apart in a simulation either."

Asha rubbed her ear. "Everyone take out your monitors. I'm getting a bad echo with everyone right next to each other."

"I'm serious, Asha," Voss said, his breathing shallow. "I almost lost it in the Focus Atrium. I can't do this again."

Claire took out her monitor. "I don't like sharks either, Voss. But we have to do it together, okay?"

"No. Not okay."

Asha took Voss by the shoulders. "You are strong, Torque. And you are going to crush this."

Voss stared at her, and she stared back at him. He nodded.

"Claire, you and I will get that sail down," Asha said, pivoting to Claire. "We don't want it keeping the boat afloat. We want to get this over with quickly."

"Freddy, Jack, there's a small cabin door there. Get down there and find axes, guns, anything that will help us sink this thing. We have a time limit, remember. Boats are not meant to sink."

Voss was looking at her apprehensively.

"Voss, you sit up at the bow and keep an eye out. Make sure there are no surprises."

Voss seemed grateful. He crawled to the front of the boat.

Asha turned to the rest of Team Thirteen and lowered her voice. "There's a chance Voss isn't going to be able to do this."

Freddy craned his neck to see past her at the formidable Voss, curled up at the front of the boat. "We can probably do this alone."

"She's not worried about that," Claire interrupted. "She's worried Voss might try to stop us."

Jack felt an odd surge of hope that Voss would stop them. He realized how much he didn't want to drown, even in a simulation. "You're okay, right, buddy?" Freddy asked.

Jack nodded, but his heart wasn't in it. Still, he followed Freddy down the short flight of steps into the cabin.

There were no working lights on the boat. Below deck was pitch black. Freddy pulled a flashlight from his pack. They discovered a larger room than Jack had expected. It was a pilot room and living space in one. The boat creaked in the water. Jack's stomach turned as the boat lolled.

Freddy shone the light around. "Whoa," Freddy whispered. "Bingo!" Freddy's light illuminated a small wooden crate, piled high with hand grenades. "That makes it easier," he said with a grim smile.

Jack picked up the heavy crate. But Freddy had moved away and was mumbling over a narrow table. Jack eased the crate back down to see what his friend was looking at.

The table was covered in large, unrolled papers. There was a map of the East Coast and the Atlantic Ocean, with positions plotted up the coastline in the northeast. There were also maps of the entire North American continent. Every state of the nation was shaded in a deep navy blue, and the color extended north into Canada and south into Mexico.

Freddy pulled another map toward him. Arrows and lines and X's marked out what seemed like troop movements. Jack picked up a folder containing mug shots of various people he didn't recognize.

Jack's gaze returned to the map of the United States covered in blue. A legend in the lower right-hand corner had two boxes of color. White represented the United States. Blue represented Pacifica. There were no white states.

Freddy looked at Jack. "What is all this?"

A shadow fell over Freddy's head, and Jack's heart leapt into his throat. From behind Freddy, a towering figure rose in the dark.

Jack shouted and dodged as the man roared and lunged for them. The flashlight was knocked from Freddy's hand, and everything went black. Jack grabbed a metal bar and swung, connecting with something. A cry filled the cabin. A body hit the ground.

The flashlight clicked on. Freddy stood, wide-eyed, looking down at the figure that had collapsed in a heap. The man lay with his face against the floor and the hood of a sweatshirt over his head.

"Nice swing," he panted.

Asha and Claire came running downstairs. "What's happening?" Asha pointed at the huge guy in the corner, unconscious. "Who's that supposed to be?"

"Just one last heart attack, care of the Dome," Freddy said, twirling his flashlight casually, which slipped out of his hand and bounced on the floor. He fumbled to pick it up. "A madman attempting to stop us from completing the simulation. Nice touch, I guess."

"More like freaky." Asha picked up the crate of grenades. "This should work well."

They followed her up to the deck, calling Voss back over. He groaned when he saw the crate of grenades.

Jack's heart pounded harder than ever. Would he be able to pull the pin? Simulation or not, this felt real. How had all the other teams done it?

Asha gave them all a quick look, then turned to Voss. She whispered something in his ear.

Jack tried to think about anything else. About the sail, about the cabin, about the maps they had found, anything. He caught Freddy staring back down into the cabin. "What?" Jack asked him.

"I'm thinking," Freddy said.

"Well stop. Let's just get this over with."

Freddy kept staring down into the cabin. He looked up at Jack. "I have to go back downstairs for a second."

"Freddy!" Jack grabbed him. "You're not going down there. That's a rabbit hole. We need you now, completing the simulation."

"I need two seconds." Freddy pulled away and ran down into the cabin. The team trailed him. Jack felt everyone's frustration and fear. None of them wanted to die, but they all wanted this to be over—quickly.

Freddy knelt next to the unconscious man in the corner. He glanced back to make sure everyone was watching. Then he pulled back the man's hood. It was the Bulgarian.

"The Dome is messing with us, and it's working," Asha said, biting her nails and fighting to keep her patience.

"Or maybe it's trying to tell us something," Freddy said.

"Yeah, that we're on a schedule," Jack told him. "We have to hurry, remember?"

Claire browsed the maps with her flashlight, ignoring the unconscious operative.

Asha was getting agitated. "We have seven minutes. We have to get upstairs and sink this boat. Now *come on!*"

On the deck the wind had picked up and the first drops of rain were falling. Asha was back with Voss, propping him up.

"You okay?" Claire shouted at him over the wind, which seemed to be building.

Voss gave a single nod. He glanced back at the hatch. "We're just going to blow up the Bulgarian?"

"It's not really the Bulgarian." Asha used her sleeve to wipe the rain out of her face. "It's a simulation."

They gathered together in the middle of the boat with the crate of grenades. Asha looked at each one of them. "Okay!" she shouted. The collapsed sail slapped against the wood deck with a bang. Asha shivered from cold and fear. "Put everything else out of your mind. Everything is about this moment. This is where we learn what sacrifice is. You ready?"

They nodded and blinked the rain out of their eyes. No one moved to pick up a grenade.

"Asha's right." Voss's voice shook. He reached down and snatched a grenade. "Let's get this over with."

"Wait!" Freddy shouted. His fingers pressed the side of his head, as if he was losing his mind. "Just wait. We can't do this!"

Jack looked at Claire and back at Freddy. "Hey, Freddy . . ."

But Freddy was scrambling around, patting the deck as if he had dropped his car keys. He stood straight back up, then charged down the steps, back into the cabin.

Voss glared at Jack. "What's he doing?"

Jack ran back, again, into the dark cabin. Freddy had his flashlight and was tossing the papers around, searching for something. Before Jack could say anything, Freddy snatched one and pushed past Jack, back up onto the deck. Jack sprinted after him to find his friend shoving the paper in Voss's face.

"What is this?" he shouted at Voss.

"How should I know?" Voss squinted at the rapidly dampening paper.

"Just *look* at it, Voss!"

Voss snatched it, checking his watch in the process.

"Freddy—" Jack started.

"Just let him answer," Freddy snapped.

Voss studied the paper for a moment. "It looks like the architecture for a power grid." He held the waterlogged plans back toward Freddy.

"You remember the night the Bulgarian attacked us in the Workshop? When you had to hack into that super-secure power grid to shut it off?" Freddy asked urgently.

"The missile defense thing," Voss said. "Yeah. So what?"

"Jack said the Bulgarian knew about that. He knew you had done that. How would he know?"

"He must have sent that fake message to Alexander," Voss answered.

"The Bulgarian *didn't* send that message," Freddy insisted. "Somebody else did. Somebody else got you to shut down the power grid. But why? And," he shoved a finger at the power grid schematic, "why would the Bulgarian have the plans to it? Why does he have military maps of Pacifica? Why does he have any of this?"

"He *doesn't* have any of this. The *Dome* does," Asha insisted.

"The Bulgarian said he never stopped working for Hadley," Freddy said. "Jack believed him. Don't you see? He has all this because he's going after Thayer. He said that she's the threat."

"He tried to kill us!" Asha reminded them.

"That doesn't mean he was working for Wyeth. He thought Jack invented the Rogue Team!"

"What's your point, Freddy?" Jack demanded.

"Why couldn't anyone ever identify the Rogue Team? There are only so many operatives, but nobody could figure it out."

Asha took Freddy by the arm. "We'll figure it out, Freddy. But our time is running out, and we have to complete this simulation. Now everybody take a grenade." The grenades were slippery in their hands in the pouring rain. "Fingers locked in the pin!"

Asha shouted over the wind. "On three, pull the pin and drop the grenades in the box."

"Wait!" Freddy squatted down, covering his ears, trying to shut out the wind, the noise. "Just *wait*!"

"Freddy." Voss leaned over and pulled him to his feet. Freddy still held his head in his hands. "Bro, if we're going to sink, let's just sink."

"On my mark," Asha called out. "One! Two—"

"What if this isn't a simulation?" Freddy shouted.

Everybody stopped.

"What if this isn't a simulation?" Freddy repeated. "What if this is real?"

"He's losing his mind," said Asha, awed.

"We've been through this before," Voss said. "We've been in the Dome before. You gotta get a hold of yourself, man."

"We walked into the Dome eighteen minutes ago, remember?" Jack asked as gently as he could over the wind and rain. "This isn't real." Jack could see the others glancing at each other. Would they need to overpower Freddy to get this done?

"Our door was different," Freddy said. "Remember what the Bulgarian told Jack? He invented an instant portal. He said the original was in the Requisition building. When Alexander made our door, he just had to change out the Corpus Christi portal chip for a Dome chip." He turned to Jack. "You saw the Bulgarian's portal. What size was it?"

"Like a thin deck of cards."

"The same size as the chip that Alexander pulled out of the Corpus Christi door," Freddy confirmed. "Don't you see? Somebody installed the instant portal prototype into our door. Our door is an instant portal!"

Jack shook his head, bewildered. "But that would mean . . ."

"We've been going through a portal every time we went into the Dome," Freddy finished. "These haven't been simulations. They've been real. We've been living out actual engagements!"

"But . . . why?" Asha asked.

"Because nobody would suspect us," Freddy said, working through it.

"One minute left," said Voss.

"Freddy, what are you talking about?" Claire whispered.

"We are the Rogue Team!" Freddy shouted into the wind. "Us! Team Thirteen! We've been the Rogue Team all along." Freddy looked like a wild man predicting the apocalypse on a street corner. His hands extended toward them, as if to pull them in, to see what he saw.

"In the cathedral, the team we fought—that wasn't the Rogue Team. That was the team of operatives," he said. "Same thing at the rally. Nobody could tell who we were because we had our hoods up. And who's expecting to see a team of recruits appearing out of nowhere? But *we* ambushed *them*, not the other way around. We were protecting Wyeth, not them!"

"But somebody would have had to install that instant portal," Voss pointed out. "Somebody at Hadley had to set all this up." For a moment nobody spoke. The rain pounded the boat.

"The dragons have been trying to get into Hadley," Freddy said more quietly.

"Yeah?" Voss asked.

"The dragons were trained to hunt down Wyeth."

Their bands beeped. Twenty minutes was up. They hadn't been extracted.

"This wasn't a simulation." Freddy was the only one with words. "The Dome has never summoned us. Wyeth installed the instant portal and triggered our bands. Only Wyeth would know where the dead zones would happen. He summoned us into the cathedral in Brussels and to the rally in DC. We ambushed the team of operatives that were already there. We were extracted while the other operatives stayed and fought to the death."

The full extent of everything they had done began to sink in.

The boat lurched. Asha was thrown to the side and Voss caught her. The wind was picking up. Then the boat hit a colossal wave that knocked them off their feet and almost clean off the boat. They slid together down the deck.

"Now what?" Voss asked, panting and gripping a rope.

Asha patted the deck. "We find out if this thing is as hard to sink as I hope it is."

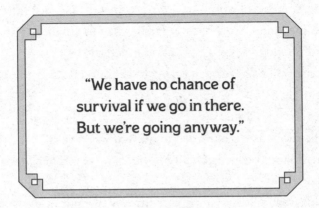

CHAPTER 30

"We have no chance of
survival if we go in there.
But we're going anyway."

HURRICANE

The storm got worse before it got better.

For hours they frantically trimmed sails and clung to wet ropes, all at Asha's shouted instructions. Wave after wave hit, and the forty-foot vessel crested each mound of water with a sickening roller-coaster motion, a rhythm of nausea.

Then the rhythm broke as the stern skidded down a wave and they lurched sideways. Another wave smashed onto the deck and the boat twisted. Claire lost her grip and slid down the deck. Just before she tumbled over the side, she snatched at a cable and swung herself back up. Somehow the boat recovered, and they returned to the sickening up-and-down dance.

Jack forgot about Wyeth. He forgot about the Rogue Team. He thought only of thirst, of the taste of salt in his mouth, of wiping his eyes with a soggy sleeve only to get drenched again. He thought of staring up into the clouds and then down into the trench of a wave. He thought of nausea and torn hands and survival.

Then it was over.

Jack sank to his knees and lay out flat on the deck. The smooth wood felt almost dry compared to his drenched clothes.

Jack replayed Freddy's revelation again and again. He thought about every interaction he had at Hadley. Wyeth had somehow installed the instant portal. But how? It seemed impossible.

Voss shook him. He had been falling asleep. His arms and legs tingled with numbness.

"You're gonna freeze out here, man," Voss said. "Come on, we're going back into the cabin. Maybe we can find some dry clothes."

Jack pushed himself up. Voss went over and lifted Asha to her feet and helped her downstairs. Freddy stood over Claire, holding out his hand to help her up. She instinctively waved it off and pushed herself partway up. "We're a team, Claire," Freddy said, his hand still extended. "You can trust me. Take my hand."

"I'm still getting used to it," Claire said.

"I get that. I've got time." Freddy plopped down, legs crossed, his hand still extended. "You just let me know. No rush."

Claire gave a reluctant smile. Then she rose to her feet and reached down and gripped Freddy's hand. She pulled him up. Freddy yelped when their skin touched. "Can't you turn that off?"

"Can you turn off your constant crazy talk?" she countered.

"Hmm. No, I guess not. But my crazy talk just saved our lives."

"Give it time, Sanchez," Claire said. "I'll save your life sooner or later."

Downstairs, they found an LED camping light in a cabinet, and soon the cabin was bathed in a pale glow. On the ground, unconscious in a gray hoodie and torn camouflage pants, lay the Bulgarian.

Voss went over and felt his forehead. "You hit him too hard."

"It's exhaustion," Jack said. "He could barely stand even before we hit him. I think he's been out on this boat for a couple of days."

The Bulgarian's eyelids fluttered, but he wasn't really there. Voss pulled him up to a seated position. His head fell forward. They peeled off his sweatshirt to find a bloodstained shirt underneath. Dark purple masses covered his ribs. One of his ankles was grotesquely swollen.

Together they lifted him onto the only bed. At least he was dry. Asha found a freezer with ice packs and set them on his raised ankle. He was breathing deeply, unconscious.

Freddy dug out a kerosene heater, Claire sparked it to life, and the small cabin warmed quickly. Voss ripped the padlock off a locker where he found a pile of musty fisherman garb and several blankets.

Once they were in dry clothes, they slid into the benches attached to a narrow, built-in table. Jack studied the navigation charts while Asha checked the GPS equipment. They were a hundred miles south of Elk Island.

The boat was stocked with tinned food and fresh water. Freddy made chicken soup in a sauccpan on the hot plate while they sipped scalding tea. Jack and Asha estimated they would have two full days of sailing ahead to get back to the Hadley Academy.

"We can't go back to Elk Island," Jack said. He had been thinking about this as he had fallen asleep up on the deck. Now he knew what they would have to do. "There's tons of intel on this boat. We can figure out where Pacifica is based. Wyeth will be there too. We have to attack them. This may be our only chance."

"You wanna *attack* them? The five of us?" Voss asked, impressed. "Man, I underestimated you, Carlson. Count me in."

"Me too," Asha said.

"You're the Guardian," Freddy added. "We can't lose."

Voss rolled his eyes. "Might wanna pump the brakes on that 'the man, the myth, the legend' junk, bro."

"I'm in," Claire said. "You're the president of the Cartography Club, Jack. Time to put that to use."

Jack wore a thick woolen sweater as he looked out over the bow toward the horizon. Asha steered while the others rested. They were heading toward the coast and gradually south, still unsure what their target destination was. They hadn't been able to discern Pacifica's headquarters from any of the papers in the cabin. Voss, Claire, and Freddy slept below, sitting upright on the benches and leaning into each other. The Bulgarian was still unconscious on the bed.

Jack went back into the cabin and peered at the maps, news story printouts, and photos laid out on the table. He examined and reexamined everything. The Dark Virus had changed the power structure in the United States. Nobody knew whom to trust. People only knew that Pacifica could protect them, and that they had access to what everyone believed was a life-saving vaccine.

Jack's vision was starting to blur. He needed a break. He stretched and rubbed his eyes with the heel of his hand. Then he flipped to one more file.

And there it was, staring at him. A Pacifica memo.

RE: Central Command

Confirmed: Security contingent to New York City. Second and Sixth Battalions to forward position. Darkened must be eliminated or controlled in a three-block radius of Times Square to allow troop movement.

Jack grabbed the paper and ran up on the deck. The sky had begun to lighten, diluting the black to a rich blue. The horizon, without a cloud to catch the rays, glowed yellow-orange.

Jack held the paper out to Asha. "We're going to New York City."

Asha took it and gave him a skeptical look. "New York City is heavily infested with the darkened. It'd be suicide, going into that."

"Exactly. That's why Pacifica moved their central command to Times Square. The city's darkened population is their fortress."

"But wouldn't they be overrun too?" Asha asked.

"Wyeth controls the darkened," Jack said. "He will protect Pacifica." Jack tapped the memo. "Wyeth will be there. Your mother too. That's where we need to go."

Asha stared out over the water, toward the brightening sky.

"You think you can do this?" Jack asked.

After a long silence she turned back to him. "I have to. I can't run from her."

Freddy popped his head out of the cabin and squinted toward the horizon, shielding his eyes with his hand. In his other hand he gripped the handles of three tin mugs, the smell of strong black coffee wafting from them. He handed one to Asha and one to Jack.

"Where are we headed?"

"New York City," Asha said.

"Right. I was thinking that's probably where Pacifica made its new headquarters." Freddy paused. "Of course, it's a suicide mission, going in there. We sure we want to do that, Asha?"

"Ask your friend."

Freddy looked at Jack. "It will be swarming with darkened."

"Wyeth is there, Freddy. I can feel it."

"Then it's settled. As good a place as any to go down fighting."

Voss and Claire came up too. "What are you dummies talking about?" Voss asked.

Freddy had lain down using a coil of ropes for a pillow and closed his eyes. He nodded toward Jack. "Just that Jack's Wyeth-detection system is tingling. Wyeth is with Pacifica, based in New York City, overrun by the darkened. And we have no chance of survival if we go in there. But we're going anyway."

Voss paused to consider that for a minute. "Yeah, alright." He shrugged. "We already survived almost blowing ourselves up and a hurricane."

"I was thinking about that, actually." Freddy craned his neck to look at Jack. "You actually would have survived the explosion, right? Because you have that blast suit. It's like you have a fairy godmother protecting you."

"A fairy godmother that would have blasted me out to sea with a bunch of boat shards and dead friends," Jack clarified. "Some lousy fairy godmother."

Voss lay down on the dry deck near Freddy. Claire sat and faced the sun for a long while with her eyes closed, soaking it in. Jack leaned against the boat's side.

And that's how they passed that first morning. Cracked lips tasting of sea salt, aching muscles, heavy eyelids. But alive. And together.

The Bulgarian woke up only rarely. When he did, whoever was with him tried to make sure he drank water before he passed back out. Their clothes were dry, and the sea was calm. They napped in shifts.

As the sun set over the western horizon, Voss burst into the cabin where Freddy and Jack were sleeping on the benches. They both leapt up, banging their legs against the low table.

"You two need to get up on deck," Voss said.

It was dark out except for a halogen lamp that cast a glow on the others. The sky was perfectly clear with only a light wind, just enough to keep them moving north.

"Static, can you make that come through any clearer?" Asha asked. Claire held the antenna of the marine radio and did whatever she did with electrons. Voices, chopped and gruff, came through the static.

Freddy leaned closer. "That doesn't sound like boaters talking about the weather. It sounds like military talk."

"It *is* military talk." Claire adjusted her grip on the antenna. They were only getting clipped phrases. But two words came through clearly: *Pacifica* and *navy*.

"Pacifica has their own navy?" Jack asked in disbelief.

"They don't have their own navy," Claire corrected. "They've taken over the US Navy."

The radio crackled and a few more words came through. "Pacifica ain't fighting the government anymore," Voss said. "They *are* the government. Our military is trying to protect people, and right now, Pacifica seems like the good guys."

Claire pointed west, toward land. "That's not the United States anymore. That's the Republic of Pacifica, under Commander Cynthia Thayer."

They kept the radio on throughout the night and all through the next day, but they picked up little else. Before dusk, off in the distance, Jack spotted it: the Statue of Liberty in New York Harbor.

They pulled into a marina among the towering skyscrapers of the financial district, waiting to be spotted. But nobody was there.

Voss jumped off as soon as the boat was close enough to the dock. He pulled the boat in and tied it off. "Where is everyone?"

"I guess the darkened don't have much interest in boating," Freddy offered.

Voss stared north up a broad empty avenue. He turned to the others. "To Times Square?"

Jack could feel Wyeth, but he didn't want to say it. He just wanted to end this. And he would—no matter what it cost him. "To Times Square," Jack answered.

"Wyeth won't have a Rogue Team anymore," Asha pointed out.

"No, just a few hundred thousand darkened." Freddy frowned.

"We can't kill that many," Voss said.

"I think they're already dead," Freddy told him. "Their souls are slaves to the Shadow now. You must have seen their black eyes up close. It's scary, that tortured look. Blazing them is a second death. It's a mercy to set those souls free."

"What are you, a darkened rights activist?" Voss asked. "Who cares what they feel? They're trying to kill us! I'm more worried about them ending *us* before we can free their souls from bondage."

Asha unzipped her pack, and Lady buzzed out. "She can at least give us a heads-up about what's around the corners," Asha said. Lady turned and bobbed ahead.

"What about him?" Voss pointed back toward the boat. The Bulgarian was still sleeping in its hull.

"We leave him here," Jack said. "He's too weak to move. If we live through this, though, we come back for him. Agreed?"

CHAPTER 31

LAST STAND

The streets of Manhattan felt like a forgotten movie set. In the six
weeks since the DC Massacre, the world had been transformed.
They didn't see a soul on the entire walk to Times Square. Lady flew
about fifty feet ahead of them as a sentry. But not once did the drone
come back to warn them.

To the north, two abandoned fire trucks blocked what had been the downtown flow of traffic. Obstructing another street was a construction site, a naked building of rust-colored beams stacked like Lincoln Logs. Huge, multistory advertising screens remained dark in the complete blackout.

"How are we supposed to find Pacifica?" Voss asked. "They could be anywhere within a seven-block radius, and all of these buildings are enormous."

Lady came zipping back. She skidded to a halt a few feet above them, spinning and indicating the way she had come with a little metal arm that popped out of her shell. She beeped rapidly.

Walking out of a side street was a young woman wobbling as if using her legs for the first time. In the silence they could hear her skin crackling. She walked to the middle of the street and faced them.

Asha drew her rune blade. The blaze shone gray. Voss held his hand out. "Careful. There might be more."

"There are more," Jack said. "They're coming." His mind was filling up like a kiddie pool overflowing when the hose was left on too long. White noise surged in his brain. A sickening dread grew in him.

"It's a trap." Claire pulled out her blade. "Wyeth has walked us right into a pit of darkened."

Freddy and Voss did the same, unleashing blue and green blazes. Freddy nodded at the hilt on Jack's hip. "Time to try that thing out, buddy."

Jack wiped a sweaty palm on his thigh and reached for the Silo Blade. It sprung off his hip and slapped into his palm. The leather was warm, as if it were a living thing. The blade leapt to life before Jack could even think it. The blaze was pitch black.

Freddy gave a low whistle. "Now that's a blade."

From both sides, the darkened streamed into Times Square and encircled Team Thirteen. They filled up the streets, packing in with unexpected efficiency, until there was no space left. The entire darkened crowd stared at Team Thirteen. They stood, swaying slightly, like large cats ready to pounce.

"We can't take them all at once," Asha warned. "I'm going to funnel them. It's our only chance. Ready?"

The darkened advanced toward them. Asha sprayed a wide circle of ice around them, ten feet thick and two stories high. She left one opening, a gap ten feet wide facing uptown. They could only see the street north of them now, and the tops of the buildings all around them, and the horde of darkened ahead of them.

"One opening!" Asha shouted to the others. "We take them as they come. This is our last stand!"

Freddy held out a closed fist toward Voss. "Last stand, bro." Voss bumped fists with him.

The first of the darkened came in. They funneled into the opening of the icy fortress like wolves into a sheep pen. Team Thirteen raised their blades. The heat from the blazes made the ice walls glisten. As one unit, they attacked the enemy.

Jack swiped his black blaze across the chest of the first darkened that came at him. The blade's impact blasted the darkened against the ice wall. The monster's eyes widened as it shrieked and crackled. Then the exoskeleton shattered into dust.

Jack stared in wonder at the Silo Blade. The speed and strength of it caught him off guard. It followed his every thought, but it also accelerated in the air as he swung it, multiplying Jack's strength.

Freddy had gotten the hang of his rune blade immediately and had already blazed three darkened in the entrance of the fortress. The darkened reacted like trapped animals. One leapt at Freddy, catching him from behind. Voss snatched the beast off Freddy and slammed it to the ground. Its hardened exoskeleton cracked the pavement before Asha blazed it.

Jack braced himself as a darkened woman ran at him. As she lunged at him, something flashed. Jack felt a blast of heat and heard a deafening crack. The woman was flung back against the ice wall. The pavement where she had stood was blackened. Jack turned around to see Claire with her palms together.

"Finish her off!" Claire hollered. "I'm going for more."

To his right, Asha and Voss fought back-to-back. Across the fortress, Freddy seemed to hardly touch the ground as he dodged the darkened, then eliminated each attacker. Their training and their gifts were taking over, and their rune blades flashed quicker than their old blades ever had.

But Jack could see beyond the line of darkened coming into the ice fortress. Thousands more waited outside. Eventually, Team Thirteen would make a mistake. Somebody would slip. They'd get tired, then exhausted, and then they would be overrun. It was a matter of time and probabilities.

"Jack!" Asha pointed up at a wide hotel balcony over a yellow-and-red Kodak sign. A lone figure stood watching. "She's up there."

Thayer. And Wyeth would be with her. Jack knew it.

But the information alone did little good. Jack couldn't leave the fortress. Even with their rune blades, they were only barely holding back the darkened now. Losing one of them would be catastrophic.

"We have to figure out a way to hold them off first," Jack said.

"Asha!" Freddy shouted. "On the wall!"

A hand appeared over the wall behind them. A darkened pulled itself up. Asha conjured a flight of hardened snow-block steps. Jack and Freddy dashed up. Freddy slid across the top of the wide icy wall, blade out, and blazed the darkened before it could get all the way up. "There are too many!" Jack said.

But Freddy was pointing south, up at the half-built skyscraper. "We may have some help!"

The massive steel beams of the construction site were shaking. The entire structure collapsed onto itself, sending up a mushroom cloud of pulverized concrete. Even the darkened paused as the ground shook.

With an earth-rattling roar the mass of debris rose into a colossus five stories high—a monster with the head of a bulldozer clutching long steel beams in its fists like drumsticks. The shovel of the dozer dropped, and the beast whooped like a celebrating rock star as it slammed the beams down into the crowd of darkened over and over. The giant's bulldozer head kept time with the beat.

Half a block away stood the Bulgarian, chest heaving from exertion but grinning. The darkened that had been piling up on the south side of the fortress now set upon the Bulgarian like jackals. The Bulgarian's monster continued to slam the steel beams down like drumsticks, keeping them at bay.

"He's distracting them," Jack said. "Maybe I can get to the hotel!"

"Jack! Freddy! We need you." Voss shouted up to them.

The darkened from the north side of the square had intensified their attacks at the opening. Jack and Freddy slid down the steps to join the others. The darkened were charging through the fortress's entrance. Thirteen was trapped.

Suddenly a heavy jet of water firing across the opening blew back the darkened, momentarily clearing the entrance. Then a blur of black passed across the opening.

"What the . . . ?" Claire started.

From the corner of his eye, Jack saw something above them on the ice wall. It leapt down into the mouth of the fortress. Jack drew up his blade. But it wasn't a darkened. It was a woman in black. She tore off her hood and a shock of spiky blue hair appeared.

"Is this what recruits are doing these days?" Operative Zhang asked with a wild grin. "Trying to get a closer look at the darkened?"

Operative Chandle appeared behind Zhang. Her eyes widened at Asha, and her glasses magnified the action. *"Quelle folie!"* She looked to her left. "Hey, Flood, *mon ami! C'est la fille qui* survived the Pit. The ice girl!"

"I'm busy, Pulse!" Flood shouted back.

"What are you doing here?" Jack asked the operatives.

"We left through the portals, but we couldn't get back. We've been fighting the darkened ever since," Zhang told him quickly. She spun and blazed a charging darkened before spinning back around. "Saw the commotion here, thought we'd come see."

"We need to get Jack to that hotel across the square," Asha told them. "No time to explain, but it's critical. Think you can help?"

Zhang glanced around, found the yellow-and-red sign on the hotel, and nodded shortly. She touched her ear. "Flood! Pulse! Blur! To me, now!"

The Kinetic was standing next to her before she finished the command, orange blaze lighting the wall of the fortress. Flood came around to the entrance, still blasting back the darkened. Pulse— Operative Chandle—raised her hand behind Zhang. *"Je suis ici!"*

Zhang pointed her blue blade to the hotel across the square. "We cut a path, straight through. One-way ticket out for Mr. Carlson." She looked around at Team Thirteen and shook her head. "First challenging operatives to a Death Match. Now taking on a hundred thousand darkened." She laughed. "Brave and stupid. You will make excellent operatives."

Zhang turned back to Jack, her eyes alight with excitement. "We leave in ten seconds. You stay right behind us. You may want to say good-bye to your team. None of us have much chance at surviving this." She turned to the others. "Team Thirteen's best chance is in this fortress. We will try to draw the darkened north. The Bulgarian will take the south."

Jack nodded. Team Thirteen huddled up.

"Survival? We're gonna do better than that. We're gonna rock this!" Freddy exclaimed. "Jack, you just make sure you kill Wyeth. Kill Wyeth and he won't control the darkened anymore. Kill Wyeth and we have a chance."

"One Life for Many," Voss said, punching his shoulder. "Jack, just make sure that Wyeth's is the life that gets sacrificed."

Asha just hugged him tight.

Claire took him by the wrist. "Keep breathing, Jack. You got this."

"Okay, Jack Carlson," Zhang shouted back. "Train is leaving!"

Jack gave them all one last look, then lined up behind Operative Chandle. They were off before he knew it. The sheer firepower between the four operatives was staggering. They blazed through the darkened at such a clip in front of him that Jack never had to slow his run. As they reached the hotel, Zhang and her team peeled off, cutting north to draw the darkened away from the ice fortress.

Jack shouldered his way through the revolving doors of the hotel, into the unlit empty lobby. He found a wide staircase and sprinted up, the sounds of the battle outside still ringing in his ears.

On the fourth floor he tumbled out of the stairwell and raced down the hall, through a bar, and out onto a wide balcony of low tables and cushioned couches.

Cynthia Thayer stood near the edge of the balcony, her back to the battle below. She stared at Jack curiously. "You came."

Jack stopped. "You knew I would come?"

"I believed you would." Her face hardened. "Now let her go," she said. "Stop those monsters, and let Asha go."

It was the last thing Jack expected her to say. "What are you talking about?"

Behind Thayer, down below, the darkened regrouped. They pushed Zhang and her team back and out of sight on the north end of Times Square. In the ice fortress Asha had created a localized blizzard in the mouth of the funnel, which slowed the attack of the darkened. But they were coming in greater numbers now.

"Where's Wyeth?" Jack deployed his blade, holding it straight out at her throat and advancing. Every second counted.

Thayer's expression went from anger to puzzlement. Then a look of wonder drew across her face. "You don't know," she said quietly. "How could you not know?"

"Tell me where Wyeth is, Thayer!"

Cynthia Thayer lowered Jack's blade with her hand. "He's right here," she said. "*You're* Wyeth."

Something in Jack's brain froze. His mind felt like it was collapsing into itself. "What are you talking about?" His jaw felt heavy. It was difficult to speak.

"You don't need to hide anymore. We've done it," she said. "But please, you have to stop them from killing Asha. The darkened are still attacking her. She's in the square."

Jack could hardly hear her. His hilt hung by his side. "I'm not hiding," he said stupidly.

Thayer snatched him by the chest. "You need to come out. Jack is still here. You need to come out and stop them. You can save my daughter, but you have to do it *now!*"

One of Jack's hands shoved Thayer backward. The other hand extended out toward the battle. An invisible surge of power cannoned out of him. Thousands of darkened below froze in place.

Jack was falling down a dark sinkhole. Somewhere in the back of his mind he recognized the feeling. He was having a blackout. But this time it was happening in slow motion. Bit by bit, the blackness swallowed him. He was at the bottom of a pit made of nothing but darkness.

"I won't save her, Cynthia. I can, but I won't."

Jack said that. He heard himself say it.

Somewhere beyond the dark, Thayer's voice echoed down to him. "I gave you everything. You swore that—"

"No. I didn't." Jack's voice was calm. "You believed that I would. And if you truly wished your daughter to be saved, you would have saved her yourself. But you are stronger than that. That is why I chose you."

"She's my daughter."

"You cannot both rule a civilization and remain beholden to your love for a single person. You have to say good-bye to her. It's time."

"You saved Claire Lacoste that night. You stopped the darkened from killing her."

"I did not save Claire Lacoste. Jack Carlson saved her." Jack heard his voice emit a putrid, cruel laugh. "Claire Lacoste will die with your daughter in that ice tomb. We begin again, together, unbound to our past. Let her go, Cynthia."

There was a long silence before Thayer's voice came through the dark. "You're right. I'm ready."

Jack had been swamped by a wave a thousand feet tall, and

there was no up and no down. He had no control over his physical body. He had no way to struggle. There was nothing but fear. Still he fought the darkness.

In the distance was a pinhole of light. He willed himself toward the last tiny glimmer of light. He could just barely see out into the world, a world that suddenly felt foreign.

"End it quickly, then." Thayer's voice was flat.

Jack could see her, blurry, as if looking through water. And then he could see the square below, filled with the darkened.

He felt his arms rising. Wyeth's arms. This was Wyeth's body. He felt another surge of energy and hate. More darkened flowed from side streets and out of buildings. They all poured down into Times Square.

The Bulgarian's monster was toppling under the weight of the darkened. The steel beams collapsed one by one, like a statue crumbling in an earthquake. The darkened were swarming the ice fortress now. They were no longer just coming in the funnel but piling up against the walls, higher and higher, a mass of darkened humanity. Then the ice walls disappeared underneath them. The darkened spilled inside. They came over the walls of the ice fortress, down on top of Team Thirteen.

From the depths of the pit that trapped him, Jack screamed. He screamed like he had never screamed before. And still the darkened tumbled over. They flooded the fortress, more and more and more.

Then the movement below stopped. There was nothing left but crushed humanity. And still Jack screamed. With no lungs and no breath, he screamed into the darkness.

Wyeth stared at the carnage. "You saw it," he whispered. "You found a way to see it, didn't you, Jack?"

Jack was empty. He was nothing.

"Good," Wyeth said. "I'm glad you did."

Cynthia Thayer gazed for a long moment at the sickening pile of darkened below. She squeezed her eyes closed. Then she opened them, inhaling a long breath before looking back at him. Her expression was calm. "It's you now?" Thayer asked. "You took yourself back?"

Wyeth turned around. "Jack was not a person. He was a disguise for thirteen years. He was no more real than a mask. And yes, he's gone."

"What are your orders, Wyeth?" Thayer asked. "We have control of US military equipment and all the administrative structures. We have replaced military personnel with the darkened, all under your control. We have injected almost thirty million civilians with the vaccine. But Hadley still has assets on Elk Island, including the Dome and some powerful instructors. We can't take any chances."

"I don't intend to. I will return to Elk Island as Jack Carlson and finish them off."

"The portals are still closed. Do I need to ask my people to restart the power grid?"

"I have the coordinates of Elk Island," Wyeth told her. "If you have a pilot who will do exactly as I say and land a plane on an invisible island, I can get back."

"I have a pilot who flew for a Colombian cartel. He's done far more dangerous landings than that. For what we're paying him, he'll land anywhere we ask him to."

"Then as Jack Carlson I will tell the Council what they need to hear. He has their trust. I will signal you to restart the power grid. You will open the portals, and the darkened will overwhelm Elk Island. We have to do it before they shut down the portals permanently."

Thayer nodded. "What happens when we take control?"

Jack felt Wyeth smile. It was cold, just an emotion of involuntary anticipation. "Destroy any remaining improbables and raze Hadley to the ground. Where is your plane?"

"LaGuardia Airport. We have a transport ready, as long as you can clear the darkened out of the way. We lost soldiers setting up our central command here, as you requested."

"I will clear a path."

Jack felt Wyeth stare over the edge of the balcony, down to the heaving ocean of darkened below. "The Order of the Grays never understood that this was the only way to save a fallen, diseased world. You tear it down and start again. Everything will be different now. Humanity will finally evolve. They will be strong, indestructible. We will finally make the world perfect."

Wyeth turned back to Thayer. "There is one last thing standing between us and that moment: The Hadley Academy. Today I will destroy it forever. Today I end the Reaper War."

CHAPTER 32

ONE LIFE FOR MANY

Jack felt them leaving Times Square. Down the steps. Out the door. Back into the square.

The ice fortress was melting. His friends were gone. He couldn't bring himself to think their names.

Jack sobbed. It was all he was, and it was all he could feel. His emotion hadn't left him. Maybe that's all he was now, an emotion. He wondered if Wyeth felt it inside him.

From the darkness that held him, Jack caught glimpses of the outside world. An armored vehicle taking them over the East River to LaGuardia Airport. A heavily fortressed wall with tanks and weapons pointed out to fend off the darkened. A long, snaking line of people. A large twin-propeller plane.

Wyeth outlined the plan to Thayer. Jack heard his voice as through a tunnel. Wyeth would crash-land the plane in the East Clearing. The blast suit would protect him—the blast suit that Alexander had given Jack, the thing that would have saved Jack's life from the grenade blast on the boat would save Wyeth now. Wyeth had planned it all from the very beginning. If the pilot didn't survive the crash, so be it.

As Jack, Wyeth would tell the Council that the rest of Team Thirteen had been darkened. Then he would get to the Workshop and open one of the portals using an outside power source. He had set everything up when he was Jack Carlson.

Wyeth had accomplished much during Jack's blackouts. There had been gaps in time that Jack had been unable to account for over the last months. There had been odd moments when Freddy had asked where Jack had been, and Jack couldn't remember. He had made lame excuses to Freddy, not wanting to worry him. It was only an hour here, an hour there, after all.

But that had been more than enough time for Wyeth. Wyeth had stolen the instant portal from the Requisition building. Wyeth had installed the instant portal in Team Thirteen's door. He'd sent the message to Alexander from inside the Workshop, making it look like Darius had sent it. The Signature Algorithm couldn't detect Wyeth when he came out because there was one place the shadow map didn't cover—the Hadley Academy itself.

Jack could almost remember those blackout moments now, when his mind belonged to Wyeth. They glinted like fleeting nightmares.

Wyeth boarded the plane. He checked on the pilot in the cockpit, a Colombian who wore a long knife on his belt and an oversized headset. As instructed, the pilot didn't turn around.

Wyeth pulled the door of the fuselage closed as the propellers started up. He sat in one of the twelve seats. Thayer and the armored truck backed off the runway.

With the door closed, Jack felt Wyeth's suspicion—not nervousness but practicality. He didn't know the pilot. He could not trust the pilot. The feeling poured over Jack through Wyeth's consciousness. Wyeth stood and walked into the cockpit.

"Do you speak English?" he asked as the pilot steered the plane down the runway.

"*Sí, senor,*" the Colombian answered, facing forward. "Commander Thayer says you will direct me, yes?"

Wyeth reached over and took the man's shoulder. The pilot jerked, then twitched. His face contorted in agony, and his eyes shut tight. His body crackled as it iced over. When his eyes opened, they were black. The man was gone. In the pilot seat was a darkened.

"I trust you haven't lost your ability to fly." No response. "Good. Follow the southern coast of Long Island, 120 miles, then north-northeast. From there I'll instruct you."

Jack wanted to stop him. But he couldn't any more than a child could have snatched the moon out of the sky. Jack was fading in and out of consciousness. Soon he would black out for good. He could feel himself slipping away. The plane rose into the air. Wyeth settled again into one of the seats.

A thunderclap woke Jack. He didn't know if a minute had passed or an hour. Wyeth looked out the window at the pounding rain. Jack could see the window. He could see the dark storm clouds against the night sky.

"Hello, David." The voice came from the front of the plane.

Wyeth's head jerked toward the cockpit. The door swung wider. The pilot had vanished, leaving only a hint of violet smoke in the air.

Who had spoken? Nobody called Wyeth by his first name. It was a name long forgotten. Then Jack saw him standing at the front of the plane. Wyeth didn't move from his seat.

"Have you come to try to stop me, Hans?"

Jack was alert and bewildered. He struggled to focus from his darkness. He thought he might be hallucinating, a last trick of his mind before his consciousness faded forever. How had Hans gotten on the plane?

"I do not need to stop you, David."

Wyeth glanced into the cockpit. "You killed my pilot. How?"

"You had already killed him. I merely helped free his soul."

"You are avoiding the question."

"I whispered to him that I could free him from your bondage," Hans answered. "All it took was a butane lighter he kept in his aviator jacket. He is at peace now."

Wyeth sat back. "You can't stop me, then. You are only a hallucination."

"The Grays would call me a vision."

"You were a hallucination to Jack Carlson. He believed you were real. He believed you brought him into Hadley, when in reality he found his own way there. He never discovered you were only in his mind, did he? Just as you are only in my mind right now."

"The mind is a powerful thing, David. You can see me now, can you not?"

"Yet you have no hold over me, as you had on Jack."

"I do not have a hold on Jack. Jack believes in something greater than himself," Hans said. "You, though, David—you believe that there is nothing greater than you. You believe you are the Guardian because you are strong. Because you have the gift of long life. Because you have a vision for the world. Because the Shadow lives in you. But you are only human, and humans are broken."

Jack listened in stunned disbelief. He tried to hold on. He hoped he wouldn't disappear without hearing this.

"The Order of the Grays were weak, Hans." Wyeth spit as he said the name. "Species that survive fight for survival. The Grays want to destroy our instinct for self-preservation. If they had succeeded, it would have ended civilization. I am rescuing humanity itself. The vaccine will usher in a new kind of humanity. A humanity that has the strength to survive," Wyeth said. "I have won the Reaper War."

"We have always known you would," Hans said.

Jack felt Wyeth swell with pride. "And now you cannot stop me—there *is* no you." Wyeth stood to face Hans. "So the question remains: Why are you here, Hans?"

Hans stood as tall and solid as a statue. "I did not come for you, David," he said softly. "I came for the Guardian. I came for Jack."

"Jack is dead. He is a vanishing mist. He is not the Guardian." Jack felt Wyeth's anger, like high-voltage electricity running through a power line. "I chose him as a baby, a baby with no parents, alone in a hospital. The day I let the Bulgarian destroy David Wyeth's body, I knew where I would go. I knew the baby was there—one that nobody would miss. The power the Grays detected in him was *me*."

"Jack chose you," Hans said.

Wyeth laughed. "He was an infant. He didn't choose anything."

"But he did," Hans told him. "You have not brought the

Guardian here. He has brought you to this moment, to fulfill the Great Prophecy. This is not the end, David. This is the beginning."

A lightning bolt hit the plane with such force that the aircraft rolled, knocking Wyeth from his feet. Hans stayed upright, a vision not beholden to gravity. Immediately another surge of lightning lit up the plane, this time so powerfully that it blasted out the windows as if they were tissue paper. Rain poured in sideways. Alarms blared from the cockpit. Even with the automatic pilot on, the plane listed sickeningly to one side.

Wyeth grabbed the blade from his hip. He twisted his wrist. The blade would not deploy. Hans watched with interest.

"The Silo Blade won't deploy for you, David," Hans told him. "It was forged for the Guardian."

Wyeth roared and threw the blade to the ground. Hans still stood between him and the cockpit. "Get out of my way, Hans," he snarled.

"You have nothing to fear from me, David. I am not really here, remember?" Hans's voice was calm in the howling storm. "I am merely the messenger. And now I will deliver my message before I leave."

"What message?" Wyeth shouted angrily.

"It is not for you, David. It is for Jack. It is to remind him who he is." Hans stared at Wyeth. Jack felt him. He was looking at Jack. He was looking through Wyeth and into Jack's very being, still alive, down in the dark.

"I am here to remind Jack that he can end all of this. I am here to remind Jack that the last of the reapers will die with you, Wyeth. I am here to remind Jack that he stopped you once already, when he stopped you from killing Claire Lacoste," Hans said.

"I am here to remind Jack what his mother once told him: He is strong. He is brave. That One Life for Many was never a motto, and it was never a creed; One Life for Many has always been a prophecy about Jack. He was born into this world to end the Reaper War. He was brought here to bring hope into despair. And just as you fulfilled your prophecy, he will fulfill his."

Then Hans was gone.

Wyeth was panting heavily, gripping the seat with one hand, knuckles white. He whirled in place. The alarms still blared. He pushed his way to the cockpit. He would pull himself in and close the door behind him.

But he didn't. Wyeth had one hand on the cockpit door frame. And he couldn't move.

From somewhere deep inside, Jack Carlson had stopped David Wyeth.

Wyeth felt a wild fear growing inside him. The fear was not Jack's. The fear belonged to Wyeth.

Wyeth's hand let go of the door frame, one finger at a time. His body straightened and balanced against the unsteady plane. "Jack." Wyeth spoke aloud. The panic rose in his voice. "Jack, I can save us—"

And then the voice was gone.

Jack Carlson stood in the plane, rain and wind whipping his skin. He felt Wyeth inside him. Wyeth shouted, trapped deep inside. "I am brave, and I am strong," Jack whispered into that dark pit. "And there is no us."

Jack took two steps to the emergency exit. He wrenched open the handle. The storm engulfed the plane, as if he were standing in a tornado. He felt Wyeth scream. Then he let himself fall. He fell through the blackness and the rain and the howling wind. He fell through the nothing, toward the sea far below.

Then he fell into something. But it wasn't the ocean. It wasn't earth.

Whatever it was, he was tearing through it, as if the air itself had hardened into a cobweb of whips that lashed his back, searing his skin. The pain was extraordinary. Then he did hit the ground, so hard that his neck whipped and his back cracked and his head smashed into the dirt.

CHAPTER 33

SILO

A CIRCLE OF STARS

The world was dark. It was cool and dry and quiet.

Jack's eyes opened, slowly and painfully. Above him was a circle, filled with the clear night sky. It was no longer raining. In the circle he could see stars. The sky was so beautiful and impossibly far away. It reminded him of home.

From the corner of his eye there was movement. But he couldn't turn his head—something was wrong with his neck.

There was a woman. The woman gathered Jack's head in her hands, gently lifting it. She cradled it in her lap. The walls surrounding him were curved.

Jack's lungs labored. Every inhale brought scorching pain to his broken rib cage. And yet he cherished that breath. He wanted to hold it inside him. The air he drew in was perfumed with earth and pine and the distant sea. Those things would exist long after he had passed on. He wished more than anything that he could remain a little longer. One more breath, one more laugh, one more cry. One more moment with people he loved.

But there was no more time. *This is what it feels like to die. This is what the end is like.* It was agony. It was separation. It was unbearably sad.

The woman gently touched his forehead, and he saw her face: his adoptive mom, Sarah Carlson. The Gray who had raised him and protected him and loved him. "You're safe now, my sweet boy," she whispered.

Jack woke up.

He was in the first soft bed he had slept in in a long time. He had forgotten they made beds this big. The ceilings were high and vaulted, and morning sun streamed through the tall, narrow windows that broke up the wall of books.

Jack eased himself up into a reclining position. His chest was wrapped in a wide bandage, but there was no pain. When he moved, he dragged with him a tangle of IV tubes. Was this another dream?

"You're not dead, you know."

Jack turned his head. Sitting to the left of him in a tall-backed upholstered chair was his mom. She leaned forward. "It's nice to see you awake. How are you feeling, Jack honey?"

He tried to speak, but nothing came out. His throat felt like sand. She handed him a glass of water, which he sipped, then gulped, water trickling down his chin and wetting his shirt. She reached behind her for a large ceramic carafe and poured him another glass. He drank again and felt his vocal chords coming back to life.

"I think . . ." he croaked. "I thought I died."

"You did die, Jack. Your heart stopped for a while there. You fell from a long way up." She took his hand and held it for a long time.

"Dr. Horn said nobody could handle that fall, even with the safety net. The only reason your body wasn't broken in two was that blast suit. You left us for three long minutes, the worst minutes of my life, but I believed you were coming back to us. I believed it."

Jack saw in her face the pain laid bare. What it must have been like, that bare-knuckled fistfight against despair for every second of those three minutes. Emotion swelled in Jack like a balloon stretched too far, squeezing against his organs until it popped and flooded his body. His throat tightened, and his eyes stung. He felt the tickle of tears on his face. What if they hadn't reached him in time? What if something had gone wrong?

But he was here. He was alive. He inhaled and exhaled slowly until his body calmed. "How long have I been out?"

"A long time. Almost eight weeks."

"Eight weeks?" He shuddered. "You've been waiting for me for two months? In here?"

"You're my son. I would have sat here for eight years."

The image of her face came back to him. It was the last thing he had seen before everything went dark. "That was you? In the Silo?" She nodded. "How did I land there? Or did I dream that?"

Jack's memories of the plane and the storm seeped into his psyche like poison gas. They had been thousands of feet in the air when he fell, in high winds. He was trying to assemble a jigsaw puzzle that was missing too many pieces.

But one piece came back to him. "Wyeth." He could barely get the word out. His heart began to pound uncontrollably. "He's inside—it was me all along."

"You killed him, Jack. He died with you. He's gone."

"How can you be sure?" he whispered.

"Because the Grays have been waiting for this moment for a thousand years. It happened exactly as it was supposed to. Wyeth died because this was when the Reaper King was always going to die. This was how he was going to die. It's why when the Bulgarian seemed to kill the Reaper King, the Grays knew he hadn't. Now it is done. Wyeth is dead."

She spoke with complete certainty. Wyeth was dead. Jack felt gratitude rush over him.

"When you adopted me," Jack said slowly. "When I was a baby, that was Wyeth, wasn't it? He had died, and he took the baby—me—and buried his consciousness inside, so he could disappear."

"Yes."

"But did the Grays know that I was Wyeth? Did you know?"

"Yes, Jack, I knew."

"And you took me anyway," he said. "Because I was the Guardian too."

His mother looked surprised. "Yes . . . that is true. I knew you were the Guardian. But that's not why I protected you." A single tear trickled down the side of her nose. "I protected you because you're my son, Jack. I brought you home when you had your black-outs. I found you, even after we had lost you for three days. I found out later that was when you made your way to the Asylum, when Wyeth recruited Thayer. Maybe others wouldn't understand why

I loved you through all of it. You're my son. That's all that matters to me."

"Who is the Guardian? Who am I?"

His mother reached over, pushing his overgrown brown hair back from his eyes. "I know it's difficult. But Wyeth is gone. You are just . . . you. You are the Guardian, and the Guardian is you. You trusted your visions."

"I don't have visions."

"No?" His mother sat back and grinned. "A thousand years ago a young monk had a vision: The Guardian would fall from the sky. The Grays would catch him. The monk saw where that Guardian would fall, and the Grays crossed the Atlantic Ocean to this island and built the Silo. You know that story."

"Yes."

"But you don't know anything about the young monk who had the vision, do you?"

Jack shook his head.

"That young monk was born to show the way to you." She paused. "You know his name, Jack."

Jack knew. "Hans."

"You saw him, didn't you? He spoke to you?"

"I was sure he was real! He was my school security guard."

His mother laughed. "I would have loved to have seen that. He was with you in spirit, Jack. On the plane, Wyeth could see him because you could see him," she said. "One day you have to promise to tell me everything you remember about him. Do you promise?"

Jack nodded, still trying to get his head around it. But thinking about Hans was bringing everything back.

"Mom, I did all of it." He fought to keep his voice steady. "During my blackouts. I almost killed Claire on the street. Wyeth wanted her dead, and I darkened that man to kill her. I woke up when it was all done, back at my bike, outside the diner."

"You also stopped him before he could."

"I darkened the bride in that cathedral. I darkened the man at that rally. I found Thayer at the Asylum and spread the virus. I led the Rogue Team. I even sent reapers to chase me into Hadley from Jersey City, so Wyeth could be inside the academy. I did all of that."

"Wyeth did it, not you, Jack," she said, taking his hand. "You were supposed to be an empty vessel. The world is forever free of reapers now because you found the strength to give your own life to end it all. *That* was you—the one who sacrificed. The rest was Wyeth."

"But there's been so much death. And the darkened are still here, and even more millions of civilians that Pacifica has injected with the vaccine." Jack's voice caught.

Then he remembered Times Square. The images struck him like live electrical wire, and he broke down. He saw the ice fortress and the darkened pouring into it.

A door on the far side of the room cracked open. A whisper came from the other side. "I heard them talking."

"Close the door, idiot."

Jack sat up so quickly he got dizzy. There was no mistaking the mop of shaggy, black curly hair poking through the door or the muscular black arm pulling it back out of the room. "Hey!" Jack's throat was so dry it came out as a squeak.

"I knew it!" Then Freddy shouted in the opposite direction. "Hey! Hey! He's awake." Freddy's body couldn't decide whether to get to Jack or to run out of the room to get the others. The convulsion looked like bad break dancing. He held a finger up to Jack. "I'm back in one second! One second. Don't go anywhere. Don't go back to sleep!"

Jack stared at his mother. "They were dead."

"I'll let them explain. They've been incredibly patient these past weeks."

A few moments later the door was almost snapped off the hinges as Team Thirteen barreled in. Freddy was pulling up the rear, but he squeezed in as they gathered around Jack's bed. Freddy fired a barrage of questions at him: How in the world did he land where he did? Did Jack know the probabilities of his landing in a stone silo that would save his life?

"Wait. You're asking me how *I* survived?" Jack cut them off. "I watched you all die."

"Short answer: Voss and Claire." Freddy threw his arms around the barrel chest of Voss Winter. Voss for once was too joyful to look annoyed.

"We were under that pile forever," Freddy said. "Claire managed to hold them off us. I thought we were all dead for sure, but then Voss just started ripping through the pavement—with his bare hands. He dug until we tumbled into a sewer tunnel. He pulled us all down into that."

Jack's eyebrows rose at Voss and Claire. "Wow."

Freddy laughed. "That's one way to put it, yeah."

"How did you get back to the island?" Jack asked.

"We were underground for a long time," Asha said. "We had to move slowly because Claire had a broken leg and Freddy had a collapsed lung. Everyone was really beat up. But finally we came up into the light." Asha looked around at the others, reliving the memory. "By the time we did, the darkened had scattered. They weren't moving together anymore. It was like an army without a general. That's when Freddy concluded that you'd killed Wyeth."

"We went back to Times Square to find you," Claire added.

"You weren't there, and we hid in an apartment near the Queens-Midtown Tunnel. Lady kept going back out to search for survivors. Two days later she came back with Instructor Suzuki."

"And Suzuki had just located Operative Zhang's team," Voss said. "They had rescued the Bulgarian."

"The Bulgarian is alive?" Jack interrupted.

"That guy won't die," Freddy said in a low voice, as if he were talking about a ghost. "He got us back here. He'd been sailing back to Elk Island when we were first transported onto his boat. He knew the coordinates, so it was just a matter of getting a boat and sneaking it out past the Pacifica navy. Took a week, but we made it."

"I did that. I sent us through the instant portal to that boat. Wyeth did, I mean," Jack told them. "So that we would blow it up and the Bulgarian could never get that Pacifica intelligence back to Hadley. I was wearing a blast suit, so I would have survived. I'm sure I would have blacked out, and Wyeth would have taken over and gotten to shore. He always had a plan."

Jack looked up at Claire and then the others, one by one.

Claire furrowed her eyebrows. "What? You look like you're trying to decide if you should say something."

Jack swallowed hard. "You guys are just . . . talking to me, like I'm not a killer," he said softly. "I was Wyeth all along. I unleashed the Dark Virus. The world will never be the same. It was my body, and I never even slowed him down."

Voss gripped his shoulder. "You couldn't have known. But we should have seen it and tried to save you."

"I almost killed you. All of you."

"*Wyeth* did that. You saved us," Asha insisted. "It must have taken a ton of strength to fight that kind of power and stop Wyeth the way you did."

Claire knelt down beside the bed. "It's true, Jack. Nobody else could have stopped him. You were born for this. And we owe you our lives."

Jack let that sink in. It would take a long time to digest everything that had happened. He looked at his mom. "One thing I still don't understand: the silo coin. I gave it to Superior Blue when I first got into Hadley. If Hans was a vision, then I imagined him giving me the coin. But the coin was actually in my pocket. Where did it come from?"

She smiled at him. "I gave you that coin, honey," she said. "The Supreme One gave me that coin on the day you were born. He told me that I would know when to give it to you. I slipped it in your pocket that morning before you left for school."

Jack's jaw fell open. "But . . . how did you know to give it to me?"

His mother patted his leg. "I'm a Gray, Jack. Sometimes I just know things."

Freddy shook the stress from his arms. "Boy. This is intense. We have a lot to catch up on, huh? We need some cookies or something."

"Chocolate chip?" Jack's mom asked.

"Yes, please!" Freddy said.

"You kids take your time. We may be on Elk Island for a while."

Jack sat up. "Why? What's happening?"

"Hadley lost all connection to the outside world some time ago," his mom explained. "When the Bulgarian activated the permanent security grid over the island, it cut all signals in and out." His mother stood. "The truth is that we don't know what's out there, Jack. And there may not be any way on or off this island."

A week later Jack was out of bed. His mother had taken care of him, along with Dr. Horn and Rufus, who had visited often. The historian was recording everything Jack could remember for the archives. Team Thirteen had moved into the house where he was staying, the grand residence attached to the Office of the Superior, overlooking the East Clearing. It wasn't far from the clinic and had plenty of room for Jack's mom and the team.

The Hadley Academy was mostly empty but for the Order of the Grays, some instructors, and the few operatives who had made it back on the boat. On one visit to Jack's bed, Superior Blue had assured Jack that he had a plan. He had created it in conjunction with the Bulgarian, Rufus, Darius, and part of the Council. They were all doing their best to keep Hadley operational. Blue had promised to share the details with Jack when he was up and about.

Well, he was up and about now. The Superior took Jack to the main gate. It stood open. "What about the dragons?" Jack asked.

"When Wyeth was alive, his presence at Hadley was like blood in the water of sharks," Superior Blue said. "That's why they were throwing themselves against the main gate every night. That's why they attacked you when you went over the wall. But with Wyeth dead, they are like any other forest predator, dangerous but without particular motivation to kill for its own sake. The Grays keep them under control."

"So they're not attacking anymore?"

"You're not Wyeth anymore. The dragons' ambivalence toward you is as much proof as anything," he said. "They are merely wandering the island now. Sushila Patel is tracking them down. It's a dangerous mission, but she is quite gifted. We'll see what happens."

"What about Pacifica?" Jack asked. "What if they restart the power grid and the portals turn on again? They could flood into Hadley and overrun Elk Island."

"The Bulgarian has permanently sealed off the portals," Superior Blue said. "Come on, I'll show you his other handiwork."

They walked slowly through the woods. Jack's heart pumped as hard as it used to when he ran, but it felt good to move and breathe fresh air. After a short walk, they arrived at the coastline, where hundred-foot cliffs bore the brunt of the crashing waves far below.

Superior Blue handed him a pair of binoculars. Warships. Three of them anchored a mile off Elk Island. They flew the flag of Pacifica: navy blue with three white stars.

Jack's heart rate rose. "They found us. Are they coming?"

"They can't." Blue picked up a rock and flung it off the cliff. It vaporized in midair.

"The protective grid," Jack remembered.

"The Bulgarian built it years ago," Blue explained. "He activated it a couple of days after we landed back on Elk Island. It's impenetrable." The Bulgarian had not only found a way to shut down the portals, he had activated an emergency lockdown of the entire island, a system he had helped developed as a cadet.

"Can he make another instant portal?" Jack asked.

"The instant portal he created used a customized atomic battery," Blue said. "We don't have the radioactive materials on Elk Island to build another one."

"So we really are trapped here."

"Maybe not. Rufus has been burning the midnight oil working through the vast collection of archives. He's going back into our predata history for possible solutions. He's found something that may help."

"What did he find?"

Blue held a cautionary finger aloft. "Not until you're fit. All of it is irrelevant until you're back to your old self. We need you in fighting shape, Jack. Rufus will share what he's found when it's time."

Jack knew better than to argue. He stared across the ocean for a long minute, a lump rising in his throat. The world would never be the same. He was grateful his mother was on Elk Island. But what about Freddy's mom and dad and Voss's sister? Would they have escaped? Would Freddy and Voss get a chance to look for them?

"Cynthia Thayer developed the Dark Virus," Jack told Superior Blue. "But she also created the vaccine. Wyeth wanted people injected with it. He told Hans on the plane that it would evolve humankind. What were they being injected with?"

Superior Blue shook his head. "We have no idea. But millions who were not darkened have received the vaccine over the past three months. We don't know what we'll discover when we find them," he said. "Or what they will have become."

———

Jack walked out into the night. A light snow was falling, the first of the early winter. He didn't care, he just didn't want to sleep; he had been sleeping for weeks. He was having a hard time allowing himself to drift off into unconsciousness. He still feared what he would become in those moments.

Jack ambled toward the main grounds. He passed the nearly empty Office of Reaper Engagement and made his way through the central part of Hadley. The academy was like a ghost town. Almost all of the operatives were on the other side of the portals, out in the world, unaccounted for. Many must have been killed. But surely not all. Jack wondered what was happening out there.

He walked along the edge of the Long Woods, toward the odd assortment of instructor houses on the Bluffs, overlooking the icy river. He approached the third house along the line, marked by a tall entry arch, lancet windows, and an onion-domed roof that reminded Jack of the Taj Mahal. He pulled the knocker, a heavy iron ring in the jaws of a wolf.

The wide door swung open. Looking tired and angry, his hair askew, stood the Bulgarian.

"Jack!" Vladimir squinted at him.

"You haven't visited."

The Bulgarian hesitated. "I have been very busy." He looked Jack over. "Are you cleared to walk around?" Jack nodded.

But Vladimir's irritation returned as he glanced at his watch. "Do you know what time it is?" he asked. "You will end up right back in a coma wandering around at night like this."

"I wanted to thank you, Vladimir. You tried to save our lives, back there in Times Square. With your giant."

The Bulgarian appeared caught off guard. "I also tried to kill you."

"I'm glad the saving part came last."

Vladimir rubbed his eyes, then swung the door open. "Come in."

The living room walls were covered with tapestries and intricately carved wooden masks of varied expressions and species. The room smelled of wood and old upholstery and spice. The Bulgarian left Jack momentarily, then walked back in and handed Jack a cup of tea.

"This was Instructor Vishnarama's home. He taught you Weaponized Chemistry, I believe." Vladimir admired the walls.

"They sent him out on one of the teams. Nobody has heard from him."

"What do you think happened?" Jack had liked Instructor Vishnarama. He was soft spoken, but he had a talent for making fatal concoctions. And his subtle delivery systems made him among the most dangerous of instructors.

"Instructors are resourceful. Vishnarama knows how to survive."

"The grid—you really think it's impenetrable?" Jack asked.

"I know it is. I designed it as a cadet project. The Council wanted a lockdown procedure, something more than just the wall, something to cover the entire island," Vladimir explained. "More importantly, I used a reverse surge to destroy the external power grid that controlled the portals. I had no choice—Pacifica had taken control of the grid. At any moment they could reopen the portals and attack Elk Island. We were vulnerable."

"If Pacifica can't reopen the portals, we can't either, right?" Jack asked. "Not without a power source. How do we get off the island then?"

"My job was our immediate survival. Rufus is working on a way off the island. You'll have to ask him."

Jack put down his tea and straightened up to face the Bulgarian. "You saw the truth, Vladimir," Jack said solemnly. "Everyone thought you were crazy, or that your shadow spade had finally shown through and turned you to Wyeth's side. But they were wrong. You were right to try to kill me. I was Wyeth."

"You were also the Guardian," the Bulgarian corrected. "If I had killed you, the world would be without hope right now."

"I thought you didn't believe I was the Guardian."

"You fell out of a plane a hundred miles south and landed in a silo on Elk Island eighteen feet in diameter. That is exactly what the Grays predicted. I am a scientist, Jack. I examine the evidence. And the evidence tells me you are exactly what they have waited for. You are something we've never seen before."

"I feel like a kid. I feel like everyone else."

"The Grays might say that's why you are the only one who can restore humanity."

"I don't know if I can do that."

The Bulgarian held up his hands. "Don't misunderstand, Jack. The Order of the Grays had only thirteen prophecies. They have all been fulfilled. There are no more prophecies, other than this one: One Life for Many. You will determine what that means. The Grays said that the Guardian would bring hope. Hope is not the same as victory. It is up to you what you do next."

Jack nodded. "Whatever happens next, thank you for trying to save us, Vladimir."

"You're welcome. I wish I had done a better job. And I owe you a great deal for saving me as well," he said. "Which reminds me. I have something for you."

Petkov pushed himself up and went into the other room. He returned and handed Jack an object wrapped in silk cloth. Jack gave him a puzzled look but carefully opened the cloth. Inside was the Silo Blade. "How did you get this? Wyeth threw it down from the plane."

"The Silo Blade has been waiting for its owner for a long time, Jack," Petkov told him. "It wasn't about to let you go so easily. Your mother found it next to you in the silo the night you fell. It followed you down. She gave it to me for safekeeping."

Jack deployed the blade. The black flame lit up the room. He retracted it again and let it magnetize to his hip. "Thanks, Vladimir."

The Bulgarian gave a short nod. Then he motioned past Jack. "Somebody's come looking for you."

Jack turned around. Claire was at the door. "What are you doing here?" Jack asked.

"I wanted to make sure you got back okay," Claire said, leaning against the door. "It's late."

The Bulgarian stood and helped Jack to his feet. He wrapped a thick arm around Jack's shoulder. "She's right. You survived falling out of an airplane. It would be disappointing to see you die of a cold."

"I'll walk him back, Vladimir, thanks." Claire looked at Jack and took him by the arm.

When they were outside, Claire slowed down. "The truth is I couldn't sleep. I came looking for you because something's been bothering me," she said. "You know that Miles Watt was mind-scraped after I started talking, right?"

"Yeah. Superior Blue demanded it."

Claire nodded. "Right. That's the thing keeping me awake. Miles had one of the shadow spades. He was a Psionic. Superior Blue said he was one of the most powerful they'd ever seen. I saw it in the eyes of the instructors, in Suzuki and Santori—even they were wary of him," she told Jack. "So of course I was so relieved when they took him and mind-scraped him. Until . . ." She paused for a long moment, watching the snow fall.

"Until what?" Jack asked.

Claire looked at him. "Until I remembered what they do with shadow spades that wash out. They're too dangerous to return to society. They don't just send them home."

Jack felt a pit in his stomach. "They send them to the Hadley Asylum."

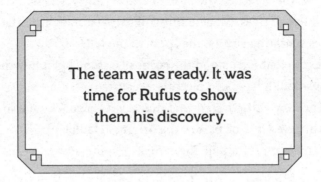

CHAPTER 34

The team was ready. It was time for Rufus to show them his discovery.

THE LAST DOOR

Little by little, Jack got back into shape. Every morning Claire showed up at his door at 6:00 a.m. Every day they ran a little longer, through snow and rain and freezing temperatures, until he was up to five miles. He had good days and bad days, but in the six months of training, Claire never left his side. She never left him behind, and she never let him give up. "Keep breathing, Jack," she'd say without stopping.

By the spring, Jack was ready. The team was ready. It was time for Rufus to show them his discovery.

Team Thirteen followed Superior Blue, Rufus, and Maggie out the main gate and down the coast. The sun was warm on their necks and shoulders, and salt water spray misted up when the waves crashed against the rocks, cooling them.

They turned inland at a wide cove. After a few more minutes of hiking, they reached the base of a towering waterfall. To its side was a grove of trees. Maggie immediately bounded into the water, her eyes squinting against the spray of the falls.

Next to the water stood the ruins of a stone hut. Only the footprint was left. It had been recently excavated.

"The Grays discovered this many years ago," Blue told them. "They believed it to be part of the original Hadley Academy."

"What's useful about the ruins of some stone house?" Voss asked.

Asha was walking slowly around the stone ring. She stopped where a doorway had once been. "It was an outpost for the academy, right? But why would they need one this far out?"

"We couldn't figure that out at first either," Blue offered. "Until Rufus suggested that it was probably used as the shelter for the first engineers at Hadley, the ones doing the most radical experiments. Then we discovered this."

They followed Rufus past the ruin to the clump of trees near the edge of the water. In the middle of a small clearing, two pine trees grew a few feet apart like lanky identical twins. A door hung from ancient iron hinges on one of the trees, swaying and creaking slightly in the breeze but never closing. The elements had polished and petrified the wood. It felt like bone. Was it possible that the door could have stood here for so long?

Voss gave it a gentle push. It groaned as it swung into the frame created by the two trees and suddenly magnetized shut, a metal plate on the side of the door locking closed with a matching metal plate attached to the other tree.

"It's a portal, isn't it?" Freddy asked, amazed. "What's it doing out here?"

"Our technology is advanced now, but back then, it must have been downright dangerous," Rufus said. "Think about how much energy it takes to run the portals—that entire power grid Voss shut down. They would have needed to generate a tremendous amount of energy to power this one." He gestured at the waterfall, which was pounding the pool below with thousands of gallons of water per minute and creating a dense mist.

Claire held out her hands to feel the spray. "Hydroelectric energy."

"Exactly," Rufus said. "And out here they could experiment far from the main grounds. No passersby would get blown to bits if something went wrong."

Asha brushed her hand against the smooth door. "Can it be fixed?"

"It doesn't need to be fixed. It never stopped working." Rufus patted the door.

"Where's it go to?" Voss asked.

"We have no idea," Rufus said. "There aren't any records of it; it's just here. All we know is that it's built by the Grays. We can't be sure it even functions like a normal portal. And we couldn't exactly test it, not knowing if we would come back."

"Wherever it goes," Superior Blue said. "It's a one-way trip off Elk Island. The waterfall only provides enough power for an exit. It doesn't produce enough energy for reentry."

"How do we get back?" Jack asked. "Vladimir destroyed the power grid."

"There's only one way," Blue said slowly. "It's dangerous, and we hoped to never have to use it. But we have no choice now; the world needs Hadley more than ever. And we need our operatives if we're going to have any chance at fighting back." Blue pointed at their wrists. "I've sent the mission details to your bands."

"And whatever you find on the other side of that portal, remember one thing," Rufus urged. "Your greatest strengths are not your individual spades. Your greatest strength is your team. That's how you'll survive: sticking together."

Jack stared at the ancient door that hung between the trees. The very first portal. And the last exit off Elk Island and away from the Hadley Academy for the Improbably Gifted.

Jack walked to the door and took the handle. It hummed with energy. Behind him he felt the rest of Thirteen line up: Asha, Freddy, Voss, and Claire.

"All right, Jack." Freddy punched him on the shoulder. "Let's go see what's out there."

Jack pulled the handle. Cool air rushed out.

ACKNOWLEDGMENTS

These are some people I would like to thank for making this book a real thing:

My agent, Trena Keating, of Union Literary, told me I needed to start writing fiction. She and her team read draft after draft and kept me going in the right direction.

My editors Laura Helweg and Ami McConnell (with help from Danielle!) had an incredible vision for this story. "Get out your pixie dust," they said. I tried to do that. The Tommy Nelson and the whole HarperCollins Christian teams have been committed and enthusiastic throughout this process.

My friend Charlie Agulla was along for this whole ride, brainstorming for hours on mind-bending concepts. Kim Mathew and Issy Kwei encouraged me in early drafts, asking the perfect questions that helped shape the final draft.

Our friend and fellow writer Cindy Halsted was the spiritual jet engine behind this book. I've never known a more dedicated encourager. The Lord used her in ways that continue to boggle the mind.

ACKNOWLEDGMENTS

There are many, many more friends and family who never let me give up, who were there to love and support me through the highs and lows of the writing process. There are far too many to thank, but I bet they know who they are.

And of course, my family:

Finn (Systemic) and Lucy (Kinetic) were tremendous brainstormers about the Hadley universe. They talked about it around the breakfast table and dinner table and everywhere in between. I always had them in mind when I wrote.

Finally, and most importantly, Lizzie (Theoric). My wife read every word, from the earliest ideas to the last polished draft. She is my first reader and greatest editor. She helped me understand how Claire and Asha felt, how the island smelled, how the food tasted. Most importantly, she protected me. The skin of a writer must be thick, but the heart has to remain vulnerable. Without her there is no Hadley Academy. She's the reason this universe exists.

CONOR GRENNAN

ABOUT THE AUTHOR

Conor Grennan is an author and a crime fighter. He used to live in Kathmandu, Nepal, where he rescued trafficked children and reunited them with their families in remote mountain villages. He wrote a book about those adventures called *Little Princes: One Man's Promise to Bring Home the Lost Children of Nepal*, which was a *New York Times* bestseller.

Conor spent his middle school and high school years in Jersey City, New Jersey, just like Jack Carlson. As a thirteen year old, Conor survived his rough neighborhood by dreaming of summer getaways on Monhegan Island, an island off the Maine coast and the model for Elk Island, home of the Hadley Academy. Today, Conor serves as the Dean of Students at the NYU Stern School of Business. He lives in New Canaan, Connecticut, with his wife, Liz; his children, Finn and Lucy; and their dog, Beasley, in a very ordinary and not-at-all-secret suburban neighborhood. Team Grennan still visits Monhegan Island every summer, hiking through the tall pine forests and helping each other discover gifts they never knew they had.